"Maresa."

Her name on his lips was a warming. A chance to change her mind.

She understood that she was pushing a boundary. Recognized that he'd just drawn a line in the sand.

"I didn't mind giving up my dream job in Paris to care for Rafe and help my mother recover," she confided, giving him absolutely no context for her comment and hoping he understood what she was saying. "And I will gladly give eighteen years to raise my niece as my own daughter." She'd known it without question the moment Jaden had handed her Isla. "But I'm not sure I can sacrifice the chance to have this kiss."

She'd crossed the boundary. Straight into "certifiable" territory. She must have cried out all her good sense.

His blue eyes simmered with more heat than a St. Thomas summer. He cupped her chin, cradling her face like she was something precious.

"If I thought you wouldn't regret it tomorrow, I'd give you all the kisses you could handle."

* * *

His Accidental Heir
is part of Mills & Boon Desire's
No.1 bestselling series, Billionaires and Babies:

HIS ACCIDENTAL HEIR

BY
JOANNE ROCK

MILLS & BOON

First Published in Great Britain 2017
By Mills & Boon, an imprint of HarperCollins*Publishers*
1 London Bridge Street, London, SE1 9GF

© 2017 Joanne Rock

ISBN: 978-0-263-92822-8

51-0617

Our policy is to use papers that are natural, renewable and recyclable products and made from wood grown in sustainable forests. The logging and manufacturing processes conform to the legal environmental regulations of the country of origin.

Printed and bound in Spain
by CPI, Barcelona

Four-time RITA® Award nominee **Joanne Rock** has penned over seventy stories for Mills & Boon. An optimist by nature and a perpetual seeker of silver linings, Joanne finds romance fits her life outlook perfectly —love is worth fighting for. A former Golden Heart® Award recipient, she has won numerous awards for her stories. Learn more about Joanne's imaginative Muse by visiting her website, www.joannerock.com, or following @joannerock6 on Twitter.

For Barbara Jean Thomas,
an early mentor and role model of hard work.
Thank you, Barbara, for teaching me the value of
keeping my chin up and having faith in myself.
During my teens, you were so much more than a boss…
You were a friend, a cheerleader and a sometimes mom
on those weekend trips with the crew. I'll never forget
my visit to New York to see Oprah, courtesy of you!
Much love to you, always.

One

"Rafe, I need you in the Antilles Suite today." Maresa Delphine handed her younger brother a gallon jug of bubble bath. "I have a guest checking in who needs a hot bath on arrival, but he isn't sure what time he'll get here."

Her twenty-one-year-old sibling—who'd recently suffered a traumatic brain injury in a car accident—didn't reach to take the jug. Instead, his hazel eyes tracked the movements of a friendly barmaid currently serving a guest a Blackbeard's Revenge specialty drink on the patio just outside the lobby. The Carib Grand Hotel's floor-to-ceiling windows allowed for views of the tiki bar on Barefoot Beach and the glittering Caribbean Sea beyond. Inside the hotel, the afternoon activity had picked up since Maresa's mad dash to the island's sundries shop for the bath products. All of her runners had been busy fulfilling other duties for guests, so she'd made the trip herself. She had no idea what her newest runner—her recovering brother who still needed to work in a monitored environment—had been doing at that hour. He hadn't answered his radio and he needed to get with the program if he wanted to remain employed. Not to mention, Maria might be blamed for his slipups. She was supporting her family, and couldn't afford to lose her job as concierge for this exclusive hotel on a private island off Saint Thomas.

And she really, really needed him to remain employed where she could watch over him. Where he was eligible for better insurance benefits that could give him the long-term follow-up care he would need for years. She knew she held Rafe to a higher standard so that no one on staff could view his employment as a conflict of interest. Sure, the hotel director had approved his application, but she had promised to carefully supervise her brother during his three-month trial period.

"Rafe." She gently nudged her sibling with the heavy container of rose-scented bubbles, remembering his counselor's advice about helping him stay on task when he got distracted. "I have some croissants from the bakery to share with you on your next break. But for now, I really need help. Can you please take this to the Antilles Suite? I'd like you to turn on the hot water and add this for a bubble bath as soon as I text you."

Their demanding guest could stride through the lobby doors any moment. Mr. Holmes had phoned this morning, unsure of his arrival time, but insistent on having a hot bath waiting for him. That was just the first item on a long list of requests.

She checked her slim watch, a gift from her last employer, the Parisian hotel where she'd had the job of her dreams. As much as Maresa loved her former position, she couldn't keep it after her mother's car accident that had caused Rafe's head injury almost a year ago. Going forward, her place was here in Charlotte Amalie to help with her brother.

She refused to let him fail at the Carib Grand Hotel. Her mother's poor health meant she couldn't supervise him at home, for one thing. So having him work close to Maresa all day was ideal.

"I'll go to the Antilles Suite." Rafe tucked the bubble bath under one arm and continued to study the barmaid, a sweet girl named Nancy who'd been really kind to him when Maresa introduced them. "You will call me on the phone when I need to turn on the water."

Maresa touched Rafe's cheek to capture his full attention, her fingers grazing the jagged scar that wrapped beneath his left ear. Her mother had suffered an MS flare-up behind the wheel one night last year, sending her car into a telephone pole during a moment of temporary paralysis. Rafe had gone through the windshield since his seatbelt was unbuckled; he'd been trying to retrieve his phone that had slid into the backseat. Afterward, Maresa had been deeply involved in his recovery and care since their mother had been battling her own health issues. Their father had always been useless, a deadbeat American businessman who worked in the cruise industry and used to visit often, wooing Maresa's mother with promises about coming to live with him in Wisconsin when he saved up enough money to bring them. That had never happened, and he'd checked out on them by the time Maresa was ten, moving to Europe for his job. Yet then, as now, Maresa didn't mind adapting her life to help Rafe. Her brother's injuries could have been fatal that day. Instead, he was a happy part of her world. Yes, he would forever cope with bouts of confusion, memory loss and irritability along with the learning disabilities the accident had brought with it. Throughout it all, though, Rafe was always… Rafe. The brother she adored. He'd been her biggest supporter after her former fiancé broke things off with her a week before their wedding two years ago, encouraging her to go to Paris and "be my superstar."

He was there for her then, after that humiliating experience. She would be there for him now.

"Rafe? Go to the Antilles Suite and I'll text you when it's time to turn on the hot water." She repeated the instructions for him now, knowing it would be kinder to transfer him to the maintenance team or landscaping staff where he could do the same kinds of things every day. But who would watch out for him there? "Be sure to add the bubbles. Okay?"

Drawing in a breath, she took comfort from the soothing scent of white tuberoses and orchids in the arrangement on her granite podium.

"A bubble bath." Rafe grinned, his eyes clearing. "Can do." He ambled off toward the elevator, whistling.

Her relief lasted only a moment because just then a limousine pulled up in front of the hotel. She had a clear view out the windows overlooking the horseshoe driveway flanked by fountains and thick banks of birds-of-paradise. The doormen moved as a coordinated team toward the vehicle, prepared to open doors and handle baggage.

She straightened the orchid pinned on her pale blue linen jacket. If this was Mr. Holmes, she needed to stall him to give Rafe time to run that bath. The guest had been curt to the point of rudeness on the phone, requiring a suite with real grass—and it had to be ryegrass only—for his Maltese to relieve himself. The guest had also ordered a dog walker with three years' worth of references and a groomer on-site, fresh lilacs in the room daily and specialty pies flown in from a shop in rural upstate New York for his bedtime snack each evening.

And that was just for starters. She couldn't wait to see what he needed once he settled in for his two-week stay. These were the kinds of guests that could make or break a career. The vocal kind with many precise needs. All of which she would fulfill. It was the job she'd chosen because she took pride in her organizational skills, continually reordering her world throughout a chaotic childhood with an absentee father and a chronically ill mother. She took comfort in structuring what she could. And since there were only so many jobs on the island that could afford to pay her the kind of money she needed to support both her mother and her brother, Maresa had to succeed at the Carib Grand.

She calmed herself by squaring the single sheet of paper on her podium, lining up her pen beside it. She tapped open her list of restaurant phone numbers on her call screen so she could dial reservations at a moment's notice. The small, routine movements helped her to feel in control, reminding her she could do this job well. When she looked up again—

Wow.

The sight of the tall, chiseled male unfolding himself from the limousine was enough to take her breath away. His strong, striking features practically called for a feminine hand to caress them. Fraternizing with guests was, of course, strictly against the rules and Maresa had never been tempted. But if ever she had an inkling to stray from that philosophy, the powerful shoulders encased in expensive designer silk were exactly the sort of attribute that would intrigue her. The man towered over everyone in the courtyard entrance, including Big Bill, the head doorman. Dressed in a charcoal suit tailored to his long, athletic frame, the dark-haired guest buttoned his jacket, hiding too much of the hard, muscled chest that she'd glimpsed as he'd stepped out of the vehicle. Straightening his tie, he peered through the window, his ice-blue gaze somehow landing on her.

Direct hit.

She felt the jolt of awareness right through the glass. This supremely masculine specimen couldn't possibly be Mr. Holmes. Her brain didn't reconcile the image of a man with that square jaw and sharp blade of a nose ordering lilacs for himself. Daily.

Relaxing a fraction, Maresa blew out a breath as the newcomer turned back toward the vehicle. Until a silky white Maltese dog stepped regally from the limousine into the man's waiting arms.

In theory, Cameron McNeill liked dogs.

Big, slobbery working canines that thrived outdoors and could keep up with him on a distance run. The long-haired Maltese in his arms, on the other hand, was a prize-winning show animal with too many travel accessories to count. The retired purebred was on loan to Cam for his undercover assessment of a recently acquired Mc-Neill Resorts property, however, and he needed Poppy's cooperation for his stint as a demanding hotel guest. If he walked into the financially floundering Carib Grand Hotel as himself—an owner and vice president of Mc-Neill Resorts—he would receive the most attentive service imaginable and learn absolutely nothing about the establishment's underlying problems. But as Mr. Holmes, first-class pain in the ass, Cam would put the staff on their toes and see how they reacted.

After reviewing the Carib Grand's performance reports for the past two months, Cameron knew something was off in the day-to-day operations. And since he'd personally recommended that the company buy the property in the first place, he wasn't willing to wait for an over-priced operations review by an outside agency. Not that McNeill Resorts couldn't afford it. It simply chafed his pride that he'd missed something in his initial research. Besides, his family had just learned of a long-hidden branch of relations living on a nearby island—his father's sons by a secret mistress. Cam would use his time here to check out the other McNeills personally.

But for now? Business first.

"Welcome to the Carib Grand," an aging doorman greeted him with a deferential nod and a friendly smile.

Cam forced a frown onto his face to keep from smiling back. That wasn't as hard as he thought given the way Poppy's foolishly long fur was plastering itself to his jacket when he walked too fast, her topknot and tail bobbing with his stride and tickling his chin. It wouldn't come naturally to Cam to be the hard-to-please guest this week. He was a people-person to begin with, and appreciated those who worked for McNeill Resorts especially. But this was the fastest way he knew to find out what was going on at the hotel firsthand. He'd be damned if anyone on the board questioned his business acumen during a time when his aging grandfather was testing all his heirs for their commitment to his legacy.

The Carib Grand lobby was welcoming, as he recalled from his tour six months ago when the property had been briefly shut down. The two wings of the hotel flanked the reception area to either side with restaurants stacked overhead. But the lobby itself drew visitors in with floor-to-ceiling windows so the sparkling Caribbean beckoned at all times. Huge hanging baskets of exotic flowers framed the view without impeding it.

The scent of bougainvillea drifted in through the door

behind him. Poppy tilted her nose in the air and took a seat on his forearm, a queen on her throne.

The front desk attendant—only one—was busy with another guest. Cameron's bellhop, a young guy with a long ponytail of dreadlocks, must have noticed the front desk was busy at the same time as him, because he gestured to the concierge's tall granite counter where a stunning brunette smiled.

"Ms. Delphine can help you check in, sir," the bellhop informed him while whisking his luggage onto a waiting cart. "Would you like me to walk the dog while you get settled?"

Nothing would please him more than to off-load Poppy and the miles of snow-white pet hair threading around his suit buttons. Cameron was pretty sure there was a cloud of fur floating just beneath his nose.

"Her name is Poppy," Cameron snapped at the helpful soul, unable to take his eyes off the very appealing concierge, who'd snagged his attention through the window the second he'd stepped out of the limo. "And I've requested a dog walker with references."

The bellhop gave a nod and backed away, no doubt glad to leave a surly guest in the hands of the bronze-skinned beauty sidling out from her counter to welcome Cameron. She seemed to have that mix of ethnicities common in the Caribbean. The burnished tint of her skin set off wide, tawny gold eyes. A natural curl and kink in her dusky brown hair ended in sun-blond tips. Perfect posture and a well-fitted linen suit made her look every inch a professional, yet her long legs drew his eye even though her skirt hit just above her knees. Even if he'd been visiting the property as her boss, he wouldn't have acted on the flash of attraction, of course. But it was a damn shame that he'd be at odds with this enticing female for the next two weeks. The concierge position was the linchpin in the hotel staff, though, and his mission to rattle cages began with her.

"Welcome, Mr. Holmes." He was impressed that she'd greeted him by name. "I'm Maresa. We're so glad to see you and Poppy, too."

He'd spoken to a Maresa Delphine on the phone earlier, purposely issuing a string of demands on short notice to see how she'd fare. She didn't look nervous. Yet. He'd need to challenge her, to prod at all facets of the management and staff to pinpoint the weak links. The hotel wasn't necessarily losing money, but it was only a matter of time before earnings followed the decline in performance reviews.

"Poppy will be glad to meet her walker." He came straight to the point, ignoring the eager bob of the dog's head as Maresa offered admiring words to the pooch. Cameron could imagine what the wag of the tail was doing to the back of his jacket. "Do you have the references ready?"

"Of course." Maresa straightened with a sunny smile. She had a hint of an accent he couldn't place. "They're right here at my desk."

Cameron's gaze dipped to her slim hips as she turned. He'd taken a hiatus from dating for fun over the last few months, thinking he ought to find himself a wife to fulfill his grandfather's dictate that McNeill Resorts would only go to the grandsons who were stable and wed. But he'd botched that, too, impulsively issuing a marriage proposal to the first woman his matchmaker suggested in order to have the business settled.

Now? Apparently the months without sex were conspiring against him. He ground his teeth against a surge of ill-timed desire.

"Here you go." The concierge turned with a sheet of paper in hand and passed it to him, her honey-colored gaze as potent as any caress. "I took the liberty of checking all the references myself, but I've included the numbers in case you'd like to talk to any of them directly."

"That's why I asked," he replied tightly, tugging the paper harder than necessary.

He could have sworn Poppy slanted him a dirty look over one fluffy white shoulder. Her nails definitely flexed into his forearm right through the sleeve of his suit before she fixed her coal-black eyes on Maresa Delphine.

Not that he blamed Poppy. He'd rather be staring at Maresa than scowling over dog walker references. Being the boss wasn't always a rocking-good time. Yet he'd rather ruffle feathers today and fix the core problems than have the staff jump though the hoops of an extended performance review.

Cameron slid the paper into his jacket pocket. "I'll check these after I have the chance to clean up. If you can have someone show us to our room."

He hurried her on purpose, curious if the room extras were ready to go. The bath wasn't a tough request, but the flowers had most likely needed to be flown in. If he hadn't been specifically looking for it, he might have missed the smallest hesitation on her part.

"Certainly." She lifted a tablet from the granite countertop where she worked. "If you can just sign here to approve the information you provided over the phone, I'll escort you myself."

That wasn't protocol. Did Ms. Delphine expect additional tips this way? Cam remembered reading that the concierge had been with the company since the reopening under McNeill ownership two months ago.

Signing his fake name on the electronic screen, he fished for information. "Are you understaffed?"

She ran a pair of keycards through the machine and slid them into a small welcome folder.

"Definitely not. We'll have Rudolfo bring your bags. I just want to personally ensure the suite is to your liking." She handed him the packet with the keys while giving a nod to the bell captain. "Can I make a dinner reservation for you this evening, Mr. Holmes?"

Cameron juggled the restless dog, who was no doubt more travel-weary than him. They'd taken a private jet, but even with the shorter air time, there'd been limo rides to and from airports, plus a boat crossing from Charlotte Amalie to the Carib Grand since the hotel occupied a small, private island just outside the harbor area in Saint Thomas. He'd walked the dog when they hit the ground at the airfield, but Poppy's owner had cautioned him to give the animal a certain amount of rest and play each day. So far on Cam's watch, Poppy had clocked zero time spent on both counts. For a pampered show dog, she was proving a trouper.

As soon as he banished the hotel staff including Maresa Delphine, he'd find a quiet spot on the beach where he and his borrowed pet could recharge.

"I've heard a retired chef from Paris opened a new restaurant in Martinique." He would be spending some time on that island where his half brothers were living. "I'd like a standing reservation for the rest of the week." He had no idea if he'd be able to get over there, but it was the kind of thing a good concierge could accommodate.

"I've heard La Belle Palm is fantastic." Maresa punched a button on the guest elevator while Rudolfo disappeared down another hall with the luggage. "I haven't visited yet, but I enjoyed Chef Pierre's La Luce on the Left Bank."

Her words brought to mind her résumé that he'd reviewed briefly before making the trip. She'd worked at a Paris hotel prior to accepting her current position.

"You've spent time in Paris, Ms. Delphine?" He set Poppy on the floor, unfurling the pink jeweled leash that had matched the carrying case Mrs. Trager had given him. He'd kept all the accessories except for that one— the huge pink pet carrier made Cam look like he was travelling with Barbie's Dreamhouse under his arm.

"She's so cute." Maresa kept her eyes on the dog and not on him. "And yes, I lived in Paris for a year before returning to Saint Thomas."

"You're from the area originally?" He almost regretted setting the dog down since it removed a barrier between them. Something about Maresa Delphine drew him in.

His gaze settled on the bare arch of her neck just above her jacket collar. Her thick brown hair had been clipped at the nape, ending in a silky tail that curled along one shoulder. A single pearl drop earring rolled along the tender expanse of skin, a pale contrast to her rich brown complexion.

"I grew up in Charlotte Amalie and worked in a local hotel until a foreign exchange program run by the corporate owner afforded me the chance to work overseas." She glanced up at him. Caught him staring.

The jolt of awareness flared, hot and unmistakable. He could tell she felt it, too. Her pupils dilated a fraction, dark pools with golden rims. His heartbeat slugged heavier. Harder.

He forced his gaze away as the elevator chimed to announce their arrival on his floor. "After you."

He held the door as she stepped out into the short hall.

They passed a uniformed attendant with a gallon-sized jug stuffed under his arm, a pair of earbuds half-in and half-out of his ears. After a quick glance at Maresa, the young man pulled the buds off and jammed them in his pocket, then shoved open a door to the stairwell.

"Here we are." Maresa stepped aside so Cam stood directly in front of the entrance to the Antilles Suite.

Poppy took a seat and stared at the door expectantly.

Cameron used the keycard to unlock the suite, not sure what to expect. Was Maresa Delphine worthy of what the company compensated her? Or had she returned to her hometown in order to bilk guests out of extra tips and take advantage of her employer? But she didn't appear to be looking for a bonus gratuity as her gaze darted around the suite interior and then landed on him.

Poppy spotted the patch of natural grass just outside the bathroom door. The sod rested inside a pallet on carpeted wheels, the cart painted in blues and tans to match the room's decorating scheme. The dog made a break for it and Cam let her go, the leash dangling behind her.

Lilacs flanked the crystal decanters on the minibar. Through the open door to the bathroom, Cameron could see the bubbles nearing the edge of the tub, the hot water still running as steam wafted upward.

So far, Maresa had proven a worthy concierge. That was good for the hotel, but less favorable for him, perhaps, since her high standards surely precluded acting on a fleeting elevator attraction.

"If everything is to your satisfaction, Mr. Holmes, I'll leave you undisturbed while I go make your dinner reservations for the week." She hadn't even allowed the door to close behind them, a wise practice, of course, for a female hotel employee.

Rudolfo was already in the hall with the luggage cart.

Cameron could hear Maresa giving the bellhop instructions for his bags. And Poppy's.

"Thank you." Cameron turned his back on her to stare out at the view of the hotel's private beach and the brilliant turquoise Caribbean Sea. "For now, I'm satisfied."

The room, of course, was fine. Ms. Delphine had passed his first test. But was he satisfied? No. He wouldn't rest until he knew why the guest reviews of the Carib Grand were lower than anticipated. And satisfaction was the last thing he was feeling when the most enticing woman he'd met in a long time was off-limits.

That attraction would be difficult to ignore when it was imperative he uncover all her secrets.

Two

As much as Maresa cursed her alarm clock chirping at her before dawn, she never regretted waking up early once she was on the Carib Grand's private beach before sunrise. Her mother's house was perched on a street high above Saint Thomas Harbor, which meant Maresa took a bike to the ferry each morning to get to the hotel property early for these two precious hours of alone time before work. Her brother was comfortable walking down to the dock later for his shift, a task that was overseen by a neighbor and fellow employee who also took the ferry over each day.

Now, rolling out her yoga mat on the damp sand, she made herself comfortable in child's pose, letting the magic of the sea and the surf do their work on her muscles tight with stress.

One. Two. Three. Breathe.

Smoothing her hands over the soft cotton of her bright

pink crop top, she felt her diaphragm lift and expand. She rarely saw anyone else on the beach at this hour, and the few runners or walkers who passed by were too busy soaking up the same quiet moments as she to pay her any mind.

Maresa counted through the inhales and exhales, trying her damnedest to let go of her worries. Too bad Cameron Holmes's ice-blue eyes and sculpted features kept appearing in her mind, distracting her with memories of that electric current she'd experienced just looking at him.

It made no sense, she lectured herself as she swapped positions for her sun salutations. The guest was demanding and borderline rude—something that shouldn't attract her in the slightest. She hated to think his raw masculinity was sliding under her radar despite what her brain knew about him.

At least she'd made it through the first day of his stay without incident. But while that was something to celebrate, she didn't want her brother crossing paths with the surly guest again. She'd held her breath yesterday when the two passed one another in the corridor outside the Antilles Suite, knowing how much Rafe loved dogs. Thankfully, her brother had been engrossed in his music and hadn't noticed the Maltese.

She'd keep Rafe safely away from Mr. Holmes for the next two weeks. Tilting her face to the soft glow of first light, she arched her back in the upward salute before sweeping down into a forward bend. Breathing out the challenges—living in tight quarters with her family, battling local agencies to get her brother into support programs he needed for his recovery, avoiding her former fiancé who'd texted her twice in the last twenty-four hours asking to see her— Maresa took comfort in this moment every day.

Shifting into her lunge as the sun peeked above the horizon, Maresa heard a dog bark before a small white ball of fluff careened past her toward the water. Startled by the sudden brush of fur against her arm, she had to reposition her hands to maintain her balance.

"Poppy." A man's voice sounded from somewhere in the woods behind the beach.

Cameron Holmes.

Maresa recognized the deep baritone, not by sound so much as by the effect it had on her. A slow, warm wave through the pit of her belly. What was the matter with her? She scrambled to her feet, realizing the pampered pet of her most difficult guest was charging into the Caribbean, happily chasing a tern.

"Poppy!" she called after the dog just as Cameron Holmes stepped onto the beach.

Shirtless.

She had to swallow hard before she lifted her fingers to her lips and whistled. The little Maltese stopped in the surf, peering back in search of the noise while the tern flew away up the shore. The ends of Poppy's glossy coat floated on the surface of the incoming tide.

The man charged toward his pet, his bare feet leaving wet footprints in the sand. Maresa was grateful for the moment to indulge her curiosity about him without his seeing her. A pair of bright board shorts rode low on his hips. The fiery glow of sunrise burnished his skin to a deeper tan, his square shoulders rolling with an easy grace as he scooped the animal out of the water and into his arms. He spoke softly to her even as the strands of long, wet fur clung to his side. Whatever he said earned him a heartfelt lick on the cheek from the pooch, its white tail wagging slowly.

Maresa's heart melted a little. Especially when she

caught a glimpse of Cameron Holmes's smile as he turned back toward her. For a moment, he looked like another man entirely.

Then, catching sight of her standing beside her yoga mat, his expression grew shuttered.

"Sorry to interrupt your morning." He gave a brief nod. Curt. Dismissive. "I thought the beach would be empty at this hour or I wouldn't have let her off the leash." He clipped a length of pink leather to the collar around Poppy's neck.

"Most days, I'm the only one down here at this time." She forced a politeness she didn't feel, especially when she wasn't on duty yet. "Would you like a towel for her?"

The animal wasn't shivering, but Maresa couldn't imagine it would be easy to groom the dog if she walked home with wet fur dragging on the ground.

"I didn't think to bring one with me." He frowned, glancing around the deserted beach as if one might appear. "I assumed towels would be provided."

She tried not to grind her teeth at the air of entitlement. It became far easier to ignore the appeal of his shirtless chest once he started speaking in that superior air.

"Towels are available when the beach cabana opens at eight." Bending to retrieve the duffel on the corner of her mat, she tugged out hers and handed it to him. "Poppy can have mine."

He hesitated.

She fought the urge to cram the terry cloth back in her bag and stomp off. But, of course, she couldn't do that. She reached toward the pup's neck and scratched her there instead. Poppy's heart-shaped collar jangled softly against Maresa's hand. She noticed the "If Found" name on the back.

Olivia Trager?

Maybe the animal belonged to a girlfriend.

"Thank you." He took the hand towel and tucked it around the dog. Poppy stared out of her wrap as if used to being swaddled. "I really didn't mean to interrupt you."

He sounded more sincere this time. Maresa glanced up at him, only to realize how close they were standing. His gaze roamed over her as if he had been taking advantage of an unseen moment, the same way she had ogled him earlier. Becoming aware of her skimpy yoga crop top and the heat of awareness warming her skin, she stepped back awkwardly.

"Ms. Trager must really trust you with her dog." She hadn't meant to say it aloud. Then again, maybe hearing about his girlfriend would stop these wayward thoughts about him. "That is, no wonder you want to take such good care of her."

Awkward much? Maresa cursed herself for sticking her nose in his personal business.

His expression remained inscrutable for a moment. He studied her as if weighing how much to share. "My mother wouldn't trust anyone but me with her dog," he said finally.

She considered his words, still half wishing the mystery Ms. Trager was a girlfriend on her way to the resort today. Then Maresa would have to take a giant mental step backward from the confusing hotel guest. As it stood, she had no one to save her from the attraction but herself. With that in mind, she raked up her yoga mat and started rolling it.

"Well, I hope the dog walker and groomer meet your criteria." She stuffed the mat in her duffel, wondering why he hadn't let the walker take the animal out in the first place. "I'm happy to find someone else if—"

"The walker is fine. You're doing an excellent job, Maresa."

The unexpected praise caught her off guard. She nearly dropped her bag, mostly because he fixed her with his clear blue gaze. Heat rushed through her again, and it didn't have anything to do with the sun bathing them in the morning light now that it was fully risen.

"Thank you." Her throat went dry. She backed up a step. Retreating. "I'm going to let you enjoy the beach."

Maresa turned toward the path through the thick undergrowth that led back to the hotel and nearly ran right into Jaden Torries, her ex-fiancé.

"Whoa!" Jaden's one hand reached to steady her, his other curved protectively around a pink bundle he carried. Tall and rangy, her artist ex-boyfriend was thin where Cameron was well-muscled. The round glasses Jaden wore for affectation and not because he needed them were jammed into the thick curls that reached his shoulders. "Maresa. I've been trying to contact you."

He released her, juggling his hold on the small pink parcel he carried. A parcel that wriggled?

"I've been busy." She wanted to pivot away from the man who'd told the whole island he was dumping her before informing her of the fact. But that shifting pink blanket captured her full attention.

A tiny wrinkled hand reached up from the lightweight cotton, the movement followed by the softest sigh imaginable.

Her ex-fiancé was carrying a baby.

"But this is important, Maresa. It's about Isla." He lowered his arm cradling the infant so Maresa could see her better.

Indigo eyes blinked up at her. Short dark hair complimented the baby's medium skin tone. A white cotton headband decorated with rosettes rested above barely there eyebrows. Perfectly formed tiny features were molded into a silent yawn, the tiny hands reaching heavenward as the baby shifted against Jaden.

Something shifted inside Maresa at the same time. A maternal urge she hadn't known she possessed seized her insides and squeezed tight. Once upon a time she had dreamed about having this man's babies. She'd imagined what they would look like. Now, he had sought her out to…taunt her with the life she'd missed out on?

The maternal urge hardened into resentment, but she'd be damned if she'd let him see it.

"Congratulations. Your daughter is lovely, Jaden." She straightened as the large shadow of Cameron Holmes covered them both.

"Is there a problem, Ms. Delphine?" His tone was cool and impersonal, yet in that awkward moment he felt like an ally.

She appreciated his strong presence beside her when she felt that old surge of betrayal. She let Jaden answer since she didn't feel any need to defend the ex who'd called off their wedding via a text message.

"There's no problem. I'm an old friend of Maresa's. Jaden Torries." He extended his free hand to introduce himself.

Mr. Holmes ignored it. Poppy barked at Jaden.

"Then I'm sure you'll respect Maresa's wish to be on her way." Her unlikely rescuer tucked his hand under one arm as easily as he'd plucked his pet from the water earlier.

The warmth of his skin made her want to curl into him just like Poppy had, too.

"Right." Jaden dropped his hand. "Except Rafe's old girlfriend, Trina, left town last night, Maresa. And since

Trina's my cousin, she stuck me with the job of delivering Rafe's daughter into your care."

Maresa's feet froze to the spot. She had a vague sense of Cameron leaning closer to her, his hand suddenly at her back. Which was helpful, because she thought for a minute there was a very real chance she was going to faint. Her knees wobbled beneath her.

"Sorry to spring it on you like this," Jaden continued. "I tried telling Trina she owed it to your family to tell you in person, and I thought I had her talked into it, but—"

"Rafe?" Maresa turned around slowly, needing to see with her own eyes if there was any chance Jaden was telling the truth. "Trina broke up with him almost a year ago. Right after the accident."

Jaden stepped closer. "Right. And Trina didn't even find out she was pregnant until a couple of weeks afterward, while Rafe was still in critical condition. Trina decided to go through with the pregnancy on her own. Isla was born the end of January."

Maresa was too shaken to even do the math, but she did know that Trina and Rafe had been hot and heavy for the last month or two they were together. They'd been a constant fixture on Maresa's social media feed for those weeks. Which had made it all the more upsetting when Trina bailed on him right after the accident, bursting into tears every time she got close to his bedside before giving up altogether. Had she been even more emotional because she'd been in the early stages of pregnancy?

"Why wouldn't she have called me or my mother?" Her knees wobbled again as her gaze fell on the tiny infant. Isla? She had Rafe's hairline—the curve of dark hair encroaching on the temples. But plenty of babies had that, didn't they? "I would have helped her. I could have been there when the baby was born."

"Who is Rafe?" Cameron asked.

She'd forgotten all about him.

Maresa gulped a breath. "My brother." The very real possibility that Jaden was telling the truth threatened to level her. Rafe was in no position to be a father with the assorted symptoms he still battled. And financially? She was barely getting by supporting her family and paying some of Rafe's staggering medical bills since he hadn't been fully insured at the time.

"Look." Jaden set a bright pink diaper bag down on the beach. Cartoon cats cartwheeled across the front. "My apartment is no place for a baby. You know that, right? I just took her because Trina showed up last night, begging me for help. I told her no, but told her she could spend the night. She took off while I was sleeping. But she left a note for you." He looked as though he wanted to sort through the diaper bag to find it, but before he leaned down he held the baby out to Maresa. "Here. Take her."

Maresa wasn't even sure she'd made up her mind to do so when Jaden thrust the warm, precious weight into her arms. He was still talking about Trina seeming "unstable" ever since giving birth, but Maresa couldn't follow his words with an infant in her arms. She felt stiff and awkward, but she was careful to support the squirming bundle, cradling the baby against her chest while Isla gurgled and kicked.

Maresa's heart turned over. Melted.

Here, the junglelike landscaping blocked out the sun where the tree branches arced over the dirt path. The scent of green and growing things mingled with the sea breeze and a hint of baby shampoo.

"She's a beauty," Cameron observed over her shoulder. He had set Poppy on the ground so he could get closer to Isla and Maresa. "Are you okay holding her?"

"Fine," she said automatically, not wanting to give her up. "Just…um…overwhelmed."

Glancing up at him, she caught her breath at the expression on his face as he looked down at the child in her arms. She had thought he seemed different—kinder—toward Poppy. But that unguarded smile she'd seen for the Maltese was nothing compared to the warmth in his expression as he peered down at the baby.

If she didn't know better—if she hadn't seen him be rude and abrupt with perfectly nice hotel staffers—she would have guessed she caught him making silly faces at Isla. The little girl appeared thoroughly captivated.

"Here it is." Jaden straightened, a piece of paper in his hand. "She left this for you along with some notes about the kid's schedule." He passed the papers to Cameron. "I've got to get going if I'm going to catch that ferry, Maresa. I only came out here because Trina gave me no choice, but I've got to get to work—"

"Seriously?" She had to work, too. But even as she was about to say as much, another voice in her head piped up. If Isla was really Rafe's child, would she honestly want Jaden Torries in charge of the baby for another minute? The answer was a crystal clear *absolutely not.*

"Drop her off at social services if you don't believe me." Jaden shrugged. "I've got a rich old lady client paying a whole hell of a lot for me to paint her portrait at eight." He checked his watch. "I'm outta here."

And with that, her ex-fiancé walked away, his sandy-gold curls bouncing. Poppy barked again, clearly unimpressed.

Social services? Really?

"If only I had Poppy around three years ago when I got engaged to him," she muttered darkly, hugging the baby tighter.

Cameron's hand briefly found the small of her back as he watched the other man leave. He clutched the letter from Rafe's former girlfriend—Isla's mother.

"And yet you didn't go through the wedding. So you did just fine on your own." Cameron glanced down at her, his hand lingering on her back for one heart-stopping moment before it drifted away again. "Want me to read the letter? Or would you like me to take Isla so you can do the honors?"

He held the paper out for her to decide.

She liked him better here—outside the hotel. He was less intimidating, for one thing.

For another? He was appealing to her in all the ways a man could. A dangerous feeling for her when she needed to be on her guard around him. He was a guest, for crying out loud. But she was out of her depth with this precious little girl in her arms and she didn't know what she'd do if Cameron Holmes walked away from her right now. Having him there made her feel—if only for a moment—that she wasn't totally alone.

"Actually, I'd be really grateful if you would read it." She shook her head, tightening her hold on Isla. "I'm too nervous."

Katrina—Trina—Blanchett had been Rafe's girlfriend for about six months before the car accident. Maresa had never seen them together except for photos on social media of the two of them out playing on the beach or at the clubs. They'd seemed happy enough, but Rafe had told her on the phone it wasn't serious. The night of the accident, in fact, the couple had gotten into an argument at a bar and Trina had stranded him there. Rafe had called their mother for a ride, something she'd been only too happy to provide even though it was late. She'd never had an MS attack while driving before.

Less than ten days after seeing Rafe in the hospital, Trina had told Maresa through tears that she couldn't stand seeing him that way and it would be better for her to leave. At the time, Maresa had been too focused on Rafe's prognosis to worry about his flighty girlfriend. If she'd taken more time to talk to the girl, might she have confided the pregnancy news that followed the breakup?

"Would you like to have a seat?" Cameron pointed toward a bench near the outdoor faucet where guests could rinse off their feet. "You look too pale."

She nodded, certain she was pale. What was her mother going to say when she found out Rafe had a daughter? If he had a daughter. And Rafe? She couldn't imagine how frustrated he would feel to have been left out of the whole experience. Then again, how frustrated would he feel knowing that he couldn't care for his daughter the way he could have at one time?

Struggling to get her spinning thoughts under control, she allowed Cameron to guide her to the bench. Carefully, she lowered herself to sit with Isla, the baby blanket covering her lap since the kicking little girl had mostly freed herself of the swaddling. While she settled the baby, she noticed Cameron lift Poppy and towel her off a bit more before setting her down again. He double-checked the leash clip on her collar then took the seat beside Maresa.

"I'm ready," she announced, needing to hear whatever Isla's mother had to say.

Cameron unfolded the paper and read aloud. "'Isla is Rafe's daughter. I wasn't with anyone else while we were together. I was afraid to tell him about her after the doctor said he'd be…'" Cameron hesitated for only a moment "'…brain damaged. I know Rafe can't take care of her, but his mother will love her, right? I can't do this. I'm going to see my dad in Florida for a few weeks, but I'll sign papers to give you custody. I'm sorry."

Maresa listened to the silence following the words, her brain uncomprehending. How could the woman just take off and leave her baby—Rafe's baby—with Jaden Torries while she traveled to Florida? Who did that? Trina wasn't a kid—she was twenty-one when she'd dated Rafe. But she'd never had much family support, according to Rafe. Her mother was an alcoholic and her father had raised her, but he'd never paid her much attention.

A fierce surge of protectiveness swelled inside of Maresa. It was so strong she didn't know where to put it all. But she knew for damn sure that she would protect little Isla—her niece—far better than the child's mother had. And she would call a lawyer and find out how to file for full custody.

"You could order DNA testing," Cameron observed, his impressive abs rippling as he leaned forward on the bench. "If you are concerned she's not a biological relative."

Maresa closed her eyes for a moment to banish all thoughts of male abs, no matter how much she welcomed the distraction from the monumental life shift taking place for her this morning.

"I'll ask an attorney about it when I call to find out how I can secure legal custody." She wrapped Isla's foot back in a corner of the blanket. "For right now, I need to find suitable care for Isla before my shift at the Carib begins for the day." Throat burning, Maresa realized she was near tears just thinking about the unfairness of it all. Not to *her*, of course, because she would make it work no matter what life threw at her.

But how unfair to *Rafe*, who wouldn't be able to parent his child without massive amounts of help. Perhaps he wouldn't be interested in parenting at all. Would he be angry? Would Trina's surprise be the kind of thing that unsettled his confused mind and set back his recovery?

She would call his counselor before saying anything to him. That call would be right after she spoke to a lawyer. She wasn't even ready to tell her mother yet. Analise Delphine's health was fragile and stress could aggravate it. Maresa wanted to be sure she was calm before she spoke to her mother. They'd all been in the dark for months about Trina's pregnancy. A few more hours wouldn't matter one way or another.

"I noticed on the dog walker's résumé that she has experience working in a day care." Cameron folded the paper from Trina and inserted it into an exterior pocket of the diaper bag. "And as it happens, I already walked the dog. Would you like me to text her and ask her to meet you somewhere in the hotel to give you a hand?"

Maresa couldn't imagine what that would cost. But what were her options since she didn't want to upset her mother? She didn't have time to return home and give the baby to her mother even if she was sure her mother could handle the shocking news.

"That would be a great help, thank you. The caregiver can meet me in the women's locker room by the pool in twenty minutes." Shooting to her feet, Maresa realized she'd imposed on Cameron Holmes's kindness for far too long. "And with that, I'll let you and Poppy get back to your morning walk."

"I'll go with you. I can carry the baby gear." He reached for the pink diaper bag, but she beat him to it.

"I'm fine. I insist." She pasted on her best concierge smile and tried not to think about how comforting it had felt to have him by her side this morning. Now more than ever, she needed job security, which meant she couldn't let an important guest think she made a habit of bringing her personal life to work. "Enjoy your day, Mr. Holmes."

Enjoying his day proved impossible with visions of Maresa Delphine's pale face circling around Cameron's head the rest of the morning. He worked at his laptop on the private terrace off his room, distracted as hell thinking about the beautiful, efficient concierge caught off guard by a surprise that would have damn near leveled anyone else.

She'd inherited her brother's baby. A brother who, from the sounds of it, was not in any condition to care for his child himself.

Sunlight glinted off the sea and the sounds from the beach floated up to his balcony. The noises had grown throughout the morning from a few circling gulls to the handful of vacationing families that now populated the beach. The scent of coconut sunscreen and dense floral vegetation swirled on the breeze. But the temptation of a tropical paradise didn't distract Cam from his work nearly as much as memories of his morning with Maresa.

Shocking encounter with the baby aside, he would still have been distracted just remembering her limber arched back, her beautiful curves outlined by the light of the rising sun when he'd first broken through the dense undergrowth to find her on the private beach. Her skimpy workout gear had skimmed her hips and breasts, still tantalizing the hell out of him when he was supposed to be researching the operations hierarchy of the Carib Grand on his laptop.

But then, all that misplaced attraction got funneled into protectiveness when he'd met her sketchy former fiancé. He'd met the type before—charming enough, but completely self-serving. The guy couldn't have come up with a kinder way to inform her of her niece's existence?

On the plus side, Cameron had located some search results about her brother. Rafe Delphine had worked at the hotel for one month in a hire that some might view as unethical given his relationship to Maresa. But his application—though light on work history—had been approved by the hotel director on-site, so the young man must be fit for the job despite his injury in a car wreck the year before. That, too, had been an easy internet search, with local news articles reporting the crash and a couple of updates on Rafe's condition afterward. The trauma the guy had suffered must have been harrowing for his whole family. Clearly the girlfriend had found it too much to handle.

Now, as a runner for the concierge, Rafe would be directly under Maresa's supervision. That concerned Cameron since Maresa would have every reason in the world to keep him employed. As much as Cam empathized with her situation—all the more now that she'd discovered her brother had an heir—he couldn't afford to ignore good business practices. He'd have to speak to the hotel director about the situation and see if they should make a change.

The ex-fiancé was next on his list of searches. Not that he wanted to pry into Maresa's private life. Cameron was more interested in seeing how the guy connected to the Carib Grand that he'd come all the way to the hotel's private island to pass over the baby. That seemed like an unnecessary trip unless he was staying here or worked here. Why not just give the baby to Maresa at her home in Charlotte Amalie? Why come to her place of work when it was so far out of the way?

Cam had skimmed halfway through the short search results on Jaden Torries's portraits of people and pets before his phone buzzed with an incoming call. Poppy, snoozing in the shade of the chair under his propped feet, didn't even stir at the sound. The dog was definitely making up for lost rest from the day before.

Glimpsing his oldest brother's private number, Cam hit the button to connect the call. "Talk to me."

"Hello to you, too." Quinn's voice came through along with the sounds of Manhattan in the background—horns honking, brakes squealing, a shrill whistle and a few shouts above the hum of humanity indicating he must be on the street. "I wanted to give you a heads-up I just bought a sea plane."

"Nice, bro, But there's no way you'll get clearance to land in the Hudson with that thing." Cameron scrolled to a gallery of Torries's work and was decidedly unimpressed.

Not that he was an expert. But as a supporter of the arts in Manhattan for all his adult life, he felt reasonably sure Maresa's ex was a poser. Then again, maybe he just didn't like a guy who'd once commanded the concierge's attention.

"The aircraft isn't for me," Quinn informed him. "It's for you. I figured it would be easier than a chopper to get from one island to another while you're investigating the Carib Grand and checking out the relatives."

Cam shoved aside his laptop and straightened. "Seriously? You bought a seaplane for my two-week stay?"

As a McNeill, he'd grown up with wealth, yes. He'd even expanded his holdings with the success of the gaming development company he'd started in college. But damn. He limited himself to spending within reason.

"The Carib Grand is the start of our Caribbean expansion, and if it goes well, we'll be spending a lot of time and effort developing the McNeill brand in the islands and South America. We have a plane available in the Mediterranean. Why not keep something accessible on this side of the Atlantic?"

"Right." Cam's jaw flexed at the thought of how much was riding on smoothing things out at the Carib Grand. A poor bottom line wasn't going to help the expansion program. "Good thinking."

"Besides, I have the feeling we'll be seeing our half brothers in Martinique a whole lot more now that Gramps is determined to bring them into the fold." Quinn sounded as grim about that prospect as Cameron felt. "So the plane might be useful for all of us as we try to…contain the situation."

Quinn wanted to keep their half siblings out of Manhattan and out of the family business as much as Cameron did. They'd worked too hard to hand over their company to people who'd never lifted a finger to grow McNeill Resorts.

"Ah." Cam stood to stretch his legs, surprised to realize it was almost noon according to the slim dive watch he'd worn for his morning laps. "But since I'm on the front line meeting them, I'm going to leave it up to you or Ian to be the diplomatic peacemakers."

Quinn only half smothered a laugh. "No one expected you of all people to be the diplomat. Dad's still recovering from the punch you gave him last week when he dropped the I-have-another-family bombshell on us."

Definitely not one of his finer moments. "It seemed like he could have broached the topic with some more tact."

"No kidding. I kept waiting for Sofia to break the engagement after the latest family soap opera." The background noise on Quinn's call faded. "Look, Cam, I just arrived at Lincoln Center to take her out to lunch. I'll text you the contact details for a local pilot."

Cam grinned at the thought of his stodgy older brother

so head over heels for his ballerina fiancée. The same ballerina fiancée Cam had impulsively proposed to last winter when a matchmaker set them up. But even if Cam and Sofia hadn't worked out, the meeting had been a stroke of luck for Quinn, who'd promptly stepped in to woo the dancer.

"Thanks. And give our girl a kiss from me, okay?" It was too fun to resist needling Quinn. Especially since Cameron was two thousand miles away from a retaliatory beat-down.

A string of curses peppered his ear before Quinn growled, "It's not too late to take the plane back."

"Sorry." Cameron wasn't sorry. He was genuinely happy for his brother. "I'll let you know if the faux McNeills are every bit as awful as we imagine."

Disconnecting the call, Cameron texted a message to the dog groomer to give Poppy some primp time. He'd use that window of freedom to follow up on a few leads around the Carib Grand. He wanted to find out what the hotel director thought about Rafe Delphine, for one thing. The director was the only person on-site who knew Cameron's true identity and mission at the hotel. Aldo Ricci had been successful at McNeill properties in the Mediterranean and Malcolm McNeill had personally appointed the guy to make the expansion program a success.

With the McNeill patriarch's health so uncertain, Cameron wanted to respect his grandfather's choices. All the more so since he still hadn't married the way his granddad wanted.

Cameron would start by speaking to his grandfather's personally chosen manager. Cam had a lot of questions about the day-to-day operations and a few key personnel. Most especially the hotel's new concierge, who kept too many secrets behind her beautiful and efficient facade.

Three

Seated in the hotel director's office shortly after noon, Cameron listened to Aldo Ricci discuss his plans for making the Carib Grand more profitable over the next two quarters. Unlike Cameron, the celebrated hotel director with a crammed résumé of successes did not seem concerned about the dip in the Carib Grand's performance.

"All perfectly normal," the impeccably dressed director insisted, prowling around his lavish office on the ground floor of the property. A collector of investment-grade wines, Aldo incorporated a few rare vintages into his office decor. A Bordeaux from Moulin de La Lagune rested casually on a shelf beside some antique corkscrews and a framed invitation from a private tasting at Château Grand Corbin. "We are only beginning to notice the minute fluctuations now that our capacity for data is greater than ever. But those irregularities will not even be noticeable by the time we hit our performance and profit goals for the end of the year."

The heavyset man tugged on his perfectly straight suit cuffs. The fanciness of the dark silk jacket he wore reminded Cameron how many times the guy had taken a property out of the red and into the ranks of the most prestigious places in the world. To have enticed him to McNeill Resorts had been a coup, according to Cameron's grandfather.

"Nevertheless, I'd like to know more about Maresa Delphine." Cameron didn't reveal his reasons. He could see her now through the blinds in the director's office. She strode along the pool patio outside, hurrying past the patrons in her creamy linen blazer with an orchid at the lapel. Her sun-splashed brown hair gleamed in the bright light, but something about her posture conveyed her tension. Worry.

Was she thinking about Isla?

He made a mental note to check on the sitter and be sure she was doing a good job with the baby. Little Isla had tugged at his heartstrings this morning with her tiny, restless hands and her expressive face. That feeling—the warmth for the baby—shocked him. Not that he was an ogre or anything, but he'd decided long ago not to have kids of his own.

He was too much like his father—impulsive, fun-loving, easily distracted—to be a parent. After all, Liam McNeill had turfed out responsibility for his sons at the first possible opportunity, letting the boys' grandfather raise them the moment Liam's Brazilian wife got tired of his globe-trotting, daredevil antics. Cameron had always known his father had shirked the biggest responsibility of his life and that, coupled with his own tendency to follow his own drummer, had been enough to convince Cam that kids weren't for him. And that had been before discovering his dad had fathered a whole other set of kids with someone else.

Before an accident that had compromised Cameron's ability to have a family anyhow.

"Maresa Delphine is a wonderful asset to the hotel," the director assured him, coming around to the front of his desk to sit beside Cameron in the leather club chairs facing the windows. "If you seek answers about the hotel workings, I urge you to reveal your identity to her. I know you want to remain incognito, but I assure you, Ms. Delphine is as discreet and professional as they come."

"Yet you've only known her for…what? Two months?"

"Far longer than that. She worked at another property in Saint Thomas where I supervised her three years ago. I personally recommended her to a five-star property in Paris because I was impressed with her work and she was eager to…escape her hometown for a while. I had no reservations about helping her win the spot. She makes her service her top priority." The director crossed one leg over the other and pointed to a crystal decanter on the low game table between them. "Are you sure I can't offer you anything to drink?"

"No. Thank you." He wanted a clear head for deciding his next move with Maresa. Revealing himself to her was tempting considering the attraction simmering just beneath the surface. But he couldn't forget about the gut instinct that told him she was hiding something. "What can you tell me about her brother?"

"Rafe is a fine young man. I would have gladly hired him even without Maresa's assurances she would watch over him."

"Why would she need to?" He was genuinely curious

about the extent of Rafe's condition. Not only because she seemed protective of him, but also because Maresa hadn't argued Trina's depiction of her brother as "brain damaged."

"Rafe has a traumatic brain injury. He's the reason Maresa gave up the job in Paris. She rushed home to take care of her family. The young man is much better now. Although he can become agitated or confused easily, he has good character, and we haven't put him in a position where he will have much contact with guests." Aldo smiled as he smoothed his tie. "Maresa feels a strong sense of responsibility for him. But I've seen no reason to regret hiring her sibling. She knows, however, that Rafe's employment is on a trial basis."

Aldo Ricci seemed like the kind of man to trust his gut, which might be fine for someone who'd been in the business for as long as he had, but Cameron still wondered if he was overlooking things.

Maybe he should confide in Maresa if only to discover her take on the staff at the Carib Grand. Specifically, he wondered, what was her impression of Aldo Ricci? Cameron found himself wanting to know a lot more about the operations of the hotel.

"Perhaps I will speak to Ms. Delphine." Cameron wanted to find her now, in fact. His need to see her has been growing ever since she'd walked away from him early that morning. "I'd like some concrete answers about those performance reviews, even if they do seem like minute fluctuations."

He rose from his seat, liking the new plan more than he should. *Damn it.* Spending more time with Maresa didn't mean anything was going to happen between them. As her boss, of course, he had a responsibility to ensure it didn't.

And, without question, she had a great deal on her

mind today of all days. But maybe that was all the more reason to give her a break from the concierge stand. Perhaps she'd welcome a few hours away from the demands of the guests.

"Certainly." The hotel director followed him to the door. "There's no one more well-versed in the hotel except for me." His grin revealed a mouth full of shiny white veneers. "Stick close to her."

Cameron planned to do just that.

"Have you seen Rafe?" Maresa asked Nancy, the waitress who worked in the lobby bar shortly after noon. "I wanted to eat lunch with him."

Standing beside Nancy, a tall blonde goddess of a woman who probably made more in tips each week than Maresa made in a month, she peered out over the smattering of guests enjoying cocktails and the view. Her brother was nowhere in sight.

She had checked on Isla a few moments ago, assuring herself the baby was fine. She'd shared Trina's notes about the baby's schedule with the caregiver, discovering Isla's birth certificate with the father's name left blank and a birth date of ten weeks prior. And after placing a call to Trina's mother, Maresa had obtained contact information for the girl's father in Florida, who'd been able to give her a number for Trina herself. The girl had tearfully confirmed everything she said in her note—promising to give custody of the child to Rafe's family since she wasn't ready to be a mother and she didn't trust her own mother to be a good guardian.

The young woman had been so distraught, Maresa had felt sorry for her. All the more so because Trina had tried to handle motherhood alone when she'd been so conflicted about having a baby in the first place.

Now, Maresa wanted to see Rafe for herself to make sure he was okay. What if Jaden had mentioned Isla to him? Or even just mentioned Trina leaving town? Rafe hadn't asked about his girlfriend since regaining consciousness. She suspected Rafe would have been walking onto the ferry that morning the same time as Jaden was walking off.

Earlier that day, she'd left him a to-do list when she'd had an appointment to keep with the on-site restaurant's chef. She'd given Rafe only two chores, and they were both jobs he'd done before so she didn't think he'd have any trouble. He had to pick up some supplies at the gift shop and deliver flowers to one of the guests' rooms.

"I saw him about an hour ago." Nancy rang out a customer's check. "He brought me this." She pointed to the tiny purple wildflowers stuffed behind the engraved silver pin with her name on it. "He really is the sweetest."

"Thank you for being so kind to him." Maresa had witnessed enough people be impatient and rude to him that he'd become her barometer for her measure of a person. People who were nice to Rafe earned her respect.

"Kind to *him*?" Nancy tossed her head back and laughed, her long ponytail swishing. "That boy should earn half my tips since it's Rafe who makes me smile when I feel like strangling some of my more demanding customers—like that Mr. Holmes." She straightened the purple blooms with one hand and shoved the cash drawer closed with her hip. "These flowers from your brother are the nicest flowers any man has ever given me."

Reassured for the moment, Maresa felt her heart squeeze at the words. Her brother had the capacity for great love despite the frustrations of his injury. Maybe he'd come to accept his daughter as part of his life down the road.

Until then, she needed to keep them both safely employed and earning benefits to take care of their family.

"It makes me happy to hear you say that." Maresa turned on her heel, leaving Nancy to her job. "If you see him, will you let him know I'm having lunch down by the croquet field?"

"Sure thing." Nancy lifted a tray full of drinks to take to another table. "Sometimes he hangs out in the break room if the Yankees are on the radio, you know. You might check if they play today."

"Okay. Thanks." She knew her brother liked listening to games on the radio. Being able to listen on his earbuds was always soothing for him.

Maresa hitched her knapsack with the insulated cooler onto her shoulder to carry out to the croquet area. The field didn't officially open again until late afternoon when it cooled down, so no one minded if employees sat under the palm trees there for lunch. There were a handful of places like that on the private island—spots where guests didn't venture that workers could enjoy. She needed a few minutes to collect herself. Come up with a plan for what she was going to do with a ten-week-old infant after work. And what she would tell Rafe about the baby since his counselor hadn't yet returned her phone call.

Her phone vibrated just then as her sandals slapped along the smooth stone path dotted with exotic plantings on both sides. Her mother's number filled the screen.

"Mom?" she answered quietly while passing behind the huge pool and cabanas that surrounded it. The area was busy with couples enjoying outdoor meals or having cocktails at the swim-up bar and families playing in the nearby surf. Seeing a mother share a bite of fresh pineapple with her little girl made Maresa's breath catch.

She'd once dreamed of being a mother to Jaden's children until he betrayed her.

Now, she might be a single mother to her brother's baby if Trina truly relinquished custody.

She scuttled deeper into the shade of some palms for her phone conversation, knowing she couldn't blurt out Isla's existence to her mom on the phone even though, in the days before her mother's health had taken a downhill spiral, she might have been tempted to do just that.

"No need to worry." Her mother's breathing sounded labored. From stress? Or exertion? She tired so easily over the past few months. "I just wanted to let you know your brother came home."

Maresa's steps faltered. Stopped.

"Rafe is there? With you?" Panic tightened her shoulders and clenched her gut. She peered around the path to the croquet field, half hoping her brother would come strolling toward her anyhow, juggling some pilfered deck cushions for her to sit on for an impromptu picnic the way he did sometimes.

"He showed up about ten minutes ago. I would have called sooner, but he was upset and I had to calm him down. I guess the florist gave him a pager—"

"Oh no." Already, Maresa could guess what had happened. "Those are really loud." The devices vibrated and blinked, setting off obnoxious alarms that would startle anyone, let alone someone with nervous tendencies. The floral delivery must not have been prepared when Rafe arrived to pick it up, so they gave him the pager to let him know when it was ready.

"He got scared and dropped it, but I'm not sure where—" Her mother stopped speaking, and in the background, Maresa heard Rafe shouting "I don't know, I don't know, I don't know" in a frightened chorus.

Her gut knotted. How could she bring a ten-week-old into their home tonight, knowing how loud noises upset her brother?

"Tell him everything's fine. I'll find the pager." Turning on her heel, she headed back toward the hotel. She thought the device turned itself off after a few minutes anyhow, but just in case it was still beeping, she'd rather find it before anyone else on staff. "I can probably retrace his steps since I sent him on those errands. I'll deliver the flowers myself."

"Honey, you're taking on too much having him there with you. You don't want to risk your job."

And the alternative? They didn't have one. Especially now with little Isla's care to consider.

"My job will be fine," she reassured her mother as she tugged open a door marked Employees Only that led to the staff room and corporate offices. She needed to sign Rafe out for the day before she did anything else.

Blinking against the loss of sunlight, Maresa felt the blast of air conditioning hit her skin, which had gone clammy with nervous sweat. She picked at the neckline of her thin silk camisole beneath her linen jacket.

"Ms. Delphine?" a familiar masculine voice called to her from the other end of the corridor.

Even before she turned, she knew who she would see. The tingling that tripped over her skin was an unsettling mix of anticipation and dread.

"Mom, I'll call you back." Disconnecting quickly, she dropped the phone in her purse and turned to see Cameron Holmes striding out of the hotel director's office, her boss at his side.

"Mr. Holmes." She forced a smile for both men, wondering why life was conspiring so hard against her today. What on earth would a guest be doing in the hotel director's office if not to complain? Unless maybe he had something extremely valuable he wanted to place in the hotel safe personally.

Highly unorthodox, but that's the only other reason she could think of to explain his presence here.

"Maresa." Her hotel director nodded briefly at her before shaking hands with Cameron Holmes. "And sir, I appreciate you coming to me directly. I certainly understand the need for discretion."

Aldo Ricci turned and re-entered his office, leaving Maresa with a racing heart in the presence of Cameron Holmes, who looked far more intimidating in a custom navy silk suit and a linen shirt open at the throat than he had in his board shorts this morning.

The level of appeal, however, seemed equal on both counts. She couldn't forget his unexpected kindness on the beach no matter how demanding he'd been as a hotel guest.

"Just the woman I was hoping to see." His even white teeth made a quick appearance in what passed for a smile. "Would you join me for a moment in the conference room?"

No.

Her brain filled in the answer even as her feet wisely followed where he led. She didn't want to be alone with him anywhere. Not when she entertained completely inappropriate thoughts about him. She couldn't let her attraction to a guest show.

Furthermore? She needed to sign her brother out of work, locate the pager he'd lost and deliver those flowers before the florist got annoyed and reported Rafe for not doing his job. Now was not the time for fantasizing about a wealthy guest who could afford to shape the world to his liking, even if he had the body of a professional surfer underneath that expensive suit.

As she crossed the threshold into the Carib Grand's private conference room full of tall leather chairs around an antique table, Maresa realized she couldn't do this. Not now.

"Actually, Mr. Holmes," she said, spinning around to face him and misjudging how close he followed behind her.

Suddenly, she stood nose-to-nose with him, her thigh grazing his, her breast brushing his strong arm. She stepped back fast, heat flooding her cheeks. The contact was so brief, she could almost tell herself it hadn't happened, except that her body hummed with awareness where they'd touched.

And then, there was the fact that he gripped her elbow when she wobbled.

"Sorry," she blurted, tugging away from him completely as the door to the conference room closed automatically behind them.

Sealing them in privacy.

Sunlight spilled in behind her, the Caribbean sun the only illumination in the room that hadn't been in use yet today. The quiet was deep here, the carpet muffling his step as he shifted closer.

"Are you all right?" His forehead creased with concern. "Are you comfortable with the caregiver for Isla?"

She glanced up at him, surprised at the thoughtful question. He really had been supportive this morning, giving her courage during an impossible situation. Right now, however, it was difficult to focus on his kind side when the man was simply far too handsome. She wished fervently he had that adorable little dog with him so she could pet Poppy instead of thinking about how hot Mr. Holmes could be when he wasn't scowling.

"I'm fine. I have everything under control." *Um, if*

only. Clearly, she needed to date more often so she didn't turn into a babbling idiot around handsome men during work hours. "It's just that you caught me on my lunch hour, so I'm not technically working."

"Unfortunately, Maresa, I am." He folded his arms across his chest before he paced halfway across the room.

Confused, she watched him. He was not an easy man to look away from.

"I don't understand." She wondered how it happened that being around him made her feel like there wasn't enough air in the room. Like she couldn't possibly catch her breath.

"I'm doing some work for the hotel," he explained, pacing back toward her. "Secretly."

Confusion filled her as she tried to sort through his words that didn't make a bit of sense.

"So you're not actually on vacation at all? What kind of work?" She could think better now that he was on the opposite side of the room. "Is that why you were in the hotel director's office?"

"Yes. My real name is Cameron McNeill and I'm investigating why guest satisfaction has been declining over the last two months." He kept coming toward her, his blue eyes zeroing in on her. "And now I'm beginning to think you're the only person who can help me figure out why."

Cameron could feel her nervousness as clearly as if it was his own.

She stood, alert and ready to flee, her tawny eyes wide. She bit her full lower lip.

"McNeill? As in McNeill Resorts?" She blinked slowly.

"The same."

"Why do you think I can help you?" She smoothed the

cuff of her ivory-colored linen jacket and then swiped elegant fingers along her forehead as if perspiring in spite of the fact she looked cool. So incredibly smooth and cool.

He hated doing this to her today of all days. The woman had just found out her brother had a child who would—he suspected—become her financial and familial dependent. What he'd gathered about Rafe Delphine's health suggested the man wouldn't be in any position to care for a newborn, and Aldo Ricci had made it clear Maresa put her family before herself.

"Preliminary data indicates the Carib is floundering in performance reviews and customer satisfaction." That was true enough. "You have a unique perspective on the hotel and everyone who works here. I'd like to know your views on why that might be?"

"And my boss told you I would talk to you about those issues?" Her gaze flitted to the door behind him and then back to him as if she would rather be anywhere else than right here.

Truth be told, he was a little uncomfortable being alone with her under these circumstances himself. She was far too tempting to question in the privacy of an empty conference room when the attraction was like a live wire sending sparks in all directions.

How could he ignore that?

"Your hotel director assured me you would be discreet."

She'd garnered the respect of her peers. The praise of superiors. All of which only made Cameron more curious about her. He stopped in front of her. At a respectable distance. He held her gaze, not allowing his eyes to wander.

"Of course, Mr. McNeill." She fidgeted with a bracelet—a shiny silver star charm—partially hidden by the sleeve of her jacket. "But what exactly did he hope I could share with you?"

"Call me Cam. And I hope you will share any insights about the staff and even some of the guests." He knew the data could be skewed by one or two unhappy visitors, particularly if they were vocal about their displeasure with the hotel.

"A difficult line to walk considering how much a concierge needs to keep her guests happy. It doesn't serve me—or McNeill Resorts—to betray confidences of valued clients."

Cameron couldn't help the voice in his head that piped up just then, wanting to know what she might have done to keep *him* happy as her guest.

Focus, damn it.

"And yet, you'll want to please the management as well," he reminded her. "Correct?"

"Of course." She nodded, letting go of the silver star so the bracelet slipped lower on her wrist.

"So how about if I buy you lunch and we'll begin our work together? I'll speak to Mr. Ricci about giving you the afternoon off." He needed to take her somewhere else. A place where the temptation to touch her wouldn't get the better of him. "We can bring Isla."

Nothing stifled attraction like an infant, right?

"Thank you, Mr. Mc—er, Cam." Maresa's face lit up with a glow that damn near took his breath away; her relief and eagerness to be reunited with the little girl were all too obvious. "That would be really wonderful."

Her pleasure affected him far more than it should, making him wonder how he could make that smile return to her face again and again. Had he really thought a baby would dull his desire for Maresa?

Not a chance.

Four

"You rented a villa here," Maresa observed as she held the ends of her hair in one hand to keep it from flying away in the open-top Jeep Cameron McNeill used for tooling around the private island. "In addition to the hotel suite."

The Jeep bounced down a long road through the lush foliage to a remote part of the island. In theory, she knew about the private villas that the Carib Grand oversaw on the extensive property, but the guests who took those units had their own staff so she didn't see them often and she'd never toured them. She turned in her seat to peer back at Isla, in the car seat she'd procured from the hotel. The baby faced backward with a sunshade tilted over the seat, but Maresa could see the little girl was still snoozing contentedly.

The caregiver had fed and changed her, and before Maresa could compensate her, Cameron had taken care of the bill, insisting that he make the day as easy as possible for Maresa to make up for the inconvenience of working with him. Spending the day in a private villa with yet another caregiver—this one a licensed nurse from the hospital in Saint Thomas who would meet them there—was hardly an inconvenience. Truth be told, she was grateful to escape the hotel for the day after the stress of discovering Isla and finding out that Rafe had left work without authorization. Luckily, she'd signed him out due to illness and found the pager he dropped on her way to pick up Isla from the caregiver. Maresa had assigned the flower delivery to another runner before leaving.

Now, all she had to do was get through an afternoon with her billionaire boss who'd only been impersonating a pain-in-the-butt client. But what if Cameron McNeill turned out to be even more problematic than his predecessor, Mr. Holmes?

"The villas are managed by a slightly different branch of the company," Cameron informed her, using a remote to open a heavy wrought-iron gate that straddled the road ahead. "My privacy is protected here. I'll return to the hotel suite later tonight to continue my investigation work under Mr. Holmes's name. Unless, of course, you and I can figure out the reason behind the declining reviews before then."

The ocean breeze whipped another strand of Maresa's hair free from where she'd been holding it, the wavy lock tickling against her cheek and teasing along her lips. What was it about Cameron's physical presence that made her so very aware of her own? She'd never felt so on edge around Jaden even when they'd been wildly in love. Cameron's nearness made her feel…anxious. Expectant.

"From my vantage point, everything has been running smoothly at the Carib." Maresa didn't need a poor performance review. What if Cameron McNeill thought that the real reason for the declining ratings was her? A concierge could make or break a customer's experience of any hotel. Maybe this meeting with the boss wasn't to interview her so much as to interrogate her.

But damn it, she knew her performance had been exemplary.

"We'll figure it out, one way or another," Cameron assured her as the Jeep climbed a small hill and broke through a cluster of trees.

The most breathtaking view imaginable spread out before her. She gasped aloud.

"Oh wow." She shook her head at the sparkling expanse of water lapping against White Shoulders Beach below them. On the left, the villa sat at the cliff's edge, positioned so that the windows, balconies and infinity pool all faced the stunning view. "I grew up here, and still—you never grow immune to this."

"I can see why." He pulled the Jeep into a sheltered parking bay beside a simple silver Ford sedan. "It looks like the sitter has already arrived. We can get Isla settled inside with some air conditioning and then get to work."

Unfastening her gaze from the view of Saint John's in the distance, and a smattering of little islands closer by, Maresa turned to take in the villa. The Aerie was billed as the premiere private residence on the island; she thought she recalled the literature saying it was almost twenty thousand square feet. It was a palatial home decorated in the Mediterranean style. The white-sashed stucco and deep bronze roof tiles were an understated color combination, especially when accented with weathered gray doors. The landscaping dominated the home from the outside, but there were balconies everywhere to take advantage of the views.

Sliding out of the Jeep, she smoothed a hand over her windblown hair to try to prepare herself for what was no doubt the most important business meeting of her life. She couldn't allow her guard to slip, not even when Cameron McNeill spared a kind smile for Baby Isla as he carefully unbuckled her from the car seat straps.

"Need any help?" she asked, stepping closer to the Jeep again.

"I've got it." He frowned slightly, reaching beneath the baby to palm her head in his big hand. He supported her back with his forearm, cradling her carefully until he had her tucked against his chest. "There." He grinned over at Maresa. "Just like carrying a football. You take the fall yourself before you fumble."

"Ideally, there's no falling involved for anyone." She knew he was teasing, but she wondered if she should have offered to carry Isla just the same.

She couldn't deny she was a bit overwhelmed, though. She didn't know much about babies, and now she would be lobbying for primary custody of Rafe's little girl, even if Trina changed her mind. Maresa knew Rafe would have wanted to exercise his parental rights, and she would do that in his place. Still, it was almost too much to get her brain around in just a few hours, and she had no one she could share the news with outside of Rafe's counselor. Oddly, having Cameron McNeill beside her today had anchored her when she felt most unsteady, even as she knew she had to keep her guard up around him.

Half an hour later, Maresa finally managed to walk out of the makeshift nursery—a huge suite of rooms adapted for the purpose with the portable crib the hospital nurse had brought with her. The woman had packed a bag full of other baby supplies for Maresa including formula, diapers, fresh clothes and linens, a gift funded by Cameron McNeill, she'd discovered. And while Maresa understood that the man could easily afford such generosity, she couldn't afford to accept any more after this day.

Today, she told herself, was an adjustment period. Tomorrow, she would have a plan.

Clutching the baby monitor the caregiver had provided, Maresa followed the scent of grilled meat toward the patio beside the pool. A woman in a white tuxedo shirt and crisp black pants bustled through the kitchen, her blond ponytail bobbing with her step. She nodded toward the French doors leading outside.

"Mr. McNeill said to tell you he has drinks ready right out here, unless you'd like to swim first, in which case there are suits in the bathhouse." She pointed to the left where a small cabana sat beside a gazebo.

"Thank you." Maresa's gaze flicked over the food the woman was assembling on the kitchen island—tiny appetizers with flaked fish balanced on thin slices of mango and endive, bright red crabmeat prepped for what looked like a shellfish soup and chopped vegetables for a conch salad. "It all looks delicious."

Her stomach growled with a reminder of how long it had been since her usual lunch hour had come and gone. Now, stepping outside onto the covered deck, Maresa spotted Cameron seated at a table beneath the gazebo, a bottled water in hand as he stared down at his laptop screen. Tropical foliage in colorful clay pots dotted the deck. The weathered teak furniture topped by thick cream-colored cushions was understated enough to let the view shine more than the decor. The call of birds and the distant roll of waves on the beach provided the kind of soundtrack other people piped in using a digital playlist in order to relax.

Seeing her, Cameron stood. The practice wasn't uncommon in formal business meetings, and happened more often when she'd worked in Europe. But the gesture here, in this private place, felt more intimate since it was for her alone.

Or maybe she was simply too preoccupied with her boss.

"Did you find everything you needed?" he asked, tugging off the aviators he'd been wearing to set them on the graying teak table.

It was cool in the shade of the pergola threaded with bright pink bougainvillea, yet just being close to him made her skin warm. Her gaze climbed his tall height, stalling on his well-muscled shoulders before reaching his face. She took in the sculpted jaw and ice-blue eyes before shifting her focus to his lips. She hadn't kissed a man since her broken engagement.

A fact she hadn't thought about even once until right this moment.

"I'm fine," she blurted awkwardly, remembering she was there to work and not to catalog the finer masculine traits of the man whose family owned the company she worked for. "Ready to work."

Beneath the table, a dog yapped happily.

Maresa glanced down to see Poppy standing on a bright magenta dog bed. Beside the bed, a desk fan oscillated back and forth, blowing through the dog's long white fur at regular intervals.

"Hello, Poppy." She leaned down to greet the fluffy pooch. "That's quite a setup you have there." She let the dog sniff her hand for a moment before she scratched behind the ears, not sure if Poppy would remember her.

"I had the dog walker pick up a few things to be sure she was comfortable. Plus, with a baby in the house, I thought she might be...you know. Jealous."

She looked up in time to see him shrug as if it was the most natural thought in the world to consider if his dog would be envious of an infant guest.

"That's adorable." She knew then that the Cameron Holmes character she'd met the day before had been all for show. Cameron McNeill was another man entirely. Although his jaw tightened at the "adorable" remark. She hurried to explain. "I mean, the dog bed and all of Poppy's matching accessories. Your mom found a lot of great things to coordinate the wardrobe."

Maresa rose to her feet, knowing she couldn't use the pup as a barrier all day.

"Actually, I borrowed Poppy from my brother's administrative assistant." He gestured to the seat beside him and turned the laptop to give her a better view. "I figured a fussy white show dog was a good way to test the patience and demeanor of the hotel staff. But I'll admit, she isn't nearly as uptight as I imagined." He patted the animal's head; the Maltese was rubbing affectionately against his ankles while he talked about her. "She's pretty great."

Coming around to his side of the table, Maresa took the seat he indicated. Right beside him. He'd changed into more casual clothes since she'd last seen him, his white cotton T-shirt only slightly dressed up by a pair of khakis and dark loafers. He wore some kind of brightly colored socks—aqua and purple—at odds with the rest of his outfit.

"The Carib is pet friendly, but I understand why you thought there might be pushback on demands like natural grass for the room." She glanced down at the laptop to see he'd left open a series of graphs with performance rankings for the Carib.

The downturn in the past two months was small, but noticeable.

"Ryegrass only," he reminded her. "I don't enjoy being tough on the staff, but I figured that playing undercover boss for a week or two would still be quicker and less painful for them than if I hire an independent agency to do a thorough review of operations."

"Of course." She gestured to the laptop controls. "May I look through this?"

At his nod, Maresa clicked on links and scrolled through the files related to the hotel's performance. Clearly, Cameron had been doing his homework, making margin notes throughout the document about the operations. Her name made frequent appearances, including a reference to an incident of misplaced money by a guest the week before.

"I remember this." Maresa's finger paused on the comment from a post-visit electronic survey issued to the guest. "An older couple reported that their travelers' checks had gone missing during a trip to the beach." She glanced up to see Cameron bent over the screen to read the notes, his face unexpectedly close to hers.

"The guy left the money in his jacket on the beach. It was gone when he returned." Cameron nodded, his jaw tense. "Definitely a vacation-ruiner."

She bristled. "But not the staff's fault. Our beach employees are tasked with making sure there are pool chairs and towels. We serve drinks and even bring food down to the cabanas. But we can't police everyone's possessions."

"On a private island where everyone should either be a guest or a staff member?" he asked with a hint of censure in his voice.

"That amounts to quite a few people," she pointed out, without hesitation. "And don't forget, many of our guests feel comfortable indulging in extra cocktails while vacationing."

"A few drinks won't make you think you had a thousand dollars in your pocket when you only had ten."

"Maybe not." She thrummed her fingernails on the teak table, remembering some of the antics she'd seen on the beach. Even before her work at the Carib, she'd seen plenty of visitors to Saint Thomas behave like spring-breakers simply because they were far from home. Her father included. "However, a few drinks could make you think you put your money in your jacket when you actually had it in the pocket of the shorts you wore into the water, where you lost it while you tried to impress your trophy wife by doing backflips off a Jet Ski."

"And is that what happened in this case?" He glanced over at her, the woodsy scent of his aftershave teasing her senses.

"No." She shook her head, regretting the candid speech as much as the memory of her father's easy transition of affection from Maresa's mother to a wealthy female colleague. Today had rattled her. Her mind kept drifting back to Isla and what she would do tonight to keep her comfortable. "I'm sure it wasn't. I only meant to point out that the staff can't guard against some of the questionable decisions that guests make while vacationing."

Cam regarded her curiously. "I don't suppose your ex-fiancé has a trophy wife?"

"Jaden is still happily single from what I hear." She couldn't afford to share any more personal confidences with this man—her boss—who already knew far too much about her. To redirect their conversation, she tapped a few keys on his laptop. "These other incidents that guests wrote about on their comment forms—slow bar service, a disappointing gallery tour off-site—I assume you've looked into them?"

Both were news to her.

"The bar service, yes. The gallery tour, no. I don't suppose you know which tour they're referencing?"

"No one has asked me to arrange anything like this." She might not remember every hotel recommendation, but she certainly recalled specialty requests. "I can speak to some of the other staff members. Some guests like to ask the doormen or the waiters for their input on local sites."

"Good." He cleared a space in front of them on the table as a server came onto the patio with covered trays. "That's one of the drawbacks of maintaining a presence as a demanding guest—I can't very well quiz the staff for answers about things that happened last month."

Maresa watched as the server quickly set the table, filled their water glasses and left two platters behind along with a wine bottle in a clay pot to maintain the wine's temperature. The final thing the woman did was set out a fresh bowl of water for Poppy before she left them to their late lunch.

"I'm happy to help," Maresa told him honestly, relieved to know that the downturn in performance at the Carib was nothing tied to her work. Or her brother's. Their jobs were more important than ever with a baby to support.

"For that matter, I can't reveal the positive feedback we've received about the staff members either." Cameron lifted the wine bottle from the cooling container and inspected the label before pouring a pale white wine into her glass. "But I can tell you that Rafe received some glowing praise from a guest who referenced him by name."

"Really?" Pleased, Maresa helped herself to some of

the appetizers she'd seen inside, arranging a few extra pieces of mango beside the conch salad. "Did the guest say what he did?"

Cameron loaded his plate with ahi tuna and warm plantain chips with some kind of spicy-looking dipping sauce.

"Something about providing a 'happy escort' to the beach one day and lifting the guest's spirits by pointing out some native birds."

Rafe? Escorting a guest somewhere?

Maresa realized she'd been quiet a beat too long.

"Rafe loves birds," she replied truthfully, hating that she needed to mask her true thoughts with Cameron after he'd trusted her to give him honest feedback on the staff. "He does know a lot about the local plants and animals, too," she rushed to add. "That's one area of knowledge that his accident left untouched."

"Does it surprise you that he was escorting a guest to the beach?" Cameron studied her over his glass as he tasted the wine.

His blue eyes missed nothing.

Clearly, he would know Rafe's job description—something he'd have easy access to in his research of the performance reviews. There was no sense trying to deny it. Still, she hated feeling that she needed to defend her brother for doing a good job.

"A little," she admitted, her shoulders tense. Wary.

Before she could explain, however, a wail came through the baby monitor.

Cam hung back, unsure how to help while Maresa and the nurse caregiver discussed the baby's fretful state. Maresa held the baby close, shifting positions against her shoulder as the baby arched and squirmed.

Over half an hour after the infant's initial outburst, the

little girl still hadn't settled down. Her face was mottled and red, her hands flexing and straining, as if she fought unseen ghosts. Cam hated hearing the cries, but didn't have a clue what to offer. The woman he'd hired for the day was a nurse, after all. She would know if there was anything they needed to worry about, wouldn't she?

Still. He didn't blame Maresa for questioning her. Cameron had done some internet searches himself, one of the few things he knew to contribute.

A moment later, Maresa stepped out of the nursery and shut the door behind her, leaving Isla with Wendy. The cries continued. Poppy paced nervously outside the door.

"I should leave." Worry etched her features. She scraped back her sun-lightened curls behind one ear. "You've been so kind to help me manage my first day of caring for an infant, finding Wendy and the baby supplies, but I really can't impose any longer—"

"You are not anywhere close to an imposition." He didn't want her to leave. "I'm trying to help with Isla because I want to."

Maresa's hands fisted at her side, her whole body rigid. "She's my responsibility."

Her stubborn refusal reminded him of his oldest brother. Quinn never wanted anyone to help him either—a trait Cam respected, even when Quinn became too damn overbearing.

"You've know about her for less than twenty-four hours. Most families get nine months to prepare." He settled a hand on Maresa's shoulder, wanting to ease some of the weight she insisted on putting there.

"That doesn't make her any less my obligation." She folded her arms across her chest in a gesture that hovered between a defensive posture and an effort to hold herself together.

Another shriek from the nursery sent an answering spike of tension through Maresa; he could feel it under his fingertips. He'd have to be some kind of cretin not to respond to that. Still, he dropped his hand before he did something foolish like thread his fingers through her brown hair and soothe away the tension in her neck. Her back.

"Maybe not, but it gives you a damn good reason to accept some help until you get the legalities sorted out and come up with a game plan going forward." He extended his arms to gesture to the villa he'd taken for two weeks. "This place is going to be empty all evening once I head back to the hotel to put the Carib staffers through their paces. Stay put with Isla and the nurse. Have something to eat. Follow up with your lawyer. Poppy and I can sleep at the hotel tonight."

She shook her head. "I can't possibly accept such an offer. Even if you didn't own the company I work for, I couldn't allow you to do that."

"Ethics shouldn't rule out human kindness." Cameron wasn't going to rescind the offer because of some vague notion about what was right or proper. She needed help, damn it.

He drew her into a study down the hallway where indoor palm trees grew in a sunny corner under a series of skylights. Poppy trailed behind them, her collar jingling. Even here, the view of the water and the beach below was breathtaking. It made him want to cliff dive or wind surf. Or kiteboard.

He ground his teeth together on the last one. He hadn't been kiteboarding since the accident that ensured he'd never have children of his own. As if the universe had conspired to make sure he didn't repeat his father's mistakes.

"Is that what this is?" She stared up at him with questioning eyes. Worried. "Kindness? Because to be quite honest, this day has felt like a bit more than that, starting down at the beach this morning."

Starting yesterday for him, actually.

So he couldn't pretend not to know what she meant.

"There may be an underlying dynamic at work, yes. But that doesn't mean I can't offer to do something kind for you on an impossibly hard day." He had that ability, damn it. He wasn't totally self-absorbed. "And it's not just for you. It's for your brother, who might need more time to deal with this. And for Isla, who is clearly unhappy. Why not make their day easier, too?"

Maresa was quiet a long moment.

"What underlying dynamic?" she asked finally.

"It's not obvious?" He turned on his heel, needing a minute to weigh how much he wanted to spell things out. Go on the record. But he did, damn it. He liked this woman. He liked her fearless strength for her family, taking on their problems with more fierceness than she exercised for herself. Who took care of her? "I'm attracted to you."

He wasn't sure what kind of reaction he expected. But if he had to guess, he wouldn't have anticipated an argument.

"No." Her expression didn't change, the unflappable concierge facade in full play. "That's not possible."

There was a flash of fire in her tawny eyes, though. He'd bank on that.

"For all of my shortcomings, I'm pretty damn sure I know what attraction feels like."

"I didn't mean that. It's just—" She closed her eyes for a moment, as if she needed that time in the dark to collect her thoughts. When she opened them again, she took a deep breath. "I don't think I have the mental and emotional wherewithal to figure out what that means right now and what the appropriate response should be." She tipped two fingers to the bridge of her nose and pressed. "I can't afford to make a decision I'll regret. This job is…everything to me. And now I need it more than ever if I'm going to take proper care of Isla and my brother."

"I understand." Now that he'd admitted the attraction, he realized how strong it was, and that rattled him more than a little. He was here for business, not pleasure. "And I'm not acting on those feelings because I don't want to add to the list of things you need to worry about."

"Okay." She eyed him warily. "Thank you."

"So here's what I propose. I'm going to need your help on this project. It's important to me." He couldn't afford trouble at the Carib with so much riding on the Caribbean expansion program. The McNeills had their hands full with their grandfather's failing health and three more heirs on the horizon to vie for the family legacy. "Take a couple of days off from the hotel. Stay here with Isla and get acquainted with her while you prepare your family and plan your next steps. I'll stay at the hotel with Poppy."

"Cam—"

"No arguments." He really needed to leave her be so she could settle in and connect with the baby. He understood the crying and the newness of the situation would upset anyone, especially a woman accustomed to running things smoothly. "You can review those files I showed you earlier in more detail. I'd like your assessment of a variety of hotel personnel."

Finally, she nodded. It felt like a major victory. And no matter what he'd said about ignoring the attraction, he couldn't help but imagine what it would be like to have her agree to other things he wanted from her. Having dinner with him, for instance. Letting him taste her full lips. Feeling her soft curves beneath his palms.

"Isla and I can't thank you enough." She backed away from him and reached for the door. "I should really go check on her."

"Don't wear yourself out," he warned. "Share the duties with the nurse."

"I will." She smiled, her hand pausing on the doorknob, some of the tension sliding off her shoulders.

"And that Jeep we used to get here actually goes with the property. I'll leave the keys on the kitchen counter and have a plate sent up from the kitchen for you." He wasn't going out of his way, he told himself. It was easy enough to do that for her.

Or was he deluding himself? He wanted Maresa—pure and simple. But he knew it was more than that. Something about her drew him. Made him want to help her. He could do this much, at least, with a clear conscience. It benefitted McNeill Resorts to have her review those reports. He was simply giving her the time and space to do the job.

"But how will you get back to the hotel?"

"Poppy is ready for a walk." He could use a long trek to cool off. Remind himself why he had no business acting on what he was feeling for Maresa. "We'll take the scenic route along the beach." He held up his phone. "I'll leave my number with the keys downstairs. Call if you need anything."

"Okay." She nodded, then tipped her head to one side, her whole body going still. "Oh wow. Do you hear that?"

"What?" He listened.

"She stopped crying." Maresa looked relieved. Happy. So it was a total surprise that she burst into tears.

Five

If Maresa hadn't needed her job so badly, she would have seriously considered resigning.

Never in her life had she done anything so embarrassing as losing control in front of an employer. But the day had been too much, from start to finish. After the intense stress of listening to Isla cry for forty minutes, she'd been so relieved to hear silence reign in the nursery. The sudden shift of strong emotions had tipped something inside her.

Now, much to her extreme mortification, Cameron McNeill's arms were around her as he drew her onto a cushioned gray settee close to the door. Even more embarrassing? How much she wanted to sink into those arms and wail her heart out on his strong chest. She cried harder.

"It's okay," he assured her, his voice beside her ear and his woodsy aftershave stirring a hunger for closeness she could not afford.

"No, it's really not." She shook her head against his shoulder, telling herself to get it together.

"As your boss, I order you to stop arguing with me."

She couldn't stop a watery laugh. "I don't know what's the matter with me."

"Anyone would be overwhelmed right now." His arms tightened, drawing her closer in a way that was undeniably more comfortable. "Don't fight so damn hard. Let it out."

And for a moment, she did just that. She didn't let herself think about how deeply she'd screwed up by sobbing in his arms. She just let the emotions run through her, the whole great big unwieldy mess that her life had become. She hadn't cried like this when the doctor told her Rafe might not live. Day after day, she'd sat in that hospital and willed him to hang on and fight. Then, by the time he finally opened his eyes again, she couldn't afford to break down. She needed to be strong for him. To show him that she was fighting, too.

She'd helped him relearn to walk. Had that really been just six months ago? He'd come so far, so fast. But she knew there were limits to what he could do.

Limits to how much he could do because she willed it. She knew, in her heart, he would not be able to handle a crying baby even if she could make him understand that Isla was his. It wouldn't be right to thrust this baby into his life right now. Or fair.

She didn't need the counselor to tell her that, even though the woman had finally returned her call and left a message to come by the office in the morning. Maresa knew that the woman was trying to find a way to tell her the hard truth—this baby could upset him so much he could have a setback.

And she cried for that. For him. Because there had

been a time in Rafe's life when the birth of his daughter would have been a cause for celebration. It broke her heart that his life had to be so different now.

With one last shuddering sigh, she felt the storm inside her pass. As it eased away, leaving her drained but more at peace, Maresa became aware of the man holding her. Aware of the hard plane of his chest where her forehead rested. Of the warm skin beneath the soft cotton T-shirt that she'd soaked with her tears. Amidst all the other embarrassments of the day she was at least grateful that her mascara had been waterproof. It would have been one indignity too many to leave her makeup on his clothes.

His arm was around her shoulders, his hand on her upper arm where he rubbed gentle circles that had soothed her a moment before. Now? That touch teased a growing awareness that spread over her skin to make her senses sing. With more than a little regret, she levered herself up, straightening.

"Cameron." Her voice raspy from the crying, his name sounded far too intimate when she said it that way.

Then again, maybe it seemed more intimate since she was suddenly nose-to-nose with him, his arm still holding her close. She forgot to think. Forgot to breathe. She was pretty sure her heart paused, too, as she stared up at him.

A sexy, incredibly appealing man.

Without her permission, her fingers moved to his face. She traced the line of his lightly shadowed jaw, surprised at the rough bristle against her fingertips. His blue eyes hypnotized her. There was simply no other explanation for what was happening to her right now. Her brain told her to extricate herself. Walk away.

Her hands had other ideas. She twined them around his neck, her heart full of a tenderness she shouldn't feel. But he'd been so good to her. So thoughtful. And she wanted to kiss him more than she wanted anything.

"Maresa." Her name on his lips was a warning. A chance to change her mind.

She understood that she was pushing a boundary. Recognized that he'd just drawn a line in the sand.

"I didn't mind giving up my dream job in Paris to care for Rafe and help my mother recover," she confided, giving him absolutely no context for her comment and hoping he understood what she was saying. "And I will gladly give eighteen years to raise my niece as my own daughter." She'd known it without question the moment Jaden handed her Isla. "But I'm not sure I can sacrifice the chance to have this kiss."

She'd crossed the boundary. Straight into "certifiable" territory. She must have cried out all her good sense.

His blue eyes simmered with more heat than a Saint Thomas summer. He cupped her chin, cradling her face like she was something precious.

"If I thought you wouldn't regret it tomorrow, I'd give you all the kisses you could handle." The stroke of his thumb along her cheek didn't begin to soothe the rejection.

Her eyes burned again, reminding her just how jumbled her emotions were right now. Knowing he had a point did nothing to salvage her pride.

"You told me you were attracted to me." She unwound her hands from his neck.

"Too much," he admitted. "That's why I'm trying to be smart about this. I'm willing to wait to be with you until a time when you won't have any regrets about it."

"You say that like it's a foregone conclusion." She straightened, her cheeks heating.

"Or maybe it's using the power of positive thinking." His lips kicked up in a half smile, but she needed air. Space.

"You should go." She wanted time to clear her head.

Tipping her head toward him, he kissed her forehead with a gentle tenderness that made her ache for all she couldn't have.

"I'll see you in the morning," he told her, shoving to his feet.

"I thought I was taking time off?" She tucked her disheveled hair behind one ear, eager to call her mother and figure out what to do about Isla.

"From the hotel. Not from me." He shoved his hands in his pockets, and something about the gesture made her think he'd done it to keep from touching her.

She knew because she felt the same need to touch him.

"When will I see you?"

"Text me when you and Isla are ready in the morning and I'll come get you. I'm traveling to Martinique tomorrow and I'd like you with me."

She arched an eyebrow. "You need a tour guide with an infant in tow?"

"We could talk through some of the data in those reports a bit more. You could help give me a bigger picture of what's going on here." He opened the door into the quiet hallway of the expansive vacation villa. "Besides, I want to be close by if you decide you want to share kisses you won't regret down the road."

He strode away, whistling softly for Poppy as he headed toward the main staircase. He left Maresa alone in the extravagant house with a baby, a nurse and all kinds of confused feelings for him. One thing was certain, though.

A man like Cameron McNeill might tempt her sorely. But he was a fantasy. A temporary escape from the reality of a life full of obligations she would never walk away from. So until her heart understood how thoroughly off-limits he was, Maresa needed to put all thoughts of kisses out of her head.

An hour later, Maresa had her mother in the Jeep with her as she pulled up to the gated vacation villa. She'd calmly explained the Isla situation on a phone call on the way over to her house, arranging for their retired neighbor to visit with Rafe for a couple of hours while Maresa brought her mom to meet her grandchild.

After hearing back from Rafe's counselor that a mention of his daughter could trigger too much frustration and a possible memory block, Maresa had simply told her brother she wanted to bring their mother to meet a girlfriend's new baby.

She'd kept the story simple and straightforward, and Rafe didn't mind the visit time with Mr. Leopold, who was happy to play one of Rafe's video games with him and keep an eye on him. The paperwork requesting temporary legal custody of the baby would be filed in the morning by her attorney, so she'd taken care of that, too.

Now, driving through the gates, Maresa enjoyed her mother's startled gasp at the breathtaking view of the Caribbean.

"I had the same reaction earlier," she admitted, halting the Jeep in the space beside the nurse's sedan. "But this isn't half as beautiful as Isla."

"I cannot wait to meet her." Analise Delphine opened the car door slowly, the neuropathy in her hands one of many nerve conditions caused by her MS. "But I'm still so angry at Trina for not telling us sooner. Can you imagine what happiness it would have given us in those dark hours with your brother if we had only known about his daughter?"

Maresa hurried around the car to help her mother out since it did no good to tell her to wait. Analise had struggled more with her disease ever since the car crash that injured Rafe. Maresa worried about her since her mother seemed to blame herself—and her MS—for the injury to her beloved son, and some days it appeared as if she wanted to suffer because of her guilt. For months, Maresa had encouraged her mother to get into some more family counseling, but Analise would only go to sessions that were free through a local clinic, not wanting to "be a burden."

Maresa had tread lightly around the topic until now, but if they were going to be responsible for this baby, she needed her mother to be strong emotionally even if her physical health was declining.

"Trina is young," Maresa reminded her as she helped her up the white stone walkway to the main entrance of the villa. "She must have been scared and confused between finding out she was pregnant and then learning Rafe wasn't going to make a full recovery."

Analise breathed heavily as she leaned on Maresa's arm. Analise had always been the most beautiful girl on the block, according to their neighbor Mr. Leopold. She'd worked as a dancer in clubs and in street performances for tourists, earning a good living for years before the MS hit her hard. Her limber dancer's body had thickened with her inability to move freely, but her careful makeup and her eye for clothing meant she always looked stage-ready.

"She is old enough to make better choices." Her mother stopped abruptly, squinting into the sunlight as she peered up at the vacation home. "Speaking of which, Maresa, I hope you are making wise choices by staying here. You said your boss is allowing you to do this?"

"Yes, Mom." She tugged gently at her mother's arm, drawing her up the wide stone steps. "He was there when Jaden handed me Isla, so he knew I had a lot to contend with today."

She wasn't sure about the rest of his motives. She was still separating Cameron McNeill from surly Mr. Holmes, trying to understand him. He'd walked out on her today when she would have gladly lost herself in the attraction. Some of her wounded pride had been comforted by his assurance that he wanted her.

So where did that leave them for tomorrow when he expected her to accompany him to a neighboring island?

"Most men don't share their expensive villas without expectations, Maresa. Be smarter than that," her mother chastised her while Maresa unlocked the front door with the key Cameron had left behind. "You need to come home."

Before she could argue, Wendy appeared in the foyer, a pink bundle in her arms. Her mother oohed and aahed, mesmerized by her new grandchild as she happily cataloged all the sleeping baby's features. Maresa paid scant attention, however, as Analise declared the hairline was Rafe's and the mouth inherited was from Analise herself.

Maresa still smarted from her mother's insistence that she wasn't "being smart" to stay in the villa with Isla tonight. Perhaps it stung all the more because that had been Maresa's first instinct, as well. But damn it, Cameron had a point about the practicality of it. The Carib did indeed comp rooms to special guests who provided services. Why couldn't she enjoy the privilege while she helped Cameron McNeill investigate the operations of his luxury hotel?

Putting aside her frustration, she tried to enjoy her mother's pleasure in the baby even as Maresa worried about the future. It was easy for her mom to tell her that she should simply bring Isla home, but it would be Maresa who had to make arrangements for caregiving and Maresa who would wake up every few hours to look after the child. All of their lives were going to change dramatically under the roof of her mother's tiny house.

Maybe she needed to look for a larger home for all of them. She'd thought she couldn't afford it before, but now she wondered how she could afford *not* to buy something bigger. She would speak to her mother about it, but first, it occurred to her she could speak to Cameron. He was a businessman. His brother—she'd once read online— was a hedge fund manager. Surely a McNeill could give sound financial advice.

Besides, talking about the Caribbean housing market would be a welcome distraction in case the conversation ever turned personal tomorrow. If ever she was tempted to kiss him again, she'd just think about interest rates. That ought to cool her jets in a hurry.

"Look, Maresa!" Her mother turned the baby on her lap to show her Isla's face as they sat on the loveseat of a sprawling white family room decorated with dark leather furnishings and heavy Mexican wood. The little girl's eyes were open now, blinking owlishly. "She has your father's eyes! We need to call him and tell him. He won't believe it."

"Mom. No." She reached for the baby while Analise dug in her boho bag sewn out of brightly colored fabric scraps and pulled out a cell phone. "Dad never likes hearing from us."

She'd been devastated by her father's furious reaction to her phone call the night of Rafe's accident.

I've moved on, Maresa. Help your mother get that through her head.

"Nonsense." Analise grinned as she pressed the screen. "He'll want to hear this. Isla is his first grand-child, too, you know."

In Maresa's arms, the infant kicked and squirmed, her back arching as if she were preparing for a big cry. Maresa resisted the urge to call to Wendy, needing the experience of soothing the little girl. So she patted her back and spoke comforting words, shooting to her feet to walk around the room while her mother left a mes-sage on her father's voice mail. No surprise he hadn't picked up the call.

"I bet he'll book a flight down here as soon as he can," Analise assured her. "I should be getting home so I can make the house ready for company. And a baby, too!"

She levered slowly out of her chair to her feet, her new energy and excitement making her wince less even though the hurt had to be just the same as it was an hour ago.

"I don't think Dad will come down here," Maresa warned her quietly, not wanting her mom's hopes raised to impossible levels.

Jack Janson hadn't returned once since moving over-seas. He hadn't even visited Maresa in Paris; she'd briefly hoped that since he lived in the UK, he might make the effort to see her. But no.

"Could you let me be excited about just this one thing? We have enough to worry us, Maresa. Let's look for things to be hopeful about." She put her hand on Mare-sa's shoulders, a touch that didn't comfort her in the least.

If anything, Maresa remembered why she needed to be all the more careful with Cameron McNeill. Like her father, he was only here on business. Like her father, he might think it was fun to indulge himself with a local woman while he was far from his home and his real life.

But once he left Saint Thomas and solved the problems at the Carib Grand, Maresa knew all too well that he wasn't ever coming back.

Cameron had new respect for the running abilities of Maltese show dogs.

He sprinted through the undergrowth on the beach the next morning, about an hour after sunrise, trying to keep up with the little pooch.

"Poppy!" he called to her, cursing himself for giving her a moment off the leash. He'd scoped the beach and knew they were alone on the Carib Grand's private stretch of shore, so he'd figured it was okay.

He could keep up with the little dog on her short legs after all. But Poppy was small and shifty, darting and zigzagging through the brush where Cam couldn't fit. The groomer was going to think he'd gotten the pup's fur tangled on purpose, but damn it, he was just trying to let her have some fun. She seemed so happy chasing those terns.

If only it was as easy to tell what would make Maresa Delphine happy. He'd spent most of the day with her and still wasn't sure how to make her smile again. The concierge had the weight of the world on her straight shoulders.

Catching sight of muddy white fur, Cameron swooped low to scoop up the dog in midstride.

"Gotcha." He held on to the wriggling, overexcited bundle of wet canine while she tried her best to lick his face.

He'd have to shower again before his day in Martinique with Maresa since he was now covered with beach sand and dog fur, but it was tough to stay perturbed with the overjoyed animal. Chiding her gently while he attached the leash, Cam turned to go back up the path to the hotel.

Only to spot Rafe Delphine walking toward the beach beside a well-dressed, much older woman.

Surprised that Rafe had come in to work with Maresa taking the day off, Cameron watched the pair from a hidden vantage point in the bushes.

"Do you know this painter I'm meeting, young man?" the woman asked, her accent sounding Nordic, maybe. Or Finnish.

The woman was probably in her late sixties or early seventies. She had a sleek blond bob and expensive-looking bag. Even the beach sandals she wore had the emblem of an exclusive designer Cam recognized because a long-ago girlfriend had dragged him to a private runway show.

"Jaden paints." Rafe nodded his acknowledgement of the question but his eye was on the ground where a bird flapped its damp wings. "Look. A tern."

Poppy wriggled excitedly. The movement attracted the older woman's attention, giving up Cam's hiding place She smiled at him.

"What a precious little princess!" she exclaimed, eyes on Poppy. "She looks like she's been having fun today."

Rafe's tawny eyes—so like his sister's—turned his way. He gave Cam a nod of recognition, or maybe it was just politeness. Effectively called out of his spot in the woods, Cameron stepped into the sunlight and let the woman meet Poppy, who was—as always—appropriately gracious for the attention.

After a brief exchange with the dog, Cameron continued toward the hotel. He'd known that Jaden Torries was probably trolling for work at the Carib, so it shouldn't be a huge surprise that one of the hotel guests was meeting him at the beach. But why was Rafe bringing her to meet him?

Given how much Maresa disliked her ex-fiancé, it seemed unlikely she would be the one facilitating Jaden doing any kind of work with hotel patrons. Especially since she wasn't even working today. Then again, what if she had found a way to make a little extra income by helping Jaden find patrons? Would she set aside her distaste for him if it made things easier for her?

Deep in thought, Cam arrived at the pool deck. He didn't want to think his attraction to Maresa would influence his handling of the situation, but his first instinct was to speak to her directly. He would ask her about it when he picked her up at the villa, he decided.

Except then he spotted her circulating among the guests by the pool. She'd been here all along?

Suspicion mounted. Grinding his teeth, he charged toward her, more than ready for some answers.

Six

Morning sun beating down on her head, Maresa noticed Cameron McNeill heading her way and she braced herself for the resurrection of Mr. Holmes. She knew he needed to be undercover to learn more about the hotel operations, but did he have to be quite so convincing in his "difficult guest" role? The hard set of his jaw and brooding glare were seriously intimidating even knowing how kind he could be.

She straightened from a conversation with one of her seasonal guests from Quebec who rented a suite for half the year. Pasting on a professionally polite smile to greet Cameron, she told herself she should be grateful to see this side of him so she wouldn't be tempted to throw herself at him again.

Even if his bare chest and low-slung board shorts drew every female eye.

"Good morning, Mr. Holmes." She reached to smooth

her jacket sleeves, only to remember she'd worn a sundress today for the trip into Martinique. *Oh, my.* Her skin had goose bumps of awareness just from standing this close to him.

"May I speak to you privately?" He handed off Poppy to the dog groomer who scurried over from where he'd been waiting by the tiki bar.

Cameron certainly couldn't have any complaints about the service he was receiving, could he? People seemed to hurry to offer him assistance.

"Of course." She excused herself from the other guests, following him toward the door marked Employees Only.

He didn't slow his step until they were in the same conference room where they'd spoken yesterday. The cool blast of air almost matched the ice chips in his blue eyes. He shoved the door shut behind them before he turned to face her.

"I thought you were taking the day off from the hotel." His jaw flexed and he crossed his arms over his bare chest, the board shorts riding low on his hips.

She tried not to stare, distracting herself by focusing on the hint of confrontation in his tone.

"I am." She gestured to her informal clothing. "I only stopped by this morning to see my brother and make sure he felt comfortable about his workday."

"And is he comfortable escorting guests to the beach?" Cameron's arctic glare might have made another woman shiver. Maresa straightened her spine.

"I never give him jobs like that. Why do you ask?" Defensiveness for her brother roared through her.

"Because I just saw him walking one of our overseas guests to the shore to meet Jaden Torries."

Surprised, she quickly guessed he must be mistaken.

He had to be. Still a hint of tension tickled her gut. "Rafe doesn't even arrive until the next ferry." She checked her watch just to be sure the day hadn't slipped away from her. "He should be walking in the employee locker rooms any minute to punch his time card."

"He's already here." Cameron pulled out one of the high-backed leather chairs for her, all sorts of muscles flexing as he moved, distracting her when she needed to be focused. "I saw him myself at the beach with one of the hotel guests just a few minutes ago."

"I don't understand." Ignoring the seat, she paced away from all that tempting male muscle to peer out the windows overlooking the croquet lawn near the pool, hoping to get a view of the path to the beach. How could she relax, wondering if her brother might be doing jobs around the Carib without her knowing? She was supposed to watch over him during his first few months of employment. She'd promised the hotel director as much. "I got here early so I wouldn't miss him when he came to work. I want everything to go smoothly for him if I'm not here to supervise him myself."

Cameron joined her at the window, his body warm beside hers as he peered out onto the mostly empty side lawns. A butterfly garden near the window attracted a handful of brightly colored insects. His shoulder brushed hers, setting off butterflies inside, too. She hated feeling this way—torn between the physical attraction and the mental frustration.

"Did you know Jaden was soliciting business from hotel guests?" Cameron's question was quiet. Dispassionate.

And it offended her mightily. How dare he question her integrity? Her work record was impeccable and he should know as much if he was even halfway doing *his* job.

Anger burned through her as she whirled to face him, her skirt brushing his leg he stood so close to her. She took a step back.

"Absolutely not. Until yesterday, I hadn't seen Jaden since I left for Paris two years ago." She frowned, not understanding why Cameron would think she'd do such a thing. "And while I don't wish him ill, my relationship with him is absolutely over. I certainly don't have any desire to risk my job to help a man I dislike profit off our guests."

"I see." Cameron nodded slowly, as if weighing whether or not to believe her.

Worry balled in her stomach and she reined in her anger. She couldn't afford to be offended. She needed him to believe her.

"Why would you think I'd do such a thing?" She didn't want to be here. She wanted to find her brother and ask him what was going on.

Did Rafe even understand what he was doing by helping Jaden meet potential clients for his artwork? Was Jaden asking him for that kind of help?

"That type of business is probably lucrative for him—"

Understanding dawned. Indignation flared, hot and fast. "And you thought I would be a part of some sordid scheme with my ex-fiancé for the sake of extra cash? Even twisting my brother's arm into setting up meetings when I do everything in my power to protect him?"

If it had been anyone else, she would have stormed out of the meeting room. But she needed this job too much and, at the end of the day, Cameron McNeill was still an owner of the Carib.

He held all the cards.

"I don't know what to think. That's why I wanted to speak to you privately." He picked up a gray T-shirt from the back of a chair in the conference room and pulled it over his head.

She watched in spite of herself, realizing he must have been doing work in the conference room earlier that morning since a laptop and phone sat on the table.

"I won't have any answers until I speak to my brother." She was worried about him. For him. For the baby. Oh God, when had life gotten so complicated?

What had her brother gotten into?

"You realize this isn't the first time he's done it." Cameron's voice softened as he headed toward her again. "That customer review that I shared with you yesterday was from someone who said he provided a 'happy escort' to the beach." Cameron's blue eyes probed hers, searching for answers she didn't have.

As much as she longed to share her fears with him, she couldn't do that. Not when he was in charge of her fate at the hotel, and Rafe's, too.

"I remember." She itched to leave, needing to see Rafe for herself. "And now that you've put that comment in context, I'm happy to speak to my brother and clear this up."

She turned toward the door, desperate to put the complicated knot of feelings her boss inspired behind her.

"Wait." Cameron reached for her hand and held it, his touch warm and firm. "I realize you want to protect him, Maresa, but we need to find out what's going on."

"And we will," she insisted, wishing he didn't make her heart beat faster. "Just as soon as I speak to him."

Cameron studied her for a long moment with searching eyes, then quietly asked, "What if he doesn't have a clear answer?"

Some of the urgency eased from her. She couldn't deny that was a possibility.

"I can only do my best to figure out what's going on." She couldn't imagine who else would be giving him extra chores to do around the hotel. Rafe had never particularly liked Jaden. Then again, her brother was a different man since the accident.

"I know that. And what if we learn more by observing him for a few days? Maybe it would be better to simply keep a closer eye on him now that we know he's carrying out duties for the hotel—or someone else—that you haven't authorized." His tone wasn't accusing. "Maybe you shouldn't upset him unnecessarily."

She wanted to tell him she already spent hours supervising her brother. More than others on her staff. But she bit her lip, refusing to reveal a piece of information that could get Rafe terminated from his position.

"I don't want him getting hurt," she argued, worried about letting her brother's behavior continue unchecked. "And I don't know who he's speaking to that would advise him to take risks like this with his job."

The day had started out so promising, with Isla sleeping for five hours straight and waking up with a drooly baby smile, only to take this radical nosedive. Anxiety spiked. Rafe was going to lose this job, damn it. She would never be able to afford a caregiver for Isla and a companion to supervise Rafe, too. Especially not once they lost Rafe's income. Heaven only knew how much he would recover from the brain injury. What kind of future he would have? How much he could provide for himself, much less a child? All the fears of the unknown jumped up inside her.

Cameron hissed a low, frustrated breath between his teeth. "What if we compromise? You confront him now, but if you don't get a direct answer or if you sense there's more to his answer than what he shares, you back off.

Then, we can keep a closer eye on him for the next week and see who is setting up these meetings."

She didn't like the idea of waiting. She knew there was a good chance Rafe wouldn't give her a direct answer. But what choice did she really have? She wouldn't be able to push him anyhow, since his health and potential recovery were more important than getting answers to any mystery going on at the Carib.

"Fine." She turned to the door, eager to see her brother, but she paused when Cameron followed her. "I'd prefer to speak to him alone."

He followed her so closely that she needed to tilt her head to peer up at him.

"Of course." He stood near enough that she could see the shades of blue in his eyes, as varied as the Caribbean. "I'm going to change for our trip. I'll have a car meet you out front in fifteen minutes."

She wondered if it was wise to risk being seen leaving the hotel with surly Mr. Holmes. But then, that wasn't her problem so much as his. She had enough to worry about waiting for the DNA tests to come back so she could finally tell Rafe about Isla. Her lawyer and his psychologist had advised her and her mother to wait until then.

Hurrying away from all that distracting masculine appeal, Maresa rushed into the employee lounge to look for her brother. She'd already called in a favor from Big Bill, the head doorman, to help keep an eye on Rafe for the next few days. Bill was a friend of her mother's from their old neighborhood and he'd been kind enough to agree, but Maresa knew the man could only do so much.

Inside the lounge, the scent of morning coffee mingled with someone's too-strong perfume. A few people from the maintenance staff gossiped around the kitchen table where a box of pastries sat open. Moving past the kitchen,

Maresa peered into the locker area between the men's and women's private lounges. Rafe sat in the middle row of lockers, carefully braiding the stems of yellow buttercups into a chain. Flowers spilled over the polished bench as he straddled it, his focus completely absorbed in the task.

Any frustration she felt with him melted away. How could Cameron think for a moment that her brother would knowingly do anything unethical at work? It was only because Cameron didn't know Rafe. If he did, he'd never think something like that for a moment.

"Hey, Rafe." She took a seat on the bench nearby, wishing with all her heart he could be in a work program designed for people with his kinds of abilities. He had so much to offer with his love of nature and talent with green and growing things. Even now, his affinity for plants was evident, the same as before the accident when he'd had his own landscaping business. "What are you making?"

He glanced up at her, his eyes so like the ones she saw in the mirror every day.

"Maresa." He smiled briefly before returning his attention to the flowers. "I'm making you a bracelet."

"Me?" She had worried he was heaping more gifts on Nancy. And while she liked the server, she didn't want Rafe to have any kind of romantic hopes about the woman. Hearing the flowers were for her was a relief.

"I felt bad I left work." He lifted the flower chain and laid it on her wrist, his shirt cuffs brushing her skin as he carefully knotted the stems together. "I'm sorry."

Her heart knotted up like the flowers.

"Thank you. I love it." She kissed him on the cheek, smiling at the way his simple offering looked beside the silver star bracelet he'd given her two years ago before she left for Paris.

He was as thoughtful as ever, and his way of showing it hadn't changed all that much.

"Rafe?" She drew a deep breath, hating to ruin a happy moment with questions about Jaden. But this was important. The sooner she helped Cameron McNeill figure out what was going on at the Carib Grand, the sooner their jobs would be secure and they could focus on a new life with Isla—if Isla was in fact his child. And even though their lives would be less complicated without the child, Maresa couldn't deny that the thought of Isla leaving made her stomach clench. "Why did you go to the beach this morning?"

She kept the question simple. Direct.

"Mr. Ricci asked." Rafe rose to his feet, dusting flower petals off his faded olive cargoes. "Time to go to work. Mom said I don't work with you today."

She blinked at the fast change of topic. "Mr. Ricci asked you to bring a guest to the beach?"

"It's eight thirty." Rafe pointed to his watch. "Mom said I don't work with you today."

Damn it. Damn it. She didn't want to throw his whole workday off for the sake of a conversation that might lead nowhere. Maybe Cameron was right and they were better off keeping an eye on the situation.

"Right. I have to work off-site today. You'll be helping Glenna at the concierge stand, but Big Bill is on duty today. If you need help with anything, ask Bill, okay?"

"Ask Big Bill." Rafe gave her a thumbs-up before he stalked out of the locker room and into the hotel to start work.

Watching him leave, Maresa's fingers went to the bracelet he'd made her. He was thoughtful and kind. Surely he would have so much to give Isla. She needed to speak to his counselor in more detail so they could brainstorm ideas for the right way to introduce them. It seemed wrong to deprive the little girl of a father when her mother had already given up on her.

For now, however, she needed to tell Cameron that Rafe was escorting guests to the beach because the hotel director told him to. Would Cameron believe her? Or would he demand to speak to her brother himself?

Cameron's seductive promise floated back to her. *If I thought you wouldn't regret it tomorrow, I'd give you all the kisses you could handle.* She'd replayed those words again and again since he'd said them.

She walked a tightrope with her compelling boss—needing him to allow Rafe to stay in his job, but needing her own secured even more. Which meant she had to help him in his investigation.

Most of all, to keep those objectives perfectly clear, she had to ignore her growing attraction to him. His kindness with Isla might have slid past her defenses, but in order to protect the baby's future, Maresa would have to set aside her desire to find out what "all the kisses she could handle" would feel like.

The flight to Martinique was fast and efficient. They took off from the private dock near the Carib Grand's beach and touched down in the Atlantic near Le Francois on the east coast of Martinique. The pilot landed the new seaplane smoothly, barely jostling Baby Isla's carrier where she sat beside Maresa in the seats facing Cameron.

Cameron tried to focus on the baby to keep his mind off the exotically gorgeous woman across from him. The task had been damn near impossible for the hour of flight time between islands. Maresa's bright sundress was so different from the linen suits he'd seen her in for work. He liked the full skirt and vibrant poppy print, and he admired that she wore the simple floral bracelet around one wrist. With her hair loose and sun-tipped around her face, she looked impossibly beautiful. Her movements with Isla were easier today and her fascination with the little girl was obvious every time she glanced Isla's way.

Before she unbuckled the baby's carrier, she pressed a kiss to the infant's smooth forehead. A new pink dress with a yellow bunny on the front had been a gift from Maresa's mother, apparently. They'd spoken about that much on that flight. Maresa had given him an update on the custody paperwork with the lawyer, the paternity test she'd ordered using Rafe's hair and a cheek swab of Isla's, and she'd told him about her mother's reaction to her granddaughter. They'd only discussed Rafe briefly, agreeing not to confront him any further about bringing guests to meet Jaden Torries. They would watch Rafe more carefully when they returned to Saint Thomas. Until then, Bill the doorman knew to keep a close eye on him.

Cameron hadn't pushed her to discuss her theory about what might be going on, knowing that she was already worried about her brother's activities at the hotel. But at some point today, they would have to discuss where to go next with Rafe, and Jaden, too. For now, Cameron simply wanted to put her at ease for a few hours while he gathered some information about this secret branch of his family. The Martinique McNeills had a home in Le Francois, an isolated compound that was the equivalent of Grandfather Malcolm's home in Manhattan—a centrally located hub with each of the brothers' names on the deed. The family had other property holdings, but their mother had lived here before her death and the next generation all spent time there.

Cameron had done his homework and was ready to

check out this group today. Later, after Maresa had time to relax and catch her breath from the events of the last few days, he would talk to her about a plan for the future. For her and for Isla, too. The little girl in the pink dress tugged at his heart.

"So you have family here?" Maresa passed the baby carrier to him while the pilot opened the plane door.

Fresh air blew in, toying lightly with Maresa's hair.

"In theory. Yes." He wasn't happy about the existence of the other McNeills. "That is—they don't know we're related yet. My father kept his other sons and mistress a secret. When his lover tired of being hidden, she sold the house he'd bought her and left without a forwarding address. He didn't fight her legally because of the scandal that would create." As he said it aloud, however, he realized that didn't sound like his father. "Actually, he was probably just too disinterested to try and find them. He never paid us much attention either."

Liam McNeill had been a sorry excuse for a father. Cameron refused to follow in those footsteps.

Cam lifted the baby carrier above the seats, following Maresa to the exit. They'd parked at a private dock for the Cap Est Lagoon, a resort hotel in Le Francois close to the McNeill estate.

"But at least he's still a part of your life, isn't he?" Maresa held her full skirt with one hand as she descended the steps of the plane. A gusty breeze wreaked havoc with the hem.

The view of her legs was a welcome distraction during a conversation about his dad.

"He is part of the business, so I see him at company meetings. But it's not like he shows up for holidays to hang out. He's never been that kind of father." Even Cameron's grandfather hadn't quite known what to do to create a sense of family. Sure, he'd taken in Quinn, Ian and Cameron often enough as teens. But they were more apt to travel with him on business, learning the ropes from the head of the company, than have fun.

Luckily, Cam had had his brothers.

And, later, his own reckless sense of fun.

Maresa held her hair with one hand as they walked down the dock together, the baby between them in her seat. Behind them, the hotel staff unloaded their bags from the seaplane. Not that they'd travelled with much, but Cam had taken a suite here so Maresa would have a place to retreat with Isla. The Cap Est spread out on the shore ahead of them, the red-roofed buildings ringing the turquoise lagoon. Birds called and circled overhead. A few white sailing boats dotted the blue water.

"A disinterested father is a unique kind of hurt," Maresa observed empathetically—so much so it gave him pause for a moment. But then he was distracted by a hint of her perfume on the breeze as she followed him to the villa where their suite awaited. A greeter from the hotel had texted him instructions on the location so they could proceed directly there. "Do you think your half brothers will be glad to see him again? Has it been a long time that they've been apart?"

"Fifteen years. The youngest hasn't seen his father— my father—since the kid was ten." Cameron hadn't thought about that much. He'd been worried about what the other McNeills might ask from them in terms of the family resort business. But there was a chance they'd be too bitter to claim anything.

Or so bitter that they'd want revenge.

Cameron wouldn't let them hurt his grandfather. Or the legacy his granddad had worked his whole life to build.

"Wow, fifteen? That's not much older than I was the last time I saw my dad." Maresa's words caught him by surprise as they reached the villa where a greeter admitted them.

Cameron didn't ask her about it until the hotel representative had shown them around the two-floor suite with a private deck overlooking the lagoon. When the woman left and Maresa was lifting Isla from the carrier, however, Cameron raised the question.

"Where's your father now?" He watched her coo and comfort the baby, rubbing the little girl's back through her pink dress, the bowlegs bare above tiny white ankle socks.

The vacation villa was smaller than the one near the Carib Grand, but more luxuriously appointed, with floor-to-ceiling windows draped in white silk that fluttered in the constant breeze off the water. Exotic Turkish rugs in bright colors covered alternating sections of dark bamboo floors. Paintings of the market at Marigot and historic houses in Fort-de-France, the capital of Martinique, hung around the living area, providing all the color of an otherwise quietly decorated room. Deep couches with white cushions and teak legs and arms were positioned for the best views of the water. There was even a nursery with a crib brought in especially for their visit.

"He lives outside London with his new wife. I spoke to him briefly after Rafe's accident, but his only response was a plea that I tell my mother he's *moved on* and not to bother him again." She stressed the words in a way that suggested she would never forget the tone of voice in which they'd been spoken. Shaking her head, she walked Isla over to the window and stared out at the shimmering blue expanse. "I won't be contacting him anymore."

Cameron sifted through a half dozen responses before he came up with one that didn't involve curses.

"I don't blame you. The man can't be bothered to come to his critically injured son's bedside? He doesn't deserve his kids." Cameron knew without a doubt that he'd suck as a father, but even he would never turn his back like that on a kid.

Maresa's burden in caring for her whole family became clearer, however. Her mother wasn't working because of her battle with MS, her father was out of the picture and her brother needed careful supervision. Maresa was supporting a lot of people on her salary.

And now, an infant, too. That was one helluva load for a person to carry on her own. Admiration for her grew. She wasn't like his dad, who disengaged from responsibilities and the people counting on him.

"What will you do if your half brothers don't want to see your father?" she asked him now, drifting closer to him as she rubbed her cheek against the top of Isla's downy head.

Cameron was seized with the need to wrap his arms around both of them, a protective urge so strong he had to fight to keep his hands off Maresa. He jammed his fists in the pocket of his khakis to stop himself. Still, he walked closer, wanting to breathe in her scent. To feel the way her nearness heated over his skin like a touch.

"I'll convince them that my grandfather is worth ten of my father and make sure they understand the importance of meeting him." He lowered his voice while he stood so close to her, unable to move away.

Fascinated, he watched the effect he had on her. The goose bumps down her arm. The fast thrum of a tiny vein at the base of her neck. A quick dart of her tongue over her lips that all but did him in.

He wanted this woman. So much that telling himself to stay away wasn't going to help. So much that the baby in her arms wasn't going to distract him, let alone dissuade him.

"I should change," Maresa said suddenly, clutching Isla tighter. "Into something for the trip to your brothers' house. That is, if you want me to accompany you there? I'm not sure what you want my role to be here."

His gaze roamed over her, even knowing it was damned unprofessional. But they'd passed that point in this relationship the day before when Maresa had wrapped her arms around him. He'd used up all his restraint then. Time for some plain talk.

"Your role? First, tell me honestly what you think would happen between us this week if I wasn't your boss." He couldn't help the hoarse hunger in his voice, and knew that she heard it. He studied her while she struggled to answer, envious of the way Isla's tiny body curved around the soft swell of Maresa's breast.

"What good does it do to wonder what if?" Frustration vibrated through her, her body tensing. "The facts can't be changed. I'd never quit this job. It's more important to me than ever."

Right. He knew that. She'd made that more than clear. So why couldn't he seem to stay away? Stifling a curse at himself, he stepped back. Swallowed.

"I need to visit my brothers' place. You can relax here with Isla and review the files I started to show you yesterday. Make whatever notes you can to help me weed through what's important." He had to get some fresh air in his lungs if he was going to keep his distance from Maresa until the time was right.

"Okay. Thank you." She nodded, relief and regret both etched in her features.

"When I get back, I'll have dinner ordered in. We can eat on the upstairs deck before we fly back tonight, unless of course, you decide you'd like to stay another day."

Her eyes widened, a flush of heat stealing along the skin bared by the open V of her sundress. He couldn't look away.

"I'm sure that won't be necessary." She clung to her professional reserve.

"Nevertheless, I'll keep the option open." He reached for her, stroking the barest of touches along her arm. "Just in case."

Seven

Just in case.

Hours later, Cameron's parting words still circled around in Maresa's brain. She'd been ridiculously productive in spite of the seductive thoughts chasing through her mind, throwing herself into her work with determined intensity. Still, Cameron's suggestion of spending the night together built a fever in her blood, giving her a frenetic energy to make extensive notes on his files, research leads on Carib Grand personnel, and review her and Rafe's performance in depth. She hadn't found any answers about Rafe's additional activities, but at least she'd done the job Cameron asked of her to the best of her ability.

Now, walking away from the white-spindled crib where she'd just laid Isla for a nap with a nursery monitor by the bedside, Maresa was drawn across the hallway into the master bedroom while she waited for Cameron to return.

What would happen between us if I wasn't your boss?

Why had he asked that? Hadn't she already made it painfully clear when she'd confided how much she wanted a kiss in those heated moments in his arms yesterday? She'd relived that exchange a million times already and it had happened just twenty-four hours ago.

Now, lowering herself to a white chaise longue near open French doors, Maresa settled the nursery monitor on the hardwood floor at her feet. She would hear Isla if the baby needed anything. For just a few moments at least, she would enjoy overlooking the terrace and the turquoise lagoon below while she waited for Cameron to return. She would inhale the flower-scented sea air of her home, savor the caress of that same breeze along her skin. When was the last time she'd sat quietly and simply enjoyed this kind of beauty, let herself just soak in sensations? Sure, the beach around the Cap Est hotel in Martinique was more upscale than the Caribbean she'd grown up with—public beaches where you brought your own towels from home. But the islands were gorgeous everywhere. No one told the beach morning glory where to grow. It didn't discriminate against the public beaches any more than the yellow wedelia flowers or the bright poinciana trees.

It felt as if she hadn't taken a deep breath all year, not since she'd returned from Paris. There'd been days on the Left Bank when she'd sat at Café de Flore and simply enjoyed the scenery, indulged in people-watching, but since coming home to Charlotte Amalie? Not so much. And now? She had an infant to care for.

If Trina didn't want her baby back—and given the way she'd abandoned Isla, Maresa vowed to block any effort to regain custody—Maresa would have eighteen years of hard work ahead. Her time to stare out to sea and enjoy a few quiet moments would be greatly limited. Given the responsibilities of her brother, mother and now the baby, she couldn't envision many—if any—men who would want to take on all of that to be with her. This window of time with Cameron McNeill might be the last opportunity she had to savor times like this.

To experience romantic pleasure.

Closing her eyes against the thought, she rested her head on the arm of the chaise, unwilling to let her mind wander down that sensual road. She was just tired, that was all.

She'd nap while Isla napped and when she woke up she'd feel like herself again—ready to be strong in the face of all that McNeill magnetism...

"Maresa?"

She awoke to the sound of her name, a whisper of sound against her ear.

Cameron's voice, so close, made her shiver in the most pleasant way, even as her skin warmed all over. The late afternoon sun slanted through the French doors, burnishing her skin to golden bronze—or so it felt. She refused to open her eyes and end the languid sensation in her limbs. The scent of the sea and Cam's woodsy aftershave was a heady combination, a sexy aphrodisiac that had her tilting her head to one side, exposing her neck in silent invitation.

"Mmm?" She arched her back, wanting to be closer to him, needing to feel his lips against her ear once more.

It'd been so long since she'd known a man's touch. And Cameron McNeill was no ordinary man. She bet he kissed like nobody's business.

"Are you hungry?" he asked, the low timbre of his voice turning an everyday question into a sexual innuendo.

Or was it just her imagination?

"Starving," she admitted, reaching up to touch him. To feel the heat and hard muscle of his chest.

She hooked her fingers along the placket of his button-down, next to the top button, which was already undone. She felt his low hiss of response, his heart pumping faster against the back of her knuckles where she touched him. He lowered his body closer, hovering a hair's breadth away.

Breathing him in, she felt the kick of awareness in every nerve ending, her whole body straining toward his.

"Are you sure?" His husky rasp made her skin flame since he still hadn't touched her.

Her throat was dry and she had to swallow to answer. "So sure. So damn certain—"

His lips captured hers, silencing the rest of her words. His chest grazed her breasts, his body covering hers and setting it aflame. Still she craved more. She'd only known him for days but it felt as though she'd been waiting years for him to touch her. His leg slid between hers, his thigh flexing against where she needed him most. A ragged moan slid free...

"Maresa?" He chanted her name in her ear once more, and she thought she couldn't bear it if she didn't start pulling his clothes off.

And her clothes off. She needed to touch more of him.

"Please," she murmured softly, her eyes still closed. She gripped his heavy shoulders. "Please."

"Maresa?" he said again, more uncertainly this time. "Wake up."

Confused, her brain refused to acknowledge that command. She wanted him naked. She did not want to wake up.

Then again…wasn't she awake?

Her eyes wrenched open.

"Cameron?" His name was on her lips as she slid to a sitting position.

Knocking heads with the man she'd been dreaming about.

"Ow." Blinking into the dim light in the room now that the sun had set, Maresa came fully—painfully—awake, her body still on fire from her dream.

"Sorry to startle you." Cameron reached for her, cradling the spot where his forehead had connected with her temple. "Are you okay?"

No. She wasn't okay. She wanted things to go back to where they'd been in her dream. Simple. Sensual.

"Fine." Her breathing was fast. Shallow. Her heartbeat seemed to thunder louder than the waves on the shore. "Is there a storm out there?" she asked, realizing the wind had picked up since she'd fallen asleep. "Is Isla okay?"

The white silk curtains blew into the room. The end of one teased along her bare foot where she'd slid off her shoes. She spotted the nursery monitor on the floor. Silent. Reassuring.

"I just checked on her. She's fine. But there's some heavy weather on the way. The pilot warned me we might want to consider leaving now or—ideally—extending our stay. This system came out of nowhere."

She appreciated the cooler breeze on her overheated skin, and the light mist of rain blowing in with it. Only now did she realize the strap of her sundress had fallen off one shoulder, the bodice slipping precariously down on one side. Before she could reach for it, however, Cameron slid a finger under the errant strap and lifted it into place.

Her skin hummed with pleasure where he touched her.

"Sorry." He slid his hand away fast. "The bare shoulder was…" He shook his head. "I get distracted around you, Maresa. More than I should when I know you want to keep things professional."

The room was mostly dark, except for a glow from the last light of day combined with a golden halo around a wall sconce near the bathroom. He must have turned that on when he'd entered the master suite and found her sleeping.

Dreaming.

"What about you?" Her voice carried the sultriness of sleep. Or maybe it was the sound of desire from her sexy imaginings. Even now, she could swear she remembered the feel of his strong thigh between hers, his chest pressed to aching breasts. "I can't be the only one who wants to keep some professional objectivity."

She slid her feet to the floor, needing to restore some equilibrium with him. Some distance. They sat on opposite sides of the chaise longue, the gathering storm stirring electricity in the air.

"Honestly?" A flash of lightning illuminated his face in full color for a moment before returning them to black-and-white. "I would rather abdicate my role as boss where you're concerned, Maresa. Let my brother Quinn make any decisions that involve you or Rafe. My professional judgment is already seriously compromised."

She breathed in the salty, charged air. Her hair blew silky caresses along her cheek. The gathering damp sat on her skin and she knew he must feel it, too. She was seized with the urge to lean across the chaise and lick him to find out for sure. If she could choose her spot, she'd pick the place just below his steely jaw.

"I don't understand." She shook her head, not following what he was saying. She was still half in dreamland, her whole body conspiring against logic and reason. Re-belling against all her workplace ethics. "We haven't done anything wrong."

Much. They'd talked about a kiss. But there hadn't been one.

His eyes swept her body with unmistakable want.

"Not yet. But I think you know how much I want to." He didn't touch her. He didn't need to.

Her skin was on fire just thinking about it.

"What would your brother think of me if he knew we…" Images of her body twined together with this in-credibly sexy man threatened to steal the last of her de-fenses. "How could he be impartial?"

Another flash of lightning revealed Cam in all his masculine deliciousness. His shirt was open at the col-lar, just the way it had been in her dream. Except now, his shirt was damp with raindrops, making the pale cot-ton cling like a second skin.

Cameron watched her steadily, his intense gaze as stir-ring as any caress. "You know the way you have faith in your brother's good heart and good intentions? No mat-ter what?"

She nodded. "Without question."

"That's how I feel about Quinn's ability to be fair. He can tick me off sometimes, but he is the most level-headed, just person I know."

She weighed what he was saying. Thought about what it meant. "And you're suggesting that if we acted on this attraction…you'd step out of the picture. Your brother becomes my boss, not you."

"Exactly." Cameron's assurance came along with a roll of ominous thunder that rumbled right through the villa.

Right through her feet where they touched the floor.

Maresa felt as if she were standing at the edge of a giant cliff, deciding whether or not to jump. Making that leap would be terrifying. But turning away from the tantalizing possibilities—the lure of the moment—was no longer an option. Even before she'd fallen asleep, she'd known that her window for selfish pleasures was closing fast if Isla proved to be Rafe's daughter and Maresa's responsibility.

How could she deny herself this night?

"Yes." She hurled herself into the unknown and hoped for the best. "I know that you're leaving soon, and I'm okay with that. But for tonight, if we could be just a man and a woman…" The simple words sent a shiver of longing through her.

Even in the dim light, she could see his blue eyes flare hotter, like the gas fireplace in the Antilles Suite when you turned up the thermostat.

"You have no idea how much I was hoping you'd say that." His words took on a ragged edge as his hands slid around her waist. He drew her closer.

Crushed her lips to his.

On contact, fireworks started behind her eyelids and Maresa gave herself up to the spark.

Cameron was caught between the need to savor this moment and the hunger to have the woman he craved like no other. He'd never felt a sexual need like this one. Not as a teenager losing it for the first time. Not during any of the relationships he'd thought were remotely meaningful in his past.

Maresa Delphine stirred some primal hunger different than anything he'd ever experienced. And she'd said *yes*.

The chains were off. His arms banded around her,

pressing all of those delectable curves against him. He ran his palms up her sides, from the soft swell of her hips to the indent of her waist. Up her ribs to the firm mounds of beautiful breasts. Her sundress had tortured him all damn day and he was too glad to tug down the wide straps, exposing her bare shoulders and fragrant skin.

Any hesitation about moving too fast vanished when she lunged in to lick a path along his jaw, pressing herself into him. A low growl rumbled in his chest and he hoped she mistook it for the thunder outside instead of his raw, animal need.

"Please," she murmured against his heated flesh, just below one ear. "Please."

The words were a repeat of the sensual longing he'd heard in her voice when he had first walked into the room earlier. He'd hoped like hell she'd been dreaming about him.

"Anything," he promised her, levering back to look into her tawny eyes. "Name it."

Her lips were swollen from his kiss; she ran her tongue along the top one. He felt a phantom echo of that caress in his throbbing erection that damn near made him light-headed.

"I want your clothes off." She held up her hands to show him. "But I think I'm shaking too badly to manage it."

He cradled her palms in his and kissed them before rising to stand.

"Don't be nervous." He raked his shirt over his head; it was faster than undoing the rest of the buttons.

"It's not that. It's just been such a long time for me." She stood as well, following him deeper into the room. Closer to the bed. "Everything is so hypersensitive. I feel so uncoordinated."

The French doors were still open, but no one would be able to look in unless they were on a boat far out in the water. And then, it would be too dark in the room for anyone out there to see inside. He liked the feel of the damp air and the cool breeze blowing harder.

"Then I'd better unfasten your dress for you." He couldn't wait to have her naked. "Turn around."

She did as he asked, her bare feet shifting silently on the Turkish rug. Cameron found the tab and lowered it slowly, parting the fabric to reveal more and more skin. The bodice dipped forward, falling to her hips so that only a skimpy black lace bra covered the top half of her.

He released the zipper long enough to grab two fist-fuls of the skirt and draw her backward toward him. Her head tipped back against his shoulder, a beautiful offering of her neck. Her body. Her trust. He wanted to lay her down on the bed right now and lose himself inside her, but she deserved better than that. All the more so since it had been a long time for her.

"Can I ask you a question?" He nipped her ear and kissed his way down her neck to the crook of her shoulder. There, he lingered. Tasting. Licking.

"Anything. As long as you keep taking off some clothes." She arched backward, her rump teasing the hard length of him until he had to grind his teeth to keep from tossing her skirt up and peeling away her panties.

A groan of need rumbled in his chest as the rain picked up intensity outside. He cupped her breasts in both hands, savoring the soft weight while he skimmed aside the lace bra for a better feel.

"What were you dreaming when I first walked in here?" He rolled a taut nipple between his thumb and forefinger, dying to taste her. "The soft sighs you were making were sexy as hell."

Her pupils widened with a sensual hint of her answer before she spoke.

"I was dreaming about this." She spun in his arms, pressed her bare breasts to his chest. Her hips to his. "Exactly this. And how much I wanted to be with you."

Her hands went to work on his belt buckle, her trembling fingers teasing him all the more for their slow, inefficient work. He tipped her head up to kiss her, learning her taste and her needs, finding out what she liked best. He nipped and teased. Licked and sucked. She paid him in kind by stripping off his pants and doing a hip shimmy against his raging erection. Heat blasted through him like a furnace turned all the way up.

Single-minded with new focus, he laid her on the bed and left her there while he sorted through his luggage. He needed a condom. Now.

Right. Freaking. Now.

He ripped open the snap on his leather shaving kit and found what he was looking for. When he turned back to the bed, Maresa was wriggling out of her dress, leaving on nothing but a pair of panties he guessed were black lace. It was tough to tell color in the dim light from the wall sconce near the bathroom. The lightning flashes had slowed as the rain intensified. He stepped out of his boxers and returned to the bed.

And covered her with his body.

Her arms went around him, her lips greeting him with hungry abandon, as though he'd been gone for two days instead of a few seconds. His brain buzzed with the need to have her. Still, he laid the condom to one side of her on the bed, needing to satisfy her first. And thoroughly.

She cupped his jaw, trailing kisses along his cheek. When he reached between them to slip his hand beneath the hem of her panties, her head fell back to the bed, turning to one side. She gave herself over to him and that jacked him up even more. She was impossibly hot. Ready. So ready for him. He'd barely started to tease and tempt her when she convulsed with her release.

The soft whimpers she made were so damn satisfying. He wanted to give that release to her again and again. But she wasn't going to sit still for him any longer. Her long leg wrapped around his, aligning their bodies for what they both craved.

He tried to draw out the pleasure by turning his attention to her breasts, feasting on them all over again. But she felt around the bed for the condom and tore it open with her teeth, gently working it over him until he had to shoo her hand away and take over the task. He was hanging by a thread already, damn it.

She chanted sweet words in his ear, encouraging him to come inside her. To give her everything she wanted. He had no chance of resisting her. He thrust inside her with one stroke, holding himself there for a long moment to steel himself for this new level of pleasure. She wrapped her legs around him and he was lost. His eyes crossed. He probably forgot his own name.

It was just Maresa now. He basked in the feel of her body around his. The scent of her citrusy hair and skin. The damp press of her lips to his chest as she moved her hips, meeting his thrusts with her own.

The rain outside pelted harder, faster, cooling his skin when it caught on the wind blowing into the room. He didn't care. It didn't come close to dousing the fire inside him. Maresa raked her nails up his back, a sweet pain he welcomed to balance the pleasure overwhelming him and...

He lost it. His release pounded through him fast and

hot, paralyzing him for a few seconds. Through it all, Maresa clung to him. Kissed him.

When the inner storm passed, he sagged into her and then down on the bed beside her, listening to the other storm. The one picking up force outside. He lay beside her in the aftermath as their breathing slowed. Their heartbeats steadied.

He should feel some kind of guilt, maybe, for bringing her here. For not being able to leave her alone and give her that professional distance she'd wanted. But he couldn't find it in himself to regret a moment of what had just happened. It felt fated. Inevitable.

And if that sounded like him making excuses, so be it.

"Should I shut those?" he asked, kissing her damp forehead and stroking her soft cheek. "The doors, I mean?"

"Probably. But I'm not sure I can let you move yet." A wicked smile kicked up the corner of her lips.

"What if I promise to come back?" He wanted her again. Already.

That seemed physically impossible. And yet…damn.

"In that case, you can go. I'll check on Isla." She untwined her legs from his and eased toward the edge of the bed.

He wanted to ask her if they were okay. If she was upset about what had happened, or if she regretted it.

Then again, did he really want to know if she was already thinking about ways to back off? Now more than ever, he wanted to help her figure out a plan for her future and for Isla's, too. He could help with that. A pragmatic plan to solve both their problems had been growing in his head all day, but now wasn't the time to talk to her about it.

The morning—and the second-guessing that would come with it—was going to happen soon enough. He didn't have any intention of ruining a moment of this night by thinking about what would happen when the sun came up.

Eight

A loud crack of thunder woke Maresa later that night.

Knifing upright in bed, she saw that the French doors in the master bedroom had been closed. Rain pelted the glass outside while streaks of lightning illuminated the empty spot in the king-size bed beside her. Reaching a hand to touch the indent on the other pillow, she felt the warmth of Cameron McNeill's body. The subtle scent of him lingered on her skin, her body aching pleasantly from sex on the chaise longue before a private catered dinner they'd eaten in bed instead of on the patio. Then, there'd been the heated lovemaking in the shower afterward.

And again in the bed before falling asleep in a tangle just a few hours ago. It was after midnight, she remembered. Close to morning.

Isla.

Her gaze darted to the nursery monitor that she'd placed on the nightstand, but it was missing. Cameron must have it, she thought, and be with the baby. But it bothered her that the little girl hadn't been the first thought in her head when she'd opened her eyes.

Dragging Cam's discarded T-shirt from the side of the bed, she pulled it over her head. The hem fell almost to her knees. She hurried out of the master bedroom across the hall to the second room where the hotel staff had brought in a portable crib. There, in a window seat looking out on the storm, lounged Cameron McNeill, cradling tiny Isla against his bare chest.

The little girl's arms reached up toward his face, her uncoordinated fingers flexing and stretching while her eyes tracked him. He spoke to her softly, his lips moving. No. He was singing, actually.

"Rain, rain, go away," he crooned in a melodic tenor that would curl a woman's toes. "Little Isla wants to play—" He stopped midsong when he spotted Maresa by the door. "Hey there. We tried not to wake you."

Her emotions puddled into a giant, liquid mass of feelings too messy to identify. She knew that her heart was at risk because she'd just given this man her body. Of course, that was part of it. But the incredible night aside, she still would have felt her knees go weak to see this impossibly big, strong man cradling a baby girl in his arms so tenderly.

Not just any baby girl, either. This was Rafe's beautiful daughter, given into Maresa's care. Her heart turned over to hear Cameron singing to her.

"It was the storm that woke me, not you." She dragged in a deep breath, trying to steady herself before venturing closer.

He propped one foot on the window seat bench, his knee bent. The other leg sprawled on the floor while his back rested against the casement.

"I gave her a bottle and burped her. I think I did that part all right." He held up the little girl wrapped in a light cotton blanket so Maresa could see. "Not sure how I did on my swaddle job, though."

Maresa smiled, stepping even nearer to take Isla from him. Her hands brushed his chest and sensual memories swamped her. She'd kissed her way up and down those pecs a few hours ago. She shivered at the memory.

"Isla looks completely content." She admired the job he'd done with the blanket. "Although I'm not sure she'll ever break free of the swaddling." She loosened the wrap just a little.

"I wrapped her like a baby burrito." He rose to his feet, scooping up an empty bottle and setting it on the wet bar. "You may be surprised to know I worked in the back of a taco truck one summer as a teen."

"I would be very surprised." She paced around the room with the baby in her arms, taking comfort from the warm weight. Earlier, Maresa had put Isla to bed in a blue-and-white-striped sleeper. Now, she wore a yellow onesie with cartoon dragons, so Cameron must have changed her. "Did your grandfather make you all take normal jobs to build character?"

"No." Cameron shook his head, his dark hair sticking up on one side, possibly from where she'd dragged her fingers through it earlier. He tugged a blanket off the untouched double bed and pulled it over to the window seat. "Come sit until she falls asleep."

She followed him over to the wide bench seat with thick gray cushions and bright throw pillows. The sides were lined with dark wooden shelves containing a few artfully arranged shells and stacks of books. She sat with her back to one of the shelves so she could look out at the storm. Cameron sat across from her, their knees touching. He pulled the blanket over both of their laps.

"You were drawn to the taco truck for the love of fine cuisine?" she pressed, curious to know more about him. She rocked Isla gently, leaning down to brush a kiss across the top of her downy forehead.

"Best tacos in Venice Beach that summer, I'll have you know." He bent forward to tug Maresa's feet into his lap. He massaged the balls of her feet with his big hands. "I was out there to surf the southern California coast that year and ended up sticking around Venice for a few months. I learned everything I know about rolling burritos from Senor Diaz, the dude who owned the truck."

"A skill that's serving you well as a stand-in caregiver," she teased, allowing herself to enjoy this blessedly uncomplicated banter for now. "You'll have to show me your swaddling technique."

"Will do."

"How did your visit to the McNeill family home go?" she asked, regretting that she hadn't done so earlier. "I was so distracted when you got back." She got tingly just thinking about all the ways he'd distracted her over the past few hours.

"You won't hear any complaints from me about how we spent our time." He slowed his stroking, making each swipe of his hands deliberate. Delectable. "And I didn't really visit anyone today. I just wanted to see the place with my own eyes before we contact my half brothers."

"But you will contact them?" She couldn't help but identify with the "other" McNeills. Her mother had been the forgotten mistress of a wealthy American businessman. She knew how it felt to be overlooked.

"My grandfather is insistent we bring them into the fold. I just want to be sure we can trust them."

She nodded, soothed by the pleasure of the impromptu foot massage. "You're proceeding carefully," she observed. "That's probably wise. I want to do the same with Isla—really think about a good plan for raising her." She wanted to ask him what he thought about buying a house, but she didn't want to detract from their personal conversation with business. "I have a lot to learn about caring for a baby."

"Are you sure you want to go for full custody?" His hands stilled on her ankles, his expression thoughtful while lightning flashed in bright bolts over the lagoon. "There's no grandparent on the mother's side that might fight for Isla?"

"I spoke to both of them briefly while I was trying to track down Trina. Trina's mother is an alcoholic who never acknowledged she has a problem, so she's not an option. And the father told me it was all he could do to raise Trina. He's not ready for a newborn." Maresa hadn't even asked him about Isla, so the man must have known that Trina was looking for a way out of being a parent.

"Rafe doesn't know yet?" he said, with a hint of surprise, and perhaps even censure in his voice. He resumed work on her feet, stroking his long fingers up her ankles and the backs of her calves.

"His counselor said we can tell him once paternity is proven, which should be next week. She said she'd help me break the news, and I think I'll take her up on that offer. I know I was floored when I heard about the baby, so I can't imagine how he might feel." She peered down at Isla, watching the baby's eyelids grow heavy. "I'm not sure that Rafe will participate much in Isla's care, but I'll have my mother's help, for as long as she stays healthy."

"You've got a lot on your plate, Maresa," he observed quietly.

"I'm lucky I still have a brother." She remembered how close they'd been to losing him those first few days. "The doctors performed a miracle saving his life, but it took Rafe a lot of hard work to relearn how to walk. To communicate as well as he does. So whatever obstacles I have to face now, it's nothing compared to what Rafe has already overcome."

She brushed another kiss along Isla's forehead, grateful for the unexpected gift of this baby even if her arrival complicated things.

"Does your mother's house have enough room for all of you?" Cameron pressed. "Have you thought about who will care for Isla during the day while you and Rafe are working? If your mother is having more MS attacks—"

"I'll figure out something." She had to. Fast.

"If it comes to a custody hearing, you might need to show the judge that you can provide for the baby with adequate space and come up with a plan for caregiving."

Maresa swallowed past the sudden lump of fear in her throat. She hadn't thought that far ahead. She'd been granted the temporary custody order easily enough, but she hadn't asked her attorney about the next steps.

A bright flash of lightning cracked through the dark horizon, the thunder sounding almost at the same time.

She slid her feet out of Cameron's lap and stood, pacing over to the crib to draw aside the mosquito netting so she could lay Isla in it.

"I'll have to figure something out," she murmured to herself as much as him. "I can't imagine that a judge would take Isla away when Trina herself wants us to raise her."

"Trina could change her mind," he pointed out. His level voice and pragmatic concern reminded her that his business perspective was never far from the surface. "Or one of her parents could decide to sue for custody."

An idea that rattled Maresa.

She whirled on him, her bare feet sticking on the hardwood.

"Are you trying to frighten me?" Because it was working. She'd had Isla in her care for a little less than forty-eight hours and already she couldn't imagine how devastated she would be to lose her. It was unthinkable.

"No, the last thing I want to do is upset you." He stood from the window seat, the blanket sliding off him. "I'm trying to help you prepare because I can see how much she means to you. How much your whole family means to you."

"They're everything," she told him simply, stepping out of the baby's room with the nursery monitor in hand. When her father left Charlotte Amalie, she had been devastated. But her mother and her brother were always there for her, cheering her on when she yearned to travel, helping her to leave Saint Thomas and take the job in Paris when Jaden dumped her. "I won't let them down."

"And I know you'd fight for them to the end, Maresa, but you might need help this time." Cameron closed the door of the second bedroom partway before following Maresa downstairs into the all-white kitchen.

She was wide-awake now, tense and hungry. She'd been more focused on Cameron than eating during dinner, and she was feeling the toll of an exhausting few days. Arriving in the eat-in kitchen with a fridge full of leftovers from the catered meal that they'd only half eaten, she slid a platter of fruits and cheeses from the middle shelf, then grabbed the bottle of sparkling water.

"What kind of help?" she asked, pouring the water into two glasses he produced from a high cabinet lit from within so that the glow came through the frosted-glass front.

Cameron peeled the plastic covering off the fruit and put the platter down in the breakfast nook.

"I have a proposition I'd like to explain." He found white ceramic plates in another cabinet and held out one of the barstools for her to take a seat. "A way we might be able to help one another."

She tucked her knees under the big T-shirt of his that she'd borrowed.

"I'm doing everything I can to help you figure out why the Carib's performance reviews are declining." She couldn't imagine what other kind of help he would need.

"I realize that." He dropped into the seat beside her and filled his plate with slices of pineapple and mango. He added a few shrimp from another tray. "But I've got a much bigger idea in mind."

She tore a heel of crusty bread from the baguette they hadn't even touched earlier. "I'm listening."

"A few months ago, I proposed to a woman I'd never met."

"Seriously?" She put down the bread, shocked. "Why would anyone do that?"

"It was impulsive of me, I'll admit. I was irritated with my grandfather because he rewrote his will with a dictate that his heirs could only inherit after they'd been married for twelve months."

"Why?" Maresa couldn't imagine why anyone would attach those kinds of terms to a will. Especially a rich corporate magnate like Malcolm McNeill. She knew a bit about him from reading the bio on the McNeill Resorts website.

"We're still scratching our heads about it, believe me. I was mad because he'd told me he'd change the terms over his dead body—which is upsetting to hear from an eighty-year-old man—and then he cackled about it like it was a great joke and I was too much of a kid to understand." Cameron polished off the shrimp and reached for the baguette. "So I worked with a matchmaker and picked a woman off a website—a woman who I thought was a foreigner looking for a green-card marriage. Sounded perfect."

"Um. Only if you're insane." Maresa had a hard time reconciling the man she knew with the story he was sharing. Although, when she thought about it, maybe he had shown her his impulsive side with the way he'd taken on her problems like they were his own—giving her the villa while he stayed in the hotel, paying for the caregiver for Isla while Maresa worked. "That's not the way most people would react to the news that they need a bride."

"Right. My brothers said the same thing." Cameron poured them both more water and flicked on an overhead light now that the storm seemed to be settling down a little. "And anyway, I backed out of the marriage proposal when I realized the woman wasn't looking to get married anyhow. My mistake had unexpected benefits, though, since—surprise—my oldest brother is getting married to the woman I proposed to."

Maresa's fork slid from her grip to jangle on the granite countertop. "You're kidding me. Does he even *want* to marry her, or is this just more McNeill maneuvering for the sake of the will?"

"This is the real deal. Quinn is big-time in love." Cameron grinned and she could see that he was happy for his brother. "And Ian is, too, oddly. It's like my grandfather waved the marriage wand and the two of them fell into line."

As conflicted as Cameron's relationships might be

with his father and grandfather, it was obvious he held his siblings in high regard.

"Which leaves you the odd man out with no bride."

"Right." He shoved aside his plate and swiveled his stool in her direction. "My grandfather had a heart attack last month and we're worried about his health. From a financial standpoint, I don't need any of the McNeill inheritance, but keeping the company in the family means everything to Gramps."

She wondered why he thought so if the older man hadn't made his will more straightforward, but she didn't want to ask. Tension crept through her shoulders.

"So you still hope to honor the terms of the will." Even as she thought it, she ground her teeth together. "You know, I'm surprised you didn't mention you had plans to marry when you wooed me into bed with you. That's not the kind of thing I take lightly."

"Neither do I." He covered her hand with his. "I am not going to march blindly into a marriage with someone I don't know. That was a bad idea." He stroked his thumb over the back of her knuckles. "But I know you."

Her mouth went dry. A buzzing started in her ears.

Surely she wasn't understanding him. But she was too dumbfounded to speak, let alone ask him for clarification.

"Maresa, you need help with Isla and your family. Rafe needs the best neurological care possible, something he could get in New York where they have world-class medical facilities. Likewise, for your mother—she needs good doctors to keep her healthy."

"I don't understand." She shook her head to clear it since she couldn't even begin to frame her thoughts. "What are you saying?"

"I'm saying a legal union between the two of us would be a huge benefit on both sides." He reached below her to turn her seat so that she faced him head-on. His blue eyes locked on hers with utter seriousness. "Marry me, Maresa."

Cameron knew his brothers would accuse him of being impulsive all over again. But this situation had nothing in common with the last time he'd proposed to a woman.

He knew Maresa and genuinely wanted to help her. Hell, he couldn't imagine how she could begin to care for a baby with everything she was already juggling. He could make her life so much easier.

She stared at him now as if he'd gone off the deep end. Her jaw unhinged for a moment. Then, she snapped it shut again.

"Maybe we've both been working too hard," she said smoothly, trotting out her competent, can-do concierge voice. "I think once we've gotten some rest you'll see that a legal bond between us would complicate things immeasurably."

Despite the cool-as-you-please smile she sent his way, her hand trembled as she retrieved her knife and cut a tiny slice of manchego from a brick of cheese. With her sun-tipped hair brushing her cheek as she moved and her feminine curves giving delectable shape to his old T-shirt, Maresa looked like a fantasy brought to life. Her lips were still swollen from his kisses, her gorgeous legs partially tucked beneath her where she sat. Yet seeing her hold Isla and tuck the tiny girl into bed had been...

Touching. He couldn't think of any other way to describe what he'd felt, and it confused the hell out of him since he'd never wanted kids. But Maresa and Isla brought a surprise protectiveness out of him, a kind of caring he wasn't sure he'd possessed. And while he wasn't going to turn into a family man anytime soon, he could certainly imagine himself playing a role to help with Isla for the next year. That was worth something to Maresa, wasn't it? Besides, seeing Maresa's tender side assured him that she wasn't going to marry him just for the sake of a big payout. She had character.

"I appreciate you trying to give me a way out." He smoothed a strand of hair back where it skimmed along her jaw. "But I'm thinking clearly, and I believe this is a good solution to serious problems we're both facing."

"Marriage isn't about solving problems, Cam." She set down the cheese without taking a single bite. "Far from it. Marriage *causes* problems. You saw it in your own family, right?"

She was probably referring to his parents' divorce and how tough that had been for him and his brothers, but he pushed ahead with his own perspective.

"But we're approaching this from a more objective standpoint." It made sense. "You and I like each other, obviously. And we both want to keep our families safe. Why not marry for a year to secure my grandfather's legacy and make sure your brother, mother and niece have the best health benefits money can buy? The best doctors and care? A home with enough room where you're not worried about Rafe being upset by the normal sounds of life with an infant?"

"In New York?" She spread her arms wide, as if that alone proved he was crazy. "My work is here. Rafe's job is here. How could we move to New York for the health care? And even if we wanted to, how would we get back here—and find work again—twelve months from now?"

"By focusing on the wheres and hows, I take it you're at least considering it?" He would have a lot of preparations to make, but he could pull it off—he could relocate all of them to Manhattan next week. He just needed to finish up his investigation into the Carib Grand and then he could return to New York.

With the terms of his grandfather's will fulfilled. It would be a worry off his mind and it would be his pleasure to help her family. It would be even more of a pleasure to have her in his bed every night.

The more he thought about it, the more right it seemed.

"Not even close." She slid off the barstool to stand. "By focusing on the wheres and hows, I'm trying to show you how unrealistic this plan is. I'm more grateful to you than I can say for trying to help me, but I will figure out a way to support my family without imposing on the McNeills for a year."

"What about your brother?" Cam shoved aside his plate. "In New York, Rafe could work in a program where he'd be well supervised by professionals who would respect his personal triggers and know how to challenge him just enough to move his recovery forward."

She folded her arms across her breasts, looking vulnerable in the too-big shirt. "You've been doing your research."

"I read up on his injury to be sure you had him doing work he could handle." Cam wouldn't apologize for looking into Rafe's situation. "You know that's why I came to the Carib in the first place—to make sure everyone was doing their job."

"It hardly seems fair to use my brother's condition to convince me."

"Isn't it less fair to deny him a good program because you wouldn't consider a perfectly legitimate offer? I'm no Jaden Torries. I'm not going to back out on you, Maresa." And she would be safe from the worry of having children with him since he would never have any of his own. That would be a good thing in a temporary marriage, right?

"We'll sign a contract that stipulates what will happen after the twelve months are up—"

"I don't want a contract," she snapped, raising her voice as she cut him off. "I've already got a failed engagement in my past. Do you think I want a failed marriage, too?" Her eyes shone too bright and he realized there were unshed tears there.

She didn't want to hear all the reasons why they would work well together on a temporary basis.

He'd hurt her.

By the time he'd figured that out, however, he was standing in the kitchen by himself. The thunder had stopped, but it seemed the storm in the villa wasn't over.

Nine

Two days later, Maresa sat behind the concierge's desk typing an itinerary for the personal assistant of an aging rock-and-roll star staying at the Carib. The guitar legend was taking his entourage on a vacation to detox after his recent stay in rehab. Maresa's job had been to keep the group occupied and away from drugs and alcohol for two weeks. With her help, they'd be too busy zip-lining, kayaking and Jet Skiing to think about anything else.

The project had been a good diversion for her since she'd returned from her trip to Martinique with Cameron. She still couldn't believe he'd proposed to her for the sake of a mutually beneficial one-year arrangement and not out of any romantic declaration of interest. Great sex aside, a proposal of a marriage of convenience really left her gut in knots.

Leaning back in her desk chair, she blinked into the afternoon sun slanting through the lobby windows and hit the send button on the digital file. She wished she could have stretched out the project a bit longer to help her from thinking about Cam. He'd been kind to her since she'd turned down his proposal, promising her that the marriage offer would remain open until he returned to New York. She shouldn't be surprised that his engagement idea had an expiration date since he wasn't doing it because he'd fallen head over heels for her. It was just business to him. Whereas for her? She had no experience conducting affairs for the sake of expedience. It sounded tawdry and wrong.

Shoving to her feet, she tried not to think about how helpful the arrangement would be for her family. For her, even. He'd dangled incredible enticement in front of her nose by promising the best health care for her brother. Her mom, too. Maresa felt like an ogre for not accepting for those reasons alone. But what was the price to her heart over the long haul? Her self-respect? Maybe it would be different if they hadn't gotten involved romantically. If they'd remained just friends. But he'd waited to spring the idea on her until after she'd kissed him. Peeled off all her clothes with him and made incredible love.

Of course her heart was involved now. How could she risk it again after the way Jaden had shredded her? Things were too murky with Cameron. There were no boundaries with him now that they'd slept together. She could too easily envision herself falling for him and then she would be devastated a year from now when he bought her a first-class ticket back to Saint Thomas. She sagged back in the office chair, the computer screen blurring because of the tears she just barely held back.

Foot traffic in the lobby was picking up as it neared five o'clock. Guests were returning from day trips. New visitors were checking in. A crowd was gathering for happy hour at the bar before the dinner rush. Maresa smiled and nodded, asking a few guests about their day as they passed her. When her phone rang, she saw Cameron's number and her stomach filled with unwanted butterflies. Needing privacy, she stepped behind the concierge stand to take the call. Her heart ached just seeing his number, wishing her brief time with him hadn't imploded so damn fast.

"Hello?" She smoothed a hand over her hair and then caught herself in the middle of the gesture.

"Rafe is on the move with a guest," Cameron spoke quietly. "Meet me on the patio and we'll follow him."

Fear for her brother stabbed through her. What was going on with him? Would this be the end of his job? She might not want to be involved with Cameron personally, but she needed him to support her professionally. She hoped it wouldn't come down to calling in the oldest McNeill brother, Quinn, to decide Rafe's fate, but they'd agreed that Cameron couldn't supervise her after what had happened between them.

"On my way." Her feet were already moving before she disconnected the call. She hurried through the tiki bar where a steel drum band played reggae music for the happy hour crowd. Dodging the waitstaff carrying oversize drinks, Maresa also avoided running into a few soaked kids spilling out onto the pool deck with inflatable rings and toys.

Another time, she would gently intervene to remind the parents they needed to be in the kids' pool. But she wouldn't let Cameron confront Rafe alone. She needed to be there with him.

And then, there he was.

The head of McNeill Resorts waited on the path to the beach for her, his board shorts paired with a T-shirt this time, which was a small favor considering how much the sight of his bare chest could make her forget all her best resolve. He really was spectacularly appealing.

"Where's Rafe?" she asked, gaze skipping past him to the empty path ahead.

"They just turned the corner. Rafe and a young mother who checked in two days ago with her husband for a long weekend."

Maresa wondered how he'd found that out so quickly. She fell into step beside him. "How did you know Rafe was with a guest? I sent him on an errand to the gift shop about twenty minutes ago."

"I hired a PI to keep tabs on things here for a few days."

Her heeled sandal caught on a tree root in the sand. "You're having someone spy on Rafe?"

"I can't assign the task to anyone in the hotel, especially if Aldo Ricci really has anything to do with assigning Rafe the extra duties." Cameron's hand snaked out to hold her back, his attention focused on the beach ahead. "Look."

Maresa peered after her brother and the petite brunette. Her short ponytail swung behind her as she walked. Rafe didn't bring her to the regular beach, but waved her through a clearing to the east. Maresa wanted to charge over there and split them up. Ask Rafe who told him to bring the woman to a deserted beach.

"What's the plan?" she asked, fidgeting with an oversize flower hanging from a tropical bush.

"We see who he's meeting and confront him when he turns back."

"We'll make too much noise tramping through there." She pointed to the overgrown foliage. "I can't believe that

woman is following a total stranger into the unknown."
Why didn't vacationers have more sense?

"He's a hotel employee at one of the most exclusive
resorts in the world," Cameron reminded her, his jaw
tensing as he drew her into the dense growth. "She paid
a lot of money to feel safe here."

Right. Which meant Rafe was so fired. Panic weighted
down her chest. Today, every penny of Rafe's check
would go to extra care for Isla—an in-home sitter to
help Maresa's mom with the baby. What would they do
when they lost that money?

She would have to marry Cameron.

The truth stared her in the face as surely as Rafe
waved at Jaden Torries on the beach right now. Her ex-
fiancé stood by the water's edge with his easel already
set up—a half-baked artist trolling for clients at the Carib
and using Rafe to deliver them off-site so he could paint
them. Rafe was risking his job for…what? He never made
any money from this scheme.

"I'm going to strangle Jaden," she announced, fury
making her ready to launch through the bushes to read
him the riot act.

"No." Cameron's arm slid around her waist, holding
her back. He pressed her tightly to him so he could speak
softly in her ear. "Say nothing. Follow me and we'll ask
Rafe about it when we're farther away so Jaden can't
hear."

She wanted to argue. But Cameron must have guessed
as much because he covered her lips with one finger.

"Shh." The sound was far more erotic than it should
have been since she was angry.

Her body reacted to his nearness without her permission, a fever crawling over her skin until she wanted to
turn in his arms and fall on him. Right here.

Thankfully, he let her go and tugged her back to the hotel's main beach where they could wait for Rafe.

"Someone is using him," she informed Cameron while they waited. "He didn't orchestrate this himself, and he doesn't receive any money. I would know if someone was paying him."

"That woman he just took down to the beach is partners with the investigator I hired," Cameron surprised her by saying. "We'll find out what's going on. But for now, ask him who sent him and see what he says. Do you want me to stay with you or do you want to speak to him alone?"

"Um." She bit her lip, her anger draining away. He was helping Rafe. And her. The PI was a good idea and could prove her brother's innocence. "It might be better if I speak to him privately. And thank you."

Cameron's blue eyes held her gaze. His hand skimmed along her arm, setting off a fresh heat inside her. "We'd make a great team if you'd give us a chance."

Would they? Could she trust him to look out for her and her family if she gave in and helped him to secure his family legacy? Sure, Cameron could help her family in ways she couldn't. He already had. But what would it be like to share a home with him for a year while they fulfilled the terms of the marriage he needed? Still, while she worried about all the ways a legal union would be risky for her, she hadn't really stopped to consider that he was already holding up his end of the promised bargain—helping all the Delphines—while she'd given him nothing in return.

Maybe she already owed him her help for all that he'd done for her. Even if the fallout twelve months from now was going to hurt far more than Jaden's betrayal.

"You're right." She squeezed Cameron's hand briefly,

then let go as she saw her brother step onto the beach. "If you're still serious about that one-year deal, I'll take it."

"Maresa?" Rafe stopped when he spotted her standing underneath a date palm tree.

She was nervous about confronting him, wishing she could talk to him about everything at once. His secret meeting on the beach. His daughter. His future.

But she worried about how he would handle the news of Isla and she wanted his counselor there. The paternity results were in, and the woman had agreed to meet them at the Delphine residence after work today, so at least Maresa would be able to share that with him soon. For now, she just needed to ask who sent him here. Keep it simple. Nonthreatening.

He got confused and agitated so easily. Which was understandable, considering the long-and short-term memory loss that plagued him. She'd be agitated too if she couldn't remember what she was doing.

"Hi, Rafe." Forcing herself to smile, she hurried over to him. Slipped an arm through his. "Gorgeous day, isn't it?"

"Nancy says, 'another day in paradise.' Every day she says that." Rafe grinned at her.

His work uniform—mostly khaki, but the short sleeves of his staff shirt were white—was loose on him, making her worry that Rafe had lost weight without her noticing. She needed to care for him more and worry about his job less. Maybe, assuming Rafe agreed, a move to New York could be a real gift for their family right now. She needed to focus on how much Cameron was trying to help her brother, mother and niece, instead of thinking about how this growing attachment to him was only going to hurt in the end.

Cameron McNeill was a warmhearted, generous man, and he'd been that way before she agreed to help him, so it wasn't as though he was self-serving. She admired the careful way he'd gone about investigating the happenings at the Carib. It showed a decency and respect for his employees that she'd bet most billionaire corporate giants wouldn't feel.

"We're lucky like that." Maresa tipped her head to his shoulder for a moment as they walked together, wanting to feel that connection to him. "What brought you down to the beach?"

Overhead, a heron flew low, casting a shadow across her brother's face before landing nearby.

"A guest wanted her picture painted. Mr. Ricci said so."

Again with the hotel director?

Maresa found that hard to believe. The man had been extremely successful in the industry for years. Why would he undermine his position by promoting solicitation on the Carib's grounds? Why would he allow his guests to think they were receiving some kind of luxury experience through a session with Jaden, whose talents were...negligible.

"Rafe." She paused her step, tugging gently on his arm to stop him, too. She needed to make sure, absolutely sure, he understood what she was asking. "Did Mr. Ricci himself tell you to escort that woman here, or did someone else tell you that Mr. Ricci said so?"

She'd tried to keep the question simple, but as soon as she asked it, she could see the furrow between Rafe's brows. The confusion in his eyes, which were so like Isla's. Ahead on the path, she could hear the music from the tiki bar band, the sound carrying on the breeze as the sun dipped lower in the sky.

"Mr. Ricci said it." A storm brewed in Rafe's blue gaze, turning the shade from sapphire to cold slate. "Why don't you believe me?"

"I do believe you, Rafe."

He shook off her hand where she touched him.

"You don't believe me." He raised his voice. He walked faster up the path, away from her. "Every day you ask me the same things. Two times. Everything. Everyday."

He muttered a litany of disjointed words as he stomped through the brush. She closed her eyes and followed him without speaking, not wanting to upset him more. Maybe she should have asked Cameron to stay with her for this.

She craved Cameron's warm touch. His opinion and outside perspective. He'd become important to her so quickly. Was she crazy to let him draw her even more deeply into his world? All the way to New York?

But as she followed Rafe up the path toward the Carib, watching the way his shoulders tensed with agitation, she knew that his job wouldn't have lasted much longer here anyway. She'd wanted this to be the answer for him— for them—until they caught up on the medical bills and she could get him in a different kind of program to support TBI sufferers. Now, she knew she'd been deceiving herself that she could make it work. In truth, she'd been unfair to her brother, setting him up to fail.

No matter how much she loved Rafe, she needed to face the fact that he would never be the brother she once knew. For his own good, she needed to start protecting him and his daughter, too. Tonight, she'd give her notice to the hotel director.

For her family's sake, she would become Mrs. Cameron McNeill. She just hoped in twelve months' time, she'd be able to resurrect Maresa Delphine from the wreckage.

* * *

Back in the Antilles Suite rented out to his alter-ego, Mr. Holmes, Cameron reread Maresa's text.

Rafe said Mr. Ricci sent him on the errand. Became agitated when I asked a second time but stuck to the same facts.

Turning off the screen on his phone, Cam stroked Poppy's head. The Maltese rested on the desk where he worked. She liked being by his laptop screen when they were indoors, maybe because he tended to pet her more often. He was going to hate returning her to Mrs. Trager when they went back to New York and his stint as an undercover boss was over.

His stint as a temporary groom was up next. He'd been surprised but very, very pleased that Maresa had said yes to his proposal. He needed to make it more official, of course. And more romantic, too, now that he thought about it. Hell, a few months ago, he'd proposed to a woman he'd never met before with flowers and a ring. Maresa, on the other hand, had gotten neither and he intended to change that immediately.

He needed to romance her, not burden her with every nitnoid detail that was going into the marriage contract. She hadn't been interested in thinking about the business details, so he would put them in writing only. It didn't matter that she didn't know about his inability to father children. She was focused on her own family. Her own child. And for his part, Cameron would make sure she didn't regret their arrangement for a moment by making it clear she had twelve incredible months ahead.

He dialed his brother Quinn to give him an update on

the situation at the Carib, wanting to lay some ground-work for his hasty nuptials.

"Cam?" His brother answered the phone with a wary voice. "Before you ask, the answer is no. You don't get to fly the seaplane yourself."

Quinn was messing with him, of course. A brotherly jab about his piloting skills—which were actually ex-cellent. But the fact that they were the first words out of his brother's mouth made Cam wonder about the way the rest of the world perceived him. Reckless. Impulsive.

And his quickie engagement wouldn't do anything to change that.

"I'm totally qualified, and you know it," he returned, straightening Poppy's topknot that she'd scratched side-wise. He'd gotten his sport pilot certification years ago and he kept it updated.

"Technically, yes," Quinn groused, the sound of clas-sical music playing in the background. "But I know the first thing you'll do is test the aerial maneuvering or see how she handles in a barrel roll, so the controls are off-limits."

Funny, that had never occurred to him. But a few years ago, it might have. Yeah. It would have. He'd totaled Ian's titanium racing bike his first time on, seeing how fast it would go. He'd felt bad about that. Ian replaced it, but Cameron knew the original had been custom-built by a friend.

He hated being like his father.

"If I stay out of the cockpit, will you do me a favor?" He thought about bringing Maresa to New York and in-troducing her to his family. Would she look at him the same way when she discovered that he was considered the family screwup, or would she take the first flight back to Saint Thomas?

"Possibly." Quinn lowered his voice as the classical music stopped in the background. "Sofia's just finishing up a rehearsal, though. Want me to call you back?"

"No." The less time Quinn had to protest the move, the better. "I'm bringing my new fiancée home as soon as possible," he announced, knowing he had a long night ahead to make all the necessary arrangements.

"Not again." His brother's quick assumption that Cameron was making another mistake grated on Cam's last nerve.

Straightening, he moved away from the desk to stare out the window at the Caribbean Sea below.

"This time it's for real." He trusted Maresa to follow through with the marriage for the agreed-upon time. "Maresa deserves a warm welcome from the whole family and I want your word that she'll receive it."

"Cam, you've been in Saint Thomas for just a few days—"

"Your word," Cam insisted. "And I'll need Ian's cooperation, too."

For a moment, all he heard was Vivaldi's "Spring" starting up in the background of the call. Then, finally, Quinn huffed out a breath.

"Fine. But the plane better damn well be in one piece."

Cameron relaxed his shoulders, realizing now how tense he'd been waiting for an answer. "Done. See you soon, Brother, and I'll give you a full report on the Martinique McNeills plus an update on the Carib."

Disconnecting the call, Cameron went through a mental list of all he needed to do in order to leave for a few days. He had to have the PI take a close look at Aldo Ricci, no matter how stellar the guy's reputation was in the industry. Cameron needed to make arrangements for a ring, flowers and a wedding. He had to find a nanny, narrow down some options for good programs for Rafe and research the best neurosurgeon to have a consultation with Analise Delphine. He could farm out some of those tasks to his staff in New York. But before anything else, he needed to phone his lawyer to draw up the contracts that would protect his interests and Maresa's, too. He felt a sense of accomplishment that he'd be able to help someone he'd come to care about. This was surprisingly easy for him. As long as they both went into this marriage with realistic expectations, it could all work.

Only when that was done would he allow himself to return to Maresa's place and remind her why marrying him was going to be the best decision of her life. He might have his impulsive and reckless side, but he could damn well take good care of her every need for the upcoming year.

With great pleasure for them both.

Ten

I need to see you tonight.

Standing in her mother's living room, Maresa read the text from Cameron, resisting the urge to hug the phone to her chest like an adolescent.

She stared out the front window onto the street, reminding herself he wanted a business arrangement, not a romantic entanglement. If she was going to commit herself to a marriage in name only, she needed to stop spending so much time thinking about him. How kind he'd been to her. How good he could make her feel. How sweet he was with Isla.

Because Cameron McNeill didn't spend his free hours dreaming about her in those romantic ways. He was too busy investigating business practices at the Carib Grand and fulfilling the legal terms of his grandfather's will. Those things were important to him. Not Maresa.

The scent of her mother's cooking lingered in the air—plantains and jerk chicken that she'd shared with Mr. Leopold earlier. Her mom had warmed up a plate for Rafe when they returned from work, but Maresa's stomach was in too many knots to eat. Huffing out a sigh of frustration, Maresa typed out a text in response to Cameron.

The counselor just arrived. Any time after nine is fine.

She shut off her phone as soon as the message went through to stop herself from looking for a reply. If she wasn't careful, she'd be sending heart emojis and making an idiot of herself with him the way she had with Jaden. At least with this marriage, she knew the groom would really go through with it since he wanted to secure his millions. Billions? She had no clue. She only knew that the McNeills lived on a whole other level from the Delphines.

Here, they were a family of four crowded into her mother's two-bedroom apartment. For now, Isla's portable crib was in Analise's bedroom so they could shut the door if she started to cry. They'd told Rafe the little girl was a friend's daughter and that Maresa was babysitting for the night, but he'd barely paid any attention since he was still upset with his sister.

"Mom?" Maresa called as she opened the door for their guest—Tracy Seders, the counselor who would help them tell Rafe about his daughter. "She's here."

Analise Delphine shuffled out of the kitchen, dropping an old-fashioned apron behind a chair on her way out. The house was neat and clean, but their style of housekeeping meant you needed to be careful when opening closets or junk drawers. The mess lurked dangerously below the surface. How would they merge their lifestyle with Cameron's for the next year? Maresa would speak to him in earnest tonight, to make sure he knew what he was getting into by taking on a whole, chaotic family and not just one woman.

"Thank you for coming." Maresa ushered Tracy Seders inside, showing her to a seat in the living area where Maresa had slept since returning from Paris. She'd tucked away the blanket and pillow for the visit.

The three women spent a few minutes talking while Rafe finished his dinner and Isla bounced in a baby seat on the floor, her blue eyes wide and alert. She wore a pastel yellow sleeper with an elephant stitched on the front, one of a half dozen outfits that had arrived from the hotel gift shop that morning, according to Analise. The card read, "Congratulations from McNeill Resorts."

More thoughtfulness from Cameron that made it difficult to be objective about their arrangement.

Now, the counselor turned to Analise. "As I told Maresa on the phone, there's a good chance Rafe doesn't remember his relationship with Trina. He's never once mentioned her to me in our sessions." She smoothed a hand through her windblown auburn hair. The woman favored neat shirtdresses and ponytails most days, and made Maresa think of a kindergarten teacher. Today, the reason for the ponytail was more apparent: her red curls were rioting. "If that's the case, we'll have a difficult time explaining about Isla."

Analise nodded as she frowned, her eyes turned to where Rafe sat alone at the kitchen table, listening to a Yankees game on an old radio and adjusting the antennae.

Maresa repositioned the crochet throw pillow behind her back, fidgeting in her nervousness. "But we don't need to press, right? We can always just end the discussion and reinforce the relationship down the road when he's less resistant."

"Exactly." Tracy Seders tucked her phone in her purse and sat forward on the love seat. "Rafe, would you like to join us for a minute?" she called.

Maresa's stomach knotted tighter. She hadn't told her mother about Cam's proposal yet, but she'd mentioned it to the counselor on the phone in the hopes the woman would help her feel out Rafe about a move to New York. She feared it was too much at once, but the counselor hadn't seemed concerned, calling it a potential diversion from the baby news if Rafe didn't react well to that.

Now her brother ambled toward them. He'd changed out of his work clothes. In his red gym shorts and gray T-shirt, he looked much the same as he had as a teen, only now there were scattered scars in his hair from the surgery that had saved his life. More than the scars though, it was the slow, deliberate movements that gave away his injury. He used to dart and hurry everywhere, a whirling force of nature.

"Ms. Seders. You don't belong here." He grinned as he said it and the counselor didn't take offense.

"You aren't used to me in your living room, are you, Rafe?" She laughed and patted the seat beside her. "I heard your family has exciting news for you."

"What?" He lowered himself beside her, watching her intently.

Maresa held her breath, willing the woman to take the reins. She didn't know how to begin. Especially after she'd hurt his feelings earlier.

"They heard from your old girlfriend, Rafe. Trina?" She waited for any show of recognition.

There was none.

The counselor plowed ahead. "Trina had a baby this

spring, Rafe. Your baby." The woman nodded toward Maresa, gesturing for her to show him Isla.

She bent to lift the little girl from the carrier.

"No." Rafe said, shaking his head. "No. No girlfriend. No baby."

He got to his feet and would have walked away if Tracy hadn't taken his hand.

"Rafe, your sister will watch over Isla for you. But the baby is your daughter. One day, when you feel better—"

"No baby." Rafe looked at Maresa. Was it her imagination, or did his eyes narrow a bit? Was he still angry with her? "No."

He stalked out of the room this time and Analise made a strangled cry. Of disappointment? Maresa couldn't be sure. She'd been so focused on Rafe and trying to read his reaction she hadn't paid attention to her mother. Gently, Maresa returned Isla to the baby carrier, buckling her in to keep her safe.

"Rafe?" the counselor called after him. "I have a friend in New York City I would like you to meet. Another counselor. She lives near where the Yankees play."

Maresa's mother drew a breath as if to interrupt, but Maresa put her hand on her mom's arm to stop her. Analise's eyes went wide while Rafe spun around, his eyes bright.

"The Yankees?" He stepped toward them again, irresistibly drawn. "I could go to New York?" He looked at Maresa, and she realized how much she'd become a parent figure to him in the last months.

"Maresa." Her mother's voice was stern, although she kept her words low enough that Rafe wouldn't hear. "You know that's not possible."

Maresa squeezed her mom's hand, while she kept her

eyes on Rafe. "We could all go if you don't mind seeing a new doctor."

Rafe raised his arm above his head and it took Maresa a moment to realize he was pumping his fist.

"Yankees." He smiled crookedly. "Yankees! Yes."

The counselor shared a smile with Maresa while Rafe went to turn up the radio louder, a happy expression lingering on his face as he sank into a chair at the table.

"Maresa?" Analise asked. "What on earth?"

They both rose to their feet to walk the counselor to the door, and Maresa gave her mother an arm to lean on. Thanking the woman for her help that had gone above and beyond her job description, Maresa waved to her while she walked to her car. Only then did she face her mother, careful to keep Analise balanced on her unsteady feet.

"I'm getting married, Mom." The announcement lacked the squealing joy she'd had when she told her mother about Jaden's proposal. But at least now, with a contract sure to come that would document what she was agreeing to, Maresa knew the marriage would happen as surely as she knew the divorce would, too. "He cares, Mom, and wants to help with Rafe however he can."

Analise bit her lip. "Maresa. Baby." She shook her head. "After everything I went through with your daddy? You ought to know men don't mean half of what they say."

Maresa couldn't have said what surprised her more—that her mother recognized her father had played her false, or that Analise sounded protective on Maresa's behalf.

"I know, Mom." Maresa watched as the counselor sped away from the curb. "But this is different, trust me. I don't have any illusions that he loves me."

"No love?" Her mother grabbed her hand and squeezed—probably as hard as her limited mobility allowed. "There is no other reason to marry, Maresa Delphine, and you know it."

Right. And fairy tales came true.

But Maresa wasn't going to argue that with her mother right now. Instead, she hugged her gently.

"It's going to be okay. And this is going to be good for Rafe. I want us all to move to New York where he can get into a supervised care program that will really help him." She remained on the front step, breathing in the hot air as the moon came out over the Caribbean. Palm trees rustled in the breeze.

"Honey, once you get your heart broke, you can't just unbreak it." Her mother's simple wisdom was a good reminder for her.

She would be like Cameron and look at this objectively. They could be a good team. And just maybe, she could keep her heart intact. But in order to do that, she really shouldn't be sleeping with her charismatic future husband. It was while she was in his arms, kissing him passionately and sharing her body with him, that her emotions got all tangled up.

"I understand," she promised, just as Isla let out a small cry. Her mother insisted on being the one to check on the baby. Before Maresa could follow, a pair of headlights streaked across her as a vehicle turned up her street.

A warm tingle of anticipation tripped over her skin, telling her who it was. What kind of magic let her know when Cameron McNeill was nearby? It was uncanny.

Yet sure enough, on the road below, a dark Jeep slid into the spot that Rafe's counselor had vacated just a short time ago.

Maresa's fiancé had arrived.

* * *

Half an hour later, Cameron had Maresa in the passenger seat of the Jeep. They'd left Isla at her mother's house since the women agreed the baby was out for the night after a final feeding. Or at least until the 3:00 a.m. bottle feeding, which had been her pattern the last few nights.

He'd kept silent in front of Maresa's mom about the fact that he'd been the one to provide that bottle to the baby two nights before. Analise Delphine had been cordial but not warm, unmoved by the bouquets of tropical wildflowers he'd brought for each of them. No doubt Maresa's mother was concerned about the quick engagement, the same way Quinn had been concerned. Both women were worried about Rafe's reaction to his daughter, which had been adamant denial that she belonged to him. Just hearing as much made Cameron's heart ache for the little girl. He knew Maresa would be a good mother figure to her. But how hard must it be for a girl to grow up without a father? Or worse, a father who was a presence but didn't care to acknowledge her?

Of course, one day, she would know that Rafe suffered an injury that changed his personality. But still…he hated that for Isla, who deserved to grow up with every advantage. With a lot of love. Cameron didn't know why he felt so strongly about that. About her. Was it because of the baby's connection to Maresa? Or did he simply have a soft spot for kids that he'd never known about? He'd never questioned his comfort with giving up fatherhood before, but he wondered if he'd always feel as adamant about that.

Now, the breeze whipped through the Jeep since he'd taken the top down. With the speed limit thirty-five everywhere, they were safe enough. Poppy was buckled into her pet carrier in the backseat, her nose pressed to the grates for a better view.

Maresa had shown him how to leave the city and climb the winding road at the center of the island to get to Crown Mountain where he'd rented a place for the night. He hadn't mentioned the destination because they weren't staying there for long, but he didn't want to give her a ring on the doorstep of her mother's home. They might be marrying for mutual benefit, but that didn't mean the union had to be devoid of romance.

She'd had a rough year with her brother's injury and now the surprise baby. And he could tell she'd had a rough evening, the stress of the day apparent in her quietness. The tension in her movements. He wanted to do something nice for her. The first of many things.

"You're very mysterious tonight," she observed as she pointed to another turn he needed to take.

"I don't mean to be." He ignored her directions now that they were close to the cottage he'd rented. He recalled how to get there from here. "But I do have a surprise for you."

She twisted in her seat, her hair whipping across her cheek as she looked backward. "It will be a surprise if we don't get lost since you didn't follow my directions."

"I've got my bearings now." He used the high beams to search for a road marker the owner of the secluded property had mentioned. "There it is." He spotted a bent and rusted road work sign that looked like it had been there for a decade.

Behind the sign lurked a driveway and he turned the Jeep onto the narrow road.

"I'm sure this is private property," Maresa ducked when he slowed for a low tree limb.

"It is." He could see the house now in the distance high up the mountainside. "And I have a key."

"Of course you do." She slouched back in her seat. "I'm sleeping on a couch while you have a seemingly infinite number of places to lay your head at night."

"It helps to own a resort empire." He wouldn't apologize for his family's hard work. "And soon you'll be a part of it. We've got properties all over the globe."

"Including a mountain cottage in Saint Thomas?" She folded her arms, edgy and tense.

"No. I rented this one." He turned a corner and spotted the tropical hideaway that promised amazing views from the terraces. "Come on. I'm anxious to show you your surprise."

"There's more?" She unbuckled her seatbelt as he parked the Jeep in the lighted driveway surrounded by dense landscaping.

Night birds called out a welcome, the scent of fragrant jasmine in the air. The white, Key West-style home was perched on stilts, the dense forest growing up underneath it, although he spotted some kayaks and bikes stored down there. The main floor was lit up from within. Visible through the floor-to-ceiling window, the simple white furnishings and paint contrasted with dark wood floors and ceiling fans.

"Yes and I'm hoping you're more impressed with the next one than you are with the cottage." He stepped down from the Jeep and went around to free Poppy, attaching her leash so she didn't run off after a bird.

"I'm impressed," Maresa acknowledged, briefly brushing against him as she hopped out, unknowingly tantalizing the hell out of him. "I'm just frazzled after the way I upset Rafe down by the beach tonight and then again when we tried to tell him about Isla." She blinked up at Cameron in the moonlight, her shoulders partly bared by the simple navy blue sundress she wore. "It hurts to be the one causing him so much distress after all the months I've tried to take care of him and help his recovery."

The pain in her words was so tangible it all but reached out to sucker punch him. He wanted to kiss her. To offer her the comfort of his arms and his touch, but he didn't want to take anything for granted when the parameters of their relationship had shifted. He settled for brushing a hair from her forehead while Poppy circled their legs.

"They say we often lash out at the people we feel most comfortable with. The people who make us feel safe." His hand found the middle of her back and he palmed it, rubbing gently for a moment. Then he ushered her ahead on the path to the house where he punched in the code he'd been given for the alarm system.

A few minutes later, they'd found enough lights to illuminate the way to the back terrace, which was the main feature he'd brought her here for.

Poppy claimed a chair at the back of the patio and Cam added an extension to the leash to give her lots of freedom to explore. She looked as though she was done for the night, however, settling into the lounger with a soft dog sigh.

"Oh, wow. It's so beautiful here." Maresa paused at the low stone wall that separated them from the brush and trees of the mountainside.

Peering down Crown Mountain, they could see into the harbor and the islands beyond. With a cruise ship docked in the harbor and a hundred other smaller boats in the water nearby, the area looked like a pirate's jewel box, lit up with bright colors.

"Would you like to swim?" He pointed to the pool that overlooked the view, the water lit up to show the natural stone surround and a waterfall feature.

"No, thank you." She wrapped her arms around herself. "It's a beautiful night. I'm happy to just sit and enjoy this." Her tawny eyes flipped up to his. "But I'm curious why you texted me. You said you needed to see me tonight?"

It occurred to him now that part of the reason she'd been tense and edgy on the ride was because she'd been nervous. Or at least, that's how he read her body language now. Wary. Worried.

He wanted to banish every worry from her pretty eyes. And he wanted it with a fierceness that caught him off guard.

"Only because I wanted to make sure we were on the same page about this marriage." He dragged two chairs to the edge of the stone wall so they could put their feet up and look out over the view. "That you felt comfortable about it. That if you had any worries or concerns, I could address them."

Also, he just plain wanted to see her again. Spend time with her when they weren't working. When the whole of the Carib Grand hotel wasn't looking over their shoulders. He didn't want her to feel like he was rushing her into something she wasn't ready for.

"I'm not worried for my sake." She tipped her chin at him as she took her seat and he did the same. "But I'd be lying if I said I wasn't worried about my family. My brother seems excited to go to New York, but my mother thinks it's crazy, of course." She wrapped her arms around herself. "And Isla... I worry that a year is a long time for a baby. How can she help but get attached to you in that time?"

It was a question that had never crossed his mind. But even as he wanted to deny that such a thing would happen, how could he guarantee it? The truth was, he was already growing attached to the little girl and he'd known her less than a week.

"She'll have a nanny," he offered, not sure how else to address the concern. "I've already asked my staff to arrange for candidates for you to interview when we get to New York. And whoever you choose will have the option of returning to Saint Thomas with you if you want to return next year."

"Where else would I go?" She frowned.

"Maybe you'll decide to stay in New York." He couldn't imagine why she'd want to leave. "I've already found a program for Rafe that he's going to love. There's a group of gardeners who work in Central Park under excellent supervision—"

"Don't." She cut him off, shaking her head. Her eyes were over-bright. "We'll never be able to afford to stay there after the year is up and—"

"Maresa." Hadn't he made this clear? The guilt that he might have contributed to her stress by not explaining himself stung. Yes, he'd kept quiet about his inability to father children since they were entering a marriage of convenience, and it wouldn't be a factor anyway. But there were plenty of other things—positive, happy things—he could have shared with her to reassure her about this union. "I'll provide for you afterward. And your whole family. I'm having my attorney work on a fair settlement for you to review, but I assure you that you'll be able to stay in New York if you choose." Maybe the time had come to make things more concrete. He dug in his pocket and found the ring box.

A jingle sounded behind them as Poppy leaped down

from her perch and dragged her leash over to see what was happening. She sat at his feet, expectant. The animal was too smart.

"That's kind of you," Maresa said carefully, not seeing the ring box while she looked down at the harbor. The hem of her navy blue sundress blew loosely around her long legs where she had them propped. "But when you say the marriage will be real, how exactly do you mean that?"

He cracked open the black velvet and leaned closer to show her what was inside.

"I mean this kind of real." He pulled out the two carat pear-shaped diamond surrounded by a halo of smaller diamonds in a platinum band. It was striking without being overdone, just like Maresa. "Will you marry me, Maresa Delphine?"

He heard her breath catch and hoped she liked the surprise, but her eyes remained troubled as she took in the ring.

"I don't understand." Sliding her feet to the stone terrace, she stood. She paced away from him, her blue dress swirling around her calves. "Is it a business arrangement? Or are we playing house and pretending to care about one another as part of some deal?" She spun to face him, her hands fisting on her hips. "Because I don't think I can do both."

Carefully, he tucked the ring back in its box and set it on the seat before he followed her.

"I'm not sure we'll be *playing* at anything," he replied, weighing his words. "My house is real enough. And I care about you or I wouldn't have asked you to do this with me in the first place."

He studied her, looking for a hint of the woman who'd come apart in his arms not once, but three times on that night they'd spent together in Martinique. He'd felt their connection then. She had, too. He'd bet his fortune on it.

"You might think you care about me, but I'm not the efficient and organized concierge that you met when you were pretending to be Mr. Holmes." She folded her arms over her chest. "Maybe I was pretending then, too. I fake that I'm super capable all day to make up for the fact that I keep failing my family every time I turn around. The real me is much messier, Cameron. Much less predictable."

He weighed her rapid-fire words. *O-kay.* She was worried about this. Far more than she'd let on initially. But he was glad to know it now. That's why they were here. To talk about whatever concerned her. To make a plan for tomorrow.

For their future.

"The real you is fascinating as hell." Maybe it was his own impulsive streak responding, but a little straight talk never scared him off. "No need to hide her from me." He reached to touch her, his hands cupping her shoulders, thumbs settling on the delicate collarbone just beneath the straps of her dress.

"Then answer one thing for me, because I can't go into this arrangement without knowing."

"Anything."

"Why me?"

Eleven

It was all too much.

The moonlight ride to this beautiful spot. A fairytale proposal from a man who promised to take care of her struggling family. A man who wasn't scared off by the fact that she'd just inherited a baby.

With her mother's warning still ringing in her ears—that there was no other reason to marry if not for love—Maresa needed some perspective on what was happening between them before she signed a marriage certificate to be Cameron's wife.

"Are you asking me what I find appealing about you?" He lifted a dark eyebrow at her, his gaze simmering as it roamed over her. "I must not have done my job the other night in Martinique."

"Not that." She understood the chemistry. It was hot enough to make her forget all her worries. Hot enough to make her lose herself. "I mean, with all the women in the world who would give their right arm to marry a McNeill, why would you ever choose a bride with a new baby, an ailing mother and a brother who will need supervision for the rest of his adult life? Why go for the woman with the most baggage imaginable?"

As she said the words aloud, they only reinforced how ludicrous the notion seemed. Women like her didn't get the fairytale ending. Women like Maresa just put their heads down and worked harder.

He never stopped touching her, even at her most agitated, his fingers smoothing over her shoulders, brushing aside her hair, rubbing taut muscles she didn't know were so tense. "Let's pretend for a moment that Rafe had never been injured and he was just a regular, twenty-two-year-old brother. How disappointed would you be in him if he chose who to date—who to care about—based on a woman's family life? Based on, as you call it, who had the least baggage?"

Was it Cam's soothing hands that eased some of her tension? Or were his words making a lot of sense? Listening to him made her feel that she'd denigrated her own worth—and damn it, she knew better than that.

"All I'm saying is that you could have made your life a lot simpler by dating someone else." She edged closer to him, drawn by the skillful work of his fingers. He smelled good. And she'd missed him these last two days. "Is that what we're doing, by the way? Dating?"

She wished she didn't need so much assurance. But she'd been jilted before. And she would be making a big leap to follow him to New York, leaving her job behind.

"Married people can date," he assured her, his voice whispering over her ear in a way that made her shiver. "And much more. The two aren't mutually exclusive."

Closing her eyes, she leaned into him, soaking up his

hard male strength. She inhaled the woodsy pine scent of his aftershave, not fighting the chemistry that happened every time he came near her. He tilted her face up to his and she closed her eyes. Waiting.

Wanting.

His thumb traced the outline of her jaw. Brushed her cheek. Trailed delicious shivers in its wake.

When his lips covered hers she almost felt faint. Her knees were liquid and her legs were shaky. She wound her arms around his neck, savoring the brush of five o'clock shadow against her cheek when he kissed her. The gentle abrasion tantalized her, reminding her of the places on her body where she'd found tiny patches of whisker burn after the night they'd spent together.

"You rented this house for the night," she reminded him, her thoughts already retreating to the bedroom indoors.

"I did." He plucked her off her feet, lifting her higher against him so their bodies realigned in new and delicious ways.

"And you haven't even asked me inside." She arched her neck for him to kiss her there, inhaling sharply as he ran his tongue behind her ear.

"I didn't want to be presumptuous." His fingers found the zipper in the back of her dress and tugged the tab down, loosening the soft cotton.

"Gallant." She kissed his jaw. "Chivalrous, even." She kissed his cheek. "But right now, you should start presuming."

He chuckled quietly as he lowered Maresa to her feet again and whistled for Poppy, unhooking the pup's leash where he'd fastened it earlier.

"Let me just grab the chairs." He opened the door for

Maresa and then jogged back to return the furniture to where they'd found it.

Cam was back at her side in no time, hauling her toward the bedroom that he must have scoped out earlier. As if walking on a cloud of hope, she followed him into the large, darkened room where pale blue moonlight streamed through open blinds overlooking the ocean, spotlighting the white duvet of a king-size bed.

It smelled like cypress wood and lemon polish and possibility. Then Cameron's arms were around her again. He slid his hands into her dress, watching with hungry eyes as the fabric slid to the floor and all the possibilities became reality. She hadn't worn much underneath and he made quick work of it now, peeling down the red satin bra and bikini panties that had been her one splurge purchase in Paris. She'd liked the feel of that decadent lace against her skin, but Cameron's hands felt better. Much, much better.

He cupped between her thighs and stroked her with long fingers until she was mindless with want. Need. She felt a deep ache for them to connect in any way possible to help alleviate the nerves in her belly. To ease her reservations about marriage that she desperately didn't want to think about.

Especially not now.

She tugged at his shirt, wanting it gone. But the longer he touched her, the less her limbs cooperated. She couldn't think. She could only feel. Or there was something inherently perfect about only feeling, about abandoning concerns and taking this moment for the two of them, only them, the rest of the world be damned for now.

When the first shudders began, he covered her mouth with a kiss, catching her cries of release. He was so generous. So good to her. He held her while she recovered from the last aftershock. She wanted to return all that generosity with her hands and lips, but he was already lifting her, depositing her where he wanted her on the bed while he stripped off his clothes.

Another time, she would ask him to strip slower so she could savor the ways his muscles worked together on his sculpted body. But right now, she craved the feel of him inside her. Deeply. Sooner rather than later. She waited until he'd found a condom, then sat up on the bed, pulling him down to her.

With unsteady hands, she stroked him, exploring the length and texture of him, wanting to provide the same pleasure he'd given her. He cupped her breasts, molding them in his hands. Teasing the sensitive tips with his tongue. Sensation washed through, threatening to draw her under again. He reached for the condom and passed it to her, letting her roll it into place.

He spanned her thighs with his palms, making room for himself before he thrust into her deeply, fully. She stared up at him and found his gaze on her. He lined up their hands and fit his fingers between each of hers before drawing her arms over her head, holding them there as she took in the moment of them, connected, as one, and a shimmer rippled along her skin.

With the moonlight spilling over their joined bodies, she had to catch her breath against a wave of emotion. Hunger. Want. Tenderness. A whole host of feelings surged and she had to close her eyes against the power of the moment.

He started a rhythm that took her higher. Higher. She lifted her hips, meeting his thrusts, relishing the feel of him as the tension grew taut. Hot.

He still held her hands, her body stretched beneath

his, writhing. He didn't touch her anywhere else. He only leaned close to speak into her ear.

"All mine." The words were a rasp. A breath.

And her total undoing.

Her back arched, every nerve ending tightening for a moment before release came in one wrenching wave after another. She squeezed his hands tight and she felt the answering shock in his body as he went utterly still. His shout mingled with her soft cries while the sensations wrapped around them both.

Replete, Maresa splayed beneath him, waiting to catch her breath. Eventually he rolled to her side but he kissed her shoulder as he went. He brushed her damp hair from her face, smoothing it, pulled the white duvet over her cooling skin and fluffed her pillow. Her body was utterly content. Sated. Pleasurable endorphins frolicked merrily in her blood.

But her heart was already heading back toward wariness. The sex had been powerful. Far more than just chemistry. And she wasn't ready to think about that right now. Not by a long shot.

Yet how long could she delay? Not more than a moment apparently. She didn't have a choice when all too soon she felt Cameron lean over the bed and dig in the pile of clothes. When he came back, he slid something cold along her hand and then onto her left ring finger.

"You should wear this." He left the diamond there and tugged her hand from the covers so they could see the brilliant glint of the stones in the moonlight.

The engagement ring.

She swallowed hard, trying not to think about what it would have been like to have him slide it into place for real, kissing her fingers to seal the moment.

Maresa turned to look at his handsome profile in the

dark, his face so close to hers. He must have felt her stare because he turned toward her, too.

"It's beautiful," she told him honestly, feeling that he deserved some acknowledgement of all his hard work to make this night special for her, even if this marriage might very well break her heart in a million pieces. "Of course I love it. Who wouldn't?"

The words were out of her mouth before she could rethink them. Cameron smiled and kissed her, pleased with her assessment.

But Maresa feared she wasn't just talking about the ring. She was talking about the night and what they'd just shared. Her emotions were too raw and this was all happening way too fast. But somehow, in spite of her better judgment and the mistakes of her past, she was developing deep feelings for him. Very real feelings.

How on earth was she going to hide it from him for the next twelve months? He'd brought her here tonight to discuss their plans for a future. A move to New York. A union that would benefit both of them on paper.

If she had any hope of holding up her end of the agreement to walk away in twelve months, she needed to do a better job of shoring up her defenses.

Starting right now.

Twelve

Two weeks after he first placed a rock on Maresa's finger, Cameron prepared to introduce her to his family. Seated in the third-floor library of his grandfather's house on Manhattan's Upper East Side, Cam sipped the Chivas his brother Ian had just handed him. The three brothers had gathered in the late afternoon to discuss the other McNeill situation before a dinner with their wives, their father and grandfather. He hadn't wanted Maresa to arrive at the house unescorted this evening but she'd been excited to visit Rafe on-site at his new work program during his first full day. It was the first sign of genuine happiness Cameron had seen from her since they'd signed the marriage certificate.

He was trying to give her time to get acclimated to New York before meeting the McNeills, not wanting to make her transition more stressful with the added pressure of a family meeting. He'd even kept the courthouse marriage a secret for the first week—a ceremony conducted by a justice of the peace in Saint Thomas to help keep the McNeill name out of the New York papers. But he could keep things quiet for only so long. Quinn had known a marriage was in the works and finally harassed the truth out of him—that Cam had relocated all the Delphines, including baby Isla, to his place in Brooklyn. Rafe was so excited to see his favorite baseball team play that Cameron had finagled a friend's corporate box for the season, an extravagance Maresa had chided him about, but not for too long after seeing how happy it made Rafe. She didn't know it yet, but Cameron was flying in Bruce Leopold, the Delphines' neighbor in Charlotte Amalie, to attend the team's next home series with Rafe.

Cameron ran a finger over one of the historic Chinese lacquer panels between the windows overlooking the street while he waited for his brothers to finish up a conversation about a hotel Ian had been working on. Cameron felt good about where things stood with all of Maresa's family now. Analise had warmed to him considerably after seeing the in-law suite, thanking him personally for the modifications he'd made so she could get around more easily. It hadn't taken a construction crew long to add handrails to the tub and a teak bench to the shower stall, along with new easier-to-turn doorknobs in all the rooms and an intercom system in case she needed anything.

Isla was sleeping longer stretches at night and Maresa had personally hired a live-in nanny and a weekend caregiver who were settling in well. She seemed pleased with them, and her legal suit for permanent custody of the baby should be settled within the week now that Cameron had gotten his legal team involved to expedite things. Trina wasn't interested in visitation, which made

Maresa sad, but Cameron told her she might change her mind one day. For his part, he enjoyed spending time with a twelve-week-old far more than he ever would have imagined. He liked waving off the nanny at 5:00 a.m. and walking around his house with the baby, showing her the view from the nursery window and discussing his plans for the day. Sometimes, when she stared up at him with her big blue eyes, Cameron would swear she was really listening.

If only his new wife seemed as content. She'd been pulling away from him ever since the night he'd slid the ring onto her finger and he wanted to know why.

"Earth to Cam?" Ian waved his own glass of dark amber Scotch in front of Cameron's nose. "You ready to join us or are you too busy dreaming of the new bride?"

Cam shook his head. "I'm waiting for you to quit talking business so we can figure out our next move with Dad's secret sons."

He wasn't going to talk about Maresa when she wasn't around. He would introduce his brothers to her soon enough and they would be impressed. Hell, they'd be downright envious of him if they hadn't recently scooped up impressive women themselves.

Lowering himself into a leather club chair near one of the built-in bookshelves full of turn-of-the-century encyclopedias that had amused him as a kid, Cameron waited for his brothers to grill him on his fact-finding mission to Martinique.

Quinn took the couch across from Cam and Ian paced. One of them must have hit the button on the entertainment system because an Italian aria played in the background. Quinn must be refining his musical tastes now that he was marrying a ballerina.

"You didn't give us much to go on," Ian noted, pausing

by an antique globe. "You said all three of them—Damon, Gabe and Jager—keep a presence in Martinique?"

Cameron remembered that day of sleuthing well. The only thing that had kept him from feeling resentful as hell about seeing the McNeill doppelgängers had been knowing that Maresa was waiting for him back at the Cap Est Lagoon villa. They'd shared an incredible night together.

"Correct. Jager runs the software empire." They'd all read the report from the PI who'd found the brothers in the first place. "Damon actually founded the company, but he's been noticeably absent over the last six months since his wife disappeared shortly after their wedding." From all accounts, the guy was shredded about the loss, even though he hadn't made the disappearance public. Talking to a few people close to the family about it had made Cameron all the more determined to figure things out with Maresa. "And Gabe, the youngest, runs a small resort property. Ironic coincidence or a deliberate choice to mirror the McNeill business, I can't say."

Frowning, Quinn set down his glass on a heavy stone coaster with a map of Brazil—a gift from their mother. "I thought they were all involved in software? Didn't the PI's report say as much?"

"They are. But they each have outside specialties and interests," Cameron clarified.

Ian took a seat on the arm of the couch at the opposite end from Quinn. He picked up a backgammon piece from a set that remained perpetually out and flipped it in his hand. "Just like us."

Quinn leaned forward. "One obvious way to bring them into the fold is to see if the one who has a resort—Gabe?" He looked to Cam for confirmation before continuing. "We ask him if he's interested in stepping into Aldo Ricci's spot at the Carib now that Cam ousted him.

With good reason, I might add." He lifted his Scotch in a toast.

Ian did the same. "Here, here. Good job figuring that one out, Cam."

Enjoying a rare moment of praise from his brothers, Cam lifted the glass in acknowledgement and took a sip along with them. With the help of another investigator, Cameron had confirmed that Aldo Ricci had been taking kickbacks from low-end artists passing their work off as far more valuable than it was to the guests. With Ricci's worldly demeanor and contacts around the globe, he was someone that guests trusted when he assured them a sitting with a famous artist was difficult to procure.

But for a fee, he could arrange it.

Ricci hadn't just done so with Jaden Torries, but a whole host of artists at the Carib Grand and at properties he worked for before coming to McNeill Resorts. Cameron had released him from his contract and the company lawyers would decide if it was worth a lawsuit. Certainly, there would be public relations damage control. But at least the Carib was free of a man who gladly preyed on employees like Rafe to facilitate meetings—employees who were working on a trial basis and could be terminated easily. Cameron was certain the performance reviews would improve with the manipulative director out of the picture.

Good riddance to Aldo Ricci. The arrogant ass.

"You want to ask Gabe McNeill to take Aldo Ricci's job?" Cameron went on to explain that the youngest McNeill's resort was on a much smaller scale.

"All the more reason to get him accustomed to the way we do business," Quinn insisted. "You know Gramps insists we bring them in—"

A scuffle at the library door alerted them to a newcomer's arrival. Malcolm McNeill pushed his way through the door with his polished mahogany walking stick before Ian could reach him to help.

"I heard my name," the gray-haired, thinning patriarch called without as much bluster as he would have even a few months ago. "Don't think you can conduct family business without me."

Cameron worried to see the toll his grandfather's heart attack had taken on him in the past months. Malcolm had booked a trip to China after initially changing his will, saying he didn't want to discuss the new terms. But having his heart attack while abroad had meant the family couldn't see him for weeks afterward, and they hadn't been able to find out much about treatments or the extent of damage until he was well enough to travel home. It had really scared them.

More than ever, Cam was grateful to Maresa for agreeing to this marriage. Crappy relationship with his father notwithstanding, Cam's family meant everything to him. And even though he'd resented having his grandfather dictate his personal life, it seemed like a small thing compared to the possibility of losing him. For most of Cameron's life, he wouldn't have been able to imagine a world without Malcolm McNeill in it. Now, he sure didn't want to, but he could envision it all too well when he saw how unsteady Gramps was on his feet as Quinn helped him into a favorite recliner.

"We need the women, I think, to really make this a party," Gramps observed once he caught his breath. He peered around the room, piercing blue eyes assessing each the brothers. "Family business needs a woman's touch."

Ian lifted his phone before speaking. "Lydia just texted

me. She and Maresa are waiting for Sofia downstairs before they join us."

Cameron resisted the urge to bolt to his feet, strongly
suspecting Maresa would rather meet the other women
on her own terms. She was great with people, after all.
It was part of what made her so good at her job. Still, it
bothered him that he wasn't with her to make the intro-
ductions himself.

"Good." Gramps underscored the sentiment by pounding his walking stick on the floor. "In the meantime,
Cameron, you can give me the update you already shared
with these two." He nodded to Quinn and Ian. "When
are the rest of my grandsons coming to New York to
meet me?"

Cameron was secretly relieved when Ian stepped in
to field the question for him. Maybe, as a recently married man himself, Ian knew that Cam was nervous about
tonight. Finishing off the Scotch more quickly than he'd
intended, he got to his feet and prowled around the room,
looking at antique book spines on the walls without really seeing them.

He was uneasy for a lot of reasons tonight. One reason was that discussion of the other McNeills stirred old
anger about his father's faithlessness to the woman he'd
married. Cam resented that his father's selfish actions re-
sulted in three other sons and a whole life they'd known
nothing about. But, as he now watched his grandfather
listen to Ian with obvious interest, Cam had to respect
the old man for refusing to limit his idea of family. Gabe,
Damon and Jager were all as important to Gramps as Ian,
Quinn and Cameron.

It didn't matter that he'd never met them.

For the first time, it occurred to Cam that he had more
in common with his grandfather than he'd realized. All

his life, Cam had been compared to his reckless, impulsive father. But Cameron would never be the kind of man who cheated on his wife. More importantly, he was the kind of man who could—like his grandfather Malcolm— embrace a wider definition of family.

Because Rafe was Cam's brother now. And Analise's health and safety were as important to him as his own mother's.

As for Isla?

Could he adore that little girl more if he'd fathered her himself? Like Malcolm McNeill, Cameron would never let go of the Delphines. He would use all his resources to protect them. Most of all, he would love them.

The insight hit him with resounding force, as sudden and jarring as the impact of that old kiteboarding crash that had stolen his ability to father children of his own. He didn't need to avoid having a real family for fear of repeating his father's mistakes. He already had a real family and he needed to start treating all of them—especially Maresa—like more than contractual obligations.

Because twelve months weren't ever going to be enough time to spend with her. Twelve years weren't going to cover it, in fact. He needed to make this marriage last and now that he knew as much, he didn't want to wait another second to let her know. Because, yes, he'd always have some of that impulsiveness in his character. Only now he knew he'd never let it hurt the woman—the family—he loved.

"Will you excuse me?" he said suddenly, stalking toward the library door. "I need to see my wife."

"We've been dying to meet you," Sofia Koslov told Maresa in the foyer of the impressive six-story Italianate mansion that Malcolm McNeill called home.

Maresa tried not to be intimidated by the tremendous wealth of her surroundings and the elegance of the beautiful women who had greeted her so warmly. Dark-haired Lydia McNeill, a pale-skinned, delicate nymph of a woman who worked in interior design, was married to Cam's brother Ian. The blonde ballerina Sofia was engaged to Quinn and due to marry within the month.

Both of them appeared completely at home on the French baroque reproduction benches situated underneath paintings Maresa was pretty sure she'd seen in art history books. Cushions of bright blue picked up the color scheme shared by the two huge art pieces. Dark wooden banisters curled around the dual stone staircases leading up to the second floor. A maid had told her the men were on the third floor and they were welcome to take the elevator.

Un-freaking-believable. Maresa had been overwhelmed by Cameron's generosity ever since arriving in New York, but seeing the roots of his family wealth, she began to understand how easy it was for him to re-order the world to his liking. He might have grown his own fortune with his online gaming company, but he'd been raised in a world of privilege unlike anything she'd ever known.

"Thank you." Maresa hoped she was smiling with the same kind of genuine warmth that her sister-in-law and soon-to-be sister-in-law demonstrated. But it was difficult to be so out of her element. Knowing she was going to be a part of this family for only eleven and a half more months hurt, too. "I will confess I've been nervous to meet Cameron's family."

Lydia nodded in obvious empathy. She wore a smartly cut sheath dress in a pink mod floral. "Who wouldn't be nervous? They are the *McNeills*—practically a New York institution." She gestured vaguely to the painting above her head. "This is a Cézanne, for crying out loud. I was a wreck my first time here."

Sofia slanted a glance at Lydia. "With good reason, since we witnessed our first McNeill brawl." She shook her head and tugged an elastic band from her long blond hair, releasing the pretty waves from the ballerina bun. She wore dark leggings with a gray lace top, but her style was definitely understated. No makeup in sight and still incredibly lovely. Sofia turned to Maresa and winked. "Your husband is a man of intense passion, we discovered."

"Cam?" Maresa asked, since she couldn't imagine him getting into a physical fight with anyone, least of all his family. He'd been incredibly good to hers, after all.

Lydia opened her purse and found a roll of breath mints, offering them each one before explaining, "It wasn't really a brawl. But Quinn, Ian and Cameron were devastated to learn that their father had a whole other family he'd kept secret for twenty-plus years. Cam landed a fist on his dad's jaw before they all settled down."

Maresa found it impossible to reconcile her knowledge of Cameron with the image they painted. But then again, he had proposed to Sofia mere months ago in a moment of impulsiveness. Maresa knew he'd gone on to extend the offer of marriage to Maresa because he thought he knew her much better. Because they had a connection. But was she really just another impulsive choice on his part?

Her stomach sank at the thought. No matter how hard she struggled to keep her feelings a secret from him these past two weeks, she feared they'd only gotten deeper. Seeing him walk around Isla's nursery with the little girl in his arms at the crack of dawn the past few mornings chinked away at the defenses she needed around him. How effective were those defenses when just the idea that he'd chosen her in a moment of rashness was enough to rattle her?

Drawing a fortifying breath, she sat up straighter on the bench seat. "He's been incredibly good to me and to my family," she said simply.

From somewhere down the hall she thought she heard the swish of an elevator door opening. Maybe the maid was returning to call them in for dinner?

Sofia flexed her feet and pointed her toes, stretching her legs while she sat. "That doesn't surprise me. We were all glad to hear that he's so taken with your little girl."

Lydia leaned forward to lower her voice. "And for a man who swore he'd never have kids, that's incredible." She reached to squeeze Maresa's hand. "His brothers are relieved you've changed his mind."

Footsteps sounded nearby. But Maresa was too distracted by the revelation to pay much attention. Her world had just shifted. Cameron had never said anything about his stance on children.

"Cam doesn't want kids?" She thought about him singing to Isla in the temporary nursery he'd outfitted for her personally while his construction crew worked to remodel an upstairs suite for her that would be ready the following week.

Had his show of caring been as fake as their marriage?

A male shadow fell over her right as her eyes began to burn. "Maresa."

Cameron stood in the foyer at the foot of the stairs, his face somber. Lydia and Sofia greeted him briefly but he didn't so much as flick a gaze their way before the other women excused themselves.

Maresa stood too quickly, feeling suddenly light-headed at the news that she was being carefully deceived. He'd never wanted children. Did that mean he'd also never wanted a wife? That their marriage was even more of a pure necessity than she'd realized? She felt duped. Betrayed.

And just how many other secrets was her husband keeping from her in order to secure the McNeill legacy?

She cleared her throat. "I don't feel well. If you can make my excuses to your family, I need to be leaving." Picking up her purse, she took a half step toward the massive entryway.

Cameron sidestepped, blocking her path. "We need to talk."

Even at a soft level, their voices echoed off all the marble in the foyer.

"What is there to talk about? Your wish not to have children? Too late. I already heard about it." Hurt tore through her to think she was letting Isla grow attached to him.

"I should have told you sooner—" he began, but she couldn't listen. Couldn't hear him explain how or why he'd decided he didn't enjoy kids.

"Please." She brushed past him. "I spent so many hours interviewing potential nannies and caregivers, I should have devoted more time to interviewing my husband." She couldn't help but remember all the ways he'd stepped into a fatherly role.

All those little betrayals she hadn't seen coming.

"It's not that I don't like children, Maresa." He cupped her shoulders with gentle hands. "I had an accident as a stupid twenty-year-old kid. And as a result—medically speaking—I can't father children."

Thirteen

Cameron was losing her.

He could tell by the way Maresa's face paled at the news. He should have told her about this sooner. He'd disclosed his net worth and offered her a prenup with generous financial terms and special provisions for her family.

Yet it had never crossed his mind to share this part of his past. A part that would have had huge implications for a couple planning a genuine future together. A real marriage. He'd been so focused on making a sound plan for the short-term, he hadn't thought about how much he might crave something more.

Something deeper.

"Please." He shifted his grip on her shoulders when she seemed to waver on her feet. "There's a private sitting room over here. Just have a seat for a minute, and let me get you a glass of water."

She looked at him with such naked hurt in her tawny eyes that it felt like a blow to him, too.

"Isla has to be my highest priority. Now and always." Her words were firm. Stern. But, thankfully, her feet followed him as he led her to the east parlor where they could close a door and speak privately.

"I understand that." He drew her into the deep green room with a marble fireplace and windows looking out onto Seventy-Sixth Street. The blinds were tilted to let in sunlight but blocked any real view. Cameron flicked on the sconces surrounding the fireplace while he guided her to a chair near the fireplace. "I admire that more than I can say."

He wanted to tell her about the realization he'd had upstairs with his grandfather. That he was more like Malcolm McNeill than he'd realized. But that would have to wait and he'd be damn lucky if she even stayed and listened to him for that long. He had the feeling the only reason she'd followed him in here was because she was too shell-shocked to decide what to do next.

He needed to talk fast before that wore off. He made quick work of pouring the contents of a chilled water bottle from a hidden minifridge into a cut-crystal glass he pulled off the tea cart.

"It's not fair to Isla to let her grow attached to you." Maresa closed her eyes as he brought over the cold drink, opening them only when he sat down in the chair next to her. "Even if what you say is true—that you like kids—I should have been thinking about it more before I agreed to this marriage." She accepted the drink and took a sip. "Not that I'm backing out since we signed a binding agreement, but maybe we need to reconsider how much time you spend with her, given that you won't be a part of her life twelve months from now."

The hits just kept coming. And feeling the full brunt of that one made him realize how damned unacceptable he found this temporary arrangement. He needed to help her see that they could have a real chance at something more.

"I hope you will change your mind about that, Maresa, but I understand if you can't." He wanted to touch her. To put his hands on her in any way possible while he made his case to her, but she sat with such brittle posture in the upholstered eighteenth-century chair that he kept his hands to himself. "I never knew how much I would enjoy a baby until I met you and Isla. I never had any experience with kids and told myself it was just as well because my father sucked at fatherhood and everyone has always compared me to him."

She looked down at the glass she balanced on one knee but made no comment. Was she waiting? Listening?

Hell, he sure hoped so.

He plowed ahead. "Liam McNeill is reckless and impulsive, and even my brothers said I was just like him. I've always had a lot of restless energy and I channeled it into the same kind of stuff he did—skydiving and hang gliding. Whitewater rafting and surfing big waves. It was a rush and I loved it. But when a kiteboarding accident nearly killed me I had to rethink what I was doing."

Her gaze flew up to meet his. She had been listening. "How did it happen?"

"Too much arrogance. Not enough sense I wanted to catch big air. I jumped too high and got caught in a crosswind that slammed me into some trees." He'd been lucky he remained conscious afterward or he might have died hanging there. "The harness I was wearing got wrapped around my groin." He pantomimed the constriction. "The pain was excruciating, but I needed to cut myself down to alleviate the pressure threatening to cut off all circulation to my leg."

"Wasn't anyone else there to help?" Her eyes were wide. She set her glass aside, turning toward him as she listened.

"Not even close. That crosswind blew me a good half mile out of the water. My friends had to boat to shore and then drive and search for me. They called 911 and the paramedics found me first." He felt the warmth of her leg close to his. He wanted to touch her but he held back because he had to get this right.

"Thank God. You could have lost a limb." She frowned, shaking her head slowly, empathy in her eyes.

For the moment, anyway, it seemed as though she was too caught up in the tale to think about how much distance she wanted to put between the two of them. Between him and Isla. His chest ached with the need to fix this, because losing his new family was going to hurt worse than if he'd lost that leg. If she chose to stay with him, she needed to make that decision for the right reasons. Because he'd told her everything.

"Right. And that's how I always looked at it." He took a deep breath. "A lifetime of compromised sperm count seemed like I got off easy—at the time. I lost my option of being a father since my own father sucked at it and I was already too much like him. Right down to the daredevil stupidity."

She eased her hand from under his, twisting her fingers together as if restraining herself from touching him again. "Do you do things like that anymore?"

"Hell no." He realized he still clutched the water bottle in his hand. He took a sip from it now, needing to clear his thoughts as much as his mind. "I channeled all that restless energy into building the gaming company.

I designed virtual experiences that were almost as cool as the real thing. But safer. I know life is too precious to waste."

"Then you're not all that much like your father, after all," she surprised him by saying. She set down the cut-crystal glass and stood, walking across the library to the fireplace where she studied a photo on the mantle.

It was an image from one of the summers in Brazil with his brothers and their mother. They all looked tan and happy. He'd had plenty of happy times as a kid and he wanted to make those kinds of memories with Maresa and Isla. Maybe he'd convinced himself he didn't care about having a family because he'd never met Maresa. He'd been holding on to his heart, waiting for the right person.

"That's what I came down from the library to tell you tonight." He crossed to stand beside her, reaching to lay his hand over hers. "It's taken me a lifetime to realize it, but I've got plenty of my grandfather's influence at work in me, too."

"How so?" She turned to face him. Listening. Dialed in.

She was so damned beautiful to him, her warmth and caring apparent in everything she did. In every expression she wore. He wanted to be able to see her face every day, forever. To see how she changed as they grew older. Together.

Cameron prayed he got the words right that would make her understand. He couldn't lose this woman who'd become so important to him in a short span of time. Couldn't afford to lose the little girl that he wanted to raise with as much love as he'd give his own child. In fact, he wanted Isla to be his child.

"Because Gramps would never turn his back on family." He gathered up her hands and held them. "He insists we bring my half brothers to New York and cut them in on the McNeill inheritance, even though he's never met any of them. I was upset about that at first, mostly because I'm still mad at my father for keeping such a hurtful secret from Mom."

"I don't like hurtful secrets." Maresa's eyes still held traces of that pain he'd put there and he needed to fix that.

"I didn't withhold that information about my accident on purpose," he told her honestly. "I didn't give it any thought. And that's still my fault for being too concerned about the physical whys and wherefores of making the move to New York work instead of thinking about the intangibles of sharing…our hearts."

"Our what?" She blinked at him as though she'd misunderstood. Or hadn't heard properly.

"I got too caught up in making this a business arrangement without thinking about how much I would come to care about you and your whole family, Maresa." He tugged her closer, trapped her hands between his and his chest so that her palm rested on his heart. "I'm in love with you. And I don't care about the business arrangement anymore. I want you in my life for good. Forever."

For a long moment, Maresa couldn't hear anything outside of her heart pounding a thunderous answer to Cameron's words. But she wasn't sure she could trust her feelings. She didn't plan to let her guard down long enough for him to shatter her far worse than Jaden could have ever dreamed of doing.

Except, when her heart quieted a tiny bit and she began to hear the traffic sounds out on Seventy-Sixth Street— the shrill whistle of someone hailing a cab and the muted laughter of a crowd passing the windows—Maresa realized that Cameron was still here. Still clutching her hands tight in his. And the last words he'd said to her had been that he wanted her to be a part of his life forever.

That hadn't changed.

And since he'd done everything else imaginable to make her happy these last two weeks, she wondered if maybe she ought to let down her guard long enough to at least check and see if he could be serious about a future together.

Her mind reeled as her heart started that pounding thing all over again.

"Cameron, as tempting as it might be to just believe that—"

"You think I would deceive you about being in love?" He sounded offended. He angled back to get a clear view of her eyes.

"No." She didn't mean to upset him when he'd just said the most beautiful things to her. "But I wonder if you're interpreting the emotions correctly. Maybe you simply enjoy the warmth of a family around you and it doesn't have much to do with me."

"It has everything to do with you." He released her hands to wrap one arm around her waist. He slid the other around her shoulders. "I want every night to be like that last night we spent in Saint Thomas when we made love in the villa at Crown Mountain. Do you remember?"

She remembered all right. That was the night she'd understood she was falling for him and decided she needed to be more careful with her heart. As much as she'd treasured their nights together since then, she'd been holding back a part of herself ever since. Her heart. "I do."

"Even if it was just us, I would want you in my life

forever. But it's a bonus that I get your mom and your brother and your niece." His touch warmed her while his words wound around her heart and squeezed. "Getting to be a part of Isla's life would be an incredible gift for me since I can't have children of my own. But I understand that could be enough reason alone for you to want to walk away. I don't want to deny you the chance to be a biological mother."

She could see the pain in his eyes at the thought. And the love there, too. He wasn't pushing her away, but he loved her enough that he would be willing to give her up so she could have that chance. That level of love—for her—stunned her. And she knew, without question, she didn't need a child of her own to find fulfillment as a mother. She was lucky to have a baby who already shared her family's DNA, something she was reminded of every time she peered down into Isla's sweet face. If they wanted more children, she felt sure they could open their hearts to more through adoption. If Cameron could already love Isla so completely, Maresa knew he could expand his sense of family to other children who needed them.

"I have a lifetime of mothering ahead of me no matter what since Isla isn't going anywhere." She would make sure Rafe's daughter grew up loved and happy, even if Rafe never fully understood his connection to her. He smiled now when he saw Isla, and that counted as beautiful progress. "Isla is going to fill my life and bring me a lot of joy so I'm not thinking about other children down the road. If I was, however, I agree with your grandfather that we can stretch the definition of what makes a family. We could reach out to a child who needs a home."

"We?" His eyes were the darkest shade of blue as

they tracked hers. "Are you considering it then? A real marriage?"

The hope in his voice could never be faked. Any worries she'd had about him deceiving her in order to secure his family legacy melted away. He might act on instinct, but he did so with honest intentions. With integrity. She'd seen the love in his gaze when he'd held Isla. She should have trusted it. He was so different from Jaden, and she'd already let her past rob her of enough happiness. Time to take a chance on this incredible man.

Even when he'd been masquerading as Mr. Holmes, she'd seen the real man beneath the facade. She'd known there was someone worthy and good, someone noble and kind inside.

"Cameron." She pulled in a deep breath to steady herself. "I've been holding back from loving you because I've been terrified of how much it would hurt to let you go a year from now."

He tipped his head back and seemed to see her with new eyes. "That's why you've pulled away. Ever since—"

"That night on Crown Mountain." She nodded, knowing that he'd seen the difference in her since then. The way she'd been holding herself tightly so she didn't fall the rest of the way in love.

She was failing miserably. Magnificently.

"I'm so sorry if I hurt you that night," he began, stroking her face, threading his fingers into her hair tenderly.

"You did nothing wrong." She cupped his beard-stubbled cheeks in both hands. "I just couldn't afford to love a man who didn't love me back. Not again. I went halfway around the world to get over the hurt and humiliation of Jaden, so I couldn't begin to imagine how much a truly incredible guy like you could hurt me."

For her honesty, she was rewarded with a hug that

left her breathless. Cameron's arms wrapped around her tight. Squeezed. He lifted her against him, burying his face in her hair.

"I love you, Maresa Delphine. So damn much the thought of losing you was killing me inside." His heart-felt confession mirrored her own emotions so perfectly she felt her every last defense fall away.

She closed her eyes, swallowed around the lump in her throat. And hugged him back, so tightly, her body tingling with happiness.

"I love you, Cam. And I'm not going anywhere in twelve months." She arched back to see his face, loving the happiness she saw in his eyes. "I'm going to stay right here with you and be as much a part of your family as you already are of mine."

He grinned, setting her on her feet again and sweeping her hair back from her face. "You have to meet them first."

She laughed, her heart bubbling with joy instead of nerves. With this man at her side, the future stretched out beautifully before her. It wouldn't necessarily be perfect or have no bumps along the way, but it was a real-life fairy tale because they would take on life together. "I do."

"And that's not happening today." He kissed her cheek and temple and her closed eyes.

"It isn't?" She wondered how she got so lucky to find a man who loved her the way Cameron did. A man who would do anything to protect his family.

A man who extended that protectiveness to her and everyone important to her.

"No." He cupped her face in his hand and brushed a kiss over her lips, sending a shiver of want through her. "Or at least, it's not happening until the dessert course."

"We can't leave them all waiting and wondering what's happened."

"They'll get hungry. They'll eat." He nipped her bottom lip, driving her a little crazy with the possessive sweep of his tongue over hers. "I have a whole private suite on the fifth floor, you know."

"Of course you do." She wound her arms around him as heat simmered all through her. "Maybe it would be a good time to celebrate this marriage for real."

"The lifetime one," he reminded her, drawing her out of the parlor and toward the elevator. "Not the twelve-month one."

"Or we could wait until we got home tonight," she reminded him. "And we could celebrate it after we tuck Isla in after her last feeding, when we are at home."

"Our home," he reminded her as he stepped inside the elevator cabin. "So you really want to go meet the McNeills?"

"Every last one of them." She didn't feel nervous at all now. She felt like she belonged.

Cameron had given her that, and it was one of many things she would treasure about him.

About their marriage.

"As my wife wishes." He stabbed at the button for the third floor. "But don't be surprised when I announce a public wedding ceremony to the table."

She glanced up at him in surprise. "Even though we're already married?"

"A courthouse wedding isn't nearly enough of a party to kick off the best marriage ever." He lifted their clasped hands and kissed her ring finger right over the diamond set. "We're going to make a great team, Maresa."

He'd told her that once before and she hadn't believed him nearly enough. With his impulsive side tempered by his loving nature, he was going to make this marriage fun every day.

"I know we will." Squeezing his hand, she felt like a newlywed for the first time and knew in her heart that feeling would last a lifetime. "We already are."

* * * * *

If you liked this story of a wealthy McNeill tycoon tamed by the love of the right woman – and baby – pick up these other McNeill Magnates novels from Joanne Rock.
THE MAGNATE'S MAIL-ORDER BRIDE
THE MAGNATE'S MARRIAGE MERGER
And the "other McNeills" stories are coming soon!
Meanwhile, don't miss these additional Joanne Rock romances.

HIS SECRETARY'S SURPRISE FIANCÉ
SECRET BABY SCANDAL

Available now from Mills & Boon Desire!

* * *

And don't miss the next BILLIONAIRES AND BABIES story THE BABY FAVOUR by Andrea Laurence. Available July 2017!

* * *

If you're on Twitter, tell us what you think of Mills & Boon Desire! #Mills&BoonDesire

Without warning, Kane's long fingers found her chin.

She glanced up but the shadows over his face didn't give her any clues to his thoughts. He simply covered her lips with his.

This simple touch sent her over the top.

He didn't grope or force his tongue into her mouth. No, Kane wasn't an overeager boy looking for an easy in. Instead, he rested against her mouth for a moment. Just long enough for her to anticipate the next move.

When it came, it left her gasping. He brushed his lips lightly across hers, back and forth until hers parted. Still he didn't force himself in. Instead he traced the outline of her lips with his tongue…and everything inside Presley tightened in response. One quick flick against her parted teeth, then he was gone.

Only then did Presley realize that her entire awareness had narrowed to the man touching her. The man she should have been scolding. But no—

She clutched the lapels of his suit jacket, wrinkling the fabric. She strained to draw air into her lungs like a horse bellowing after a race.

And the man before her stood with his hands loose at his side, appearing completely unmoved.

"See? Nothing to worry about."

UNBRIDLED BILLIONAIRE

BY
DANI WADE

MILLS
&
BOON

First Published in Great Britain 2017
By Mills & Boon, an imprint of HarperCollins*Publishers*
1 London Bridge Street, London, SE1 9GF

© 2017 Katherine Worsham

ISBN: 978-0-263-92822-8

51-0617

Our policy is to use papers that are natural, renewable and recyclable products and made from wood grown in sustainable forests. The logging and manufacturing processes conform to the legal environmental regulations of the country of origin.

Printed and bound in Spain
by CPI, Barcelona

Dani Wade astonished her local librarians as a teenager when she carried home ten books every week—and actually read them all. Now she writes her own characters, who clamor for attention in the midst of the chaos that is her life. Residing in the Southern United States with a husband, two kids, two dogs and one grumpy cat, she stays busy until she can closet herself away with her characters once more.

To my beautiful baby sister ~ Following our dreams
runs in the family...never give up on yours!

One

"You can take me on a stroll through the gardens…"

Kane Harrington glanced toward the large arched windows along the back hall of Harrington House, darkening from gray to black as the sun disappeared. "I don't think there's quite enough light for that."

The little imp—Joan was her name, if he remembered correctly—sidled a little closer. "I don't mind."

I do. And so did all the eligible women and their mothers who had hoped for a few minutes of his time. After all, he was the only Harrington man who was still single. That made him the center of attention at this open house for the new estate and stables he and his brother, Mason, were holding for prominent local families. Suddenly the four hours he'd already endured started to wear on Kane.

"I'm sorry, hon," he said, trying to infuse his normally stern expression with a sincere regret. "I just remembered I need to make a business call tonight. I'll be right back."

He quickly escaped down the hall to the large office they had marked off-limits during the earlier tours. Though Kane had his own desk and computer to work from in the office, he didn't live at the estate with Mason and his fiancée, EvaMarie.

Thankful for the heavily carved door that kept out unwanted visitors, he dropped into his desk chair with a squeak of leather and a sigh. His sudden exhaustion reminded him of why he had been avoiding social events over the last few years. To his eternal consternation, his dark, brooding looks seemed to attract the attention of more women than he wanted. And as soon as word spread that he and his brother had inherited enough money to be labeled billionaires, the number of potential wives chasing him had become obscene.

He'd agreed to take one for the team if his mixing and mingling got their newly established stables noticed by pretty girls and their families. Money wasn't the only thing they needed to keep building—although his father had ensured that they had plenty of that. No, they needed to build a reputation among the movers and shakers of racing society here in Kentucky bluegrass country. Kane would do whatever he had to in order to ensure their names were on every pair of lips at this year's biggest events surrounding the race to the Triple Crown.

After he'd had a few minutes to himself...

What surprised him was how utterly boring he found the women here today. The newly minted billionaire was looking for a bit of a challenge, a sassy remark or, hell, anything outside the cookie-cutter norm...but he hadn't found that yet.

And the fake helpless act...he shuddered. Kane had more protective instincts than most men, but he could see right through to the calculating performances that did nothing more than turn his stomach.

Idly, he clicked on his email icon and glanced over the notifications. The usual mix of ads, business replies and such filled the screen. Geesh—it didn't matter how often he checked his inbox; the thing just kept filling up.

Suddenly the name Vanessa Gentry caught his eye, and his world went still for long, long seconds.

He recognized it, of course, even after several years. *Kinda hard to forget the woman who would have been your mother-in-law.* Immediately his mind's eye filled with a picture of her with her daughter, both of them laughing, heads close together. They'd looked so much alike, only Vanessa's dark hair had gone silver gray at an early age. Her daughter Emily's had still been black as night. Just the thought saddened Kane.

Though he probably shouldn't, he clicked on the email and read it while a photo began downloading.

Kane, I know it is presumptuous of me to send this to you. But after the way things ended... Well, I just wanted you to know that all is well and that Emily has been able to move on.

Kane braced himself, straightening his spine against the back of the chair. Sure enough, as he glanced down at the picture that appeared, it was as though someone had landed a blow square in his solar plexus.

There she was, the beauty he'd thought to one day call his own. Odd—he'd thought he would never stop loving her then. Now love wasn't the emotion he felt. No, instead it was the familiar wave of weakness, the helplessness that had first plagued him during his mother's illness and death from cancer. Then Emily had had her accident, which sent all his fix-it instincts into overdrive. But she'd wanted none of his help. She'd interpreted it all as pity.

Beside her in the photo was an average-looking man, nondescript except for the tux and boutonniere. There was a happy glow in his eyes. Over Emily's shoulder Kane could see the handle of her wheelchair. So she was still at least partially paralyzed…

And a beautiful bride to someone who could apparently meet her needs better than Kane, no matter how hard he'd tried.

The anger hit quick and hard. Even though he didn't want to, Kane conceded that Emily had a right to move on. But Kane had a right to be left out of it, instead of being reminded of all the ways he hadn't measured up.

Surging to his feet, he ignored the slam of his chair against the wall behind him. Stalking across the expensive carpets without a thought, he continued out the door and down the hall without acknowledging the few guests he passed. He imagined his facial expression wasn't particularly welcoming at the moment.

The way people fell back as if he were the beast at the ball only confirmed his thoughts—and exacerbated his anger.

But his body knew what it needed. The peace and quiet he'd always found in the stables. The acceptance of the horses. The earthy smell that grounded him in the present. And today, the realization of the dream he hadn't been willing to give up—even after his ex-fiancée had fallen off her horse and been left paralyzed for life.

There was no one in the stables. They'd allowed tours earlier. After all, this would be the heart of their operations. Kane and Mason were rightfully proud of the building, the renovations they'd done here and the stock they'd started housing in the stalls. As soon as he entered, Kane's steps slowed, his breath evened out, his heart rate returned to normal.

He paused, savoring the quiet shuffle of horses' feet and their gentle calls to him as they sensed his presence. This time when he moved forward, his footfalls were almost silent. He was meditative as he strolled through the space. It was the realization of a dream he and his brother had for so long: premium-grade stables and the stock to one day race a championship horse.

He only wished his father had lived long enough to share it with them.

A sudden high-pitched squeak broke the silence. Then he heard a voice coming from the right-hand fork of the aisle. Kane wasn't as alone as he'd thought. Had a sneaky couple decided to play some games in the stables while the party was going on? Normally he would just ignore it, but that wing had been declared off-limits to visitors earlier in the day.

Because that's where their new breeding stud was being kept.

Sun was a very new addition, having only arrived yesterday, and Kane hadn't wanted him disturbed by a rush of onlookers. The horse needed time to get used to his new digs.

Picking up speed, Kane rounded the corner and made his way toward the noise. The closer he got, the more his calm melted away, because the voice seemed to be coming from the stud's stall. Singular and soft, it had to be a woman's. Either she was talking to the horse or some man was getting an earful of sexy whispers.

The stall was about halfway down the aisle, but as Kane approached, something farther down caught his attention. The back door to this wing sat ajar, giving him a glimpse of the black night...and the glint of the stable lights off metal. A truck? A trailer?

Was this woman stealing his horse?

His big body automatically adopted stealth mode, his feet almost silent on the hard-packed earthen floor. He gave the stall door a wide berth, coming around it in the shadows across the aisle so he could see without being seen. As he paused, a sudden awareness of the pumping of his heart and an intense curiosity flooded over him.

He wasn't bored now.

Over the half wall, Kane could see the massive stallion standing unusually still, almost as if mesmerized by the woman's voice. She spoke continuously as she worked—from what Kane could tell since she faced away from him, she was indeed readying Sun for transport. But the whole time she touched him, steadying him with a firm hand that bespoke familiarity and authority.

She wasn't dressed to steal a horse. Through the barely open door Kane caught a quick peek of the flat soles of the woman's sandals. The straps across her feet were bejeweled; he could see them peeking out through the straw. A loose sundress of nondescript gray-blue material skimmed her lightly muscled body instead of hugging her curves.

Her back was to him, but from what he could tell, she was pretty but not flashy. She certainly hadn't caught his attention earlier tonight. If she'd been present at the party—as the dress suggested—he couldn't remember her. And he had a feeling he would have remembered the wealth of caramel-colored hair pulled back into a thick ponytail. He wanted to see what her face looked like, but first, he needed to know what she was up to.

Many people didn't realize that behind his stoic exterior, Kane was an exceedingly patient man. He stood for a good ten minutes in silence, cataloging the woman's movements and actions, guessing at her intentions. She had an incredible talent for soothing the giant horse they'd nicknamed the Beast, but the breakaway-style halter, blanket and leg wraps on the animal left no doubt that she planned to leave here with his horse.

As if the truck and trailer didn't make that plain enough. As she finished the last of her preparations, Kane decided it was time to make his move. Stepping out of the shadows, he moved to block the open stall door. The Beast caught sight of him first, lifting his head with a little jerk that conveyed his uneasiness at Kane's appearance.

The little thief didn't catch on as quickly. She placed her palm flat on the horse's neck and spoke to him in a low voice. He whinnied, seeming to nod, though Kane wasn't sure if it was in agreement or to warn her of his presence. Without a sound, Kane leaned against the door frame and let his sternest stable-manager voice boom out into the silence.

"What have we here?"

The voice jolted Presley's system. She'd been so caught up in Sun that she'd forgotten the threat posed by the Harringtons. One look over her shoulder told her she'd been caught by one of the actual brothers rather than a stable hand.

Remembering the papers in her pocket, she raised her chin and turned to face him fully. "I'm Presley Macarthur. And you are?"

She already knew. After all, Kane Harrington had made the social pages a few times already, though his brother, Mason, had appeared many more times…and would probably garner a precious full-page spread after today's announcement of his engagement to EvaMarie Hyatt.

She could recite the entire story of the stable hand brothers who had moved away from here after their jockey father had been blackballed, only to move back last year after inheriting a huge sum of money upon their father's death. They were set to make a big splash in the horse racing world.

The giant of a man loomed in the doorway, letting the silence stretch, but she refused to give in with a rambling explanation of what she was doing here. That would only make him think he had power—which he didn't in this situation.

Pushing away from the door frame, Kane stalked closer. "I would think, since you're in my barn, stealing my horse, that you would know who I am."

A sudden return of the heated anger and embarrassment Presley had felt when her stepmother had told her what she'd done with Sun had Presley's sight dimming momentarily. "Actually, I'm not stealing anything. I'm simply collecting what's rightfully mine."

"I don't think so, little girl," Kane said, his chuckle skating over her nerves in an unfamiliar way. There was an undercurrent signaling more to his attitude than mere disdain. A whole lot more she didn't want to acknowledge.

Kane went on, "You see, I have the paperwork that shows I bought this horse, fair and square."

Presley felt Sun shift his big body next to her, as if sensing the gist of the conversation. She rested her palm against his withers. "Fair? Are you sure about that?" she asked.

Kane's only response was to lift a darkly arched brow. Her stomach dropped, but she kept her expression as blank as possible. The intimidation she felt in the face of his stoic self-assurance was new to her. She'd been dealing with men—and their attitudes when they realized a woman was in charge—for many years now. Fear was foreign to her in a business setting. Yet this man evoked it with a simple look.

Not good.

She swallowed hard, but the fear got the better of her. "If those papers don't list the seller as Presley Macarthur, then I'm afraid you've bought this horse illegally."

Yikes. Presley immediately wished the words back. That wasn't the tack she'd meant to take. All the calm prepa-

ration she'd done before coming here was flying out the
window. "What I mean is, there seems to have been a misunderstanding—"

"I'd say so. Because I bought this horse from the home
farm run by the late Mr. Macarthur's widow, Marjorie."

While I was out of town on a consult...

"I'm sure you did, Mr. Harrington." Boy, that name
was hard to force out from her constricted throat. "But it's
a matter of public record that Sun is owned by me, Mr.
Macarthur's only daughter. *Not* his widow." She smiled as
sweetly as she could fake. "Though we do own the business jointly, so I can see where such a misunderstanding
could occur."

The sudden brooding look he shot her made her want
to stammer, but she fought for control. Reaching into the
side pocket of her skirt, she pulled out a copy of her ownership papers. "If you need proof, I have it right here."

To her consternation, he stalked forward. Though she
knew he was coming for the papers, her heart sped up and
her palms grew damp. Once more she knew it wasn't all
from the stress of this situation. This felt...personal. His
long fingers brushed over hers as he took the pages, and
a hot flush spread like wildfire through Presley's limbs.

What the heck was happening here?

Granted, Presley wasn't one to swoon. She was too
busy taking care of business. But she could honestly say
she'd never reacted to a man the way she had to Kane Harrington. It felt as if a tornado had taken up residence inside her body, swirling her emotions and reactions into a
maelstrom she couldn't control—or even make sense of. As
Kane read over the papers, she had a brief reprieve to com-
pose herself before he pinned her with his gaze once more.

"Well, it seems we are at an impasse, Miss Macarthur."

"No." She drew the word out as if he were a child in

need of instruction. "This situation is very clear-cut. I'll be taking Sun home, where he belongs."

"And the check I gave to Ms. Macarthur?"

Presley struggled not to wince. "I assure you, your money will be returned to you in full." No matter how much of a hit the business took because of it. Presley had a sneaking suspicion her stepmother had spent as much as possible before Presley could get wind of what happened.

"And what about my reputation?"

She cocked her head to the side, tightening her hand around Sun's lead rope. "Excuse me?"

Kane stepped closer, close enough to cast a shadow over her. "I bought this particular horse for a reason, Miss Macarthur. I'm sure you are fully aware of the jump start a stud of this caliber would give to our breeding program. That's not the kind of thing I can find just anywhere."

"I do understand, but don't really see where that is my problem."

But one look from Kane Harrington told her he was about to make it her problem. "I think the people around here would disagree with you."

"What do you mean?"

"We both know our businesses," he said with a smooth confidence. "We know they run on reputation almost as much as the performance of our horses."

Oh, Presley knew all about that, having experienced the struggle to keep her stepmother out of the business of running their stables since her father's death more than six months ago. Her stepmother didn't know the meaning of tact or, hell, even business. All she saw were dollar signs, and she wanted more and more—no matter what she hurt in the process.

They can scent a weak link better than a hound dog

and will extort it worse than a lawyer. Never let them see weakness.

Her father had repeated those words to her again and again, so why had he decided that his daughter and his wife should *share* the business he had worked so hard to build since before Presley was born? Her stepmother was the weakest link of all—and Presley had a feeling Kane Harrington knew that all too well.

Wielding his power without noticeable effort, Kane moved closer, then had the gall to pace around her, making her temperature rise. The urge to move away became unbearable.

Just as Kane reached her back, she slipped beneath Sun's neck, putting the horse between them to avoid the unfamiliar arousal this man evoked deep inside. Yes, as much as she hated to give the feeling a name…

Kane's thick, dark eyebrows rose, but he didn't call her out on her cowardice. "The way I see it, your stepmother has done something illegal. And then there's the embarrassment of retracting the announcement that Sun would be joining the Harrington stables." He loomed over the horse's high back, pinning Presley with a steely-eyed glare that should have made her mad but instead sent intriguing shivers up and down her spine.

"If my reputation is gonna take a hit over this, so is yours," he assured her.

Anyone who thought the customer was always right had never been in just this situation with just this man. One look told Presley she was about to make many concessions—whether she wanted to or not.

Two

Kane could tell the moment Presley Macarthur realized he wasn't letting her off the hook without consequences. She was pretty good at hiding her expression—but her gorgeous, moss-green eyes gave her away.

They told him she was going to try to get out of this somehow.

"I'm really s-s-sorry about that—"

Kane shouldn't be happy about that stammer, shouldn't wish it was from more than just the pressure he was bringing to bear. It marked him as a bad person, surely. But it didn't stop the satisfaction from rushing in. The curiosity.

Whoa. This game is fun.

"So you're sorry your stepmother made a mistake. How do you plan to make it up to me?"

Only as her eyes widened did he realize how that might sound—and not just the words. An attraction, a need sparked by this woman had given his voice a husky quality. He hadn't had this type of reaction with a single debutante since he'd moved back to Kentucky.

Hell, years before that, even.

Why this particular woman? She wasn't flashy like the diamond-studded princesses in the main house. Her dress was pretty enough, made of a nice-quality material, but its loose style didn't reveal a single curve. Kane was intrigued by what might be waiting underneath for him to discover. And this close, he noticed another significant difference. Whereas every woman he'd met tonight wore makeup to a greater or lesser extent, Presley Macarthur's face was clean and clear, without so much as tinted lip gloss to highlight the sexy curves of her naked lips.

Suddenly her gaze narrowed, and she pulled herself a little taller. "What do you mean, exactly?"

The pushback intrigued him, too. The last thing he wanted was a weak woman, one who needed taking care of—that type was his kryptonite, as Emily had proven all too well. Before him was an attractive woman who obviously knew and ran her own business. If the gossip he'd heard was correct, Presley also did consulting on equine and stable management. So she was smart, not easily intimidated. Kane was going to have to get creative to recoup this loss.

He shook his head, ignoring her question while he worked out the puzzle in his head, well aware his silence would be intimidating in and of itself. What was happening to him? First his earlier anger. Now he was contemplating…what?

Blackmail?

Sure, that would get him a long way toward acting on this attraction, toward finding out what was beneath Presbley's loose dress. *Not*. The sudden idea that popped full-blown into his head was very naughty. As if reading his thoughts, Presley leveled a suspicious gaze squarely in his direction. Kane relied on his instincts, but he wasn't usually quick to act. He thought things through, weighed the consequences, made plans. Impulsiveness was more Mason's style.

Not tonight.

This was too delicious an opportunity. "I'll need you to fix this for me—"

"I would think good and hard before you try to force me into anything inappropriate," she interrupted.

"Oh, I wouldn't do that." Kane let his deceptively soothing tone confuse her while he, too, slipped beneath the horse's neck to invade her safe spot. She stiffened even more.

Apparently she didn't like that at all…

Or did she? This close, he couldn't miss the uptick in her pulse at the base of her delicate throat or the way her tongue peeked out and slid slowly over her parted pink lips. He also caught the dip of her gaze to his fitted dress pants and button-down shirt before quickly returning to his face with a flash of guilt darkening her eyes.

Surely it wasn't terrible to use that interest to his every advantage? Selfish, maybe. He wouldn't let that sway him. "But I do think we will be getting to know each other very, very well."

"What?" The squeak in her voice and the hot blush that rushed into her cheeks told Kane he'd struck a nerve.

"Macarthur." He stepped closer, herding her toward the wall. "I recognize your name, Presley. Your stables, your family." He had a feeling his grin was not putting her at ease. "So does everyone else in the state, and beyond."

"So?"

Ah, he loved that breathless tone. "So, if we were together, it would put your seal of approval on Harrington stables."

"Together?"

Her voice was high and nervous. He propped one of his hands on the slatted wall above her shoulder. Had he reduced her to a one-word wonder? The thought made him grin even more. His proximity threw her off, and she seemed to squirm under his direct attention. And not in fear, which made the knowledge a delicious treat.

"Presumably together," he qualified. "As in, give the impression that we have a thing going." At her frown, he pushed farther. "Let everyone think we're lovers."

Suddenly, the beauty before him shut down. "Um, no."

"Are you sure about that?"

"I'm pretty sure I can think of another way to endorse your stables."

But that wasn't what he wanted. *Not anymore.* "Without sounding like you're being forced to?"

"Better than I could pretend to be your...ugh..."

"Lover?" Kane was getting the feeling that personal topics made Miss Macarthur very uncomfortable.

"Absolutely not."

Kane stepped back, palms out in a hands-off gesture. "Okay. We can simply tell them the real story instead. How your stepmother tried to swindle me out of an incredible amount of money—"

"She did not." Presley planted her fists on her hips, with the unintended effect of pulling her dress tighter over her body, giving him a glimpse of firm curves that set off interesting sparks in his brain.

Presley was oblivious. "She simply...well..."

"What?" Kane challenged, crossing his arms over his chest. "Made a mistake with a million-dollar horse that didn't belong to her?"

The expressions of indecision and ultimate acceptance that played out on Presley's face in that moment told Kane a hell of a lot about the woman before him. He knew plenty of men and women alike who would have thrown their hands up and declared the situation not of their making, so they weren't taking any responsibility. Not Presley. She could have thrown her stepmother to the fishes, but instead she tilted her chin and asked, "Exactly what expectations are we talking about here?"

Well, since he'd just thought this up on the fly, he wasn't sure. "We can discuss that."

"Now's as good a time as any." She moved to mimic his stance, crossing her arms beneath a surprisingly abundant chest.

He was beginning to see that this was a woman of contradictions. Soft woman. Smart woman. Hard worker. Astute business manager. Timid on an interpersonal level. Which of these was the truest part of Presley Macarthur? The puzzle had his full attention, and it was the first time he'd been drawn away from his goals since—he didn't want to think about that.

"I already planned to spend a substantial amount of time making the social rounds over the next racing season," Kane said, softening his tone. He could afford to ease up when his instincts told him he was about to get what he wanted. "You could accompany me—"

"As in a date?"

He quickly suppressed a smirk. It wouldn't help to appear pompous. "Quite a few dates, actually. You can introduce me around, engage me in conversations that help showcase my business—"

"All while making you look like a stud yourself."

"If you underestimate the value of personal connections, you haven't been in this business long enough."

Despite being much younger than him—he'd guess almost ten years—he could see she understood. She knew how this industry operated. Potential customers wanted to work with people they knew, people who had already been vetted and accepted.

"We will attend together, and if I'm satisfied at the end of the season, all will be forgiven."

"No," she said, to his surprise, as she caught him in that narrow gaze once more. "Seems to me you'd be getting a lot of value for very little effort on your part."

"Is there something else you'd like me to…offer?"

"Yes. A ten percent discount on your refund."

Kane waited, almost amused at the vibration of energy holding her taut. What would that much emotion feel like? Taste like?

"Attending a bunch of events is going to cost me a good bit—of time *and* money. I think it's only fair to be compensated since you are the one getting the positive publicity."

Kane nodded slowly as he thought. He could afford to be generous at this point. "I think a consultation fee would be even more than that. Let's make it forty percent."

Those green eyes widened, which made Kane want to chuckle. Obviously she hadn't expected him to be so generous, but the facts were: he had more money than he knew what to do with and he wanted to spend more time with this woman. No matter what it cost him.

"But you will pretend to be my lover."

This time her protest was clear in her expression. He cut her off before she could speak. "No one is going to care about your endorsement if they know you've been paid to give one. And lovers touch. So this is part of the deal. Take it or leave it."

"Then one other condition," she said, holding her finger up in warning—as if that would ever hold him back. "You keep your hands to yourself."

"I'll keep my hands to myself, except when necessary."

"You mean when *you* think it's necessary?" Her disgusted tone told him just how she felt about his caveat.

She was a smart one. Considering the volatile extremes

of this encounter, Kane wondered just how long that condition would last.

Or how long he'd be able to talk himself into obeying it. "But Presley, you are welcome to touch me any time you see fit."

"Since I'm being so generous," Kane said before Presley had a chance in hell of processing everything that had happened in the last half hour, "I propose we go into the house and get started."

"What?" Yeah, processing was not her strong suit at the moment. Which she didn't like. Being in control meant a lot to her.

"If you want to take Sun home tonight, there's no time like the present."

Why did his arrogant expression make her want to both smack him and rub the pad of her thumb along the arch of his raised eyebrow?

"Once we've made an appearance, I'll even make sure he gets properly loaded myself."

He gave her clothes a once-over. She'd come dressed to fit in with the party crowd, even though she had no intention of setting foot in the house. The irony wasn't lost on her. Kane thought he'd gained a sidekick who would give him an entrée into the tightest circles of racing society.

What would happen when he found out Presley was far from a social butterfly?

Large groups of people made her break out in hives. She'd only attended parties when her father insisted and usually spent the time doing her best wallflower impression. The men who constantly called her for advice and dropped by the stables to ask about their mares' latest ailments seemed to grow blinders the minute she slipped into a dress.

Not that she could blame them. Formal clothes looked bad on her and made her uncomfortable. Still, she was well enough known now that plenty of people would drop by her corner to talk business. But the endless conversations about horses dried up when prettier women entered the picture, making parties a minefield Presley had no ability or desire to navigate.

Maybe Kane wouldn't realize that until she had Sun safely home…

"Shall we?"

Kane graciously waved a hand to indicate she should precede him out of the stall. But Presley had now had an up-close encounter with the power and stubbornness behind the manners. They might have an agreement, but one look into his dark eyes told her he'd release the information about her stepmother and ruin her if she didn't cooperate.

A wolf tended to hide behind the good ol' boy facade here in the South.

She picked her way out of the stall, taking care not to dirty her sandals. The soothing cocoon of familiarity she always felt in the presence of animals immediately disappeared as she slipped into the wide alley that cut through the stables. As she passed Kane, she was once more impressed with his height; she barely reached his chest.

What little she knew of the Harrington brothers had come from local gossip after they had taken over the manor, and then it had mostly covered Mason. Kane hadn't moved here full-time until very recently, and lived in his own home in the historic district downtown. According to the gossip mill, he had yet to hook up with anyone, but that wasn't for lack of trying on the ladies' parts. More than a few were eager to take Kane for a test drive.

Which meant Presley would not be their favorite person. Her steps slowed as she came back to the major flaw in his plan: she was not the best person to help Kane gain acceptance. And though she'd never admit it in a million years, the thought of this virile, astute man seeing just how inadequate she was in this situation had her cheeks burning already.

But she also couldn't let her reputation be ruined because of her stepmother's greed and ineptitude.

When she got close to the main door of the stables, Presley let her trepidation bring her to a full halt. Kane got a little ahead of her, then paused. He threw a look over his shoulder that seemed to ask what the problem was. How could he say so much with just a look? She had the feeling time spent with Kane Harrington would not be filled with idle chitchat.

Which would be a welcome prospect after endless hours of it with her stepmother.

Shoot! She'd forgotten her stepmother had spent all week expounding on what an event the Harrington's open house would be, which meant Marjorie would be a witness to this command performance. And she was a woman who was more than aware of Presley's faults and not shy about bringing them up when she had the chance. Not vindictively—it just never occurred to her flighty little self that what she was saying embarrassed Presley to no end.

Presley just couldn't do this. She'd end up falling flat on her face, literally and probably physically, too.

"What is it, Presley?"

If he had demanded, she might have lied. Instead his coaxing tone brought the most unexpected words to her lips. "How can I possibly pretend to be the—" she choked a little "—lover of a virtual stranger?"

Kane didn't seem the least bit fazed by her naive question. Instead he retraced his steps until he was all too close and her body was a jumble of sparks she didn't recognize.

"Would you like to practice first?" he asked, his husky tone sending a singular shiver down her spine.

Yes. "No! I just need time—"

"And I need everyone to talk about something else besides why the prize stud horse won't be making an appearance in my stables. The surest way to distract people from that is if we have a captive audience."

"That's what I'm worried about."

His unexpected chuckle had her stomach doing somersaults. What was wrong with her tonight?

Without warning, Kane brushed her chin with his long fingers. Startled at the warm contact, she glanced up, but the shadows over his face didn't give her any clues to his thoughts. He simply covered her lips with his.

Sensations immediately assaulted Presley, as if her body weren't already on overload. This simple touch sent her over the top.

He didn't grope or force his tongue into her mouth. No, Kane wasn't an overeager boy looking for an easy in. Most of her experience had been like that. Instead, he rested against her mouth for a few moments. Just long enough for her to anticipate the next move.

When it came, it left her gasping. He brushed his lips lightly across hers, back and forth, until she opened to him. Still, he didn't force himself in. Instead he traced the outline of her lips with his tongue…and everything inside Presley tightened in response. One quick flick against her parted teeth, then he was gone.

Only then did Presley realize that her entire awareness had narrowed to the man touching her. The man she should have been scolding like a chaste maid from the seventeenth century. But no—

"How dare you?" she breathed.

He glanced down. Her gaze followed his and her cheeks started to burn.

Her hands clutched the lapels of his suit jacket, wrinkling the fabric. Her lungs strained for air as though she were a horse bellowing after a race. Her heart beat hard in her chest, the pounding of her pulse finding an embarrassing echo lower in her body.

And the man before her stood with his hands loose at his side, appearing completely unmoved.

Mortification that she could be overwhelmingly affected while he was completely cool hardened her attitude. "I told you to keep your hands to yourself."

"I wasn't using my hands," he said, holding them out to his sides. "See? No harm, no foul."

Despite herself, the deep tone of his voice gave her just a smidgen of satisfaction, even when he was lying through his teeth.

Three

"Sir, there's a trailer out—"

The words barely registering, Kane turned to find his stable manager, Jim Harvey, standing in the doorway of the barn. Jim's gaze moved from Kane's face to Presley.

His eyes widened.

"I'm so sorry to interrupt—"

"No problem," Kane cut him off quickly. He had a feeling Presley was on the edge of bolting at any moment. He needed this to be short and simple to set her at ease.

"Jim, this is Presley Macarthur."

Jim nodded. Recognition softened his expression, and he slipped off his cowboy hat. "Pleasure, ma'am."

He looked back and forth between the two of them, obviously curious about what he'd walked in on but smart enough to know when something wasn't his business.

"Give us about an hour, if you don't mind," Kane went on, "then load Sun up for Miss Macarthur in the trailer so she can take him home."

Despite his confused look, Jim didn't question Kane in front of Presley. "Yes, sir." He turned to the woman who hadn't spoken a word. "I'll be right nearby, ma'am. We'll inspect the trailer when you get back."

"Thank you, Jim."

Ah, they were back to the confident, businesslike voice now. Probably for the best, though the off-guard squeaky one was Kane's favorite so far. What would she sound like if he kissed her again? Touched her more intimately? Cutting off the interesting train of thought, he offered Presley his arm and escorted her out of the stables.

They had barely stepped into the night air when she paused. "I don't understand. You're just gonna hand him back over to me?" She waved toward the brightly lit house. "Don't you want to test the goods before you make that decision?"

Kane couldn't help smirking. "I believe I already have."

Feeling the wave of shock shoot through her, he patted her hand in a benign gesture and continued on. As they crossed the drive back to the house, Kane found himself hyperaware of the woman at his side. The top of her head barely reached his shoulder, which made her taller than the average woman. She would fit right into the crook where his chest met his arm. The faint scent of honeysuckle teased his nose, an unusual perfume and one that reminded him of some of his happiest times on a horse in the countryside near his childhood home.

Honeysuckle had also grown on the edge of the yard at the house where he'd grown up before his mother died. He could still vividly remember her first attempts to teach him the gentle force needed to get the liquid from the honeysuckle flowers—and the tiny burst of sweetness on his tongue when he succeeded.

"Besides," he continued on, "I never go back on my word. Sun will be home tonight." They'd reached the covered side entry, and Kane paused with his hand on the doorknob. "This situation is tricky, but I know you'll do what's best for your family and your business."

Blackmail wasn't a sexy subject, but before they stepped onto the stage, Kane wanted Presley to remember exactly what was at stake here. The stiffness of her body told him more about her state of mind than her simple nod of acquiescence.

He ushered her inside with a hand at the small of her back, and the lights from the Swarovski crystal chandeliers left her blinking. In fact, her whole demeanor changed the minute they walked through the door. If someone had told him a person could become invisible, he wouldn't have believed them—until he saw Presley practically pull off the impossible.

They'd barely made it halfway down the back breezeway when Mason and EvaMarie stepped out of the office. "Kane," his brother called.

Only as he stopped and registered the concern on Mason's face did Kane remember that he hadn't taken the time to shut down his computer before storming out the door. The knowledge sat between them like a lead brick. Mason knew exactly what that email from Vanessa Gentry would have done to Kane—he'd been there when Emily had left him behind, and watched as Kane systematically let everything disappear from his life except their shared goal.

Because life was easier that way.

Hoping to ward off any questions from his impulsive sibling, Kane preempted the conversation. "Mason, this is Presley Macarthur."

His brother blinked, then focused on the woman on Kane's arm. "Oh, from Macarthur Haven?"

Presley's hand tightened on Kane's elbow. But she relaxed a touch when EvaMarie nodded and smiled. "Hello, Presley."

"Congratulations, EvaMarie."

The lovely woman, who had been Mason's first love

and had been the epitome of a woman defeated by life when they'd returned to Kentucky, now practically glowed. "Thank you."

As the women chatted for a moment about the engagement, Mason looked at Kane with a raised brow.

"There's been a change of plans," Kane murmured, keeping his voice low though he'd moved slightly away from Presley.

"As in?"

Kane turned to face his brother. "It appears Ms. Macarthur didn't have the proper authority to sell Sun."

Mason cursed. "That's a helluva mistake to make."

An understatement if ever there was one. But then, Kane was being generous when he labeled Marjorie Macarthur's actions a *mistake*.

"What are we gonna do now? Our plan going forward hinged on having a celebrated stud for the stables." Mason's worry practically vibrated in his voice.

"Never fear," Kane assured him, as he had many times in the last two years. They'd been through a lifetime of ups and downs together. Kane wasn't about to let them fail. "I've got a new plan that will work just fine."

His brother's gaze followed him as he turned back to the women and slipped his arm around Presley's shoulders. The muscles beneath his palm tightened and her smile faltered for a moment, but he didn't move away. The sooner she became used to his touch, the better.

The more he touched her tonight, the sooner word would start to spread. Nothing overtly sexual. He'd keep it completely casual—not that anyone would interpret it that way.

Kane wanted his name linked with hers from this moment forward…for however long this situation remained beneficial to them both.

Mason continued to watch him with interest and just

a touch of shock. Not surprising, since Kane hadn't been publicly involved with a woman since Emily left.

He hadn't wanted to be and was actually shocked by how much he wanted it now. But then he spotted Presley's stepmother over Mason's shoulder. When her stepdaughter's presence registered, Ms. Macarthur trotted their way with the grace of an overadorned poodle, and Kane had only a moment to wonder if he really knew what he'd gotten himself into.

Her loud greeting only confirmed it. "Lordy, Presley! Is that really hay in your hair?"

As her stepmother's words echoed throughout the long, open back hall of the Harrisons' home, Presley wished she could sink into the floor.

Not that embarrassing her was anything new for Marjorie. No, it actually seemed to be her regular pastime. But repeated experience didn't take away the sinking feeling in Presley's stomach or the hot flush that flooded her cheeks so quickly that she was surprised she didn't pass out from blood loss.

Her stepmother practically shoved herself between Presley and Kane. "Look at you. Hay on your dress, dirt on your sandals. What were you doing out in the barn, you silly girl?"

"I think the answer to that might be just as embarrassing as the question."

With that single answer, Kane caught the attention of everyone within hearing distance. Presley wished she could fade into the flowered wallpaper as his laser gaze inspected her from head to toe, no doubt noticing her lack of style and ability to attract dirt no matter how hard she tried to stay clean. But he didn't mention it. Oh, no. Kane had embraced this pretend relationship wholeheartedly.

If he only knew what a mistake he was making—though it was beneficial for her that he didn't. The sooner he realized she wasn't going to be the perfect princess on his arm at all these events, the sooner she'd have to repay him in full.

"Sorry, sweetheart," he murmured near her ear, though his voice still seemed to carry. "I didn't mean to get you all dirty."

Holy Moses. The heat that swept through her as she heard him talk should have been an embarrassment. She should have been wishing he would quit making a spectacle of her. Instead, she wished he would keep on talking and make her forget about their audience.

He reached out to snag the small piece of hay from the tip of her loose ponytail—the only hairstyle she could comfortably create—and then held it up as he smiled into her eyes. There was mischief in that look, and also something deeper, darker, that tempted her to join him in his game.

Only she'd never learned how to play.

Her stepmother was just as nonplussed, which was the first time Presley had ever seen that happen. Marjorie watched Kane's actions with a kind of wide-eyed fascination, then glanced back and forth between the two of them as confusion clouded her expression.

Finally she focused solely on Presley, frowning. "Well, you should have at least told me you had a date. I could have helped you find something more appropriate to wear."

Apparently the embarrassment wasn't going to end any time soon. Over Marjorie's shoulder Presley could see a group of women—the same debutantes who had haunted her existence since she was about fourteen—whispering furiously and grinning. All except one: Joan Everly. She simply stared through narrowed lids, anger slowly taking over her polite society mask.

"Oh," Kane said, his amused tone warning Presley she wouldn't like what was coming. "I think her dress suited *my* purposes just fine."

Judging from the few gasps she heard out of the debs, Kane's voice had carried. But Presley could sense the disbelief in people's reactions. And now she was done being put on display.

She turned around and blindly grasped the nearest door handle and pushed her way through. She didn't care where she went, as long as it was away from prying eyes. But the shuffle of feet and the click of dress shoes on the floor behind her told her she hadn't escaped. She had company. Great. More confrontation was just what she wanted right now.

Give her a stubborn horse or an uppity ranch hand and she met the challenge like a trouper. Social settings and public displays of anything, much less affection, were definitely not her forte.

A familiar weariness seeped into her muscles. The feeling had made its first appearance as soon as her father's funeral was over and all the guests were gone. Since then it returned regularly, but she always pushed it back. She didn't have time to be tired, especially not with the task of taking care of her stepmother on top of her already heavy schedule managing the business.

So just as she had a hundred times in the past six months, she pushed the gray cloud back and straightened her spine. When she spun around, she saw that only their small group had followed, but it was Marjorie who spoke first.

"Presley, what is going on here?"

Confusion still reigned in Marjorie's expression, but years of being ridiculed for not living up to Marjorie's expectations, not being feminine enough, being too smart

and serious all the time…none of that made Presley want
to confide exactly what had happened in the barn earlier.
Her tongue stuck to the roof of her mouth. How in the
world could she possibly say out loud that the only way
she could attract a man of Kane's caliber was because her
stepmother had tried to swindle the Harringtons out of a
large amount of money?

Of course, given the result, Marjorie would probably
see that as doing a good deed.

To Presley's surprise, Kane spoke up. "The fact is, Presley wouldn't even be here without your criminal lack of
judgment, Ms. Macarthur."

Shock rippled through the room, settling in Presley's
core. No one had ever stood up for her. Not even her daddy.
When he'd brought Marjorie into their lives, he'd hoped
that she'd teach his daughter to be a woman. Marjorie's ab-
ject failure in that area was considered all Presley's fault.
And though he had loved her, her father hadn't hidden his
disappointment from her.

The look of shock on Mason's face was priceless. Especially when Kane stepped closer to Presley and draped
his arm around her shoulders again. But Kane ignored
his brother as he said, "Oh, don't get me wrong. I'm very
grateful she did show up."

Marjorie wasn't buying it. "If you expect me to believe
that my Presley snared the catch of the county in thirty
minutes, in that dress, you must think I'm really stupid."

Presley wasn't sure what set off her normally dormant
outrage. The stress of the day. Kane's blackmail. Or everyone's obvious disbelief even as Kane insisted they were interested in each other. *If you had to sell it that hard, might
as well not sell it at all.*

Without thought Presley stomped forward, invading
her stepmother's personal space. "What I think is that you

couldn't care less how your actions affect me or anyone else who has to put up with your antics."

"Well, I knew that my very smart stepdaughter would smooth everything out," Marjorie whined.

"Excuse me?" Suddenly all the tension and upset of the night became too much and Presley was the one who couldn't control her voice. She made a desperate attempt to contain the words but couldn't keep them back. "You bargained with an animal you knew didn't belong to you, but that's okay because Presley will figure it all out?"

Marjorie blanched. "I know you love the horse, but money is—"

Presley stepped uncomfortably close, lowering her voice. "Not something you have an unlimited amount of anymore. And if you ever pull a stunt like this again, I'll do everything in my power to have Grant break Father's will. Do you understand me?"

"He couldn't."

"He's a great lawyer. I'm sure he could manage it for me."

Something in her expression must have scared Marjorie, because she focused on Presley's face and remained silent for a long moment. Finally she gave a stiff nod, then blinked, and the flighty society lady was back in action. "No need to be so serious, dear. This is a fun night. For you more than most, am I right?"

It was no use. All the anger and frustration flooding Presley's veins had nowhere to go, no way out. Some days she thought running around in endless circles with her stepmother would never end. Why her father had subjected her to this particular hell, she'd never know.

And despite the threat she'd just made, she had little expectation of any change. The next shiny diamond to cross Marjorie's path would catch her attention and block out all reason.

Leaving Presley with another six-foot-four-inch problem to solve—a magnitude totally out of her league.

Kane's response didn't exactly put her fears to rest. "I assure you, Ms. Macarthur, Presley and I have gotten off to a very good start. And we will be seeing a great deal of each other in the future."

His words should have heaped another helping onto her pile of worry. Instead anticipation tingled in her stomach, warming her from the inside out. This was wrong. All wrong.

Presley preferred situations she could control.

"That settles that, then," her stepmother offered with a toothy grin.

Marjorie's problems always disappeared. Presley's merely grew. And she had a feeling she was way out of her depth on this one.

Four

Kane wasn't sure he was surprised when the woman who answered the Macarthurs' front door told him, "Miss Presley is almost always in the barn." The Presley he'd met the night before certainly wasn't a Miss Kentucky pageant type. But he had to admit he didn't have a lot of experience with daughters of bigwigs who were willing to get their hands dirty.

He was used to the daughters of fellow laborers, who loved animals and worked just as hard as any of the men.

He certainly hadn't expected to hear Presley's raised voice as he closed the stable door behind him. Several hands at the far end of the aisle kept their heads down and focused intently on their work, pointedly ignoring the noise. A lone man stood in the aisle closer to Kane, stance rigid, arms crossed over his chest, gaze trained tightly on the open stall in front of him until Kane walked into his peripheral vision.

Their eyes met as Presley's hardened voice continued to boom out from inside a nearby stall. She was scolding someone Kane couldn't see. "I realize she doesn't like her hooves cleaned. First of all, if you can't work around that, you aren't good enough or experienced enough to be em-

ployed here. Second of all, if you ever lay a hand on any
of my horses like that again, it's the last horse you'll touch
in this barn. Do I make myself clear?"

There was a silence, and Kane saw the man in front of
him tense up even more, if that was possible. From within
the stall, the employee being reprimanded replied with a
tight "yes, ma'am."

Then Kane's companion in the aisle relaxed.

"Now," Presley said, her voice turning indulgent as
though she was trying to teach something to a particularly hardheaded child, "I'll do one hoof for you, then you
can do the others while I watch."

No argument was forthcoming. Kane grinned, imagining the grown stable hand being taken back to Hoof Cleaning 101 and the ribbing he would get from his coworkers
later today. Sounded like he deserved it, though.

The man who stood before Kane in the aisle finally held
a hand out to him. "Hello there. I'm Bennett, the Macarthurs' stable manager."

Kane shook, introducing himself in turn. He jerked his
head in the direction of the stall. "Shouldn't you be dealing with that?"

Bennett shrugged. "Usually I do, but Miss Presley is
a very hands-on owner. Has been since her daddy first
brought her into the stables." He turned his gaze back
to the stall door as if checking progress. "There are certain things she will always handle herself. Mistreatment,
no matter how small, is something she's adamant about
being informed of immediately. We have a zero-tolerance
policy here."

"But she didn't throw him out on his ass at the first
sign?"

"Depends on what happens. She's also a fair employer.
She understands that many of these men have families to

support or are just learning their trade." Bennett's craggy face softened with approval. "The men know it, too. They don't cross her. We rarely have problems, but she's quick to handle whatever comes along."

So she had experience along with her degree in equine management. No wonder she was well respected. Kane had done a little digging before showing up this morning, just to double-check the information he'd gathered from the grapevine. But he hadn't just been after her business credentials—EvaMarie had known a lot more about Presley personally, piquing Kane's interest on a totally different topic.

Her reluctance to make personal appearances at parties had been well noted throughout the years, often leaving her open to ridicule from other women in their social circle. While her business reputation had been solid long before her father's death, her social reputation had often floundered. After watching Presley for those few moments with Marjorie the night before, he could easily guess why.

She'd never been allowed to find her true footing. To be herself in the face of peer pressure from society's little darlings. Kane's sudden desire to help her set off alarm bells in his head. The last thing he should do was attempt to fix anyone. He'd been down that road before, and he simply wasn't built for it.

It was the only thing he'd ever failed at in his life.

But Presley was a whole different ball game from Emily. The last thing she needed was taking care of—as her management skills attested. If Kane could help her tweak her public persona while they were together, it would simply be an added bonus of their arrangement. He was way more interested in what would happen in private when their time in the spotlight was done.

"See, you just have to know how to handle her. Now go help Arden get the water tank fixed," he heard Presley command.

Something about her confidence made Kane smile—and his body come to attention. Presley wouldn't be a limp, lazy princess who expected someone to make her happy in bed. Oh, no, this woman would be a full participant.

Not that he should be considering that so soon...

As a shamefaced man came out the stall door with his thumbs hooked in his jeans pockets, Bennett directed him down the aisle with a jerk of his head. He glanced as Kane. "That could have ended very badly, with fussin' and fightin'. But not with Miss Presley. Somehow she can take 'em to task, put 'em on the right path and get everyone movin' forward without a knock-down-drag-out." He winked. "But I'm always nearby, just in case."

Bennett followed his employee down the aisle, leaving Kane to approach the stall door all alone.

Presley's murmured words to the mare soothed Kane's nerves, which he now realized had been standing at attention from the first moment he'd heard her raised voice. Unfortunately, the sight of her as she bent over and carefully inspected each of the horse's hooves had other things coming to attention, too.

Last night, Presley's flowy dress had been hiding some serious curves. Today she wore a very soft-looking T-shirt tucked into a pair of jeans. Rounded hips blossomed from a tiny waist hugged by denim. When she stood to pat the horse's back, he saw that the cotton of her shirt clung just as faithfully in all the right places.

Holy hell. He was in trouble...so why was he grinning like an idiot?

He forced his gaze upward, only to encounter a glare

directed his way. Funny, it didn't dampen his excitement. "Hello, Presley."

"What are you doing here?" she asked, narrowing her gaze on him.

"Watching you in action," he replied, fully understanding how much that would aggravate her. "I'm impressed."

To his surprise, she had quite a sarcastic mouth on her. "I'm so glad you liked what you saw."

But her bravado didn't stop a flush spreading over her cheeks. Perhaps as a gentleman, he should clarify his previous comment. "There's a difference between appreciating a woman and disrespecting her—my mama taught me that."

"So you're respectfully blackmailing me?"

"Considering the concessions I've made, isn't it more of a mutual agreement than blackmail?"

"An agreement I'm forced to enter into if I don't want my family and business reputation ruined… I think that does qualify as blackmail."

That bossy tone should not be so arousing. And he couldn't deny her logic. "Maybe I wanted to spend time with you."

"A woman you didn't know?" She scoffed. "You'd be the first."

With just those few words, she confirmed EvaMarie's story from this morning. Kane kept silent.

Sticking to his stance might take away his gentleman card, but he wouldn't miss what was coming for the world.

Presley skirted around the horse's rump, making her way to a clipboard on top of a cupboard by the door. "Most men are only hoping for one thing when they spend time with me," she said, studying the papers with unnecessary intensity. "My expertise with horses."

Kane nodded, even though she pretended she wasn't

watching him. But he saw the quick sideways glance, no matter how brief.

She continued, "Not frilly dresses and small talk."

Deciding she'd had enough time to spout nonsense, he crossed the threshold of the stall. To her credit, she didn't retreat as he neared. He didn't box her in but got close enough that he could smell her shampoo. "There are things a lot sexier than social niceties."

It was too soon, but he couldn't stop himself from reaching out to sample some of the thick blond strands of hair in her ponytail. Silky—just as he'd imagined.

"Why are you touching me?" she asked.

Her tone wasn't quite as breathless as he'd have liked. He sensed just a hint of excitement.

"You're right," he murmured. "I'm sorry. I'm simply fascinated by the color, texture."

She smoothed her hands over her hair. "I don't know if I can do this."

That's what her mouth said, but as soon as he looked up to catch her eyes, she glanced away. Avoidance. At least it confirmed what he suspected was happening here. Time for a different approach: honesty. "Look, Presley. I know that this might be uncomfortable. I'm simply trying to make things more natural between us."

"I don't think I like it."

"But you aren't sure?"

She stiffened, her look transforming into a glare. "That's incredibly sexist."

"Or incredibly honest." He pushed on, leaving the inference of his own interest behind for the moment. There was another way to get her riled up, which he enjoyed far too much. "I told you, touching is expected. Would you rather we practice in public?"

"I'd rather not practice at all."

"But practice makes perfect. Besides, I find I enjoy touching you. It's okay if you like it, too. It doesn't have to go any further than, well, public displays of affection."

Presley opened her mouth to speak, then paused. She studied him for a moment, but he had the feeling she wasn't really looking at him. "Why do I feel like we've covered this before?"

He let his amusement mold his mouth…just a little. "Guess it's something we'll have to keep doing until we get it right between us."

Her perfect bow-shaped lips twitched, lush in their natural state. He could swear she was holding in laughter. "Like, practice?"

"Maybe."

Her entire face opened up, letting her enjoyment of the moment shine through her earlier irritation. Seeing Presley give in to her amusement was sexy as hell. Her smile was wide and unself-conscious, her eyes bright and seeking his. When he laughed with her, the glow increased like a power surge.

Gorgeous.

A noise interrupted them. Kane turned to see Bennett in the doorway. Presley's laughter shut off instantly.

"Miss Presley, Sun is ready."

Kane watched from the corner of his eye as she nodded. Bennett left, but Presley continued to stare at the doorway. She shifted. She swallowed. Kane waited her out.

"Was there something you needed, Kane?" she finally asked.

Did she worry about him being too close to the stud? "I did want to speak with you. Iron out a few details."

"Well, I have things I need to do right now."

As if that would stop him. "I don't mind tagging along."

From the look on her face, Kane could tell she wasn't sure what to feel. Ah, he was making progress…

Presley preceded Kane down the barn corridor, feeling flustered. Why in the world hadn't she told him to hit the road? She should have. After all, the man was completely taking advantage of a situation she had no control over.

But she couldn't forget the look in his eyes when she'd first spotted him in the doorway. He could have leered. He could have been indifferent. But the pure male appreciation wasn't something she'd encountered before today. Oh, men had told her she was pretty, though it never rang true. But something about Kane's gaze, unsullied by greed or arrogance, was special.

Maybe that was why she hadn't fought this harebrained scheme harder. Maybe she was more than a little interested to see exactly how this would all go. There was probably something very wrong with that line of thinking, but Presley was nothing if not honest with herself.

When they got to Sun's stall, Kane didn't force his way in or try to take over. She'd come across a lot of men who thought they knew better than a woman in the stables… until she taught them they were wrong. It didn't take a huge confrontation or butting of heads. She simply let them go on until they ran out of steam, then stepped in and quietly set them straight.

Unless she needed to raise her voice. Then she did.

Nodding to Bennett, who was already in the stall, Presley put her hand on Sun's withers and whispered near the horse's ear. He whipped his head around fast, and Presley heard Kane's step behind her, but she didn't flinch. They'd played this game before, her and Sun. The horse didn't bite or hit her with his heavy head. Instead he corrected at the last minute and pressed the side of his muzzle against her shoulder, pushing hard. She stumbled, chuckling, then reached up to give him a rough rub behind his ears.

"Likes to play, does he?" Kane asked.

Bennett laughed from his position on Sun's other side. "Believe it or not, he's like a big kid. And she's incredible with him."

Presley felt warmth creep into the pit of her stomach. No matter how often someone complimented her on her knowledge, it was this connection with the animals in her care that meant the most to her. Especially with Sun.

She checked him over quickly, just to make sure in the daylight that there were no adverse effects from last night's quick trip. Then she and Bennett discussed what he needed over the next week. Her big baby got a good rubbing and a piece of apple she was hiding in her pocket before they left.

After locking Sun back down, Bennett said goodbye to them outside the stud's stall door and went to tend to the other horses.

"He's right, you know," Kane said, "I've never seen anyone so in tune with horses."

Presley ducked her head, embarrassed by Kane's compliment, even while that warm glow spread. "They can be sensitive creatures. It's all about knowing them, what they need. Of course, Sun and I go way back." Maybe that's why the horse was the one thing her daddy had willed to her alone. "Daddy bought him for me the year my mother died," she found herself adding.

Wow, what a maudlin subject to introduce. But Kane didn't hesitate before he asked, "How old?"

Though she now regretted bringing it up, she answered, "Six."

"I was fifteen when my mother died after a long fight with cancer."

She glanced at him in surprise. Somewhere in the back of her mind, she might have remembered this about the Harrington family but had forgotten in the loads of other, more recent, gossip. His dark eyes were solemn, his gaze direct. It almost made her feel as though she could actually talk to him about things—private things she mostly kept to herself now that her daddy was gone.

"Did your father also insist on bringing in a new mommy?" she murmured, though she did add a bit of a smirk to lighten the impact of her question.

Kane smiled too, but his dark gaze remained serious. "Nope. From then on out, it was just us guys. Action movies and baseball games. When we were older, beer and pizza nights."

"That must have been nice…"

"What must have been nice?" Marjorie's voice was jarring, not just because it was so close and loud, but because Presley could only remember one other time her stepmother had ventured into the stables. She'd never been back.

Presley quickly closed her gaping mouth as Marjorie appeared from behind Kane.

Kane didn't flinch, of course. "We were just talking about remarrying."

"I see," Marjorie said, nodding as if she had all the knowledge in the world. Her bejeweled pantsuit and heels were completely out of place in her surroundings. "I'm afraid our girl has never appreciated what her father and I tried to do for her. I'm sure you were more grateful to your father…"

"He never remarried."

Short and sweet. No apologies. Presley was beginning to enjoy this.

The shocked look on Marjorie's face melted into confusion, but she quickly recovered. Presley suppressed a sigh as her stepmother prattled on about her own marriage and how she couldn't understand why Presley had never taken to her. *There ya go. Tell all our dirty little secrets.*

"Did you need something, Marjorie?" Presley finally cut in.

"Oh." Marjorie blinked, obviously reorienting herself to her mission. "I saw you arrive, Kane, and wanted to make sure there were no hard feelings from last night."

No *I'm sorry for stealing your money.* But why would Marjorie think she needed to apologize for that?

"I'm over the moon to have my Presley taking care of things and wouldn't want you to think otherwise," Marjorie said. "She keeps this place running..."

Presley raised a single brow, surprised Marjorie tore herself away from her society lunches long enough to notice, much less be grateful.

"If I could just get her to listen to me more—"

Please, stop talking.

But no, Marjorie just had to keep going. "She has so much potential, you know."

"And she's living up to it every day," Kane replied.

Marjorie and Presley both focused in on Kane. Presley couldn't tell which of them was more shocked. No one had ever defended her against Marjorie's inane yet often hurtful prattle in this house. Her father had let it go on and never gave a clue to his own thoughts. At times, he had even reiterated Marjorie's message in his own way.

Oh, he'd loved Presley. She had no doubt. But he'd thought she'd be better off as a prissy princess, not a tomboy, even though she could run this business better than any man here. She'd never understood that.

Kane broke into her thoughts. "Now if you'll excuse us, we have a lunch date."

What? she almost asked, but Kane's steady gaze kept her mouth shut. Presley gave a short nod. Anything to get her away from Marjorie and this uncomfortable conversation.

"Surely not dressed like that?" Marjorie asked, eyeing Presley's dusty jeans and T-shirt.

Presley glanced over to find Kane doing the same, with a far different look in his eyes than she expected. "Why not?" he asked, his voice just a touch husky. "Love the jeans, hon."

That wink would have made any woman swoon. Presley recognized it as a weapon against her normally strong defenses. How long could she hold out against all this Harrington appeal?

Five

Presley soon realized that Kane wasn't kidding. He nodded when she said she wanted to wash up, but he encouraged her not to change—the restaurant wouldn't care.

What kind of restaurant was that? Surely the world's newest billionaire wasn't taking her out for fast food? She did at least upgrade from a dusty shirt to a clean one with a Wonder Woman logo. Both out of defiance and a deep-down desire for Kane to see the real her. The girl who couldn't care less about society chatter but enjoyed action movies and riding and comic books.

Eventually it would bore him and he'd leave her alone, especially if he had to take the real her out in public, right?

The quicker disillusionment set in, the quicker she'd be free of this dang bargain.

When she rejoined him at the front of the house, he glanced down at the front of her shirt and grinned but didn't say anything. She wasn't sure exactly what his reaction meant. He led her to a dark burgundy luxury SUV and let her in the passenger side like a true gentleman. As she waited for him to join her, she took a deep breath. The inside of the vehicle smelled of new leather seats and the cologne Kane had been wearing the night before. As he opened the door, she breathed again.

Boy, did he smell good. She probably still smelled like the barn. Now she wondered if she should have changed into a dress, but then she would have been completely uncomfortable and self-conscious. As if she wasn't self-conscious now—

"Let's just relax and get to know each other, okay?" Kane asked, interrupting the momentum of her thoughts.

Her nod was a little jagged. In the barn, she'd been fine. Not totally in control, but confident in her surroundings. Now she didn't have that, and the need to second-guess everything meant she'd be on edge the entire time.

Just let it go.

"You should feel lucky," she blurted out as he turned around in the wide drive.

"How's that?" he asked, flashing her a grin that took at least half a dozen years off his features. Kane was often solemn-looking. *Why was that?*

"Marjorie hasn't been in the barn in a long time. Years, I think. But she made a special trip just to see you."

To her amusement, his brows shot up. "I don't know if I'd call either of us lucky for that."

Laughing with him felt good. She hadn't done that with many people since her father died. He'd been one of the few who actually got her off-the-wall sense of humor. She missed that feeling of communal amusement.

Kane directed the conversation back to horses as they drove through the heart of town and out the other side. The west end of town was just as rural as the east, but the farms were smaller. Usually the families over here raised cattle or did specialty farming on a more modest scale than the elite horse farms on the east. There was also a small community college out this way that Presley had only visited a time or two for concerts.

Kane drove with confident ease. His hands on the wheel were things of masculine beauty. She could watch his sure grip and the slide of his palm against the leather all day. To her surprise, he shared some of what he and his brother were planning to do with their own farm.

When he suddenly pulled into a lot and parked, Presley glanced around, having been distracted by their debate over different animal supplement techniques. The gravel lot was a tiny triangle at the intersection of two roads. There were only a few vehicles besides theirs. Several people had congregated on the tiny outdoor porch of the restaurant at the widest point of the lot.

"Um, I haven't been here before," she said, studying the place with a bit of skepticism.

In Kentucky, it wasn't a stretch to say some of the best food came from some of the most run-down-looking joints. Her daddy had often picked up food for her from restaurants like this when they traveled. One of his protective measures had been to bring it back to the hotel. He never let her go to a part of town he didn't feel was safe for her. But this place was in her own backyard, and she'd never heard of it.

Guess her high-class snobbery was showing.

"We'd better get in line," Kane advised. "We've got about ten minutes before this place is packed."

Um, okay.

The main wing of the two-story building was small, with a weathered, pointed roof. A square addition had been fitted against the back to form a stubby L shape. While relatively clean, the place showed a lot of wear. "What kind of food is it?" she asked as they crossed the lot.

Eyeing the casual attire of those already lined up, she

realized Kane had been right. No need to worry about her barn clothes here.

"They have some different things, but the main fare is southern-style barbecue," Kane said with obvious enthusiasm. "I've been eating here since I was about ten years old."

Well, if this restaurant had been around that long, they must be serving something good. And the cuisine explained some of the grubbiness—the barbecue smoke had been building up for a long time.

Kane grew quiet while they waited, but it wasn't an uncomfortable silence. He pointed out a menu on the wall so she could get a preview. Then he held his tongue until the door opened and they followed the small crowd to the hostessing stand, if one could call it that. The timber walls were covered with handwritten messages left by numerous patrons. Quarters were close, and the line behind them promised to make things even cozier.

But they shouldn't have trouble getting a table, if the hostess's big grin and hug for Kane were any indication. He and the older woman chatted a few minutes, getting caught up. "The usual spot?" she asked, her gaze flicking curiously to Presley and back.

Kane nodded, and the hostess handed menus and wrapped silverware off to a younger waitress without a word. Kane gestured for Presley to follow the woman, his firm hand at the base of her spine leaving her all too aware of him as she contemplated the very tight spiral staircase they had to climb.

"Hope I don't meet anyone on their way down," she joked.

There truly was only space for one-way traffic. "That's how you get to know your neighbors," Kane deadpanned.

Yeah, this man would surely get her sense of humor.

The stairs opened onto a narrow aisle on the second floor lined with rustic booths. The slanted roof lent an interesting angle to the ceiling, and one side of the floor looked out over the room and bar below. The waitress seated them in the far corner in front of a triangular window that fit into the angles of the room.

As she took her seat across from him, Presley caught Kane watching her. He didn't speak, but somehow she knew he was wondering what she thought. Country music cranked up from the jukebox downstairs. Presley grinned. "This is interesting." Like some of the honky-tonks she'd heard the stable hands talk about but had never gone to herself.

Kane nodded. "I love things with character. This place has it in spades. Just wait until you taste the food."

He didn't try to direct her in what she should eat. Instead he waited while she read every inch of the menu.

"Anything especially good?" she asked.

Kane shrugged. "Over the years I've had just about everything. But the ribs are my favorite. Oh, and the mac and cheese." He nodded slowly as if he were a wise sage imparting an eternal truth.

Presley smothered a grin and went back to her menu. Kane didn't even crack his.

"This is where we had all of our fancy dinners growing up," Kane said almost absently. "My dad loved it here."

Presley couldn't help but compare the worn decor and friendly atmosphere with the stuffy yet impressive restaurants where she'd been forced to celebrate her birthdays over the years. "Things must feel a lot different now." After all, Kane could probably buy this place fifty times over if he wanted.

He focused in on her for a moment, the intensity of his

look causing her to catch her breath. "Some things haven't changed at all."

Before she could even question his statement in her own mind, their waitress returned to take their order. Anxious to revisit her own barbecue memories with her father, she chose the one food Marjorie would have thoroughly admonished her for eating in public: ribs. Though she ordered hers with a milder sauce than what Kane was having.

Her simple decision made Presley want to smile. She was a grown woman and didn't need anyone's permission for the choices she made. Being with Kane made her want to explore a different side of herself. Maybe it was his open acknowledgment of Marjorie's lack of parenting skills. Maybe it was the teasing or casual use of sexual innuendos. Something about Kane made her want to take pleasure in life instead of being all business for a change.

"I figured you'd want more definitive details about our agreement since you're a businesswoman," Kane said.

Heat swept over her skin. Apparently she was the only one ready to leave business behind. How embarrassing. After all, a man like Kane would certainly not be interested in a real date with a woman like her.

"Right. Yes, I would," she managed.

She'd gotten lost in the personal conversation and forgotten that she was only here for business. Kane just preferred to conduct his business over barbecue rather than at Pierre's downtown.

Presley tried to push the discouraging thoughts away and focus on what Kane was telling her.

"It occurred to me, after I was able to give this arrangement more thought last night," he said, his face once more solemn, without a hint of his earlier wink, "there might be another way to work off your family's debt."

For a moment, Presley was paralyzed all the way to

her core. She wasn't sure if she was worried he was about to disrespect her or if she was worried he was about to give her a way out. Which was wrong, but somehow she couldn't help it. She couldn't stop herself from wondering if he'd spent all night trying to find a way out of spending so much time with her.

"You mean my stepmother's debt?" she said, wincing at the slight croak in her voice.

No matter how he'd grown up, Kane couldn't have looked more regal than when he gave her a single, solemn nod. "There might be another way to preserve her reputation—and mine."

Presley narrowed her gaze on him. This little meeting had taken on a completely different tone with just a few words. "I'm listening."

"You can keep the money I paid you for stud service."

Her eyes widened as her dirty little mind went in a totally different direction than it should have. "Excuse me?"

"For Sun."

Of course. He wouldn't have meant anything else. And if it had been anyone else speaking, that was the first thing she'd have thought. But this was Kane Harrington. And somehow, in the past twenty-four hours, Presley had gone from viewing this as a business arrangement to wishing for something Kane probably wouldn't enjoy as much— kiss or no kiss.

Before she could do something stupid, like voice her disappointment, their waitress set two steaming platters on the table between them. Presley looked down at the juicy half rack of ribs and wondered what the hell she'd been thinking. Surely she'd make a complete mess out of this. The way she had of her personal perceptions about what was happening here.

Just as her worries escalated, her hands trembling with

that unmistakable performance anxiety she often suffered in social situations, Presley took a deep breath and forced herself to stop and focus on the business at hand.

Business. It was only business, and that she knew how to handle. *That's all it ever could be, right?*

Presley forgot about the food between them. "How much?"

Kane's impassive expression wasn't giving much away. "I've got the paperwork in the SUV. You can invoice out every use of Sun for stud, and we will subtract the normal fee from your balance. If at any time this arrangement no longer suits you, just pay the balance in full and we're done."

"And you again have free rein to ruin my reputation?" she asked, not buying this simple fix. At all.

"As you'll learn, I always do what is required. But in this case, I don't think that will be necessary. Do you?"

Kane relaxed into the worn leather-upholstered booth, watching Presley carefully pick her way through the ribs on her plate. She tried so hard to be neat, to not make a mess. He expected her to break out a fork at any minute.

He'd figured the business discussion would put a damper on what was happening between them, but the matter had needed to be addressed. Kane had always been a fan of getting the necessary ugly stuff out of the way first.

Presley had gone from the comfortable and confident woman who had climbed into his SUV with a mild sense of rebellion, wearing jeans and a T-shirt, to self-conscious and stiff the minute he'd brought up their arrangement. He'd been able to see the transformation in her expression, the way she held herself.

The dichotomy fascinated him, kept him on the edge of his seat in a way few things had lately.

"We can start small on the social scale. Practice, if you will." He flashed a small grin even though she'd gone stock-still. "A small party shooting pool in the basement at my house tonight. You didn't get to see the entertainment area downstairs, did you?"

Presley was still holding two rib bones in her fingertips. Was she ever going to just eat? Despite her surprise, she wasn't just accepting his request.

"What if I have plans for tonight?" she asked.

Like she could fool him. "Do you?"

She frowned. Had she really thought he wouldn't challenge that?

"No, but—"

"Good. You can be there about eight. It'll just be a few people."

She didn't move. Didn't agree. And it didn't matter— he wasn't giving her the chance to back out.

"And by the way, if there should be any side effects to our spending time together—"

"Side effects?" That squeak reminded him of their first encounter, which had only been last night. They'd packed that short time full of interesting things, hadn't they?

Kane didn't repeat himself. Instead he gave her a direct look, letting her see his intent front and center.

Kane loved to challenge her, just to watch her think. Her expression only hinted at what was happening inside, but he could tell she was trying to figure out how to handle him.

"Anything that happens will be by mutual consent."

Now she had his word.

"Aren't you gonna dig in?" he asked.

Presley blinked. Then he nodded at her plate, and she glanced down at her fingers. She was still gripping the bones as if it was the only sure move she knew.

"Like this," he said, then tore several ribs off his rack and lifted them to his mouth, biting into them unceremoniously with a mock growl.

Presley didn't quite giggle, but it was close. Kane considered his playfulness worth it. He was on a mission to see Presley smile and laugh. It was an honorable mission. A counterbalance to his demands. But also a slippery slope to becoming too invested.

That he could never do, because Kane wasn't built for long term.

But he was built for this. He kept things light for the rest of the meal and enjoyed it when Presley finally got her hands dirty. When they stood to leave, instead of leading the way down the aisle, Kane stepped closer. "I'm glad you had a good time."

Presley had gotten comfortable enough over the last thirty minutes to raise a sassy eyebrow at him. "What makes you think that?"

Leaning toward her, he snagged a clean napkin from the stack on the table. "Because you actually have sauce on your face."

Her eyes widened, and she glanced around them as if someone would spot her indiscretion and judge.

"Relax," he admonished. "This is a rib place, after all." Then he rubbed the outer edge of her mouth with the napkin, knowing all the while that he really wished it was his mouth on those luscious full lips.

But it was a little too soon to press his luck. Instead he escorted her to the car and took her home like a true gentleman. No one could say he didn't know his place—even though he didn't always stay in it.

After stopping in the drive close to the barn, Kane got out of the SUV. He didn't want to take up the rest of Presley's afternoon, especially since he would be commandeering her evening, but he really wasn't a drop-'em-off-and-drive-away type of guy. Not waiting on him to open her door, she came around the vehicle with a hesitant look on her face. An awkward expression that asked what the heck type of response this situation called for, because she wasn't really sure.

Neither was he. A fact that he found intriguing. Actually, he knew what his response *should* be, but it wasn't what he wanted.

Before either of them could speak, muted shouting erupted from the vicinity of the stables. They shared a startled glance, then took off at a run.

Kane got to the barn first, so he swept the door open for Presley to sprint through. Half a dozen men stood with a sort of agitated energy at the opening of the stall where he'd first found Presley this morning. A couple of loud thumps emanated from inside. Then Bennett spilled from the darkened doorway with the ranch hand from this morning clinging to him. Not for long, as Bennett unceremoniously dumped the man on the ground.

Bennett stood for a minute with his hands on his hips, watching the man lie there. "There was pretty dang stupid," he finally said.

"What happened?" Presley asked, alerting the group to their presence.

Kane glared when the man on the ground mumbled what he was pretty sure were some choice curse words.

Bennett nodded at the stable hand. "Brilliant here decided to give himself another go at cleaning the mare's hooves. Went even worse than the last time."

"It kicked me," the man ground out.

"Did you deserve it?" Presley asked. "Bennett?"

"Sure did," her stable manager said in a grim tone. "He took a crop to her when she wouldn't stay still."

Everyone tensed. Kane felt the urge to step in, take control and give this idiot a lesson he'd never forget. Just in time, he checked himself. This wasn't his barn. The lesson wasn't his to give—but he would if it wasn't properly learned this time.

The stable hand struggled to his feet. From his movements, Kane guessed the mare had gotten him in the thigh. He was lucky she hadn't caught his knee.

Then the guy had to open his mouth. "Crops are for putting animals in their place."

Yep, he was going to be sore tomorrow...and out of a job.

Presley stepped forward. "Here we use crops sparingly. They are for training and racing—not an instrument of punishment. As a matter of fact, the only place to find one here is in the tack room. Not this stall."

Oh, she was a smart one. Even Kane hadn't caught onto that.

"I refuse to have someone working at Macarthur Haven that I can't trust. Boys, escort him to his truck, please." She stared the injured man down for a moment, matching his glare and almost daring him to say anything more.

Inside, Kane cheered.

"You can come by tomorrow for your gear and final paycheck. Go straight to Bennett and he will supervise your visit."

Apparently that didn't go over well, because the man took a halting step in her direction. He didn't get far. Kane moved forward and blocked his path, arms crossed over his chest to display muscles from years of hard labor, an intent look on his face that dared the man to try any monkey business. Kane didn't even have to speak.

The stable hand immediately lost his steam. Bennett nodded at the group of men, and they ushered the now ex-employee toward the door in a tight formation that brooked no argument.

In minutes, the trouble was under control and Presley thanked Bennett for stepping in before the situation got out of hand.

"I just wish it hadn't occurred at all," he replied with a shake of his head.

"I made my feelings over the treatment of our animals very clear this morning," she said. "Not everyone gets it."

Bennett nodded. He shook Kane's hand, then turned back toward the stall. "I'll check her over and get her settled down."

Presley's heavy sigh told Kane just how much the confrontation had taken out of her. Still… "I'm proud of you for not backing down," he said.

She tossed a surprised look his way, then shrugged. "It's not the first time. Probably not the last. But it's a shame, regardless."

"Does that authoritative stare come naturally, or did you have to cultivate it over the years?"

Her smirk was sassy, sexy. "You may not know this, but if you don't stand up for yourself in a male-dominated environment, they will assume you can't. So I did what was necessary."

"I'm sure your dad was very proud."

Her smile flatlined instantly. "You know, that's the first time you've been wrong about me."

Six

Presley frowned into her rearview mirror as she tried to get her lipstick on without making a mess, for a change. Usually it took her several attempts, when she even bothered to try. Why she was doing this tonight, she wasn't sure. She'd worn nothing but Chapstick for months now. But she did want to look better than usual tonight, even if this was a casual get-together. Thinking back to this afternoon didn't help steady her hand, though.

Her last words to Kane had gone too far, revealed way more than she wished. She'd never talked with anyone about her father's disappointment in her…and he'd never displayed it openly in public. He'd reserved that for his private suggestions to wear a dress instead of pants or to spend more time at the country club than in the barn. While he'd been undeniably proud of her accomplishments, there was no doubt about his disappointment that Marjorie's feminine tendencies hadn't "taken" with Presley. And he had certainly never let her make any final management decisions in the stables, despite her degree and extensive experience.

But she'd kept that secret to herself…until today.

Had Kane seen her as just a little girl whining? He

hadn't given any indication, simply studying her for a moment before nodding slightly and turning to go. What did that mean? The man was so hard to read. He kept his reactions close to his chest, leaving her in guessing mode so that when he did let something through—like those occasional glimpses of male interest—she was left to wonder if she'd really understood what had just happened.

The man was blackmailing her! She needed to remember that and stop looking at this like a friendship. Or even worse, a relationship.

One thing was certain: she wasn't getting comfortable with him any time soon. Which would probably suit him fine.

Forcing herself to stop fiddling, Presley got out of her truck and stomped toward the front entrance of the Harrington estate. Of course, the sound wasn't as satisfying when she wasn't wearing her boots. *Dang dress shoes!* And the wait after she rang the bell didn't help her mood. Her stomach churned from nerves as she stood there.

She wasn't quite sure what to expect, but when she heard the word *party*, she wanted to run. Heck, if she was ever lucky enough to get married, she'd probably elope to avoid the ceremony. Because if there was anything worse than a party, it was a party where she was supposed to be the center of attention.

The door swung open, and Presley found herself face-to-face with Kane. His piercing gaze, combined with her thoughts about marriage, sent a flush to her cheeks. Maybe he wouldn't notice it if she stepped in quickly.

"Welcome, Presley."

His deep voice was counterbalanced with EvaMarie's higher one as Presley scooted into the foyer. The light from the sparkling chandelier wasn't as harsh as she'd expected, and EvaMarie's smiling face was a welcome sight. At least she wouldn't be the only woman here.

"Hey, EvaMarie."

From directly behind her, Kane spoke. "What about me?"

Presley hesitated, then glanced over her shoulder. "Oh, hi."

His half grin teased her. "That's a bit more like it, I guess."

"Were you looking for something else?" Was she really flirting with her blackmailer? It kind of felt like it.

Before she could prepare, Kane tucked an arm around her shoulders and pressed his lips against hers. Her squeak reverberated in her own ears, prompting embarrassment to wash over her. He didn't press for more but also didn't back down.

Remembering that this was just business, Presley relaxed. The first sensation to sweep through her was the tingling of her lips. Then the heat where he was touching her thin silky shirt. Both spread across and down like a slow-moving burn. Just as her whole body was engulfed, he pulled back. A mere fraction. Enough for her to feel his breath across her lips.

Then he was gone.

The first thing she saw was EvaMarie's wide-eyed stare. The burn in her cheeks returned. *Great.*

She spent the trip downstairs trying to calm herself. Realizing she was the last to arrive didn't help, but she saw that the only other guests were the Rogers brothers, whom she already knew well. As long as she could keep from embarrassing herself, she'd be okay.

But then again, knowing the other guests as well as she did put her in a bit of a quandary…

"Jake, Steven, this is Presley Macarthur."

"We've known each other since grade school," Jake said, tipping his head at Presley in greeting.

"Most people around here have if they live on the same side of town," EvaMarie confessed to Kane. "Or they at least know of each other."

Presley nodded her own greeting, her attention distracted by the gorgeous antique pool table at the far end of the room. She quickly pulled herself back to the conversation. "How's Princess, Steven?" she asked.

"Good," he said. "That trick you gave me got her back on track. Her speed is up already."

"What trick?" Jake demanded. "Are you holding out on me?"

"You bet I am," Steven said with a grin.

The men mock argued with each other while Mason helped EvaMarie set up food and drinks on the bar. Kane once again closed in. "Are you gonna share this great trick with me?" he asked in a low voice that gave the question a whole new meaning.

Presley tried to look him in the eyes, she really did. But those lips kept drawing her attention. "Depends."

"On what?"

"On whether you can beat me at pool…"

Did she really say that? For a second, panic pressed hard against Presley's chest, but for once she refused to acknowledge it. If Kane was going to go all in on this Lothario routine, why make it easy for him? He certainly wasn't cutting her any slack. And he seemed to have accepted everything he'd seen of her today—hadn't he?

"That sounds like a challenge," he said, but he didn't look put off by it. Instead, that glitter in his eye seemed to indicate…excitement?

Would nothing go according to plan?

"Shall we play?" Kane announced to the room as a whole.

Presley turned to see the others watching them. Jake raised his empty glass as if in salute. "I think I'll get a drink first. You two go ahead."

As Kane crossed the room to prep the table, Jake shot her a wink—he and Steven were aware of her little talent. She just hoped nerves didn't ruin her performance.

"EvaMarie?" she said, hope lightening her voice.

The other woman gave a soft sigh and wrinkled her nose. "You first," she conceded. "I'm not ashamed to admit I'm horrible."

"And nothing I have done has made her any better," Mason said.

Presley laughed as EvaMarie swatted her fiancé with a towel, then turned toward the pool table with a touch of dread. Kane waited until she got close before holding out a pool stick to her. "Ladies first."

Time to dance.

At least Presley was better at this than regular dancing. Though she was confident in her abilities, she didn't normally perform under the watchful gaze of the most striking man she'd ever met. Drawing in a deep breath, she studied the table, zeroing in on its unfamiliar surface. *Let everything else fade away.* Then she lined up her shot with deliberate care and let loose.

After four successful shots, she glanced up from the far side of the table to see her audience. Jake and Steven chuckled with knowledge of the coup. Mason and EvaMarie exchanged surprised glances. Kane stood almost frozen, brows raised, his gaze trained on the table as if he couldn't figure out what voodoo she was using to accomplish this feat.

Four moves later, the table was clear. With each clink of

the balls into the pockets, Presley felt her satisfaction grow. She didn't often get to let her true self out, and it was even rarer for her to enjoy the experience. So this was a treat.

Feeling every ounce of her win, she leaned against the stick and glanced Kane's way. "Guess you won't be finding out that trick today…"

His half grin should have warned her. "Oh, the night isn't over yet, sweetheart."

Presley smiled as she heard Mason teasing EvaMarie over her pool-playing skills. Presley had enjoyed several games, winning her fair share, but the men had eventually poked some holes in her strategy. As usual, the opposite sex always saw a female pool player as a challenge to be faced and overcome at all odds. At least this group was friendly. Sometimes things could get ugly, which was why she was usually careful about the places she played. And whom she played with.

But now it was time to let someone else be the center of attention—a place Presley never relished.

Crossing back over to the bar, she surveyed the dent already made in the food and started gathering platters.

"You don't have to do that," Kane said as he came up beside her. "I'll take them upstairs for a refill."

"I don't mind helping."

They evenly distributed the serving dishes between them and Kane led the way to the kitchen. The limestone countertop was obviously new, as were the stainless steel appliances. Really nice dark wood floors complemented the red, black and silver color scheme.

"This kitchen is gorgeous."

"Thanks," Kane said as he opened the fridge and started pulling out various containers. "It's not just easier to cook in now, it's a pleasure."

That gave her pause. "You cook?"

"Of course."

She nodded, unsure how deeply she should probe into his actual home life, so she remained silent. Opening the containers and refilling platters at least gave her something to do with her hands.

Luckily Kane volunteered more information so she didn't have to endure the awkward silence much longer.

"EvaMarie and I usually split the duties when I'm here for dinner. If I'm not here, I usually eat out. Doesn't seem to be much point cooking for one, especially after I cooked for grown men for so many years. Mason doesn't have the cooking gene, so I usually fed our hands back home."

Presley thought back to how much she'd seen the stable hands eat on various occasions. Since he'd brought up the subject, maybe she could push a little further. "Yeah, I can see how that would be a big difference. When did you learn to cook?"

Kane refilled the homemade salsa and carefully spread tortilla chips on a platter. "I started when my mom got sick. She and my dad were gone a lot for appointments, and Mason still needed to be fed."

"Very few teenage boys would voluntarily take on that task."

"Well, I'm not gonna say we didn't eat our fair share of frozen pizzas before I figured a few things out. But it had to be done. My mom taught me some things."

And he'd stepped up to the plate.

"Dad wanted me to learn to cook," she admitted.

Kane tilted his head toward her. "You didn't want to learn?"

She barely held back a giggle. "I did try, but nothing good ever came of it."

"That bad?"

"I know it's a disgrace to admit this to an acknowledged cook, but I can't even manage boxed macaroni and cheese."

"Wow," Kane said, slowly shaking his head, but his half grin told her he wasn't judging. "But you obviously have other talents." He nodded toward the basement stairs. "I bet your dad was pretty proud of that."

Presley felt her amusement fade. "Actually, he refused to let me learn how to play pool. He said it wasn't for girls."

Kane raised a brow. The story didn't reflect well on her, but his very silence pressured her to explain.

"He started taking me to horse shows and racing events with him not long after my mother died. But he was very protective. He brought food back to the hotel and didn't go drinking or anything while I was with him. Well, until Marjorie came along—then it was back to staying at home until he decided I was old enough to show horses and compete myself."

She dipped a chip and chewed while she thought back on those times. "One day he left me with one of the newer guys while he went to negotiate the purchase of a horse. The man ordered some takeout food from a local bar. It was the middle of the day, and I got to watch people playing pool while we waited. To my dad's dismay, I was fascinated…"

Again, with the half grin. Why did that look on Kane's face have to be so sexy? "Did the employee get fired?" he asked.

"Close," she remembered. "I think the thing that saved him was he was a young guy who had never dealt with kids before then. And he explained that he'd been afraid to leave me alone while he went for the food."

"Sounds reasonable."

"My dad rarely was reasonable when it came to me.

But from then on, billiards, as he called it, was a forbidden subject."

"But you're damn good at it."

She gave a rueful grin. "I learned to play while I was at college—actually took a class. Some of my fellow students started including me in trips to the local pool hall. My dad would have killed me if he saw the place."

"I bet."

"But it sure was fun."

"And you're fun to watch. He missed out."

Presley didn't want to think about that. She'd loved her dad more than anything. Why had he refused to accept so much about her?

"Ready to take this stuff down?" she asked, changing the subject.

Kane laid his hand over hers on the platter. "I'm serious, Presley. This is fun."

"Yeah, for me too." A day hanging out in the barn, lunch at a barbecue dive, then playing pool. Not at all what she'd expected from Kane Harrington. Something told her this was too good to be true.

"One night I'll cook dinner for you."

A sparkle of nerves ignited in her core, warning her this was getting too personal. "Is that part of the agreement?" she asked, suddenly desperate to get them back to business.

"Does it need to be?"

In the kitchen's soft lighting, his dark eyes met hers. Somehow she could tell he didn't care about business—he simply knew what he wanted. But could she trust him?

Could she trust any of this?

Then Mason's voice erupted from downstairs. "Food!"

And Presley was given a reprieve…but not for long. An hour later, Kane insisted on walking her to her car, though she reminded him that the driveway was perfectly safe. Lots of other men would have done the same, and she wouldn't have thought twice about accepting their escort, but being alone with Kane in the dark set those nerves in motion once more.

"I hope you had a good time," he said as they reached her truck.

In the dark, his voice played over her skin, making their conversation feel more intimate than it should. He'd been pleased with her performance tonight. That's all this was.

"You know," she said before she could think too hard about it. "It won't always be this way…" She turned toward him, her back against the driver's side door. "I don't always fit in—okay, I hardly ever fit in."

He seemed to be standing closer than was comfortable, yet she didn't want to push him away. For some reason, she wanted him to know the truth about her.

"I think we'll fit just fine," he said.

"I mean—"

He stepped closer, but somehow they still weren't touching. "I know what you mean. Don't worry about it."

"I've always worried about it," she murmured, distracted by the notion that she wished they *had* touched.

"I know…"

The knowledge in his voice left her worried.

Seven

Kane settled Presley into the front seat of his Escalade, shut the door, then let his grin break through as he skirted the SUV on his way to the driver's side. She'd come to the door with no makeup, her hair in its usual ponytail. For the luncheon of the local chapter of the American Horse Racing Society they were attending, she'd chosen to wear a long skirt with no shape and an equally loose blouse. He didn't even have a description for them except…gray.

Did she even realize how obvious this ploy to remain invisible was? Probably not, since according to EvaMarie she'd been dressing like this for many years. She'd probably forgotten why she started wearing clothes that wouldn't flatter anyone, much less a woman of her natural beauty.

So how would she feel about stop number two today?

He suppressed a grin as he slid behind the steering wheel. He'd worry about that when the objections started—because he knew good and well they would.

Presley chatted pleasantly with the lady at registration when they arrived, then automatically headed in the direction of their table. Those who were already seated smiled and greeted her companionably. He had a feeling she had a set routine at these events that eliminated any unease and minimized any contact with people who would point out her lack of social aptitude.

As she introduced him, he slipped easily into his role of Harrington Farms representative. Even Presley seemed a little dazzled.

The food was above average for a large catered event, and the speaker was interesting. Kane had never actually attended a society event of this caliber. He and Mason had several memberships, but the American Horse Racing Society had certain expectations and heavy entry fees that had kept them out before.

Not a problem now.

The speaker had barely finished when Presley turned to him. "All righty, let's go."

Kane glanced around the room at the small clusters of people forming to signal the usual social hour that followed these types of events. "You don't want to stay?" he asked.

"Um, no." Her raised brows told him how ludicrous the question was.

His little introvert. "Shouldn't we at least speak to Madame President?"

"Right."

He loved the sheepish cast to Presley's expression. It told him so much about the push and pull between her business side and her natural avoidance of anything social, despite her heavily ingrained manners.

Ms. Justine Simone, as Presley introduced her, was every inch a southern maven intent on allowing only limited access to her kingdom until she had more of an idea whom she was letting in.

"Ah, Mr. Harrington. I knew it was only a matter of time before you tried to join our ranks here at the American Horse Racing Society."

"Try?" He gifted her with one of his rare smiles, which

he knew had softened up many a detractor. "On the contrary, Ms. Simone, I will *definitely* be joining this lovely organization."

"We shall see about that, Mr. Harrington. We shall see." She smiled, flashing a full set of teeth that rivaled her diamonds in their sparkle. "While I am utterly charmed by handsome men such as yourself, I am a business owner first, and as always, looking out for the good of this organization."

"I do understand."

He could afford to be patient while he grew on her. Eventually, with enough time, he would work magic on those in this room with his natural business acumen and ease in presenting his extensive knowledge. Presley was his key to gaining that time.

Her presence legitimized him in a place where he wouldn't have fit in before, a place where many were accepted based solely on their family name. He, on the other hand, would make a place for himself, regardless of outdated notions of social standing. He'd done it before in his life, and he would do it again as necessary.

"I think you will be suitably impressed," Presley said from his side, drawing the woman's attention her way. "I've been out to the farm, seen the quality of the stock they have already. And I've talked with Kane and his brother, Mason, extensively. Harrington Farms is going to be a premier stable within a few short years—I assure you."

Kane was shocked. Her verbal recommendation wasn't part of the deal. There'd been no requirement for her to sponsor him or endorse him with anything other than her presence. He and Ms. Simone both knew that Presley would never say this if she didn't mean it. Kane found the experience humbling.

"And this young woman would know," Ms. Simone said with a gracious smile in Kane's direction. "I'm not sure her daddy realized what a gem he had in this one. She understands the animal—its needs, its instincts—which is something book learning cannot teach you."

The older woman linked her arm with Presley's. "And she's never been one to be swayed by a pretty face." She threw a discreet wink in Kane's direction. "Not that I would blame her…"

Kane got the distinct feeling Ms. Simone might pinch his cheeks if he stepped any closer.

"And do I hear the infamous Sun might have a hand in building these stables?" Ms. Simone went on.

"He will be a part of the bloodline, yes," Presley admitted, her sudden stillness making him aware of a growing tension in her body.

She could have said no. She could have said there was a misunderstanding. She could have told him Kane was on his own. Instead she was championing his case in a way he hadn't asked for, which was sweeter and sexier than if she'd offered him something else—something he shouldn't be thinking about in this setting.

"So he isn't being sold?" Ms. Simone asked sweetly, though Kane could see her sly quest for knowledge.

He easily set her straight. "A simple miscommunication. Sun has been with Presley since he was weaned. That would be like selling part of the family."

He returned Presley's wide-eyed gaze with steady calm. What happened before was between the two of them. He wasn't even sure he could change that if he needed to, since his growing instinct was to protect her. Standing here, sharing this connection with her, he acknowledged the truth.

This was deeper than he'd planned.

"What are we doing here?"

Kane frowned. He'd expected objections once they

got inside the town's most exclusive clothing store, but he
hadn't expected the battle to start in the parking lot. And
they'd been having such a pleasant afternoon...

"I need to pick up my tux for the gala at the museum
this weekend."

Presley crossed her arms firmly over her stomach. Her
set expression wasn't encouraging. "I'll wait here."

"Why?"

She frowned. "Why not?"

Kane relaxed back into his seat, giving Presley his full
attention. Her fists clenched, suggesting she wasn't happy
about that, either. "Don't you want to see what I'm wearing? Make sure we don't clash or anything?"

"Is that really a thing outside of prom?"

"Look, I don't have all day," he said, cutting to the
chase. "Why don't you just tell me what's wrong so we
can move on."

"So we can move on? Seriously?"

"Yes."

Her expression conveyed shock over his stubbornness,
but Kane wasn't budging. This behavior had gone on too
long. If her daddy couldn't break her of it, he sure as heck
would.

"I'm waiting, Presley."

She scrunched her eyebrows together. "Just go get your
tux."

"Not happening." He kept his gaze steady and serious.
This trick worked pretty well on Presley. "I don't like
this store."

"This store? Or this *type* of store?" He needed to be
sure about what he was dealing with here.

"Well, I'm not thrilled about any formal dress store,"
she said tartly, "but this one is a particular nuisance to me."

Kane glanced at the front of the stately building modeled after the style of the elegant manor houses dotting this end of town. "Someone recommended this store to me as one of the oldest in town, with the best reputation."

Looking back at Presley, he could see a slight wobble in the stubborn tilt of her chin. "Mrs. Rose has been very helpful and attentive every time I've been in here."

"I don't care."

"I do. Spit it out."

Presley rolled her eyes at his masculine ultimatum, but he didn't miss the glint of moisture before she blinked.

"Marjorie insisted on buying all the clothes for her and Dad's wedding here. We came. I sat. Marjorie shopped with her girlfriends. It was a horrid experience, repeated often."

He glanced back at the building. "You refuse to go inside because you were forced to shop here as a kid? Seems extreme to me."

"Well…"

He waited. He was good at that.

"The last time she brought me here was for a fitting for my bridesmaid's dress. I was a token junior bridesmaid so they could say I had actually been included in the wedding." Presley rubbed her palms down her skirt, stretching the material. "It was an awful froufrou dress with multiple layers of ruffles for a skirt. I felt like one of those Barbie cakes in that stupid thing. When I refused to wear it, Marjorie and I got into a yelling match in the store."

"That must have been embarrassing."

"Not at the time, but I've never been back. Marjorie got tired of me fussing, so she shook me by the shoulders. I pulled away and fell right into a rack of jewelry. Knocked the whole thing over and tore my dress when I fell."

"Let me guess? You didn't have to wear it?"

She worried her lower lip between her teeth, but a smile

threatened to break free. "I'm ashamed to say I did not. The new dress wasn't as comfortable as jeans, but Mrs. Rose picked out something much simpler."

"But you've still never been back?"

"Would you go back? After behaving that way?"

"You were a child. You're a grown woman now. Right?"

She gave him a wary look. And she was right to be suspicious. But he wasn't backing down.

"So let's go."

Kane gave her the space to hang back as they went through the front door with its delicate chime and down a ramp into the heart of southern-formal world. Mrs. Rose herself stood talking to a younger woman behind the counter. Her little wrinkled face lit up when she saw him. "Mr. Harrington! I've been impatiently waiting for you and Ms. Macarthur to arrive."

She rounded the counter with a much sprier step than one would anticipate from a seventysomething. "I have the most wonderful selection for her to try on—"

The sharp, choked note from behind him caught the older woman's attention. "Hello, Ms. Macarthur," the proprietress said with a beaming smile. "It's lovely to see you in my store again."

Kane glanced back over his shoulder and almost choked himself at Presley's glare. He was busted. But this would be good for her. She'd see.

Mrs. Rose didn't seem to notice the silent communication. "I'm so excited," she prattled on. "I see your mother in here often, but never you."

Kane saw Presley's lips tighten when Marjorie was mentioned and silently applauded her for not correcting the older woman's description.

"And your tuxedo is ready for your fitting, Mr. Harrington."

Kane nodded as they followed Mrs. Rose farther into the store. He would try on the clothes later. Leaving Presley by herself right now wasn't a good idea.

They came to a small sitting area. Mrs. Rose gestured for them to be seated on a plush semicircular bench. "I'll just go get everything ready," she said before scurrying away.

Presley glanced at the bench then turned away with a shudder. Kane figured he'd be better off meeting her resistance on his feet. The blows weren't long in coming.

"I thought we were getting your tux," she said, her sharp tone giving him a good gauge of her temper levels.

"And I asked if you wanted us to match."

"No, no, I don't. I want to be the least—" she stared at him in frustration, obviously searching for the words she wanted "—matchy couple there."

If her temper made her any cuter, he was going to do something that might make her head explode. "So are you gonna be rude to a sweet little lady and not try on her clothes?" he asked, attempting to stay calm and not give in to his amusement.

"Yes." Presley glanced around at the overflow of dresses and mirrors. "No."

Kane simply nodded. "It is a conundrum."

The sound that came from her throat was suspiciously like a growl, but before he could respond, Mrs. Rose returned and gestured them toward a separate fitting area along the back wall. More privacy, as Kane had requested.

"This way," she said smartly. "We're all ready."

As Kane studied the tight, straight line of Presley's back, he couldn't help thinking some of them were more ready than others.

Eight

Presley stared at the rows of dresses hanging on the rack in front of her as if they were snakes. Actually, that wasn't true. Snakes she knew how to handle. Ambushes at local formal boutiques…not so much.

She should have known better than to start thinking Kane was a guy who might just accept her for the person she was. Instead they had their first formal public appearance tomorrow night, and he'd done the unthinkable. She hadn't looked at even one dress, and already anger and embarrassment were building.

She had a feeling making a scene wouldn't work as well with Kane as it had with her stepmother.

Honestly, she'd let her inner angry child show way too much today. She didn't like flashing her issues around like a sign that her world had been screwed up long before her father died. The few times they'd discussed her family, Kane had been understanding. At the moment, though, she got the feeling he was laughing at her, leaving Presley to feel like a child throwing a tantrum.

Maybe that's what she was…

She could be an *adult* about this. She'd try on a few dresses, decline them, then they'd be on their way. She nodded to herself, ignoring the dozen or so candidates waiting on the rack. Good strategy.

"Let's get started, shall we?" Mrs. Rose said, grabbing a surprisingly large armful for such a small woman and heading into a dressing room that had the curtain thrown back away from the entrance.

Presley sheepishly followed, watching as Mrs. Rose arranged her choices on another, smaller rack. Not a ruffle in sight, much to Presley's relief. Also none of the pale colors she gravitated toward. A wide array of jewel tones hung before her, begging for attention.

The very thing Presley did not want.

She stared long after Mrs. Rose left, drawing the curtain closed behind her. Where should she start? Should she start at all? What in the world was she doing here?

Just as her insides started to shake, she heard Kane from right outside the curtain.

"Let me see them, Presley."

"No." Her voice had a way-too-embarrassing squeak in it.

Without another word, Kane pulled the curtain back, just enough to stick his head through.

"What are you doing?" she hissed.

"You *will* let me see you in the dresses," he insisted. Though his voice was only loud enough for her to hear, it still carried the weight of authority. "If you don't, I'll just pull the curtain back at random moments and the whole store can listen to you squeal."

In desperation, she glanced at the edge of the curtain in search of a way to keep it closed, but there was none. Kane chuckled. "No lock to keep me out, sweetheart."

He was enjoying this—and unfortunately for her, she knew he would follow through on his threat. No matter how much embarrassment that would cause her.

"Or I could simply come in and help."

Presley's mouth went dry. Visions of him wrangling a dress over her head made her cringe. That wasn't the way she wanted him to see her naked the first time.

Not that she wanted him to see her naked at all. Absolutely not.

Shoot, who was she kidding?

"I'm not gonna like this," she said through gritted teeth.

"Look at me," Kane said, his voice going dark and serious.

She found herself compelled to obey.

"Trust me. I think you'll be pleasantly surprised."

By him invading her dressing room? That might be the only fun thing to come out of this.

"I'll be out in a minute," she said, ignoring the flames licking her cheeks.

Hearing him chuckle on the other side of the curtain didn't make her feel any better.

Blindly she reached out and grabbed the first dress she touched. Taking off her clothes left her feeling vulnerable, but oddly stimulated. Knowing Kane was on the other side of the curtain with full knowledge of what she was doing had her brain sending out tingling signals of awareness.

Stop. It.

This situation was hard enough without adding unwanted arousal to the mix. One look in the mirror made her sigh. She hated trying on clothes. Hated looking at herself in the mirror. Clothing was functional for her. The rest was a mystery.

"Presley, now."

At least he didn't sound like he was standing right outside. When she pulled the curtain back, she saw him leaning casually against a pillar behind one of the padded benches nearby. She forced herself not to wrap her arms around her middle and tried to avoid any other self-conscious gestures.

"What do you think?" he asked, his tone and expression neutral.

She'd barely looked in the mirror, but the sight was burned into her retinas. "Not a big fan," she said with a grimace.

"Why?"

Her defenses were up, but his stance remained neutral. "I like green, but this shade reminds me of Jolly Ranchers. And I have no idea what to do with this." She waved the ends of a sash in the air.

Kane's lips twitched. "I agree. Green is a good color for you, but not this one. Next."

Presley blinked, not moving. Most people—the few she'd ever let go shopping with her—spent their time arguing as to why a particular piece was right for her, despite her protests. This was new.

He didn't change his mind. He just stared with raised brows until she turned away. Presley couldn't get her mind to process what had just happened, so she pulled out another dress and robotically started the complicated process of getting it on.

Three was usually her limit for items she was willing to try on before grabbing the loosest thing in the vicinity and rushing to the checkout counter. But Kane's opinions on everything she came out in fascinated her. She actually started looking through the options and picking things that might work instead of just grabbing the next in line.

And then she found it.

First, the blue definitely complimented the green color of her eyes—even she could see that. Second, it slid on easily, without any complicated pieces and parts. And third, she could actually see her shape in it without feeling like she was in a full-body stranglehold.

The silky material followed her curves like water running over her skin. There were actually multiple layers, which gave the silhouette a little movement without twisting, another major annoyance of hers.

It was beautiful.

Presley held her breath as she came out of the dressing room this time. Afraid she was wrong, afraid he would hate it…simply afraid.

Kane held still for long moments, studying her with that inscrutable look he got sometimes. Then he took her hand and led her to a raised platform before a three-way mirror toward the back of the little alcove. The added height almost allowed her to look him straight in the eyes. The mirror let her watch as he stepped up onto the platform behind her.

She felt him fumbling with the hair tie holding her ponytail. As he released it, her heart started to pound. Still in fear, but also…anticipation. The thick weight of her hair spread across her shoulders. Seeing Kane's long fingers in the mass sparked a feeling of intimacy, almost as if he were undressing her.

Then those same fingers skimmed downward, tracing the hourglass shape revealed by the material, leaving a trail of goose bumps in their wake.

"Do you feel comfortable?" he finally asked, a deep note in his voice she couldn't recognize but that she wanted to hear more of.

Unable to put words to what she was feeling, she simply nodded.

"Restricted?"

"No," she whispered, as if the word was a betrayal of her long-held clothing beliefs.

He stepped back down off the platform, then returned with a shoe box. Presley could barely hear for the blood rushing in her ears. *Please, don't ruin this.*

She wasn't quite sure if the plea was for her or for him. Kneeling before her, Kane lifted an especially sparkly sandal from the box, then held out a hand for her foot. She had to lift her skirt up, and her psyche flooded with the sense of exposing secrets to the dark man before her. Her hands clenched into the material, but she didn't resist as he lifted her foot and slid the shoe onto it. The warmth of his palm against her ankle increased that sudden sense of intimacy.

After securing both shoes, he returned to stand behind her. "Do the shoes hurt?"

The slight kitten heel felt a little odd. She was used to either flats or boots. But the heels weren't high enough that she was afraid she would fall. The straps were soft on the inside, not rubbing like most of the dress shoes she endured for these events. "No. They're pretty."

The view in the mirror entranced her for a moment. The bright brilliant blue of her dress and her blond hair stood out in contrast to Kane's dark good looks and black dress shirt and jeans. But it was the look in his eyes that caught and held her attention. Definitely lust. She'd never seen it directed at her, but she recognized it nonetheless. But there was also something else. Something just as brilliant as the color of her dress.

Understanding, maybe?

His fingers returned to her hair, testing the texture in long, soft strokes. "I've always felt that dressing up isn't about changing—it's about creating an enhanced version of who you really are."

"So you're speaking from experience?" she asked quietly, her tone almost hushed in the intimate space between them.

His half grin made a reappearance, but it didn't reach his dark eyes. "I didn't grow up with money, Presley. My version of formal clothes was a new pair of jeans once a year." His gaze shifted to his reflection in the mirror. "This new reality took me a while to wrap my head around. But I am who I've made myself—no one else."

His hands rested lightly on her shoulders. "You can present anything you want to the world, Presley," he continued. "Dressing down was your quiet form of rebellion. But your father isn't here anymore. Now is the time to let it go."

The next evening, in her bedroom, Presley stared at her face in the mirror, more than a little shocked.

Once she'd chosen a few dresses, Mrs. Rose had introduced her to a young woman at the store tasked with showing her how to put on makeup, and all her childish protests had risen once more.

"I really don't like the feel of makeup on my skin," she'd objected. Which was the truth. And only one of the reasons she'd never learned to put any on. The horses and stable hands didn't care, so why should she?

"Oh, you don't need it all over," the young woman had assured her. "You have gorgeous skin. I can just show you a few ways to give yourself a more polished look for formal occasions."

Skepticism rode her hard, but Presley had decided there wasn't any harm in letting the woman have her way. She could just wash it off when she got home—before Marjorie could see.

But she hadn't. Not only that, she'd been able to replicate the techniques today with minimal effort.

Following the step-by-step instructions, Presley had added the exact colors to the exact places they needed to go, then rubbed a bigger brush over her lids, resulting in some pretty shading that made her green eyes stand out even more. She'd finished with a barely there dusting of blush that gave her face some color and sheer, dark pink gloss that emphasized the curves of her lips.

Seeing herself in the mirror had her straightening her back, smiling a little. Polished? Yeah, that was the right word.

Now she crossed to the bed and got dressed with enough excitement and nerves that her fingers shook slightly. She couldn't help imagining what people would say tonight. She'd always hated being the center of attention, but tonight would be different.

Kane was right. Not caring about her appearance was her own form of rebellion against her father, Marjorie, and their insistence that she should be more feminine. But it was time to move on to another phase of her life.

She held up a pretty pair of panties and studied the matching bra on the bed. Luckily, Mrs. Rose had banished Kane to try on his tux before breaking out the undergarments yesterday, but at that point Presley had been in a pliable enough mood to go with the flow. In line with what she'd already seen Presley pick out, Mrs. Rose hadn't presented a full seductress line of lingerie, just some simple, pretty support pieces with an ultra-soft texture Presley fell in love with immediately. She'd ordered a full range to be delivered with the dresses she'd chosen.

Which made her both proud and slightly ashamed—because she couldn't help wondering if Kane would see them on her…or not.

The desire she'd seen on his face had been very real, but that didn't mean he would ever act on it.

She couldn't help noticing that getting dressed tonight was just as quick as throwing on jeans and tucking in a T-shirt, all thanks to Kane's acceptance of her clothing quirks and Mrs. Rose's efforts to find things that worked for her. No matter how this all started, she had a feeling she would end up owing Kane far more than the money her stepmother had taken for Sun.

Seeing the lights from Kane's SUV flash across the front of the house at dusk, she hurried out the front door and down the stone steps. The clack of her jeweled kitten heels was unfamiliar, but it added to a slight Cinderella feeling. For the first time she could remember, Presley felt like a woman from head to toe. The swish of her hair, thick and loose around her shoulders, made her wonder if Kane would touch it again.

In the dim light outside, she watched as Kane cataloged her new look as she approached him. She'd picked out a cocktail dress for tonight's event. The jewel-green dress had a flowy skirt that hit right at her knees and a blousy top with slits in the sheer arms. An elastic waist added to the comfort, but a jeweled attachment looked like a belt around the front without the tight confinement of one.

It was the most comfortable dress she'd ever put on, but it didn't look as though comfort was the goal of wearing it.

Kane let out a low wolf whistle. "You chose well," he added.

She should have been offended, but she'd never been whistled at before, and his response made her warm all over. Which was something she should definitely ignore. "Only with your help. You knew good and well I'd never pick this or any of the other dresses out for myself," she said, not quite able to attain her desired tartness in the face of his appreciation.

"Or any dress in that store," he replied, softening his know-it-all attitude by kissing the back of her hand after helping her into the passenger seat.

But he didn't go over the top with the attention. As soon

as he settled behind the wheel, conversation returned to normal. If he'd made a big deal out of her transformation, she would have felt uncomfortable—but then, the insufferable man probably knew that as well.

Instead he started talking about a mare at Harrington Farms that was about ready to foal. Then they discussed some training techniques she'd been researching. But on the drive, Kane threw more than a couple of admiring glances her way.

Presley returned more than a few of her own. Kane didn't look so bad himself. The tux he'd purchased fit him to perfection, squaring off across his broad shoulders then skimming the muscles of his back, pulling a little as he gripped the wheel. Her awareness of him grew until she could sense his every movement without even looking in his direction. The occasional whiff of a barely there cologne and the low timbre of his voice in the darkened car only set her further along the edge of arousal.

At least the sensations distracted her from her nerves. Thoughts of whether people would notice her and make comments left her stomach a little hollow. She didn't want to be in the spotlight, but she was also tired of fading into the background. Their time at Mrs. Rose's formal shop had taught her that much. But that didn't mean she wanted people making a big deal of her transformation—especially Marjorie, who had left for the party a full hour before her so she could enjoy cocktails with some friends.

Luckily the first faces they saw as they walked into the marble rotunda of the museum were Mason and EvaMarie.

"Hello," EvaMarie greeted them, her smile widening as she took in Presley's new look. "Wow. You look great."

"Thank you," Presley said, her cheeks stinging until the conversation moved on. Surreptitiously she took a deep breath, trying to calm herself. It was just a dress, for goodness' sake.

No big deal.

Things settled into a more normal rhythm as EvaMarie asked about the association luncheon the day before, though Presley noticed that Mason kept shifting from one foot to the other. Was he nervous about something, too?

A few new arrivals joined them, and Presley weathered another round of questions about her dress more easily this time. She managed okay but quickly lost interest when the other women embraced fashion as a full-on topic. Presley was proud of her clothes, but she wasn't at all interested in discussing them. Her glance around told her that the two men had abdicated the discussion themselves, stepping to the side to hold a private conversation.

Presley was ashamed of her curiosity, but a lifetime of eavesdropping to learn things people wouldn't tell her came in handy sometimes.

"Why won't you talk about this with me?" Mason demanded of his brother.

Kane's tone didn't match Mason's intensity. "What's to tell?"

"Well, your ex-fiancée got married. No one should have to find that out via email, Kane."

Shock held Presley very still, very quiet. On an intellectual level, she recognized that this was a piece of gossip that hadn't been passed around in their social circles. After all, Marjorie would surely have mentioned if Kane had been engaged before now.

But on a personal level, her curiosity grew. What kind of woman wouldn't want Kane? *Why* had she not wanted Kane?

"There's no need to make such a big deal out of things," Kane insisted. "So she got married. So what?"

Apparently he wasn't interested in answering his brother's questions, just deflecting them. Which meant she had a snowball's chance in hell of finding out what she shouldn't want to know in the first place.

"This is a really big deal," Mason continued, not seeming fazed by his brother's lack of response. "He's our business manager, and has been for over fifteen years. Of course he's worried about you. He called to make sure you would handle finding out okay."

"Notice he didn't call me."

"Because he didn't want his head chewed off." Even in his low tone, Presley could tell Mason was both irritated and laying the sarcasm on thick.

Kane didn't respond. Presley ached to turn in their direction, away from the distracting nuisance of the women talking fashion right in front of her, but instinctively she knew the brothers' conversation would end the minute that happened. As sad as it made her, she wanted to know more.

"Seriously," Mason finally continued, "he's worried. After the accident and everything that happened, I'm worried."

"I don't understand why." Kane's words were short, clipped.

Mason wasn't put off. "Because I know you aren't made of stone. After she was hurt, you just shut down. But now—look, are you okay?"

Nothing. Presley couldn't stand the pressure, the anticipation. Finally, she turned to look at the men, but Kane was walking away.

Nine

Is she trying to kill me?

Kane couldn't miss the woman in green as he stepped into the ballroom. Instead of looking like a drab bird, she stood out from the crowd. Not just because of the color of her dress, but because of the sheer glow about her. The extra attention might have made her nervous at first, but that was rapidly changing.

He couldn't even take the credit. Once they'd gotten over her initial reluctance, she'd taken matters into her own hands. The results were simple and stunning, as he'd suspected they would be.

One thing was for sure: she was definitely seducing him, without even trying.

And it was so much more pleasant than thinking about Emily, the specter Mason had brought to the party. She had no place here. Not anymore. Kane only needed Presley—closer, right now.

Without thought, he crossed directly to her, clasped her hand and led her to the dance floor. His own dance style was simple, so he was able to focus on her nearness, the feel of her. He could hear the fabric of her dress swish against his pant legs. He could feel the movement of her body beneath his palm. Every sense tuned in; he was desperate to soak in her essence.

If he had his way, he would experience all that was Presley Macarthur before the night was done.

As if she felt it, too, she glanced up to meet his gaze. Her eyes were wide, vulnerable, and Kane could see an answering need reflecting back at him. "How much longer until we can leave?" he mumbled.

A wine-colored blush spread across her cheeks, telling him he was right, even as she dropped her gaze and worried her lower lip with the edge of her teeth. Without thinking, he let his feet stop, drew her in close and conveyed his desire with a kiss. It felt so good to slide his hands up the back of her neck and into the thickness of her hair. The return pressure and slight parting of her lips told him she felt the same.

Surely it was time to go now...

Unfortunately he didn't see the obstacle before there was enough time to avoid it.

"Presley, oh, my goodness!"

Marjorie stepped right into their path, blocking Kane's progress toward the door. "Look at you. I almost didn't recognize you properly dressed up for a change. So beautiful."

Kane felt Presley's automatic withdrawal, and not just because of the closed expression on her face and the step backward she took.

"And you, Kane," Marjorie continued in an overly loud voice that made Kane want to cringe on Presley's behalf, "aren't you the most handsome man here? Isn't it nice she's finally made an effort to be worthy of being seen with you?"

What was this woman's problem? And how could she not see the effect she was having on Presley? No wonder

Presley had adopted whatever strategy she could to keep Marjorie at arm's length.

"Presley doesn't need to make an effort—" he started.

"Nonsense. I've been telling her she needs to make an effort her entire life. Not that she would listen," Marjorie finished.

Then a new voice entered the conversation. "Oh, we all tried." Joan Everly's singsong cadence ramped up Kane's irritation. "But sometimes growing up takes a while."

Kane wondered if he imagined Presley's step closer to his side.

Marjorie, however, smiled at the newcomer. "Well, I know who I have to thank for that," she said, pointing in Kane's direction. "Why, I haven't seen her covered in horse manure in days. I can't believe someone has finally taught her how to be womanly."

The target of Marjorie's comment remained silent. But not Joan.

"Let's hope he hasn't taught her too many things," she mumbled, loud enough for Kane to still hear her.

Marjorie's nonexistent brows shot up.

"Of course, I never had to be taught," Joan continued, turning her gaze directly toward Kane. "To be feminine, that is. It's always come naturally to me."

Kane was very careful not to drop his gaze, because if he wasn't mistaken, little Joan was arching her back to put her cleavage more on display.

"But Presley was always a horsey girl, you know." She glanced at the object of her ridicule with a small smile. "I doubt it will be long before she's back in jeans."

Just then, the hand tucked into his slipped away.

"Oh, goodness, I hope not," Marjorie said. "Leave a woman some hope."

Kane reached out and found Presley's hand once more.

He kept his grip firm. She wasn't getting away, and he wanted her to know it.

"Actually, I hope she's back in jeans tomorrow," he interjected. "It would be silly to work in a dress in a barn. And since Presley is the reason Macarthur Haven is still kicking, I'd think you might change your mind about that, too, *Marjorie*."

His pointed look actually had the older woman's cheeks filling with ruddy color. *Let her remember exactly what her stepdaughter is doing for her.*

Finally, he glanced Presley's way, keeping quiet until she raised her gaze to meet his. It wasn't for long, just a few seconds before it dropped again, but maybe it was enough for her to see the truth. A truth he wasn't hiding any longer.

He wanted her.

"Presley and I have gotten to know each other very well," he said, leaving the women to decide what he meant. "She's an excellent business manager, animal lover and daughter. I didn't teach her anything. I simply gave her permission to be her best self."

He turned a piercing gaze on Joan. "There's more to a woman than a dress," he said, not bothering to hide his annoyance. "If not, what's the point in hanging around?"

There was no stopping it. His own wicked way of looking at things wouldn't be held back. So he said the very thing he knew would get into Joan's craw. "Besides, Presley is sexy no matter what she's wearing…or not wearing, for that matter."

He quickly sidestepped the two women as if they were an unwanted encumbrance and led Presley on a single-minded trek to the front doors. She didn't protest. Didn't say anything, in fact. By now, she should have been talking smack, but she wasn't.

That's what worried him.

* * *

Presley wasn't sure how long she'd been riding in the SUV, shaking on the inside, concentrating on not letting the tremors show. As she became more aware of her surroundings, she also realized that her feelings weren't as cut-and-dried as they should be.

She'd been subjected to ridicule from Joan since the moment Joan realized just how powerful it made her feel. Of course, normally her taunts were more veiled and more private. Presley had overlooked the comments about her clothing choices and lack of ability to compete on any kind of sexual level for what seemed like forever. Their potency had been weakened by years of repetition.

But not tonight. For some reason, knowing Kane wasn't just the witness but the recipient of Joan's comments changed everything. Joan's first words had made her heart pound, but everything else was now lost in a red sea of embarrassment. As if Marjorie and Joan had stripped her naked so they could point out all of her flaws—to Kane.

He wasn't the type to walk away. Oh, no. Instead he'd defended her—she remembered every word of that part of the exchange in detail. But she wished she couldn't.

Presley and I have gotten to know each other very well...

"Why would you tell them that?" she choked.

She could feel Kane glance her way in the dark, but she didn't turn to look at him.

"Which part?" he asked.

You don't remember, because it doesn't affect you. "They're going to think we're sleeping together," she mumbled, almost afraid to say the words aloud. But a force deep inside—maybe anger, maybe need—wouldn't let her stay quiet any longer.

Kane wasn't helping. "So?"

"The season's just started." Why was she pursuing this line of questions? It could only lead to an embarrassing rejection. Right? "Do you really want to keep this pretense up for months on end?"

"Will it be a pretense?" he asked.

For a moment, her breath caught in her throat. "What?"

Instead of answering, Kane turned the wheel, then pressed on the brakes. Presley's stomach lurched as the SUV jerked and went still. Kane twisted in his seat to face her.

"I haven't made any secret of the fact that I'm attracted to you, Presley."

She shook her head as if to deny what she already knew. "But I thought that was..." Her throat closed.

In the lights from the dash, Kane looked even darker, more dangerous and determined. "I have absolutely no need to pretend," he said. "This is me, Presley. I'll always be honest with you."

She thought back to all he'd told her since they'd first met. *And by the way, if there should be any side effects to our spending time together—mutual consent...* The doubt returned, clouding her thinking.

"Did you say all that just to get in my pants?"

His chuff of laughter made her ears burn. "No. I said it because it's the truth. But while we're talking, is it working?"

"Is what?"

"My attempt to get in your pants."

"Of course it is."

Did she really just say that? She should have been embarrassed; she should backtrack. Instead the internal pressure from earlier faded away, leaving only an aching need for him to be telling the truth.

"Good," he said simply, then reached across the console for her.

Presley didn't resist, couldn't resist. Her lips met his halfway, eager for another taste of Kane's dark essence.

His kiss was soft yet strong. Eager and hungry. Anticipation swelled to match the pounding of her blood. Kane's hand slid up into her hair, burying deep in the loose thickness, holding her still for his thorough exploration.

It wasn't the overzealous fumbling of a boy, but the firm lead of a man who knew what he wanted. His tongue teased along the seam of her lips, and she allowed him inside. He conquered every new inch of territory with a sensual purpose that allowed her to concentrate on the way he made her feel.

Suddenly Kane pulled back, breathing hard as he rested his forehead against hers. His fingers flexed against the back of her skull, eliciting a moan from deep in her throat. His obvious struggle for control sent a thrill rushing through her. No one had responded to a simple kiss with her like that—certainly not someone as strong and single-minded as Kane.

For the first time, she heard Kane erupt into full-bodied, rolling laughter. Everything in her froze, almost waiting for the *gotcha* like an awkward high school girl lured under the bleachers, only to find herself the object of ridicule. Instead, Kane wiped a hand over his eyes, then gestured toward the windshield.

"Apparently my subconscious knows what I want, too."

Huh? Her gaze followed the light, and she blinked for a moment, then suppressed a smile. Illuminated in the glow of the headlights was the columned porch of Kane's house in town.

The walk into Kane's house wasn't nearly as uncomfortable as it was once she got inside. Presley wished she could go back to the mindless passion of moments ago, instead of feeling the self-conscious awareness that they were moving into territory that had never worked out for her the way it was depicted in romantic movies.

Kane secured the front door, then asked quietly as he removed her wrap, "Would you like a drink?"

"Yes. No."

Ugh.

Kane grinned at her. "Not sure, huh?"

"Well, yes, I feel the need for one, but not for a good reason. No, I don't want one, because then I might not be as in control as I need to be and..." She breathed in deep. "I'm rambling."

The way he studied her made her feel even more uncomfortable. Why did she have to be so socially awkward? Give her a room full of guys wanting to hear step-by-step instructions on how to bit train a horse, and she could give them exactly what they wanted. Give her one man in a room with passion on his mind, and she completely flaked out and failed to deliver.

This was her experience of womanhood...

Kane offered his trademark half grin and took her hand, leading her up the stairs that rose along the left side of the foyer. "Don't worry," he said. "I don't think you'll need alcohol to have a good time."

"I hope you feel the same later," she mumbled.

He didn't even hesitate but continued upward.

Please, please don't let him be disappointed.

Her heart pounded, and she felt as far from aroused as possible by the time they reached Kane's bedroom. She distracted herself by examining the surroundings: antique wooden floors, a tapestry of a hunting scene over the fireplace, the heavy mahogany bed frame and furniture against the creamy walls.

A small lamp from the hallway let her see inside, but

Kane didn't move to turn on any more lights. *Thank goodness.* Her stomach churned. Kane's presence surrounded her from behind. She could feel him finger individual strands of her hair and wanted so badly to close her eyes, to slip under his spell.

But she was afraid. This was one area where confidence in her job would not help her.

But then those big hands began to knead her shoulders, her neck, her scalp, and liquid sparkles melted into her blood. By the time he released the single clasp on the back of her dress, she was beyond protest.

The dress could only come off over her head, but that didn't seem to worry Kane. She felt the brush of him against her back, then warm palms pressed against her naked thighs. He traced up and over the curve of her hips, cupping them so his fingers cradled her hip bones. His fingers lay just inches from the part of her body that told her in no uncertain terms this was what she wanted.

Her body jerked involuntarily. Kane's hold tightened. Then, to her surprise, he guided her back against him. His thigh pressed firmly against that most intimate part of her, eliciting a rush of need. Presley didn't know whether to be grateful or regretful of the clothes still separating them. The urgency to feel Kane's skin, all over, grew with each touch.

But he made it clear he was running this show.

He guided her in a rocking motion until her breath was shallow and staggered. Then those wicked palms moved farther upward, taking her dress with them, until the only thing covering her most intimate parts was a thin, silky pair of panties.

The dress continued inching up her body, until the sheer momentum lifted her arms. Then it was over her head and her hair fell back around her shoulders. Kane didn't leave her time to be self-conscious.

One moment he was glued to her, then he was gone. Before she had time to think, he swept her up in his arms and strode to the bed. This was definitely new... He came down with her until Presley felt surrounded by the heat and musk of him. He buried his face against her neck.

Presley found herself staring at the darkened ceiling as the sensation of Kane's open mouth on her skin left a trail of fire. A sudden awareness of his clothes brushing over her bare skin flooded through her. Soft with just a touch of starch, the fabric of his shirt made every one of her nerve endings take notice. The knowledge that she lay beneath him in just bra and panties while he was fully clothed left her vulnerable, yet...not.

Closing her eyes, she concentrated on the sensations. She grabbed his upper arms, her fingers digging into the muscle as she pulled him closer.

"Yes, Presley," he groaned against her skin.

Suddenly she wanted to give him her all, not just lie there waiting on him.

She reached farther, burying her fists into the back of his shirt. Though she pulled against him, he didn't fall, but his body began to rock. She recognized the motion from earlier, but the full-on version was a whole different experience. A preview of exactly where they were headed. Kane's sucking kisses moved down her collarbone to her cleavage, causing her nipples to tighten in almost painful need.

Her grasping hands moved to his collar, then around to the buttons. But she wasn't dexterous enough for this particular exercise at the moment. No problem. Kane reared up to balance on his knees, then jerked his shirt open from collar to hem.

His urgency echoed her own, and a small part of her sighed in relief, finally letting go of the self-conscious worry that he was somehow only humoring her.

He didn't try for her bra clasp, but instead pulled the cups down to expose her shaking breasts. Her cries filled the dim room as he teased first one nipple then the other in a synchronized dance that brought them to taut red points. Presley snaked her hands between them until her fingers found his belt buckle.

Then Kane stilled. Presley's breath caught. Was he upset? Frustrated? She could feel the press of his hardness against the backs of her knuckles.

"Unzip me," he demanded.

Her sudden tension melted, and her fingers fumbled before finally achieving her goal. Kane's hand brushed hers away to complete the task of freeing himself. Watching Kane kneel between the vee of her legs to yank down his pants was gratifying in the extreme.

Eager and ready, Kane reached for Presley's panties. She expected him to yank them down or something. Instead his fingers slid around the edge, and Presley's world zeroed in on the feel of him brushing against her wetness. He bent close and breathed against her through the fabric. Presley's heart pounded hard; her hips lifted as her need spiked.

Then the rip came, and Presley's new panties were nothing but shredded fabric. Kane covered himself quickly. Then her. Nothing could have prepared her for the feel of his hardness pressing against her, into her. Presley reached for his hips without thought, only aching need. One hard pull of her hands, and he drove into her.

Her back arched. Her head strained back as everything within her tightened around him. Kane's deep, guttural groans filled her senses. Then his weight came down on her as he started to pump.

Time and space gave way to sensation. The heat of his body. The smell of musk and cologne. The rough texture of his skin against her inner thighs. The delicious pressure of his body inside hers.

Kane shifted up on his arms, and the change made Presley's world explode. She had a vague sense of the frantic working of his hips and a sudden pressure as he cried out. It was all wrapped up in the intense wonder of the moment as Kane collapsed into Presley's arms.

For a brief moment in time, everything was perfect in her world.

Ten

Kane didn't look in the mirror over his bathroom sink as he washed up. He focused instead on one task at a time. Wash his hands. Button up his shirt. Zip up his pants. Buckle his—ah, the belt was missing.

But he couldn't ignore the slight, almost imperceptible, shaking of his fingers.

He hadn't realized that, by encouraging Presley, he would unleash a tigress—not in a kinky way, but in the fierce way Presley made love. That intensity had reached a part of him Kane hadn't been prepared for her to touch.

I need a moment...just a moment more. The mantra was the only refrain in the stunned silence of his mind.

He would not think of Emily. Would not think about how this act, with this woman, far surpassed anything he had experienced before. How was that even possible?

I need a moment.

Far from ready, he stepped back into his bedroom, only to realize he might have been gone longer than he'd thought. Presley sat primly in the chair by the floor lamp, fully dressed. The small pool of light in the darkened room emphasized her isolation. At first glance, she looked exactly how she had when she'd come in here, but a closer look revealed the difference. The disheveled thickness of her hair. The slight twist at the waistband of her dress, giving it an off-kilter look. The shoes she had yet to slip onto her carefully placed feet.

"I need to go home."

The husky edge to her voice stirred him again, almost obliterating the actual words as he remembered her cries echoing in his ears. Then what she said truly registered.

Trying to keep things light, he asked, "Isn't that usually the man's line?"

Her eyes widened slightly, planting guilt in his heart for teasing her.

"I'm not really used to the protocol of these situations," she finally murmured.

Boy, he was an ass. But he'd been trying to ease her into being comfortable with their new, well, whatever this was. It certainly wasn't business. But it wasn't wholly pleasure, either, if their current strained conversation was any indication.

For a moment, Kane's fists clenched.

He hadn't intended things to go this far—though that was a lie if he thought long and hard about it. This woman held a unique attraction for him that he didn't understand and wasn't sure he was entirely comfortable with. In truth, he hadn't intended things to go this far *tonight*. But the sensations had quickly swept him away, like a river with category-four rapids.

He didn't realize he'd been staring until she reached up to smooth her hair back into place. When that didn't seem to work, she instinctively gathered it and put it back into its regular ponytail. Only she had no tie to hold it.

Without thought, he stepped to his chest of drawers. He took a ribbon from the valet box and extended it toward the woman who'd just rocked his world.

"Thank you," she murmured, then tied her hair back. She didn't ask where the ribbon was from.

Kane didn't offer.

Instead he knelt before her, resting his palms against her elbows. She had folded her arms over the front of her body, as if to protect herself from whatever came next. Her expression was carefully neutral. He could feel a slight tremble beneath his touch and wanted to smile. It reminded him of his own off-balance reaction just minutes earlier, but he kept his amusement to himself.

Instead he strove for a semiserious tone. "There isn't one particular protocol," he assured her. "Only whatever makes you the most comfortable."

Presley acknowledged him with a nod, but it was a few moments before she spoke. "I'm not really a stay-all-night kind of girl."

So why was he wishing she was? That she would spend the night in his arms and really reel him in? Which was exactly what he didn't need. Shouldn't want. Yet he couldn't deny his strongest inclination.

Except in the face of her own needs.

He wasn't the sharpest tool in the shed, but Presley knew what she needed right now. Kane would give it to her.

Guiding her back downstairs, he bundled her up into her wrap once more. The silence between them on the drive to her family home wasn't comfortable—Presley fiddled, squirmed just a little—but Kane found himself reluctant to break it.

He simply couldn't shut down the thoughts whirling in his brain enough to make intelligent conversation.

Like a sneaky teenager, he turned off the SUV's lights and kept down any unnecessary noise as he approached the house. Somehow he knew Presley was too fragile for another confrontation with her stepmother. What she probably needed right now was simply to be alone.

Oddly enough, he didn't resent that. Even though he wanted the complete opposite.

He pulled right up to the side door, so she wouldn't have far to walk to get inside. He knew she'd be even quicker to slip out of the vehicle than normal.

He finally found his words when she stood just inside the open door, blinking in the glare of the cab lights as she gathered her sparkly clutch from the floor. He just couldn't let her go without telling her.

"Presley…"

She froze, her gaze caught in the intensity of his as if she couldn't look away. He didn't want her to. She needed to see that he meant every word he said.

"Presley." He swallowed. "You were beautiful tonight. And I'm sure as hell not talking about your dress."

Kane stared at his hands gripping the steering wheel for long moments, shocked to realize he was second-guessing himself.

Normally, he'd never drop in on someone this early unannounced. But he knew enough about Presley to know she'd been up for a while and was probably already in the stables. Plus, this was a working racing establishment. More people than just Presley would be up and running.

This doubt was ridiculous.

He'd woken this morning with Presley on the brain—and his body had not been happy about his empty bed.

He was a grown man, unconcerned about appearing too eager. Besides, his interest would probably be the best thing for Presley to know. He'd made no mistake about wanting her, enjoying her, last night. He'd definitely like a repeat—a lot of repeats far into the future—regardless of contracts, agreements or money.

So get your ass out of the SUV and find her.

As soon as Kane opened the door, the sounds of early morning he'd heard every day of his adult life washed over him. Even though these weren't his stables, his horses, those sounds still brought peace, belonging and anticipation of a job he loved—no, not a job. A way of living.

Did Presley share those same feelings as she greeted her mornings?

Wow—philosophical Kane was getting damn touchy. Kane focused on the crunch of his boots on the gravel as he crossed to the already bustling barn. One of the hands on his way out held the door for him. The lowered light of the stables made Kane pause and blink to adjust.

Curious, he stepped to the stall that had been the focus of so much drama the other day and glanced inside.

The mare turned her head his way, curious about the new visitor. By way of greeting, he clicked his tongue softly; the sound caught her attention, and she neighed a quiet hello. This conversation of no words continued for several minutes before she deemed it safe enough to approach him.

"Hello, lovely girl," he crooned.

After a few strokes of her head and neck, she turned to nudge her lips against his palm.

"Sorry, girl. I came totally unprepared this morning."

That was probably an understatement. He had no idea what he would say to Presley, no idea what he would do. He'd simply woken with a need to be near her. So here he was.

"Ah, a cardinal sin when visiting the stables," Bennett said from his left. The stable manager stepped closer. "But then again, animals always think they're the reason you dropped by, so why wouldn't you bring a gift for them while you're at it."

He reached into his pocket and held a sugar cube out to Kane. They shared a grin, because they both knew Bennett spoke the truth, then Kane fed the treat to the mare. No sooner had she lifted it delicately from his palm and crunched a few times before she returned to search for more. Kane shook his head as her searching lips tickled his palm.

"Sorry, girl." He turned to Bennett. "She doing okay? No ill effects?"

Appreciation flashed in Bennett's expression. "Doesn't seem like it. Her usual handler came back from vacation two days later, and that settled her down pretty good."

Kane nodded. "I'm glad."

"You here to see Presley?" Bennett asked.

"If she's not busy."

"She's always busy, but if you're willing to wait her out, you might get somewhere." He gestured toward the inner recesses of the building. "I'll show you where to find her."

Kane steeled himself for any awkwardness. Her virtual sprint from his place last night concerned him. Knowing Presley, she'd probably done some second-guessing herself this morning—hell, all night—and he wanted to put her at ease.

Bennett took a left turn at the large cross aisle Kane remembered from before, then headed down to the open double doors at the end. Stepping back out into the bright morning sunlight left Kane blinking for a moment, then he noticed he was on the side of the stables where several training paddocks were set up. The white-painted railings looked neat and in good repair.

"Presley is down in the far paddock, where the jumps are set up."

A flash of heat engulfed Kane. His stomach turned. "Jumps?"

Bennett nodded. "She's working with a new horse, training him for shows for a client."

No matter how harshly Kane told himself this was a common activity for any horse owner, he could not bar the images that flooded his brain. Emily preparing herself and her horse for the approaching jump. Emily's eyes going wide the minute she realized something was very wrong. Emily's body twisting as she hit the hard ground in an unnatural position.

He sucked in a breath, drawing Bennett's attention. "You okay, Kane?"

From somewhere beyond his boiling emotions, Kane dug out a smile and a "sure thing."

Bennett seemed to buy it. "I'll let you walk on down, if you don't mind. I need to head back in."

Kane thought he said, "No problem," but he honestly wasn't sure. Bennett smiled, waved and went back the way they'd come, so Kane's response must have been adequate. He stood where he was, braced against the storm inside him, afraid the minute he relaxed he would either collapse or lose the contents of his stomach. And he wouldn't be able to explain away either.

He tried to think logically but couldn't at the moment. So he stood baking in the heat—outside and in his head— just trying to survive the next few minutes.

He could see the horse and rider making rounds in the paddock. Warming up, maybe? The jumps weren't that high. It was a standard early training setup. People jumped horses and went to competitions all the time. Kane had even attended a few since the accident and experienced no discomfort whatsoever. So why did he still feel like he was going to puke up the breakfast he'd wolfed down?

The horse paused, Presley holding him at rest. Would she be able to tell Kane was here if she looked this way? Suddenly the steel traps on his legs loosened. He walked to a nearby stand of trees, but the shade didn't give him any relief.

At least, not that he noticed.

The horse started forward again. *She's fine. Everything's fine.* The mantra didn't help. The approach to the first low jump was flawless, but Kane didn't stick around for the execution.

He didn't remember the walk back to his SUV. Didn't even remember much of the drive. He only remembered the grip of his hands around the steering wheel as the SUV took him as far away from Presley as possible.

Eleven

"So what did you do to ruin this relationship? Or are you the only woman in history who could make a deal that was purely business with that man?"

Presley stared at Marjorie, startled for a moment to have her own fears spoken out loud. "What?"

"Well, he hasn't been here since the party the other night. Maybe he's just tired of having to defend you everywhere he goes."

Her stepmother had been more than a little irritable since Kane's rebuke the other night. Presley had hoped she would get over it, but she'd apparently decided instead to take her ire out on Presley.

"Everything's fine. I'm sure he's just busy."

"So it *is* solely business."

Presley's cheeks started to burn as memories of their one night together rose in her mind. She did her best to push them away. The last thing she wanted was to think about that while Marjorie watched her for any clue as to what was really happening between her and Kane.

She hadn't talked to Marjorie about sex, even during puberty. She had no intention of starting now.

"I forgot something in the barn."

She turned on her heel, but Marjorie continued to speak behind her. "Presley, you come back here and tell me what's going on right now."

So you can tell all your friends and they can all smile sympathetically every time I walk into a room for the next six months?

Presley kept right on walking, all the way to her truck.

It had been three days since Kane had dropped her off that night. She hadn't expected him to rush right over, but a phone call, maybe…a text, even… Some acknowledgment of what had happened between them.

Nothing. Not a single word in three days. And call her old-fashioned, but an innately feminine part of her wanted Kane to make the first move. Somehow prove to her that he was still interested.

It looked as though she wasn't going to get her wish.

But they still had a contract, and as uncomfortable as this meeting might be, Presley needed to know if the deal was still on…or if she was going have to find the funds to pay the Harringtons what Marjorie owed in full. That could be a purely business conversation, right?

She was still wondering how the heck she would pull that off when she drove her truck into the circular driveway of his house in town. Part of her wondered if he would even be here. But it was the end of the day, and she'd figured there was a fifty-fifty chance that he'd finished his work at the Harrington stables. His SUV by the garage told her she'd guessed right.

As she climbed the front steps, the clip of her boots on the stone reminded her she was still in her work clothes. Great. She was just reinforcing the image of not being good enough, with dirty clothes and muddy boots and hay in her hair. This plan might have been poorly thought out.

But this was her. He could take it or leave it.

The thought brought a smirk to her lips, and she forced herself onward. Kane might not be interested in her as a bed partner after having tasted her once, but that didn't mean they couldn't still be business partners. She'd spent three days wondering if he'd renege on his contract. It was time to put the doubts to rest.

Kane didn't look surprised when he opened the door. Presley only hoped her expression was giving away as little as his. He didn't speak, simply stepped back and motioned her inside. *Not very promising.*

She stomped over the threshold but quickly caught herself once she realized what she was doing. Neither leaving a trail of tiny dirt clumps nor walking like a three-year-old having a tantrum would reflect well on her. But the more her nerves jangled, the more anger crept in.

Turning to face him across the foyer, she noticed that she'd crossed her arms over her middle but allowed herself the defensive gesture. She needed comfort, to say the least, as she jumped right in.

"Wanna tell me what's going on, Kane?"

"Hey, Presley."

His even response as he closed the door threatened to wiggle through all the defenses she was building. She did her best not to read anything into it as he gestured her into the living room. She got a quick impression of leather furniture complimenting the dark wood floors before she turned her focus back on him.

She refused to soften her tone as she asked, "Have you been okay, Kane? Sick?"

"No," he said with a shake of his head. "I wish I had that kind of excuse. But we both know I don't."

"I don't know anything. Care to enlighten me?"

Instead of giving her an excuse, any excuse, he started to pace. His own boots beat out a tattoo across the floorboards. The view of his strong back and tight rear made her mouth water. But the scowl on his face when he turned around was enough to make her look away.

Her heartbeat picked up speed like a train leaving the station. She had to face the fact that this wasn't about business, as much as she might wish it was. No, this was personal. Very personal.

Her arms squeezed even tighter over her chest, only giving the illusion of security. She averted her gaze, looking off toward the doorway, no longer able to handle Kane and his silence.

"I'm sorry, Kane," she finally said. "I'm sorry if you were disappointed the other night."

Her quiet words landed like a firecracker in the room. Kane jerked to a halt, finally showing one emotion. Shock. And something else, something darker that she couldn't make out.

He shook his head a few times. "Are we remembering the same night?" he asked. "Because from my viewpoint that isn't even an issue."

Presley blinked. How was that possible after the way he behaved? "Look, I'm used to guys not calling, so you don't have to feel bad. But I'm not usually under contract with them, so…"

"Not usually?" Kane asked, his brow rising.

How could one look make her feel like such a ditz? "Okay, never. Which is why we need to get this, um, figured out."

There, that was pretty close to businesslike.

But Kane still didn't answer. He squeezed his eyes closed and rubbed his hand against the back of his neck. Presley waited while her stomach churned, her mind tumbling through the possibilities of what he would say next.

Patience had never been her strong suit. "I just don't

want anything that happened between us personally to affect our contract. What we expect from each other."

"Why would it?"

Was he really this dense? Or just being difficult?

"I don't know, Kane," she suddenly exploded. Her breath came hard and fast as her emotions outstripped her control. "I have no idea why you're suddenly being an inconsiderate jerk, okay?"

She swallowed hard, but the feelings refused to be locked back up inside. Turning around, she rushed for the doorway, intent only on getting out of there before she did something stupid—like bursting into tears.

A firm grip on her arm whirled her back around. In seconds Kane was hard against her with the wall at her back. And all her anger detonated into a white-hot passion inside her.

His lips met hers as if he felt it, too. No polite inquiry or gentleness here. He insisted she open for him, then conquered every inch of the territory within. Need spiked as his tongue met hers.

He pressed closer, his hips grinding against her. If she'd thought their one night together was all they had, his body told a whole different story. Her groans echoed in her ears. She clutched at his arms, desperation shoving aside everything but desire. Kane reluctantly pulled away from her lips, only to dive for the vulnerable length of her neck.

His ragged breathing hitched as he nuzzled, suckled and nipped at her skin. Presley rose on her toes, eager for more.

Luckily Kane didn't settle. His hands fumbled at her shirt, jerking it from her waistband, then up over her head.

She didn't have time to think about bare skin in daylight or what bra she had on. Kane stripped her of it soon enough.

His hands kneading her breasts made everything in her tighten, her body aching for Kane's rough passion.

Her nipples tingled in anticipation and were rewarded when Kane drew first one, then the other into his mouth. Presley's head fell back against the wall, her hands buried in Kane's hair.

Only in these moments could she forget her own hangups and just let herself feel.

With a grunt, Kane's hands moved to the button on her jeans. Relief flooded through her when he finally got the fly open and started to wriggle them down her hips.

She wanted to cry when he paused. Then he stepped back, allowing cool air to drift over her skin. He glanced down, then back up to meet her wide-eyed gaze.

To her pride, he looked a little dazed as he gave her a half grin. "I don't think this is gonna work," he murmured.

"What?" Her question was slightly slurred.

Kane glanced back down. So did she—only to see their boots.

Yep. That would make getting out of her pants a bit of a challenge.

Instead of stepping away or letting her go, Kane pressed close once more. He spoke against her ear, reviving the goose bumps across her skin. "If I haven't made myself clear, I have no problem with you or what happened the other night. Got it?"

"Then why the hell didn't you call?" she mumbled.

"We'll get to that. Just don't ever think that I don't want you, Presley. Ever."

Seriously? She found herself pushing him back, even though the move exposed far more than she was comfortable with. "What else am I supposed to think, Kane? It's been three days. Three days without a word."

In true male fashion, Kane glanced down but then met

her gaze once more. "That's because I'm a jerk. Nothing to do with you. Got it?"

She shook her head. Because she didn't get it. She didn't understand. "That's not good enough. Tell me why."

He took a deep breath, then turned away. "That's a very good question."

Kane didn't look back as he heard Presley scramble for her clothes. The least he could do was give her a chance to make herself decent after he'd almost stripped her bare.

The pull was strong, the desire to return to the heat of her skin and the eager passion she gave him when he touched her.

But he couldn't. Not now.

Just the thought of what he had to tell her killed the desire racing through his body like a fire extinguisher putting out a flame. But if he wanted to undo the damage he'd inflicted on Presley, on her self-esteem, he had to own up to why he'd stayed away. She deserved his honesty.

Which totally sucked.

Kane didn't like talking about Emily. He didn't even talk about her with Mason, who'd been there through every stage of the relationship. Discovery, bliss, tragedy and absolute rejection. Could Kane make his actions toward Presley understood without having to reveal all the nitty-gritty details about Emily?

He hoped so.

Finally the sounds behind him stopped. Kane turned to face his punishment. "I did come by, actually."

Presley tilted her head to the side, wisps of hair that had come loose from her inevitable ponytail dancing around her head. "What? When?"

"The next morning."

He could see her try to think back, probably searching

for what she'd done that morning and how it could have run him off. There was no point in speculating, but she didn't know that yet.

"Bennett led me through the stables out to the paddock where you were training."

Recognition dawned in those pretty green eyes, but no understanding. *He* didn't even understand his extreme re-action himself.

"You were working on jumps and I—" Kane paused as his throat closed. In his mind, he cursed. Why the hell couldn't he keep it together?

"Yes," she said slowly. "Black Jack's just started."

The jumps were low. There was nothing dangerous about what she'd been doing. Nothing upsetting. He could almost hear her think, *what's the big deal?*

"I was engaged once."

His words sounded too loud in the room, as if they echoed off the hardwood floors and walls. Her green eyes flared. She sucked in a deep breath. "I know."

"You knew that?" he asked, delaying the inevitable.

Her nod was cautious. "I just heard Mason mention that you'd had a fiancée the other night. That's it."

"What kind of lover are you?" he asked, trying to lighten the mood. "Not even a single internet search?"

Her cheeks turned a delicate pink that entranced him. "Well, I didn't have much to go on."

At least she was honest. "I wouldn't have blamed you if you had. But anyway…" Where should he start? How much should he say? "It was a few years ago and we were together—" More years than he cared to remember.

"She was an accomplished rider. We had big plans. Emily loved horses as much as I did."

A movement brought his gaze back to Presley, even though he hadn't realized he'd looked away. Tentative steps brought her closer, though her arms were still wrapped around her waist. She hadn't bothered to tuck in her shirt, but everything else seemed to be in place.

"We were at a competition when it happened. Something went wrong with the jump. I'm still not sure what. It surprised her, too, and she couldn't recover properly."

"Oh, Kane," Presley said, shaking her head as if in denial. She'd been around animals long enough she probably didn't need more details. Just the important one. "But she lived?"

He nodded. "Permanently paralyzed from the waist down."

Ignoring Presley's gasp, he forced himself to go on. "But she no longer wanted anything to do with me or the dreams we had together. She moved to a city where she never had to see another horse. Got a job. Married a man. Built a new life. And I don't blame her one bit."

Liar.

"So my jumping upset you?" Presley asked, confusion in her tone.

"I don't know why," Kane said with a shrug. "I'm around animals a lot. Been to plenty of competitions since then. Shouldn't be a problem." He met her gaze head on. "Won't be a problem."

She wanted to say something. He could tell. But she shook her head, then suddenly changed tack. "So we're good?" she asked.

Kane switched gears immediately, grateful to leave the subject of his stupid behavior and broken engagement far behind. He stalked toward her, enjoying the sensation of control as her eyes widened. "No."

Presley blinked. "No?"

"I think it's a little soon to be good."

She wasn't following, so he gave her a demonstration. First he swooped her up into his arms, then dropped her onto the leather couch. Her cry quickly turned into a giggle. Then she gasped as he straddled one of her legs, bringing his thigh high between hers. "Kane," she said, breathless, "I came straight from the stables. I'm dirty."

He leaned in close, bracing his palms on the smooth surface on each side of her head. The urge to imprint himself on her was overwhelming, but he maintained just a few inches of distance. "Let's get this straight," he said, bending his elbows so he could bring his mouth to her skin. "I spend regular parts of my day getting sweaty and dirty."

He grinned as she sighed from the sensations of having him this close.

"I find you fascinating, Presley. I told you before, it's not about the dress."

His hips dipped briefly to press into the cradle of hers. "I like you messy. I like you clean. I like you fancy. I'll take you however I can get you."

"Yes," she moaned, arching to press his lips harder against her.

He nibbled his way up to her earlobe. After giving the soft flesh a firm nip, he whispered in her ear. "And right now, I have only one thing on my mind."

"What's that?"

"Getting you out of these boots."

Twelve

"Are you using this trip to force me to stay the night?" Presley asked as she looked around their elaborate suite in the boutique hotel Kane had chosen in Louisville.

The question was a little tongue in cheek, but her nerves were very real. This would be her first night to stay in Kane's arms. Her first time to wake up with him. Was she crazy?

To hide the jitteriness invading her limbs, she strode over to the balcony doors. Each room had its own individual balcony with side walls made of wrought-iron covered in clinging ivy. Gorgeous.

"Hey, whatever works," Kane said from directly behind her.

With a natural ease that still discomfited her, Kane slipped his arms around her and pressed his lips against her temple. Affection came as naturally to him as sex—something she hadn't expected.

"Men are devious about getting their way," he added, amusement in his voice.

And for some reason, this was something he wanted. Not in a pushy way, but he'd asked her every night they were together to stay. She never did. There were no demands, no fuss. But the question came like clockwork.

"What devious men want is rarely the best for everyone involved," she quipped, then automatically wished she could take the words back. They were too revealing for her comfort.

Her instincts told her that sleeping beside him all night would be the end of her ability to stay detached. Thus the nerves that had her eyeing the king-size bed with something akin to fear, mixed with an excitement she couldn't deny.

Honestly, was her current state really, truly detached? No...but it was comforting to delude herself.

When he wrapped his arms around her, it chipped away at her resolve, as did his low whistle when she came out of the dressing room a little later. She was wearing the very dress that had made her stare into the dressing room mirror weeks ago. The deep jewel-blue, silky material, and flowing length made her feel special, especially when Kane complimented her. Every sexy, whispered word of praise made her ache to dive in headfirst and not think about later. Why did she have to be such a practical kind of girl?

She tried to put practicalities aside and enjoy the luxury of the limo that took them to their first event in Louisville—the annual dinner put on by the American Horse Racing Society to kick off the festivities leading up to the Kentucky Derby race.

She savored his hand at the small of her back. The assurance that this dress— her breakthrough dress, she often called it —actually looked and felt good on her.

As the dinner got into full swing, she tried to loosen up enough to consider tonight magical, even if the thought made her practical, party-hating self choke a little on her champagne.

To her surprise, it was magical for a couple of hours. With Kane at her side, they chatted with her friends whom he'd already met. She introduced him around to acquaintances in the business. They even sat with Justine Simone during the meal.

But the magic ended the minute she stepped out of a stall in the ladies' room to find Joan applying lipstick at the mirror.

"Oh," Presley said, "I didn't even realize you were here."

Judging from the frown that appeared on the other woman's face, that wasn't the right choice of words.

"I'm not surprised," Joan said with an exasperated drawl.

"Um, excuse me?"

"Mooning like a cow is not becoming—or ladylike. But we both know that's not one of your strong suits."

Presley stood for a moment, perplexed. Joan hadn't been this direct in her attacks since they were teenagers. Teenage girls weren't subtle; they didn't hold anything back. Oddly, the words didn't upset Presley, but only confused her.

Her body made up her mind for her, and she automatically moved forward to wash her hands. Whatever was stuck in Joan's craw would just have to stay there. Presley wasn't in the mood.

Ignoring the woman watching her, she carefully straightened her dress, making sure no part of it had gotten tucked into her underwear by accident. Then she reached into the little clutch she carried and retrieved a new lip gloss—praying the whole time someone else would come in and break up the tension.

No such luck.

As Joan continued to stare, a flush of anger ignited in Presley's core. Joan and her like had always made Presley feel ashamed, as though she were less than them. Not today. Somehow her self-esteem had gotten Kane's message.

Apparently her application of the lip gloss was the catalyst to break Joan's silence.

"Makeup? Really, Presley?" Joan shifted to rest against the counter as if taking up a front row seat. "The girl who has always gone au naturel is wearing makeup for a man?"

Presley studied the mirror. Most women wouldn't even consider what she wore now as true makeup. Some powder, lip gloss and eye shadow, applied using the very basic technique she'd managed to master. That was all. She smiled, watching her barely red lips move in the mirror. But beneath the smile was something very, very different.

"And that dress," Joan continued. "Are you seriously attracting a man with that?"

"Everyone else likes it."

"They're just being polite."

Kane picked it out.

Joan wasn't finished. "It's embarrassing how hard you're trying—only to fail so publicly."

Presley watched her own brows rise in the mirror, as if her reflection were questioning this new accusation. "Fail?" Presley could only be proud that her tone and expression were calm, since her insides were anything but.

Joan shook her head from side to side, as if in pity. "Kane could have simply paid you for your expertise, if that's what he was after. It seems to be the only thing other men want from you. But he is a man, after all… They're gonna take what's on offer, if it's free."

Presley's breath caught hard in her chest.

"Until something better comes along," Joan added with an arch smile.

I don't think so. "And that something is you?"

The fake shock Joan adopted wasn't fooling Presley. "Well," Joan said, drawing the word out as if she were reluctant to continue, "I don't see why not."

"Right. Because you have so much to offer, I guess?"

Now Joan turned to the mirror to straighten her own dress. The preening nauseated Presley.

"Honestly, I don't see much on offer besides a pretty face and stylish clothes. The problem is there's not a single original thought in your head."

"What?" Joan gasped, her expression more shocked than it should be. She probably hadn't been prepared for Presley to fight back.

"I didn't stutter," Presley said, her tone only a little shaky.

"Look here, you—"

Presley stepped forward. "No, you listen." She straightened her posture a notch, using her extra inch over Joan to her advantage. "I've put up with a lot over the years. I've ignored, pouted and, yes, even cried a few times."

She pressed a little closer, which caused Joan's eyes to widen.

"But we aren't children anymore, Joan. And I don't have to put up with the manure you're shoveling. Do not talk to me again, or I will not hesitate to make your life as miserable as you've made mine in the past."

Presley didn't wait for an answer. She swung toward the exit and kept walking. Only when she'd pulled back the door did Joan shout, "You won't win."

"I already have."

"He won't stay long."

This time, Presley looked back, giving Joan her full attention. "See, that's how silly you are. That doesn't matter. This isn't about Kane."

"Yes—"

"It's about you and me, Joan. And at the end of the day, you still have to live with yourself. But I don't." She stepped forward, letting the door go so it could slowly swing shut. But the last word was still hers as she caught Kane's gaze on her from a few feet away. "So, yeah, I win."

Kane smiled slightly at Presley's words, though they obviously weren't spoken to him. The door to the ladies' room slid silently shut as she walked straight to him and took his arm, her expression calm and almost triumphant. He glanced back over her shoulder, catching a glimpse of Joan storming out the door to glare at them.

Or, rather, Presley.

But she never looked back, and Kane was damn proud of her. He didn't know what had transpired in there, but Presley had obviously come out on top. He took a couple of steps to meet her.

"Did you put someone in her place?" he murmured.

Presley paused in her forward push and blinked at him. He could see her register her surroundings for the first time.

He couldn't help but tease. "Well, she seemed to have all her hair. You must not have tried hard enough."

That brought her up short. "I wouldn't resort to hair pulling."

Kane grinned. "Sometimes they deserve it."

"I'm fine just using words," she said, but she did match his smile with a sheepish version of her own.

"That's my girl. Let's go."

"Already?" she asked.

He bent close to her ear as he took her arm. "You deserve a reward."

But as he turned toward the door, their plans were interrupted.

"Great to see you again, young lady," the man Kane had been speaking with said as Presley came so close she almost settled against him.

"Mr. Stephens," she exclaimed, moving away long enough to give the graying man a hug. "I didn't see you earlier."

"Oh, we arrived a bit late," the man said. "A little car trouble on the way, but we finally made it."

"That's good. Kane, have you met Mr. Stephens? He was my original trainer, but has been a friend of the family for many, many years."

"Oh, yes," Stephens said as he shook Kane's hand. "So wonderful to meet the newest celebrity in our little club."

Kane watched as the two shared a look that spoke volumes he wasn't privy to—and found himself surprised by the sudden questions peppering his brain.

"So how's the training going?" Mr. Stephens asked Presley. "That new young'un getting a hang of things?"

A cold sensation seeped into Kane's chest. He knew exactly what kind of training Stephens was referring to.

"Yes," she said, enthusiasm coloring her voice. "Just a little more work and I think we will lick that hitch. Once he gets some maturity on him, he'll be a champion jumper. Your jockey will be thrilled."

Stephens turned to Kane with a beaming glow. "She's one of the best students I ever worked with. All those trophies aren't just for show."

Kane forced a smile, though his feelings were already in deep freeze. He'd gone out of his way not to mention Presley's jumping practices again. Sometimes he could almost convince himself that they didn't happen. And he was okay with that, for now. After all, he wasn't delusional enough to think the issue wouldn't come up at some point…far in the future.

They talked about the gelding's finer points and what Presley was doing to correct his approach. Kane let the words swirl around him, let the confusion and remembered

pain melt away as they moved on to other subjects, let himself admire the confident woman who stood by his side.

By the time they left Stephens, Kane was more than
ready to cut their evening short. Presley didn't protest as he
led her to the lobby and called for the limo. They'd barely
made it inside before Kane took her lips with his, an unmistakable need rising like a tide inside him. However long
he had her, he would make it the best time they'd ever had.

Her lips were soft, but the grip of her hands was strong.
She pulled him closer, her eagerness leaving him gasping.
The dark taste of the wine she'd drunk at the party and the
delicate smell of honeysuckle intoxicated him.

He buried his face in the crook of her neck, breathing
deep, then licked along the ridge of her collarbone, taking in her flavor. Her gasps played on the air like music.
Kane pulled her close, struggling for control. How much
longer was it to the hotel?

He was proud he didn't drag her through the lobby to
the elevator at high speed. The instinct was there, but he
controlled himself. Barely. No need to spoil the surprise.

They came through the door to a darkened room, only
a couple of lamps casting a dim glow. Her shy smile as
he led her to the balcony doors intrigued him, urged him
to push this further than she might be comfortable with.

He led her through the door the staff had left open to
find the soft glow of electric candles on the small table
outside. The ivy created a sense of a walled-in space, iso-
lating them from the city around them, darkening the area
to a level of intimacy that heightened Kane's senses.

Presley stepped toward the table for two. "What's this?"
she asked, surprise lightening her tone.

Kane didn't even have to look. More champagne. Slices
of decadent coconut cake. "Your favorite," he said simply.

She glanced back at him, but he couldn't make out her

expression in the dark. When she spoke, her voice had grown husky. "What if I had eaten dessert already?"

"You didn't," he said, stepping closer. "Chocolate cake doesn't seem to appeal to you."

"You noticed?"

"I notice everything about you, Presley." *Even the things I don't want to see because they worry me.*

He lifted a bite to her lips, the candlelight glinting off the silver fork. Over and over he fed her, appeasing her hunger more important to him than feeding his own.

"You're spoiling me," she murmured between bites.

"Good. Someone should."

Suddenly the night flared to life, sparkling lights and the popping of fireworks filling the sky. Presley turned to look, giving Kane a brief glimpse of her profile. He switched the candles off and led Presley to the rail, abandoning their dessert. She gripped the support, face lifted for the famous fireworks show preceding the Kentucky Derby.

Kane was much more interested in creating some fireworks of their own.

The thickness of her hair as he pulled it to the side made him anticipate seeing it spread across a pillow in the early hours of the morning. He tasted the light sheen of salt on her skin as he kissed the back of her neck. He stood close enough to feel the shiver that traveled down her spine at his touch.

It was more intoxicating than the champagne. Hell, it was more intoxicating than a good bottle of scotch.

He sucked lightly, moving to the sensitive junction where her neck met her shoulders. She arched back into him. Her softness molding to his hardness made him groan. He heard a slight huff of air, as if she were smothering a laugh, and decided he'd be happy to make her pay for her amusement.

Pressing closer, he used his body to bend her toward the rail. She didn't protest. Her breath sped up as his hands found her hips. Slow and sure, he let his palms follow the silky-soft material down the outsides of her thighs. Then he bunched it up so he could slip beneath the hem and indulge his desire to feel skin against skin.

"What are you doing?" she murmured, turning to watch him over her shoulder. Her voice only conveyed a hint of dismay, far less than what he'd been expecting.

He couldn't help but chuckle. "What do you think?" He lifted back up to align his body close against hers, whispering in her ear. "Trust me."

Trust me?

Presley wasn't so sure about that, but Kane's touch convinced her to leave the worry to him. Though she knew no one could see them, her brain automatically equated outside with being in public, Kane didn't seem to care.

Pretty soon, his mouth and hands convinced her she didn't care, either.

She tried to breathe, tried to hold on to her sanity, but it simply wasn't happening. His hands roamed her thighs, massaging the muscles in a way that made her want to turn into jelly. Her heels made her the perfect height, so she fit neatly against his body. He was aroused. He wanted her.

And she wanted this.

She didn't protest when she felt the cool night air against the backs of her thighs. The front of her dress still fell straight from her waist, which calmed her irrational fears of being seen. His hands briefly clasped her hips, as if positioning her for his pleasure. She had to press her lips together to hold back the moan that ached to escape.

The fireworks continued in the distance, but Presley hardly even saw them. Her focus turned inward to the need buffeting her body. Behind her she heard the rasp of a zipper, the rustle of clothing, the rip of the little foil packet.

Kane nudged the inside of her ankle, spreading her legs a little wider, leaving her exposed. One of his hands meandered around the front, sliding beneath the scrap of lace between her thighs. The throb of her core deepened. She panted through the need to beg.

Back and forth his fingers played, leaving her aching and wet. Without thought, she shifted, tilting herself back in invitation. Taking advantage, Kane fitted himself against her and slid home. Everything inside Presley tightened, desperate to keep him with her.

"Yes," he hissed, giving her little nub a flick with his fingers as a reward.

This time she couldn't cut her cry off before it escaped. It was followed quickly by Kane's groan of satisfaction. Ever so slowly, he withdrew. Then he returned at the same pace, allowing her to feel every inch of delicious fullness. She expected him to pick up the pace, but he didn't. For what seemed like an eternity, he played with her. The push forward filled her and also bumped her against his hand. The increase in pressure sent ecstasy coursing along her nerves, but never quite enough to send her over the edge.

The pullback shot her need higher, the glide eliciting a whimper just short of begging. But Kane wasn't in the mood to hurry, it seemed. Instead of speed, he added force, taking her up on her toes with each thrust. She tracked his climb by the harsh tempo of his breath with the intimate recognition only a lover would have—a fact that added to her awe.

Then all thought was lost. Waves of pleasure rolled over her body, crashing deep inside just as the crescendo of fireworks exploded before her eyes. Her cry was lost in the roar of the explosion and the distant applause of the crowd across the city. One thrust, two, then Kane joined her, pressing himself deep inside her and holding hard as his body gained release. She soaked in his groan, the tight grip of his hands.

As she stared out into the night, she knew that everything had changed. *She* had changed. The barriers were gone, leaving her heart exposed. It was his for the taking.

She had a feeling she'd never get it back.

Thirteen

Presley walked through the beginning half of Derby Day feeling off kilter, as if she were on a cruise and couldn't find her sea legs.

It wasn't a physical sensation, though. Her body moved with a languid ease that she'd never experienced before but could definitely attribute to Kane's TLC. If last night hadn't been satisfying enough, the way he'd woken her up this morning definitely finished the job.

She'd thought she was dreaming as dawn crept into the room. A slow coming to consciousness prompted by the smooth glide of warm skin against her own. Kane's leisurely, silent loving this morning, being surrounded by his scent, only made her crave him more. His touch had lit a fire inside her that pushed all sleepiness aside, replacing it with white-hot need. A need Kane had more than met.

No, the problem this morning was definitely a mental game.

She'd been afraid to stay with Kane overnight, and her fears had been justified. Despite knowing this was a business arrangement, she'd managed to fall hook, line and sinker for the gentleman behind the contract. A man who seemed to have no interest in making this a long-term arrangement.

He was kind, attentive, sexy—and completely closemouthed about anything to do with his emotions or history beyond business. He'd never again mentioned his ex-fiancée, nor Presley's training pursuits, even though she secretly wished his comments meant he was interested in her personally.

No such luck. The only true depth of emotion they experienced was in bed.

"Mint julep, ma'am?" a meandering waiter asked, balancing his tray of gorgeous cut-glass tumblers. Though it wasn't even noon, she eagerly reached for one, hoping it might calm her nerves. She sipped the signature concoction while she and Kane waited for lunch to be served in Millionaires Row.

Kane eyed her drink, then let his gaze drift over the sea of hats and fancy clothes surrounding them. "Pretty impressive," he murmured.

So was he. The white suit and pale purple shirt and tie set off his dark good looks in a mouthwatering way.

"You've never been here for Derby Day?" she asked instead of giving voice to her appreciative thoughts.

"Definitely not like this," he said, surveying the room a second time.

The announcement that lunch was about to be served produced a surge of three hundred guests toward the doors to the dining area. Kane took her arm.

"I've only witnessed the race in person once, though we watched it every year on television," he continued as they headed in to lunch. "My father brought us here the year after my mother died. We were in the infield with a picnic from a fast food chicken place. But we each got brand-new dress clothes for the occasion and stayed in a

run-down motel across town—the only rooms available
that Dad could afford."

His smile took Presley's breath away as he went on.
"We didn't care. We were at the derby. I remember every
moment of that weekend."

Presley swallowed hard against the lump in her throat.
"You're amazing, you know?"

Kane settled her into her seat, then pulled his own chair
out. He removed his suit jacket and sat down beside her.
As their dining table slowly filled, he leaned close, so their
heads were almost touching. "How so?"

"It takes a special kind of person not to be resentful of
that, heck, of everything that happened to your family,"
she said, holding his dark gaze for the first time today.

Kane smirked, though the look in his eyes remained
somber. "I think Mason has proven that revenge only back-
fires."

Presley thought back to the rumors surrounding Mason
and EvaMarie's reunion romance. "Guess so."

Kane frowned at his water glass. "There are still times
I don't understand why my father did what he did. Why
didn't he use the money from my mother to make life easier on himself?"

"Did he ever give you a reason?"

Kane's smirk grew into a grin. "Besides honoring my
mother's wish that the money be used for us boys? His
only other answer was pride."

Presley lowered her voice as the seats around them
filled. "What? Why?"

Kane leaned a little closer. "Since he moved back to
her hometown to finish raising us, he didn't want her
parents and people in that town accusing him of being
a gold digger, just as they had when he'd married her.
He knew that if he suddenly had money to spare, they'd

gossip, and that gossip would eventually get back to Mason and me."

Kane absently fingered one of the loose strands of her hair. She knew he loved it down, so today she'd worn it with just a simple turquoise fascinator with feathers and ribbon pinned to one side, instead of the traditional hat worn by most of the ladies in attendance.

"I'm sure he would have withdrawn some funds if he'd needed it to feed us," Kane continued, "but once he was working again, our situation wasn't dire. Things became easier, and he really just left the money where it was and forgot about it for long periods of time."

Flash. Flash.

Presley squinted as an unexpected flare of light surprised her. She glanced across the table as Kane turned in the direction of the light. A grinning man with a camera covering half his face snapped another picture. Presley eased closer to Kane as a wave of unease swept through her.

"Gorgeous couple," the man said as he lowered the camera. "Bernie with the *Louisville Scene.*"

He strode around the table to shake Kane's hand. "I recognized you right away, Mr. Harrington. I've been following the opening of the Harrington stables since the big announcement a couple of months ago."

"That's very flattering," Kane said.

"News isn't what gets hits anymore," Bernie said. "In this digital era, we've gotta reel 'em in, and stories like yours are just the ticket. Working man turned billionaire overnight. Who wouldn't want to see themselves in that story?"

Presley noticed the other occupants of their table blatantly watching and listening to the overeager photographer. She felt herself blushing.

"Let's get a few more of you with your lovely date. What's your name, sweetheart?"

Kane glanced her way, his smile stiff this time. "Presley?"

"Yes?"

It took a moment before she noticed his gaze pointedly slip from hers to her hand curved around his upper arm. Her fingernails were digging into the fabric of his shirt. She immediately released him and drew in a subtle breath. It was as if the muscles in her hand had stiffened into a permanent position, but after a few seconds of concentration, she was able to relax them.

"Presley?" Bernie's voice boomed loud enough now to catch the attention of people at other tables in their general vicinity. "That's an unusual name. I've only known one woman with that name, and I seriously wanted to give that woman the name of a beauty consultant. Sad, really."

As he grinned at her expectantly, Presley wanted to crawl under the table and disappear.

Kane stood, holding his hand out to her. As much as she didn't want her picture splattered all over the internet, maybe if they got this over with quickly, the photographer would go bother someone else. To her surprise, Kane unobtrusively positioned her at his side, using a heavy palm against her back. Then he reached around and flipped her hair forward over her shoulder before briefly catching her chin with his fingers.

"Just smile pretty," he murmured.

A few flashes later and Presley wanted to collapse back into her seat, feeling like a baby for making a big deal out of nothing. But the churning of her stomach and burning of her cheeks took a while to subside.

Kane shook the man's hand again, and Bernie turned to go. *Free!* But she had a sinking feeling she'd celebrated too soon as he pivoted back toward them after a few steps.

"Miss, I didn't get your full name for the caption," he said, smiling in a way that should have set her at ease, but didn't.

"Presley Macarthur," Kane supplied.

Bernie paused, his pen hovering over his little notebook, staring at her with his mouth agape. "No. You can't be Presley Macarthur."

Presley braced herself for what she could see coming. Not an apology for what he'd said earlier. Only more insults. "Why not?"

"You don't look anything like her—um, yourself." He glanced up and down, studying her as if trying to find something. "I mean, I've seen her—you—at lots of races. You look beautiful. Before you were…"

"Careful." Kane's voice had gone guttural.

Bernie glanced at him with wide eyes. "Right. Must be going. Lots of people to get on camera."

Kane shifted as if to return to the table, but Presley couldn't move. He stepped close for a moment. "Just ignore him," he said, solely for her ears.

Luckily the noise level in the room was higher now that the tables were full of hungry partygoers. It gave Presley a sense of protection, of privacy.

Still she found herself staring blankly over Kane's shoulder. "Do you think everyone is talking about me like that?"

She didn't want to sound like a whiny child seeking attention, but she was very afraid that was how she came off. Except it hadn't occurred to her that the changes she'd made would put her at the mercy of people like Bernie, people she felt compelled to be polite to, even though they didn't play by the same rules.

Once more Kane nudged her chin with his fingers until she looked up to meet his gaze. "If they can't see how beautiful you are, how beautiful, smart and talented you've always been…you don't need 'em."

And she didn't. But she was afraid she might need Kane for a long, long time to come.

After the whirlwind of derby weekend, Kane desperately wanted to relax. He didn't mind people. But there was too much of a good thing. His body needed rest; his eyes needed tranquil green; his ears needed nature.

He knew Presley felt the same. Just remembering her face when the photographer had questioned her made Kane ache. By the end of the weekend, she'd been more than anxious to get home.

So much for spending the night.

Such a strong woman shouldn't be made to feel low by a reporter's thoughtless words. While Kane was glad he'd helped her show her true beauty to the world, he understood better now why she'd never taken that step on her own.

He'd watched the *Louisville Scene* website to make sure no derogatory remarks were posted. Though the pictures did appear and correctly identified them both, nothing else was said.

Good thing, for Bernie's sake.

But now Kane had an inexplicable need to spend time with Presley out of the spotlight. It was dangerous—just as dangerous as sleeping beside her each night. But he couldn't seem to stop himself.

He didn't even want to try…

Kane watched her approach the barn across the drive, his mouth watering at the faithful lie of her jeans over shapely hips. And those boots…

"What's in the bag?" he asked, desperate to distract himself.

Her grin was a little shy, a little sly. "My contribution to the picnic."

Kane peeked inside, and the heavenly aroma of fried chicken greeted him.

"It's not fast food," she offered, "but I hope you still like it."

Their eyes met, forming an almost tangible connection between them that set off warning bells in the logical part of Kane's brain. He shouldn't be this close. Shouldn't be this invested. It could lead to him taking over, stepping in where she didn't want—or need—him to go. Only he couldn't look away.

Her murmur was a little breathless. "Sounded like it was your favorite picnic food."

"Yes, ma'am." The obvious enjoyment in his tone made her smile even bigger.

"Then I suggest we get going before the food gets cold," she said.

He led her inside, where EvaMarie and Mason were already saddling their own horses. He and his brother had added more than a few horses since taking over the stable. For tonight's ride, Kane had chosen a mare with spirit that he knew Presley would appreciate. Nothing docile for her, but not enough of a challenge to make their ride hard work.

The goal was to relax, after all.

The four of them headed out the west side of the stables and along a well-worn path. The world around them was fresh with young leaves filling in the once empty spaces from winter. Kane soaked in the fresh air, still comfortably cool, and the sight of Presley swaying in her saddle in front of him.

As they arrived at a small clearing with a stream running through it, Presley exclaimed, "How pretty! I didn't realize y'all had water on the property."

"It starts at a spring up that hill," Mason explained "Nice, huh?"

"If we had a spot this nice on our property, I'd never want to leave," Presley said.

"Oh, we don't, either," Mason said, winking over at EvaMarie.

Though he'd been teasing his fiancée, Mason was right They didn't want to leave. And the day was just right for a picnic. The chicken went perfectly with the rest of the food EvaMarie had packed. They dipped their bare toes in the ice-cold water before indulging in dessert. Then they lay on blankets to stare up at the fluffy white clouds in the blue spring sky. It was peaceful. Kane hadn't felt this happy in a while—at least, outside Presley's arms.

Kane wasn't ready to end it and face reality, but work still had to be done. He and Presley were going to an event this weekend and a house party in a couple of weeks, so he needed to get ahead.

"This is where we used to have to run," Mason said as they rounded a curve near the end of their return trip "since we were always cutting it close to your curfew. Re member, EvaMarie?"

"Lord, do I?" his fiancée confirmed. Her laughter sub sided quickly. "Funny now, but I sure was scared Daddy would tan my hide if he found me gone, much less with you."

Things had turned out so well for his brother that Kane often forgot for long stretches that EvaMarie and Mason had dated when they were teenagers, leading to a very bitter breakup. Seeing them happy now, after many years apart, could almost make a man believe in destiny.

Almost.

"It usually became a race to see who could reach the

edge of the woods first, without bursting from the tree line for everyone to see and hear," Mason explained to Presley.

"I won most often," EvaMarie bragged.

But Mason wasn't having it. "You did not."

"Yes, I did. I know these woods and this trail better than anyone," She glanced in Mason's direction with a brow raised in challenge. "Even you."

"Oh, really?"

Kane could see the slight tightening of Mason's hands on his reins. It was on now.

"Let's see about that," Mason yelled, then urged his horse to a full gallop.

EvaMarie gasped while Presley laughed. Both women pushed their horses to follow. Kane joined the chase, too.

Exhilaration flooded Kane's body. There was nothing like riding a horse at a full run. He and the animal moved as one, which wasn't surprising, since they'd done this many times in the past. He noticed Presley moving in tune with her horse, too. She was a natural horsewoman.

Kane had almost caught up with the others when he noticed they were approaching a part of the path that narrowed before opening onto the field near the stables. The three horses before him continued full throttle. His heart skipped a beat, fear taking over. The bottleneck wouldn't allow all three to pass. None of them seemed to be slowing down. Did Presley remember the narrow part from the ride out here?

Maybe not. She seemed to be urging her horse to go faster. Kane did the same, desperate to stop her even though he knew he couldn't reach her in time. EvaMarie suddenly reined in her horse, trying to make room for Presley, but there simply wasn't enough time.

Without a hitch, Presley guided the mare into a jump

approach and sailed over the overgrown ravine that blocked her path. Kane missed seeing the landing somehow.

After a moment he realized he'd squeezed his eyes shut.

He flicked open his eyelids. Instead of the broken body he expected to find, he saw that Presley and her horse had continued on the path unharmed. Kane swore under his breath and swept past EvaMarie and Mason, both of whom had slowed significantly. By the time Kane emerged from the trees, Presley was reining in her mare near the stables.

Adrenaline, fear and anger pulsed through Kane, pushing him forward. He gave his horse its full head and sped across the sloping ground. Only as his horse rushed in close did he pull back hard on the reins and yell, "Presley! What the hell were you thinking?"

Startled, Presley and her mare shied away. But not quickly enough. Kane's horse bumped against the mare. Though Kane grabbed at Presley, he wasn't able to stop her from falling to the ground.

Fourteen

Presley glared up at the horse and man towering over her, wondering if her legs were long enough to kick him. But she couldn't risk hitting the horse instead.

"Why would you do that?" she demanded. The throb of pain in her backside annoyed her, but she was also grateful she'd landed where there was some padding. At least nothing had broken. "You know better."

He should. Kane had been around horses even longer than she had. Rushing one while yelling was a good way to get someone hurt. As it was, her mare had hightailed it for the stables she knew were safe and quiet.

"Me?" Compared to her, Kane's voice was even. Deadly calm and cold. "You're the one who should know better. Taking a blind jump in unfamiliar territory."

Presley struggled to her feet despite protesting muscles. Tomorrow she'd be stiff and sore, but today she'd rather fight on her feet. After dusting off her legs and attempting to quell the urge to throw a tantrum like a toddler, she said, "It wasn't unfamiliar to me. I remembered it from the trek out."

On the periphery of her vision, Presley saw Jim, the Harringtons' stable manager, sprint from the stables in her mare's direction. He held something in his hand and his mouth moved, though she couldn't hear the words this far away. After a moment's hesitation, the mare allowed herself to be lured close enough for him to take control of her reins.

Several other stable hands exited the building. Great. An audience.

"Presley," EvaMarie gasped as she and Mason pulled their horses to a stop nearby, "are you okay?"

"She's fine," Kane snapped. "Despite making a stupid choice."

Presley felt her anger flare, and she put her fists on her hips. "I'm not stupid."

"I didn't say you were," Kane corrected. His jaw looked too tight to let the words out. "But that was a stupid, headstrong jump that didn't give a thought to safety—yours or the horse's."

Mason groaned.

Presley ignored him and waved toward her now captured mare. "Look who's talking. You yelling like that got me tossed on my rear. Is that safe, crazy man?"

"Kane," Mason said as he urged his gelding forward a few steps. "She's not Emily."

Brother glared at brother as understanding trickled through Presley, but that didn't make any of this okay. Fear like that had no place around these powerful animals. They rode all the time, but like cars, these animals could be dangerous under certain circumstances. Like now.

Kane needed to remember that. "He's right," Presley chimed in. "I'm not your ex-fiancée. I don't need you to take care of me, fix me or protect me. I've been handling those jobs myself my whole life."

Kane finally swung a leg over his horse's rump and dismounted. Then he faced Presley with his arms crossed tightly over his chest, biceps clearly defined through his T-shirt. She pretended not to notice…or be intimidated.

Now was not the time.

"I realize that, Presley," he said, his voice softening a little. "But that was a dangerous choice."

"No, it was fun. Until you ruined it." Presley wasn't sure why or where her next words came from, but she couldn't hold them back. "Kane, I took a risk. I'm fully aware of that. But it was a risk backed by knowledge."

Kane swept his hat from his head, giving her a better view of his impassive expression. His hands worked over the brim, crumpling it.

"I have a lifetime of knowledge, Kane," she continued. "That doesn't mean an accident won't happen, but I play it safe in every area of my life. This is the only one where I've learned to trust myself, my instincts. I won't start questioning them now."

Kane had taught her that, almost as much as her father. "I thought you trusted me, too…" she murmured.

As soon as the words reached him, Kane slapped the hat hard against his thigh. His jaw worked, clenching and unclenching in waves of tension that she could feel radiating off him. She wanted to relent, wanted to give in to his need to keep her safe. But somehow she knew if she did that, it would never end. Kane needed to remember the capable woman she was, not see his ex-fiancée every time he looked her way.

Then Kane shook his head with a jerk. "I don't know if I can live with that," he declared. Then he turned and walked away, leaving Presley with a throb in her heart that rivaled the one in her backside.

Presley wasn't sure if Kane would actually pick her up for the house party this weekend in Baltimore or not.

She hadn't actually spoken with him since that day at the Harrington stables. Frankly, she'd expected to open the mailbox and find a bill and nullified contract from him any day now.

Then she'd received his terse call thirty minutes before he arrived. "I'll pick you up at noon" was the only warning she'd gotten.

Good thing she'd decided to pack—just in case.

There was a strained silence between them as he opened the car door for her and stowed her luggage in the trunk. He'd taken the luxury sedan instead of the usual SUV for the ride to the private airfield. It wasn't until they were settled and on the road that he said, "I wasn't sure you would go."

All you had to do was call and ask...

"I don't back down from my obligations."

"Is that what this is?"

It was certainly the only thing that had her in the car at the moment. Her emotions mixed and mingled even more forcefully than they had over the last week. Kane had finally broken through her wall of reserve—now she wanted nothing more than to rebuild it, to keep out one more person who would tell her how to live...but she couldn't.

So maybe she wasn't just here out of obligation.

After a long, tense moment, she finally murmured in the direction of the window she kept staring out, "I'm not sure."

Kane didn't speak. He only nodded his head.

That infuriated her. She was digging into her psyche but he offered nothing of his own. And that wasn't acceptable. As the hot anger swept over her, she knew she needed answers. "What about you, Kane?"

He didn't look her way, but she saw his hands tighten on the steering wheel, knuckles turning white. "What do you want to know, Presley?"

Wasn't that a loaded question? There were so many things she'd wanted to ask for ages, but she stuck with the one question that was most pertinent to the moment.

"If this is only a business arrangement to you, why did you care if I fell?"

She sensed that wasn't the question he'd been expecting. She wouldn't be surprised if he chose not to answer, and for a long time he didn't. When he did speak, his voice was low and had an uneven rumble. "I would care if anyone got hurt, Presley, but especially you."

What did that mean? But he didn't offer anything else, and Presley had used all the courage she had to ask the one question.

Where did they go from here? The miles sped by in a flash of green hills. Kane turned on the radio, and soothing instrumental music filled the car. She doubted it was his first choice for ambience, but at least it calmed Presley's mood somewhat.

On the short flight out, Kane sat in the front with the pilot, leaving her alone with her spinning mind. Luckily she knew the family they were visiting well and had accepted their invite a while before she and Kane had become an item. The last thing she'd imagined was a weekend spent in the same room with him, this strained silence between them.

But when their hostess came to meet them under the portico while their luggage was being unloaded from the limo they'd taken from the airfield, an inkling of concern whispered through Presley.

"Hey, girl," LaDonna said as she hugged Presley. Her friendly greeting contradicted her strained smile. "So glad you made it."

LaDonna waited until after she'd greeted Kane before urging Presley a few steps away. "I didn't know Marjorie was coming."

Presley took in her hostess's worried expression. "Um, I didn't, either."

"She showed up several hours ago."

Presley squeezed her eyes shut for a moment, willing away a headache, then gave LaDonna a sympathetic look. "I'm so sorry. I hope that won't put you out."

"Well—" LaDonna glanced over her shoulder toward the doors as if to make sure the rest of the party—or the offending guest—hadn't shown up to listen. "The thing is, we have a full house this time. Every room is taken."

Great. Presley knew exactly what that meant. A weekend spent listening to her stepmother pick over every piece of clothing she'd brought to wear, or asking her a million times if Kane had picked out something she approved of "Maybe I should just go home," she groaned.

"Why would you do that?"

Presley's eyes opened to see Kane's curious expression over LaDonna's shoulder.

"We've had an unexpected guest show up," LaDonna confessed.

"Marjorie," Presley sighed.

Kane's expression was neutral. "I realize she can be difficult, but why would that be reason to abandon ship?"

LaDonna glanced back and forth between them as if unsure what to say, but Presley wasn't in the mood to spell it out herself. "It's messed up our sleeping arrangements."

"Shouldn't." Kane's voice was more matter-of-fact than she would have expected considering the strain between them. She anticipated his next words as much as she dreaded them. "Presley will be staying in my room."

LaDonna's eyes widened, but thankfully she didn't express disbelief or ask questions. She gave a polite smile. "That'll work, then."

But as LaDonna turned away from Kane, her wide eye

met Presley's. Her mouthed *oh my gosh* would have been comical if Presley didn't have so much weighing her down. She didn't want to make LaDonna uncomfortable—she'd always been a sweet woman, who had been a friend of Presley's mother and stayed in touch despite their living so far apart. Their shared investments in horse racing gave the families even better reason to continue their longstanding friendship. Presley didn't want to inconvenience her or spill the details of her currently troubled relationship—if one could call what she and Kane had a relationship. Deep down, she was very much afraid that's exactly what she wanted.

But now Presley had to figure out what to do with Kane—and the king-size bed they would soon share.

Fifteen

As Presley eyed him warily, Kane had the first urge to smile he'd felt in days. He wasn't sure why—the situation between him and Presley hadn't improved. But the look on her face implied he was a big bad wolf who would more than likely take advantage of her in their shared room.

By damn, she was probably right.

Not that she'd forgiven him for his behavior. She might be able to sleep with him, but her spirit wasn't quite willing. Kane had wavered about a solution to this problem—not to mention the cause—a lot over the last few days.

The answer wasn't making itself known quickly enough.

"Presley! You finally arrived."

The sound of Marjorie's voice when they were only halfway up the main staircase made Kane smother a groan. As if this weekend wasn't complicated enough... Marjorie wasn't his favorite person, but he tried to be polite to her. But add in the strain between him and Presley at the moment, and his patience with her stepmother was bound to be a little thin.

Presley seemed to feel the same way, as she said in a voice that held no warmth, "We didn't know you were going to arrive at all, Marjorie."

The older woman's titter set Kane's teeth on edge, as did the light glinting off all the sequins on her top.

"A last-minute decision," Marjorie assured them. "You shouldn't mind, Presley. After all, you have a place to sleep, don't you?"

The way she eyed Kane over her stepdaughter's shoulder made him distinctly uncomfortable. Either she didn't notice Presley's clenched jaw or she simply didn't care. Kane leaned toward the latter explanation.

Marjorie moved on to her next topic, one of her favorites. "Please tell me you're on your way to dress for dinner, Presley. You shouldn't wear slacks in this type of company—"

"We are actually on our way to our suite," Kane interrupted, gesturing toward the man who waited at the top of the stairs with their luggage. "We'll be down for drinks once we're settled."

Presley didn't resist as he ushered her up the remaining steps. He handled the luggage while she crossed the suite to stare out the picture window overlooking the impressive gardens just coming into full bloom. Kane saw the waning sunlight darken to dusk in just a few minutes, giving the room a more intimate quality.

Knowing only that he had to reach her in some small way but unsure of how to go about it, Kane crossed to stand behind Presley. Though they weren't touching, standing like this reminded him of their trip to Louisville. He wanted to use his body to bend her just where he wanted her. Connect with her from head to toe, get them both too revved up to be able to go down to dinner.

But now wasn't the time to focus on sex. He could easily make her feel satisfied—but more importantly, he needed to make her feel respected. Their conversation in the car had told him that loud and clear.

So he did the one thing he didn't want to do. He started to speak. About his feelings.

"When my mother died, I was fifteen—" He paused for a deep breath. "No, it started before that. She'd been sick with cancer for almost two years before she was taken from us."

Presley shifted slightly, but he couldn't tell what she was thinking so he continued. With only a lamp on in the far corner of the room, there wasn't any light to see her reflection in the glass.

"My father worked full-time. Took care of all her medications, appointments, treatments…and he had me and Mason. But there are only so many hours in the day, and he had no relatives nearby to help him. Some of the neighbors would bring over food sometimes, but the longer an illness goes on, the easier it is for people to forget that you're in need."

He edged a little closer, drawn to her warmth.

"I wanted to help, so I begged my mom to teach me to cook the things she wanted to eat, whatever she thought she could keep down. Soups, mashed potatoes, pudding— soft foods to start. Soon I was making entire meals for everyone. I helped Mason with his homework every night so he wouldn't get behind. Took out the trash. Cleaned the bathrooms. Did laundry. Taking care of people just came naturally to me."

Kane sucked in another deep breath, momentarily distracted by the brush of his chest against Presley's back. The light scent of her hair, tied back into a thick ponytail, enticed him. He should stop talking before he revealed too much. Why didn't he stop talking?

"When Em fell, I ended up in the same place, the same head space. Like if I just worked hard enough, I could fix it."

"Since you didn't prevent it?"

The murmured words were quiet, but their impact was massive.

Kane's whole world tilted, leaving him dizzy. "Logically I knew I couldn't have stopped it, but that message didn't translate to my heart. So I tried to make up for it instead. Which didn't go over so well."

At all. Instead of bringing them closer, he'd driven Emily away. She'd needed space, time to heal…without him. The memories sent Kane back across to the dresser, pulling at his hair as he paced the expanse of the big room, his steps eerily silent on the plush carpets. "I should have handled it differently. Tempered my response to what she needed, what she wanted." He jerked to a halt, bracing his hands on hips. "It's just who I am, Presley."

"No."

Surprised, he braced himself to face her.

"That was your normal response on steroids. You felt yourself losing her, so you pumped it up."

And made myself into a fool.

"The truth, Kane, is that she probably would never have accepted your help."

"Why?"

Kane hated the plaintive note in his voice, yet it was also a relief to say the word out loud after listening to it echo inside his head for three years. Presley glanced back out the window, hesitating for long moments before she answered. Kane felt every second of that wait in his bones.

"I'll admit, I looked up the details of Emily's fall." Presley shrugged. "I was curious. But there were things that puzzled me for a while. How could someone so invested in horses go completely in the other direction after what was obviously an accident?"

"She wanted nothing more to do with them," Kane

choked out. "When she left, she said she never wanted to see another animal or stable again."

"She moved to a big city, didn't she?"

Kane nodded.

"See, it could have gone the other way. There are lots of rehabilitation programs she could have worked with, helping her overcome her fears if she'd wanted to. But she didn't."

Presley took a few small steps closer to him. "And she couldn't ask you to give up your dreams, either, Kane. She wasn't pushing you away after her accident—she was pushing you in the direction of the future she knew you deserved. A future she couldn't handle being a part of anymore."

The truth hit Kane like lightning, jolting him from the inside out while freezing him in place. For so long, he'd had it in his head that Emily simply wanted nothing more to do with him, nothing to do with the essential parts of him. So those parts of him had to be buried—until the pressure of watching Presley accelerate toward that jump had his protective instincts spewing forth again like a shaken soda.

The implications whirled inside Kane's brain, making him dizzy. Through sheer force he shut down his mind. He could dwell on it later, when he was alone. Right now Kane needed to focus on the uncomfortable present and lock away the devastating past for another time. "I thought I'd buried my triggers," he admitted, not acknowledging the turbulence inside himself. "Obviously I was wrong."

A weak apology at best, but all he could manage at the moment.

This time Presley advanced on him with sure steps. "You know, Kane, there's a difference between taking care of people and taking them over."

Wise woman. "I forget sometimes." With the best of intentions, but still...

"Then you'll just have to live with me putting you back in your place...when it's appropriate, of course."

Her moss-green gaze met his. A little vulnerable. A lot strong. And like a snap of his fingers, Kane's hesitation vanished.

He strode back to her, cupping her face to hold her captive for his kiss.

Once he started, there was no turning back. Passion, need and something deeper drove him forward. He made short work of stripping off their clothes. Her every gasp, every moan added an extra spark to his excitement. Luckily the bed was a soft landing place.

For a woman who worked so hard, Presley's skin was silky soft, drawing his hands, his mouth. Kane might have spent time dressing Presley, but undressing her was a unique pleasure. Her body was firm, muscled from her hard work. Her long, lean legs felt like heaven wrapped around Kane's hips.

He couldn't wait to have her there again.

Stepping to the edge of the bed, Kane made a place for himself between Presley's thighs. She was like the sweetest of treats laid out before him; Kane surveyed every inch before leaning over for a taste. He plumped her breasts with his hands. Her nipples tightened, begging for him. His kiss covered her delicate mounds, but he saved the little pink buds for last.

As he closed over one tip, Presley arched up to meet him. The dusky darkness of the room grew heavy with her moans and his ragged breath. She buried her hands in the thickness of his hair at the base of his skull, drawing him closer. He sucked at her tightened nipples until they darkened to rosy red.

Something about the feel of her, the sound of her, fit perfectly into the empty place in Kane's soul. He didn't want it, but there was no denying it. No way to stop himself from reaching out and taking her.

After slipping on a condom, he guided her legs around his waist. She locked her ankles together at the small of his back. Her core was wet and eager for him. Sliding inside felt even better than coming home.

It was just right.

The heat surrounding Kane lit an urgency inside him that he couldn't control. Spurred on by the pressure of her legs pulling him closer, he plunged deep inside her. His world stopped. All he knew was that he didn't want this to end. Didn't want to face the day when he would never again connect with Presley's very essence.

But his body wasn't interested in the emotions.

In and out, each thrust became an automatic drive to detonate their explosion. He leveraged his stance for maximum force, losing himself in the clutch of her hands and the exquisite pull of her body. Every thrust to the hilt threw them closer to the edge.

Kane knew he wanted nothing more than to jump into the free fall with Presley.

Just a minute more, and he felt the impact hit her, the clamp of her muscles around him a direct jolt to his own ecstasy. Kane felt suspended in a maelstrom of pleasure and pain before slowly returning to the softness of the woman beneath him and the solid foundation of the floor under his feet.

Never had reality felt so good.

Apparently she shouldn't have worried about that canceled contract.

Presley was pretty sure what they'd been doing upstairs

shone from every pore on her face, but no one so much as hinted at it over dinner. Instead they all chatted pleasantly from cocktails to dessert, eager to meet the newest up-and-comer in the racing world when Presley introduced Kane.

As she watched him over the rim of her wineglass after dinner, she had the sinking feeling that Kane didn't truly need her anymore. He was far more comfortable in social situations than she was and quickly connected with whomever he met. Yes, she'd helped him gain entry to a couple of places it might have taken him longer to break into, but his name and reputation had spread rapidly.

When it was just the two of them, their connection felt almost tangible. Their lovemaking upstairs had left her with no barriers against her true feelings for him. But it was hard seeing him work a room full of people when her natural instinct was to hide in a corner. How long would it be before babysitting her grew old?

But she certainly wouldn't object to calling it an early night when she knew what was waiting for her upstairs.

LaDonna approached Presley's quiet corner. "Wow, Presley. I'm thoroughly impressed," she said as she eyed Kane, who was in conversation with a couple of high-powered horse brokers from Ireland.

"You should see him with his brother."

"I'd heard there were two of them," LaDonna said with a playful wink. "Don't tell hubby that I'm salivating already."

She turned her focus fully on Presley. "I'm sorry about the mix-up with Marjorie, but I didn't know you and Kane were together when you asked for the invite. Why didn't you tell me, Presley?"

"I wasn't...sure." Heck, she still wasn't sure, if she admitted the truth.

"Are you happy?"

In some ways, very much. In others… But she couldn't tell LaDonna that. Instead she protected herself and the complicated situation she was in by saying, "Yes, why?"

"Well, I've tried hard not to malign Marjorie over the years."

Haven't we all?

"But as a mother, she was never quite right for you."

Marjorie's piercing laugh from across the room only punctuated that truth. Presley sighed, then said, "I'm glad I'm not the only one who saw it."

"Oh, your father had all the excuses for why you wouldn't take to his new wife, and Marjorie adopted them for herself from the beginning."

Presley tilted her head to the side, studying her stepmother in her sequined attire. Marjorie liked to glitter when she moved. "Do you think so?"

"I'm afraid so," LaDonna said. She indicated Presley's silky shirt and skirt with an elegant gesture. "And then I saw you like this, and I worried."

Presley glanced down, expecting to feel self-conscious to have someone talking about her new clothes, but she fell back into the knowledge that the outfit was lovely and felt good, too.

Then an unexpected vulnerability swept over her. "Do you think my mom would have liked it? Liked me?"

LaDonna stepped closer, reaching for Presley's ponytail and pulling it forward so it fell in a golden swath over her shoulder. "Most definitely, honey. But then again, she loved you in jeans and T-shirts, too. She didn't care much for fashion herself."

"She didn't?" Presley struggled to remember more about the mother she'd lost so long ago.

"Oh, no," LaDonna said with a soft smile full of memories. "She much preferred the comfort of her work pants.

She dressed up when she had to, but she really wanted to be at ease most of the day. Formal clothes made her constantly worry about buttons coming loose, pockets poking out or the fabric twisting and not lying right. That stuff seemed to happen to her constantly."

Presley chuckled. "Like me."

"Like you." LaDonna shook her head. "I always wanted you to go with your gut, Presley. Still do. So would your mother."

Presley eyed the darkly handsome man across the room. Could she? Should she? Would she risk missing the most spectacular opportunity to ever come her way?

"You look beautiful, Presley. Don't forget that." Again LaDonna fingered her ponytail. "So like your mother. But most importantly, you finally look like you, comfortable in your own skin."

The little pep talk, which might have been insignificant to most people, stuck with Presley the rest of the night, prodding her into action. But it wasn't until she drifted in soft waves of approaching sleep, comfortable in Kane's arms, that she finally listened.

"I love you," she whispered, speaking the words that had been weighing on her conscience all day.

But when she finally slipped into slumber, his silence in return haunted her.

Sixteen

Kane's energy waned late the next afternoon, forcing him to excuse himself a few minutes early from the tour of the hosts' stables. They had some gorgeous animals, but Kane's focus was nonexistent at the moment. His uppermost need was to get a few minutes alone in their suite—some time to regain his equilibrium and figure out what the hell he should do now.

He'd been distracted since hearing Presley's whispered words the night before.

Kane had struggled to keep his body from reacting. He hadn't wanted her to think he was rejecting her precious gift, so he'd held perfectly still, letting her think he was already asleep.

He wasn't sure the ruse had worked. Presley had been subdued today, but that could also have been a natural consequence of Marjorie's over-the-top presence this weekend. The woman seemed to be everywhere they went. And her laugh—Kane had never known a sound that grated on his nerves so badly.

The thought of Presley having to manage this woman—her outrageous spending, constant criticism and, yeah, that laugh—all in an attempt to honor her father's wishes that Marjorie be supported and part of the Macarthur busi-

…ess made Kane's respect for the man take a nosedive.
Of course, he'd probably known that Marjorie would sink
within a year if Presley wasn't taking care of her.

As if his thoughts had conjured her, Kane heard that
…igh-pitched, nail-scraping sound in the foyer at the end
of the hall. He had a strong urge to turn around and find
a back way upstairs, but that might take him a while in
…he unfamiliar expanse of the sprawling mansion. It was
a gorgeous place but not the easiest to navigate.

Straight ahead was the quickest route.

The deep rumble of a male voice assured Kane that
Marjorie wasn't alone. Perhaps he could squeeze through
with just a quick acknowledgment. Except what he heard
…s he reached the spot where he could make out the actual
words stopped him in his tracks.

"Sun is one of the most well-known and well-respected
…tallions in the industry, Ms. Macarthur. I'm shocked you
…on't have buyers lining up a mile deep."

"Oh, he's such a special animal—we don't want him to
…o to just anyone, so we're keeping the sale inquiries dis-
…reet, if you know what I mean."

Kane glanced around the corner to see a balding gentle-
…an he'd met at dinner the night before. Peter, he thought
…is name was. His vague race predictions and lack of
…ands-on knowledge left the distinct impression that Pe-
…r's wife was the brains of that operation.

The thought that Marjorie would try to sell Sun again,
…nowing the problems it had caused for Presley the first
…me, confounded Kane. The thought that she would sell
…uch a beloved animal to a clueless stable owner was be-
…ond his understanding.

"Well, I know he's a derby champ and renowned stal-
…on," Peter said. "Y'all must want a pretty penny for him."

As she mentioned a figure almost twice what she'd

charged Kane, his blood went from simmer to boiling. Somebody was getting bold. The fact that she'd do it while Kane and Presley were under the same roof proved she simply didn't care about the consequences.

Peter must have realized the price was over-the-top because he shook his head.

"I do have a couple of other interested parties," Marjorie added for good measure.

"Still, I can't commit to that kind of money without consulting my wife. Will tonight be soon enough for an answer?"

Smart man. Before Marjorie could answer, Kane stepped from his hiding place into the foyer.

"That's a very good idea," he said, his voice echoing in the dome of the rotunda. "In the meantime, would you leave me with Ms. Macarthur for a moment? We have a pressing matter we need to discuss."

The man nodded, walking away with a smile and a light whistle, completely unaware of the tension he left behind. Marjorie eyed Kane warily as he approached, and rightly so. His anger had grown to the point he couldn't hide it from his expression anymore.

"Doing a little business, Marjorie?" he asked, his voice quiet but forceful. He wasn't yelling, which was a good sign he was keeping his rage under control.

"I don't believe that's any of your business."

"Then you'd be wrong."

"No," she countered, her voice squeaking a little as he stepped closer. "No, I'm not wrong. You are not part of Macarthur Haven."

"Actually, you are wrong. You just tried to sell a horse that doesn't belong to you—for the second time."

"You must have misheard the conversation," she said, tilting her chin up.

"Really?" Kane mimicked Marjorie's high-pitched tone. 'I'll settle for that price, even though he's worth far more.'" He groaned, shaking his head. "Marjorie, that's twice what you charged me. I think you're getting a little greedy."

"Presley asked me to do it," Marjorie said, changing her tune. "She couldn't face doing it herself."

"Now you must think I'm ignorant." He stalked close enough to see the tremble of Marjorie's lower lip, but it didn't evoke any sympathy from him. "Presley loves that horse. She'd never sell him. That's the difference between us, Marjorie. I see Presley's heart, not just dollar signs."

That had her narrowing her gaze. "How in the world could you know Presley better after two months than someone who has known her most of her life?"

"Maybe because I actually see her."

"Really?" Marjorie planted her hands on her well-endowed hips. "Well, doesn't that make you sound like an awesome guy? Even though we both know you're only dating her because of a contract. It's all a business deal."

"A business deal that happened because you stole her horse and sold it to me illegally."

"You're welcome."

"Excuse me?"

Her eyes widened, but Marjorie didn't back down. "You've gotten a lot out of that deal, haven't you? An awful lot."

"So you're just going to—what? Keep forcing her to fix your mistakes so you don't go to jail?"

Marjorie gasped. "Presley would never do that to me."

"No, she wouldn't," Kane agreed. "She also wouldn't put a stop to your illegal activities. So I'll make sure this never happens again."

Marjorie rolled her eyes. "And how do you plan to do that, tough guy?"

"I'll shut you down permanently. Your easy access wil be over once I marry her."

That caught Marjorie's attention, her eyes widening Then she stared over his shoulder, her look turning almos calculating. Kane didn't care what she planned to throw at him next. He had the upper hand now.

Only Marjorie wasn't afraid of delivering low blow that were only true in her own mind. "That's almost as ba as forcing her to give the money back and sign a contrac saying you could escort her all over town, change how sh looked, use our horse as stud—all with the added bonu of sex on demand."

"Marjorie!"

LaDonna's voice rang through the foyer, causing Kar to turn around with dread settling in his stomach like stone. A group of half a dozen people watched from th doorway leading to the foyer.

Right in the middle of them stood a white-faced Presle

"What do you want?"

Presley should have been surprised by LaDonna words, but she wasn't. She could even make a guess as who was at the door to their suite, since she had no dou her stepmother would not be coming around to apologiz Heck, she probably wouldn't even go home but would cor tinue to enjoy her weekend and the race tomorrow, obliv ous to the looks and whispers cast her way.

No, the person at the door would definitely be Kan He was too responsible to back down from his obligation

Whatever he said must have been sufficient, becau LaDonna glanced over her shoulder at Presley. The que tion in her expression was obvious, even though she didr speak. Presley replied with a short nod.

LaDonna opened the door. "You have ten minutes," she warned before slipping outside herself.

Presley didn't turn around again to watch Kane cross the room. It would remind her too much of the day before, and the stride of those long legs as he came for her. No. She couldn't face those memories right now.

Instead, she continued packing her suitcase.

"Leaving?" he asked.

Whatever she'd been expecting, it wasn't the soft, apologetic note in his voice.

"What's the point in staying?" she countered. "I can't be much help to you now that everyone knows I'm only with you because of a contract."

"Everyone?"

"This business is a pretty tight circle, as you well know," Presley said, tossing her extra pair of jeans into the suitcase with more force than necessary. "Word has already spread through the house by now, I'm sure. It will hit basically everywhere by the end of the race tomorrow."

Kane stepped close, halting the jerky movements of her hands with an arm across the front of her body. "Presley, I'm so sorry you had to hear that."

"Not as sorry as I am to be humiliated in front of people who have known me my entire life."

"That was not my intention. When I heard what she was doing—"

"You know what's even worse, Kane?" Glancing down, she noticed that the garment she kept worrying between her fingers was actually the silky nightgown she'd brought, knowing Kane would see her in it at some point. The old Presley would never have dreamed of wearing such a thing. Yet she'd thought about wearing it with excitement just two days ago.

She dropped it as if it burned her hands. "The worst

part is that for some of them, this will explain exactly why you would choose to date someone as frumpy and uninteresting as me."

"Presley, that's not true."

She tilted her head up to meet his gaze. It hurt, having him this close, seeing the eyes that had stared her down with lust and laughter now dark and guarded.

"It is," she said softly. "They've known me forever as a smart businessperson, but not as a woman, Kane. I won't be able to pretend any longer that I'm truly a person you would want to be with for—" her breath shook for a moment "—for more than a business arrangement."

"Did you not hear what I said down there? None of this will be an issue anymore. I want to marry you, Presley."

She stepped away, unable to tolerate being this close to him while he said those words. Words she'd only dreamed of hearing. Words that she knew didn't hold the same meaning for him as they did for her. "Oh, I heard. And just a day ago I heard you tell me this was just about a contract."

"That wasn't me, sweetheart. That was you."

"I believe I told you I didn't know what this was really about, Kane. But that's changed."

"For me, too."

Kane didn't give any quarter this time. Gone was the man reaching out to her with soft words and kid gloves. Here was the man plowing over her boundaries with passion.

His forceful advance backed her up against the nearby wall. Not because she wanted to retreat, but because she was afraid of what one touch from him would ignite inside her. She was right to be afraid.

As Kane pressed close, her body ignited with heat and need. Presley was perilously close to losing her head in he desire for the things Kane could make her feel. Without her permission, her hands clasped his upper arms tight. She didn't protest as he buried his mouth against her neck.

Could she possibly live without this? How would she survive without the heady passion Kane had brought into her life? His body was backing her against the wall, mouth pushing aside the collar keeping his lips from her skin, hard need pressing into the cradle of her hips—and Presley wanted nothing more than to lose herself in the drive to ecstasy she'd only found with this man.

For long moments, she gave desire free rein. Her nails dug into his shirt. Her thigh clamped around the leg he slid between hers. When his mouth captured hers, she opened to him without hesitation. No matter how much she questioned Kane, this, she knew, he couldn't fake.

But even as he tasted and tempted her, she could not hold back the doubts of a lifetime. The fear of never being loved. The fear of never being pretty enough. The fear of never being truly seen. Doubts proven true again and again…until Kane.

If she didn't walk away now, new doubts would creep in, and she didn't want to live like that anymore. Didn't want to wonder if this was a business deal with a side dish of desire. No. She wanted love.

Somehow she found the strength to push him away, to step around him, to walk to the bed. Alone.

She snapped the suitcase closed. Whatever was left, LaDonna could ship to her. Right now, she simply had to get out before this humiliation gave way to the river of pain lurking beneath her careful control.

Pulling the suitcase from the bed, she rolled it toward the door. But she only made it halfway before she turned back. "What hurts even worse is that you think I would settle for a marriage that wasn't everything I deserve."

"And exactly what is that?" His soft tone was completely gone now.

"A man who respects me enough to trust I can fix my own problems, who will stand strong with me when I need him to and make decisions *with* me…not *for* me."

This time she didn't pause until she reached the door. "I'll have what's left of your money for the stud services returned to you in full by Monday."

Seventeen

The last person Presley expected to knock on their door on the following Wednesday evening was a lawyer she recognized from town. James Covey was well liked among the racing community, though he didn't actually own any horses. He was known to be fair, and Presley knew from seeing his name on the envelopes on Kane's desk that he was also the Harringtons' lawyer.

"Who is it?" Marjorie called from the hallway leading to the foyer. They'd been in the middle of dinner when the bell rang.

"No one," Presley called back as she opened the door.

"Ms. Macarthur?" the man asked, a more pleasant smile on his face than she would have anticipated.

"Mr. Covey?"

"I have a package for you from Mr. Kane Harrington."

She was shaking her head before he even finished. "I returned his money to him by cashier's check on Monday, delivered by courier," Presley said, anxiety churning in her stomach despite her certainty that she'd done more than was legally required of her. "Mr. Harrington should have no further need to contact me, much less through legal channels."

Unless he'd decided to insist on using Sun as a stud. She'd taken a significant hit to her business to return Kane's original sum to him in full. It hadn't been required according to their contract, but she'd wanted no further ties between them, which meant Sun would not be serving as a stud for the Harringtons' new stables. She hated to back out of any business deal, but right now, her sanity was more important to her than her bank account. Remembering that it was only a temporary loss that the business would recover from helped.

No matter how much writing that check had stung.

"I cannot say why Mr. Harrington chose this way to contact you, ma'am," the lawyer said.

Again, Presley wondered about his benign expression. Either he was quite good at masking his true thoughts or the envelope didn't contain a subpoena or any other legal threat.

He continued, "I was simply instructed to deliver it to you personally."

Presley barely registered his parting "Good evening" as she studied the oversize envelope in her hands. It was creamy white with the lawyer's logo in one corner and her name scrawled in Kane's bold handwriting across the center. Just seeing the strong curves and almost sharp lines brought to mind an image of watching him write. Kane's script wasn't messy, like a lot of men's. Instead it was indicative of his personality, daring and smooth and elegant.

No matter his family's class growing up, Kane had pride and expectation of quality that had shone through consistently. His quality of character had come through again in the fallout from the gossip about their original contract. From the gossip Marjorie had shared, when questioned at a cocktail party the other night he'd refused to speak about contracts that were nobody's business but the parties involved.

At least Kane was protecting her. The same couldn't be said for her stepmother. Presley's threat to once more talk to their lawyer seemed to have kept Marjorie quiet—for now.

"What's taking so long?" Marjorie asked from her elbow, startling Presley. She hadn't realized Marjorie had joined her.

"It's nothing. Just some business papers."

Her stepmother studied the envelope, but Presley knew she wouldn't know where it was from, since the Harrington name didn't appear on it. She set the package on a side table and went back to the dining room as if it were truly unimportant, but it wasn't as easy to put the contents out of her mind. Still, she forced herself to wait until Marjorie had finished eating and retired to her room for the evening. She had a lunch date the next day that it would take her all night to prepare for, she said.

Presley still couldn't imagine putting that much thought and time into her appearance, even if she was enjoying her new clothes. Mrs. Rose had helped her build quite a closet full. Though she wasn't looking forward to any social events any time soon. She imagined whatever she wore from now on would be examined and talked about, but she refused to go backward.

She'd just have to learn to deal with it with a straight face.

Her hands trembled as she took the envelope to the privacy of her office. Why? She had nothing to be concerned about. She'd fulfilled her obligation to Kane per their contract and returned everything to him in full. Why he was contacting her now, she had no idea.

But this was business. She needed to suck in her emotions and handle whatever needed to be done.

The first thing she noticed as she dumped the contents onto her desk was the check she'd had delivered to Kane on Monday. Only now it was stamped with a big black "Void" across the front.

Her heart started to pound in earnest. If he was refusing her payment, then he must want something else. Although what that something would be, she couldn't imagine. She'd given him his freedom. He should be grateful.

She picked up the sheaf of papers and began to read the top page. The impersonal *Ms. Macarthur* on the Harrington Farms letterhead didn't bode well.

Receipt of your cashier's check surprised me, even though you warned me it would be arriving. In truth, the money does not interest me, so I am returning it to you in the form of a voided check.

Why? Why would the money not interest him? Unless he thought there was some other way she needed to fix whatever damage might come to his business after the weekend's revelations made the rounds.

In the interest of opening further negotiations, I'm having my lawyer deliver a new document for you to consider. Not a contract, per se. More of an agreement.

This is the only agreement I am willing to entertain, with mild adjustments at your discretion. I will only accept this document if it is returned by you, in person, at your convenience.

Sincerely, Kane Harrington

What kind of jerk thought he could dictate the terms of their further business dealings after humiliating her in public? Presley flipped to the next page with such force that the cover letter tore.

It is the wish of Kane Harrington to enter into a romantic agreement with Presley Macarthur that includes, but is not limited to, living in the same home, discussing business and personal interests with each other, being seen in public together, and, in general, allowing all intimate activities that would be acceptable and agreed upon between two people who wish to spend their lives together. This agreement may or may not include marriage, at Ms. Macarthur's discretion, but Mr. Harrington would prefer that a permanent romantic agreement occur in order to publicly acknowledge his devotion and love for her.

In acknowledgment of previous behaviors, Mr. Harrington agrees not to bring undo public attention to Ms. Macarthur in any way except during a wedding ceremony, should both parties agree. Should their previous contract ever be mentioned to him by interested parties, he will explain in no uncertain terms that their business arrangement was for the couple's mutual benefit and was of no concern to anyone but the two of them.

It is Mr. Harrington's responsibility to support and encourage Ms. Macarthur, but to in no way make her decisions for her. He agrees to only come to her defense when she is not able to defend herself, and to discuss disagreements in a calm and approachable manner, rather than dictating.

Mr. Harrington acknowledges that Ms. Macarthur is a smart, sexy woman who has years of knowledge and business acumen on her side. He will trust her to use that knowledge to her benefit and for her safety, and he will do his best not to infringe on that in any way.

It is Mr. Harrington's utmost wish to spend the rest of his life with Ms. Macarthur, loving her and caring for her to the best of his ability, in hopes that she will help him to become the best man to meet her needs and desires for all of eternity. He requests that she support him during all of his future business decisions, offering her knowledge as he builds Harrington Farms to the scale he and his brother have always dreamed possible.

All previous agreements between Mr. Harrington and Ms. Macarthur are furthermore null and void, requiring no further obligations to be fulfilled.

The rest of the page went on with more details tha blurred through the tears in her eyes, but it was the last bi handwritten across the bottom, that struck her the mos
Presley, I admit I'm hopelessly addicted to you—you strength, your common sense, your professional exper tise and most of all the way you give me your all when yo are with me. I want to be brave, to move on from the pa: into the most incredible future I could imagine—a futur with you. Be brave with me. I need you... Kane.

It took Presley an entire day to respond to Kane's pacl age—and Kane felt every minute from sunrise to suns(in the depths of his soul.

When he glanced out the window of his office at Ha: rington Farms and saw her truck in the driveway, his hea' stopped for a beat. Part of him wanted to know her answe art of him didn't want to know if the answer was negative. e could just live in this anxious limbo for eternity, right?

When EvaMarie showed her into the room, Presley's xpression didn't offer him any glimmers of hope. Her oker face was pretty good. She held the envelope he'd ad James Covey deliver lightly in one hand. Despite in- eriting an incredible sum of money, Kane was a realist. is life had been hard, often struck by tragedy. He had a eling today would be the hardest of them all.

In business, he could always push through and turn ings around. On the personal side, Kane knew life didn't ork that way.

"I received your package—" she started, but that wasn't here Kane wanted to begin.

"Before that, please accept my apology."

He must have disrupted a script in her head, because esley blinked for a moment. "What?" she asked.

"Before we go any further," Kane said again, "I would ke for you to accept my apology."

Another slow blink.

"I did not mean to embarrass you or harm you, Presley. ealize my instincts to protect you had those unintended onsequences, and I'm very, very sorry. No matter what ppens today, I hope you know that."

"I do, Kane," she said, sounding dishearteningly formal. know you saw what was happening and only wanted to otect me from further harm. Thank you."

"I never would have said any of that if I had realized I d an audience."

She nodded, her pale cheeks flushing beneath his gaze. was the first sign of emotion he'd seen. That was a little icouraging, at least.

Then she lifted the envelope. "This told me a lot. But also brought up some questions."

"How so?"

"Kane…" She glanced away, her delicate throat work-ing. "I want to believe, because of this, that my fears are unfounded. But I can't quite let them go."

He clenched the edge of his desk, desperate to go to her. To wrap her up in his arms and prove to her that fear didn't matter, that the past didn't matter. But that wasn't what she needed—and for once he wasn't letting his emo-tions push him into action.

With a deep breath, he let her lead by saying, "What can I do to help?"

"Tell me, Kane. I need to know that I wasn't just a fun bonus to a business deal you needed. That I wasn't just a doll to be dressed up to make you look good. A woman you would have defended no matter who I was personally."

Damn. "I'm sorry, Presley. I won't tell you that."

Her businesslike mask was stripped away in an instant, and Kane saw the blatant pain he'd caused her in full color. But he couldn't back down now.

"I won't tell you that because you know, deep down, none of that is true. It never has been. We may have started this as a business arrangement, but it turned into some-thing else quicker than wildfire."

His unexpected answer grabbed her attention, pulling her focus back to him. "Before I knew it, I was in love with a tomboy who knows horses inside and out, a daughter who is doing her best to fulfill her father's last wishes, and a woman who is as beautiful outside as she is on the inside."

This time he let himself stand, let himself circle his desk and take the seat next to her. Tears welled in her eyes as she leaned toward him. "I can't change who I am, Kane."

"I know."

"I don't want to spend my life with someone who can't accept me the way I accept me. My father—he gave me a life of opportunities to explore my own interests. Horse camp and 4-H club and jeans, but there was always a persistent undercurrent of pressure to be more like the other girls. The casual remarks that told me he wished I had preferred cotillion and cheerleading."

"And you shouldn't have to live like that," Kane said.

He brushed away the single tear that trembled on her cheek. Then he pushed aside a few strands of the gorgeous blond hair she'd left loose around her face.

"I felt that, at Mrs. Rose's, you saw me," she said, her voice barely above a whisper. "You helped me find what worked for me, instead of dressing me up to fit your image. I was just…" She shrugged weakly. "I was afraid to trust that experience when so many people told me it couldn't be right."

He cupped his hand against her cheek. "Presley, I can't spend a lifetime reassuring you that you're the woman for me. My presence, my fidelity, my love are all the proof you need. You'll simply have to trust me, give me time to prove it to you."

There was no holding back from meeting her lips with his, a kiss that was just as much a pledge as it was a pleasure.

"Just like you can't spend a lifetime reassuring me that your every decision will keep you safe and sound. I have to trust that your knowledge and skills will bring you home to me safely."

"I don't want you to live in fear," she murmured against his lips.

"I've been there enough," he agreed, "and I'm ready to move on."

"I do understand, though."

Pulling back, he held her glistening gaze for long moments. "Understand what?"

"Why you behaved like you did. I just didn't see it at the time." Her deep breath gave her next words the air of a confession. "You wouldn't have been so upset about the jump if you didn't care. You wouldn't have defended me so fiercely, without thought to who was listening, if some pretty strong feelings weren't involved."

"How do you know?"

Her smile captured his heart. "Because I feel the same way."

Kane couldn't hold back. His lips covered hers as he sought both to take and be taken. Her soft surrender empowered him. Yet he strove in every way to please her, to show her the love he'd never thought to experience after a lifetime of pain.

When they finally came up for air, Kane was surprised to hear Presley say, "I think our agreement needs a new clause."

"What's that?"

"That whenever fear starts to take hold, we have to tell the other immediately."

He liked that plan. "Sounds good."

"And we have to find the best way possible to calm those fears and move past them, without letting them rule our world."

If he wasn't mistaken, judging by the increased color in her cheeks and the sexy arch of her brow, the little negotiator in front of him had some pretty interesting ideas how to do that already. He liked this plan more and more.

"I'll have James draw that up immediately." He stood, anxious to be closer to her, to feel her body against his own. "Do you have any other demands?"

She stood as well. "Only one."

"What's that?" he asked, not surprised that his voice had deepened with her nearness.

"We go somewhere more private—" she glanced around his office with a blush and a shy smile "—and spend the next few hours exploring exactly what else this merger might need to be successful. Every possible avenue should be explored."

Yes, ma'am. "Good plan. I have a few ideas we should definitely discuss."

Epilogue

A year later

"Push, girl. Push!"

Mason's cheering scraped over Presley's nerves, followed by the more soothing, soft encouragement offered by Kane. "Come on, girl. You can do it."

The men stood side by side, coaching, sweating and just generally making a mess of themselves. Any woman could have told them it wouldn't help.

"I think she knows what she's doing," Presley said through clenched teeth. Being this close to a birthing while her own belly was swollen with her first child set her on edge for the first time in her life.

Mason smirked at her over his shoulder, not realizing how close to physical injury that put him. "Woman's intuition and all that jazz, huh?"

Presley wasn't amused. "You say that during labor and you'll likely find yourself kissing the floor," she assured him.

"You wouldn't do that to me, would you, love?" he asked, eyeing EvaMarie as she rubbed a hand over her distended belly in slow circles.

"Maybe…" She smiled sweetly, but there was a slight menace beneath the surface Mason didn't seem to notice

You remember those films they made us watch in birthing class, right?"

Mason grimaced. "Don't remind me."

"There are certain parts you better remember pretty darn well, buddy," EvaMarie said. Presley had a feeling he'd be needing that knowledge sooner than he realized. If she wasn't mistaken, EvaMarie had been having contractions for the past two hours, at least. Mason had been too focused on the horse to notice.

Kane eyed Presley's matching tummy with a wary expression. "Is it too late to change our minds?"

"You bet, mister," Presley said.

The horse in the stall beyond the men whinnied, reminding everyone why they were actually here in the stables in the early hours of the morning. Mason yawned wide. "I could use some coffee," he said.

Presley glanced over at EvaMarie. "Oh, you're definitely going to hurt him in the delivery room," she said.

EvaMarie gave her a knowing look.

"Here it comes," Kane interrupted.

They rushed to the half door, peering inside as the mare made her final push to get her baby into the world. A vet watched from inside the stall, and Jim stood next to him. They weren't taking any chances with this mare or her foal.

She was special.

She was also a very good mommy, moving right away to free her baby from his sac and ensure all was well. As the four of them stood long minutes later watching the foal struggle to his feet for the first time, Presley's eyes filled with tears. "Look at that," she breathed.

The foal was the spitting image of his sire.

Kane rubbed her aching back. "Sun's first foal here at Barrington Farms."

Bending over with a little difficulty, EvaMarie lifted

wineglasses and two bottles from a cooler nearby. "Tim
to celebrate," she said.

Mason filled the men's glasses with champagne whil
Kane did the same with a nonalcoholic version for th
women. They all shared bright smiles as the gentle sound
of the mother and baby getting to know each other wafte
around them.

"To new beginnings," Mason said as they lifted thei
glasses for a toast.

"And a future without fear," Kane added, resting hi
hand on Presley's tummy.

They clinked glasses and drank, knowing that they wer
doing everything they could to make both of those pledge
come to pass. Before their glasses were even empty, Eva
Marie gasped, jerking her hand so the last of her drin
spilled to the floor.

"Sweetheart, are you okay?" Mason asked.

The women shared a look, then Presley started to gig
gle. Watching Mason go through this was going to b
quite amusing.

"What's so funny?" Kane asked.

Presley eyed her brother-in-law with a touch of glee. '
think someone is going to experience an up-close versio
of labor a little sooner than he thought."

EvaMarie nodded. "My water just broke."

Mason's eyes went even wider. "Are you serious?"

"Don't worry, brother," Kane said, slapping Mason o
the back. "The vet's already here."

"Oh, hell, no," he said, grabbing EvaMarie's hand an
rushing her out the door.

Well, as fast as one could rush a pregnant woman i
labor.

But all amusement was gone later that night as Presle
stood holding her new niece, Kane's arms wrapped tight

around her. Mason lay crowded against EvaMarie in the hospital bed across the suite as the two tried to catch a little bit of sleep before visiting hours were over.

"She's beautiful," Presley whispered, slipping her finger against the baby's palm. Her heart felt like it was overflowing. Even asleep, the child gripped her as if holding her hand. "Bless her heart. She's all tuckered out." She smiled at her husband, the father of the child they would soon have. "New beginnings are hard work," she said.

Kane kissed her softly, then stared into her eyes. "They definitely are...but they're more than worth it."

* * * * *

Don't miss any of these dramatic
southern romances from Dani Wade:
REINING IN THE BILLIONAIRE
EXPECTING HIS SECRET HEIR
THE RENEGADE RETURNS
THE BLACKSTONE HEIR
A BRIDE'S TANGLED VOWS

Available now from Mills & Boon Desire!

***

If you're on Twitter, tell us what you
think of Mills & Boon Desire!
#Mills&BoonDesire